W9-CJF-665
3 5674

My Heart Shall Not Fear

by JOSEPHINE LAWRENCE

Peoples Book Club
CHICAGO

MY HEART SHALL NOT FEAR

This is a special edition published exclusively for the members of the PEOPLES BOOK CLUB, P. O. BOX 6570A, Chicago 80, Illinois, and 228 Bloor Street West, Toronto 5, Ontario, Canada. It was originally published by Whittlesey House, a division of the McGraw-Hill Book Company, Inc.

Printed in the United States of America

Morning

Chapter One

"GOOD morning, Mrs. Garrison." Miss Coburn, the floor nurse, charged briskly into No. 33 like a crusader with banners unfurled. "I was sure you'd be awake," she trumpeted. "This is the day you'll have lots of company."

Young Mrs. Garrison, slim and narrow again after months of bodily clumsiness, rested motionless in the high bed to the left of the window. The smallest and cheapest private room in the maternity wing of St. Luke's Hospital accommodated, in addition to the bed, a dresser, washbasin, and one chair. When for a moment the nurse ceased chattering, the soft, hesitant ticking of a small ivory clock on the dresser punctuated the silence that blanketed the little cubicle.

The window opened on a court, but it captured the reflection of the early March sun as the pale light touched the opposite sills and windowpanes. Miss Coburn, sturdy and square in her fresh uniform, her flourish of energy temporarily checked, perceived that her patient slept. She bent over the lovely, serene face, unconsciously pitying, as she always did, the sleeper defenseless and off guard.

"She looks different from anyone I've ever known," Miss Coburn had told her girl friend in the linen room the day before. "I think it's her eyes."

Certainly the deep-set eyes in their shadowed sockets gave the features something of the calm, clear quality of marble. The smooth, broad forehead and heavy golden eyebrows further accented the shadowed eyes. As the nurse watched, the lips so lightly closed parted in a smile. Patience Garrison opened her eyes, and they were gray, with the limpid depths of spring water.

"Hello, Miss Coburn." Recollection pricked Patience fully awake. "Is the baby all right?" she asked.

"Wonderful. He's been asking for you." Miss Coburn's subdued rustle as she turned on the basin faucets increased to a joyous whirlwind as she went into her dance—so her less sedate patients labeled her routine.

An excellent maternity nurse, she brought enthusiasm, good nature, rugged energy, and insatiable personal curiosity to her profession. Patience, hospitalized for the first time in her life with the birth of a son on her twenty-first birthday, told herself that Miss Coburn might be living vicariously in the lives of her patients, a situation not without pathos: the trouble was that Miss Coburn insisted on living so many lives at once that sympathy yielded to nerves.

"Your husband coming this morning, Mrs. Garrison?" Miss Coburn, her capable hands busy with washcloth and soap, did not wait for a reply. "The girls think he's so cute. You make a nice couple. I hope things always go right for you, but you never can tell."

"No," Patience said, deeply shadowed gray eyes inscrutable. "You never can tell."

She had been helping out in the wards the day before, Miss Coburn confided. "Some of the private patients raise Cain if I get them up too early, so after I leave you I go down where they're not so fussy. I will say for you, Mrs. Garrison, that you've been swell about cooperating."

"I want to be ready when Mr. Garrison stops on his way to the office, you know." Patience took the toothbrush handed her. "I suppose other women—"

Miss Coburn snorted. Other women wanted lady's maids, not nurses. The attention they expected from a floor nurse would bankrupt Elizabeth Arden. "What was I saying just before you started to brush your teeth?"

"The wards." Patience found it difficult to brush her teeth and talk at the same time. She wished she could wheedle Miss Coburn into bringing Nicholas across the hall for a moment—a mother ought to know how her son looked at half past six in the morning.

"There's a girl in the ward just about your age," Miss Coburn was saying. "Let me take the basin—you want to do your hair? She had her first baby, a little girl, about the time you did, too—maybe you saw her in the delivery room. Well, yesterday her husband was killed—on his way to see her, they say—and there she is with a child to keep and not a cent of insurance."

Patience, supported by the plump, white pillows, let the hand glass and brush slip down into her lap. She had thick, soft golden-yellow hair, and it was her secret grief that at twenty-one it had begun almost imperceptibly to darken. Her new haircut, in honor of the baby, was short and close with wide, deep waves brushed forward over her small ears and curls tumbled loosely over her forehead.

"Does the girl know?" she asked.

Miss Coburn could bathe a patient with the fewest possible motions and without in the least disrupting her own train of thought. She had already assembled everything she needed, and as she set skillfully to work, the pitiful, commonplace little story of the girl whose tragedy had briefly singled her out among the ward beds took shape for Patience.

"They married on a shoestring, you might say," Miss Coburn said, whisking washcloth and towels dexterously. "Then along comes the baby, and of course he loses his job. And now she'll have to board it out and get a job to support it."

The hospital would keep the mother until she had regained a measure of strength, and the out-patient department would probably take hold after she was discharged. No one could say St. Luke's didn't have a heart, Miss Coburn said. "They get grand care in the wards. If I couldn't afford a special, I'd rather go into the wards myself. You get looked after there."

Patience, who considered the luxury of privacy worth the cost of occasional neglect, murmured gratefully. She was being looked after and liked it.

"You!" Miss Coburn shook talcum with an indulgent hand. "You know this is the first morning it's really felt like spring. Not that it isn't snappy enough, but there's something mixed with it. If this keeps up, we'll be going out to my sister's summer place to stay week ends soon."

Her sister had a lovely home in a lake development. She was well fixed, a widow with a foolproof trust fund.

"I was up with her my last day off, just to go over the house, and did we get a surprise! I never saw such a sight, and my sister says she never did."

Patience, the bath finished, lay back against the pillows refreshed and yet conscious of the strange new weariness that seemed to follow even slight exertion. The doctor had told her it would not last, and she had resolved that it could not last. Once home, she must be vigorous and strong and do everything herself to make up for the rent of the new apartment.

"You see, the house was closed up tight for the winter." Miss Coburn at the washbasin raised her voice above the rattle of glass as she tidied the shelves. "And when we walk into the living room, what do we see but the window frames completely ruined! The windows are Colonial style, divided into six panes, upper and lower, and all the woodwork enameled white."

Every section of the frames had been gnawed and chewed beyond hope of restoration. It would be necessary to replace each window—six of them—completely, Miss Coburn said.

"And do you know what did it? At first we thought it was boys, whittling, but no, it was squirrels. They came down the chimney, and they couldn't get out. They bit and chewed and clawed at the windows, but they never did get out. We found them dead on the floor."

"Oh, no!" Patience sat upright. "Oh, Miss Coburn, you mean to say they were trapped like that? They could see the snow and the trees outdoors, and they couldn't break the glass or loosen the putty so that one pane would fall out! They must have gone mad—and so should I."

Squirrels were dumb, Miss Coburn shrugged. "If they could come down the chimney, why didn't they know enough to go back that way? Next winter my sister's going to have netting put on top of the chimney to keep them out. Squirrels can do an awful lot of damage. It'll cost her plenty to get new window frames."

"If you can't find the way out, it might as well not be there," Patience said.

"There! You're all set, and the room's halfway decent." Miss Coburn, her labors completed, had already dismissed the subject of squirrels. "Your husband will be along any minute, and after that your tray will be up. It's time I tackled Her Royal Highness in 31. She's got an awful crush on her doctor, and if he should pop in before she gets her make-up on, the Lord help me."

Patience, smiling, heard her cheerful "Good morning" and the rather querulous response of her next patient two rooms away. The door of Patience's own room, directly in line with the bed, had been left half closed. Outside in the corridor subdued noises marked the transition from the night to the day routine in a large city hospital. *The squirrels got in, but they couldn't get out,* thought Patience. How many times had those wild, furry bodies hurled themselves against the glass, before—starved and beaten —they had died?

The odor of coffee drifted in from the diet kitchen farther down the corridor, and someone clattered silver and trays.

"Patience!"

The nameless apprehension, no heavier than a cloud, vanished as a cloud dissolves in sunlight.

The tall young man reached the bed and leaned over her. "Patience!" he said again.

"Good morning, Mr. Garrison." Her arms around his neck, her cheek to his, she laughed a little shakily. It might so easily have been a dream that they had a son now ten days old.

"I don't suppose we can ask the nurse to let you see him," Patience said.

The privilege of visiting your wife before breakfast at St. Luke's did not include a special glimpse of your son, Jesse reminded her. "Besides, Nicholas needs his beauty sleep to be in form for the daily reception."

"I hope"—Patience settled herself comfortably against her husband's shoulder—"that he looks exactly like you."

Jesse was more than handsome. Even the nurses said he was "cute," their highest form of praise. He was tall enough to be able to sit on the side of the bed and brace one foot against the floor, so that he held her exactly right. Perhaps he was too thin, but all young people were too thin, her mother said, and the good lines of his alert, intelligent face might have been lost if thickened.

"Your mother," Jesse was saying in his low voice that could never be compressed to a whisper, "sends her love, and I'm to tell you that she won't come today. There's something she has to attend to—very hush-hush, I gather. She told me this morning that the relatives will drop in, so you won't be lonely."

Patience laughed. "She means relatives other than grandparents, darling. Doctor Guye said that after the ninth day I can have visitors, one at a time. Mother's going to take Pauline and clean the apartment for us—but we must pretend to be surprised."

"Nicholas and I will never be able to keep secrets from you," Jesse sighed. "Or from your mother. Do you two communicate by thought waves?"

Patience shook her head. It had been her mother years ago who had opened the window after a summer storm and released a frightened bird imprisoned by its own wild haste to find sanctuary. The frenzied beating of wings against ceiling, walls, and window glass had terrified the little girl, who for the duration of the heavy downpour had shared the torment of that small creature gone mad. The bird had escaped, Patience remembered, it had been more fortunate than the trapped squirrels.

She said, hearing the steady strokes of Jesse's heart as he held her, "That girl in the ward—she must be sorry for her baby."

"What girl and whose baby?" Jesse wondered if his wife's shadowed gray eyes concealed some anxiety or doubt. That square-faced nurse had said to him the third day, "Your wife thinks too much, Mr. Garrison," and Patience and he had laughed together, for she had overheard the strident whisper.

"Well, of all the gay and cheerful before-breakfast stories!" he grumbled, when Patience had explained the tragedy. "Sure, I'm sorry for the poor kid, but I don't see any reason why you should be told a thing like that. You're here to be taken care of, not have your feelings harrowed."

Patience, her yellow head tucked beneath his chin, spoke hesitantly. "What do you want most for Nicholas, darling?"

"What do I want for him? Why—a good life, I suppose." Jesse, uneasy, wriggled. "I'm hardly used to him yet," he apologized.

"More than anything else in the world, I want him to have security." Patience hesitated. "If he feels secure, he'll feel free. Always."

That was one reason why having an apartment meant so much, she added after a moment's silence. "If it were twice the rent, I'd go without everything else, to have a place of our own, Jesse."

"You care that much, darling?" said Jesse's steady voice above her head.

"Not for myself—or us. For Nicholas. He must feel from the first that he's in his home and that nothing can frighten him. He's like a plant—he has to put down roots. I can't wait to fix up his room for him—a real boy's room."

The eager young voice trailed into the silence of dreaming, and Jesse, holding his wife so lightly and firmly, unconsciously sighed.

"Is anything the matter?" Instantly Patience stirred. "That's your worried sigh—I recognize it. You'd tell me if anything was wrong, wouldn't you, Jesse? We promised to tell each other things."

If a man couldn't take a deep breath without alarming the wife of his bosom, her nerves must be in a fine state, Jesse scolded. "What on earth could be wrong? You tell me."

"You might have decided we couldn't afford the apartment," Patience said. "Or the superintendent might have let someone else have it. You did sign a lease, didn't you, Jesse?"

"And paid six months' rent, spot cash in advance," Jesse testified.

Patience's body relaxed. "Then don't be giving those deep sighs," she commanded. "We're the luckiest people in the world."

Again the odor of coffee seeped into the room, a slightly acrid flavor and too strong. Somewhere in one of the rooms a woman's voice rose to a shriek, was silenced by the slam of a door. Patients occasionally lost their tempers and screamed at the nurses, Miss Coburn had said.

"Look here, maybe you need your breakfast or something," Jesse suggested. "Your mother doesn't think you get enough to eat."

"My mother—" Patience faltered, the new tenderness for her mother filling her heart unexpectedly and making speech difficult.

No one had told her how a woman felt toward her mother, with her first child in her arms. As the youngest and the only child at home—her sister had been married for many years—Patience had taken the love of her parents for granted, had been no more critical of her background than the usual adolescent. Since her marriage two years ago, she and Jesse had lived with her father and mother because there was no other place for them to live. Patience had kept her job, and the familiar pattern, followed by most of the young couples she knew, had worked out comfortably for herself and Jesse.

She had almost forgotten her mother in the first rapturous year of her married life. Her mother asked nothing, and Jesse asked a great deal. Even in her pregnancy she had found herself relying on her obstetrician and the "modern" ideas of her contemporaries, in preference to her mother, who might be bound by tradition.

The hunger for sight of her mother when she woke from her

twelve hours' sleep following the arrival of Nicholas had been a new experience. She had not been conscious of a veil between them, until her mother's kiss had sealed an understanding intangible yet complete. Remembering, Patience, for all her youth, knew with a sudden swift prescience that, though it might never happen again, the miracle could not be denied. *We were one spirit,* she thought.

She felt Jesse's arm tighten around her, and then his deep voice said, "Good morning, Miss Coburn."

"I thought you'd be here," beamed the nurse. "Your wife had a grand night, and the baby's breaking records. We call him 'Butch.' "

Jesse, grateful for the time she had allowed him, assured her that he was on his way, and she warned that the breakfast trays were due in five minutes. "It's getting warmer out, isn't it?" she added and as a final friendly gesture closed the door tightly behind her.

Patience giggled, and Jesse stood up, his dark hair ruffled. "Have a happy day, darling." His smiling brown eyes laughed with her. "Your mother was sure you'd have lots of company. Aunt Nellie plans to come this morning, I know."

Even if they couldn't afford it, a private room was worth the extra cost, Patience decided in a flurry of recklessness that communicated itself to her farewell kiss. "I *love* having you come in mornings," she declared.

But when he had reached the door and turned, she said hurriedly, "I mustn't get too used to having breakfast in bed—I don't want to become a pampered woman. And we need so many things for the apartment."

The nurse had been right, Jesse thought. He could never be sure what Patience had on her mind until she put her secret anxiety into words. Behind her shadowed gray eyes and that tranquil look of listening, she often went far away from him, walking alone and perhaps afraid. But she came back, he told himself exultantly, she always came back to him; it might be his imagination or vanity, but he fancied that since her marriage to him she was slowly, timidly, learning to feel more safe. Or she had been—until the birth of her child.

"Dishes," said Nellie Lake to the black cat, "just naturally gravitate to me."

The cat blinked eyes green as traffic lights and carefully re-adjusted his tail to make a neater coil. So arranged, he fitted exactly into the spot of sunlight he had discovered beside the kitchen sink.

"Mother! And I meant to help you." A young woman in a quilted red house coat stood in the kitchen doorway. She had dark hair and eyes, and her rouge and lipstick emphasized a total lack of color in her skin.

There was nothing to be done, Nellie assured her daughter-in-law. "If you're going to the doctor's, Rhoda, mind you undress and go to bed as soon as you get back. I'll be home in time to bring up your lunch."

The doctor charged a double fee for a house call, and Rhoda tried to go to the office for at least one of the four weekly treatments. She and Chris fretted because they couldn't pay board and doctor bills too, but Nellie made light of that.

"I don't think the first few years of married life are ever too easy, Rhoda," she had once said with the middle-aged philosophy that her sons' wives agreed was always consoling. "You look at other young couples—they have sickness to contend with, or their husbands are out of work, or they lose their furniture in a fire and have no insurance."

Rhoda objected that she knew older people who had it none too easy. "You and Dad, for instance."

"Oh, heavens, that's different. At first trouble is a new experience—gradually you learn that—that it isn't fatal." Nellie laughed. "Young folks are entitled to be helped over the first rough spots. The road gets better as you go on, Rhoda. You'll find it so."

Of course, Nellie admitted to herself, she and Luther had still to face the problem of their old age. They had been so confident, as the young, hopeful parents of three small boys, that in their middle years they could prepare for independence when old. The war had wrecked those plans, had disrupted their lives and those of their children, and had cost them all more, Nellie had begun to suspect, than any of them were willing to confess.

Now she told Rhoda to dress without hurrying and to take a cab. "There's always a taxi at the corner, dear."

The girl lingered in the doorway. "Are you going out, Mother? The twins said you gave them money for lunch at school."

It had been the twins, Rhoda's six-year-old daughters, who had brought her to paper napkins, Nellie reflected, the last dish dried and put away. She set the table for ten at breakfast and dinner regularly, and she had had to cut down on the laundry. Besides Luther and herself, Rhoda and Chris and their twins, there were Barry and Violet, Jerry and Seth. The house bulged at the seams, Luther said, but Nellie thanked God every night of her life that they had resisted the temptation to sell and move into an apartment.

She let fresh water run into her pan, put the dish towels to soak.

"I'm going up to St. Luke's, to see Patience Garrison's baby. This is the first day they've allowed anyone except grandparents to visit her."

"How lovely!" Rhoda smiled, remembering her own happiness. "They named him Nicholas, didn't they? Maybe Chris will take me over to see her after she gets home."

Nellie said, "Jesse finally found a beautiful apartment," and instantly wished she had kept still.

But Rhoda, dragging herself up the stairs, thought only that Patience had all the luck. She and Chris and the twins had been with Chris's people for four months, and all of that time she had been ill. They couldn't afford an apartment, even if they found one, and if Chris's parents had not been angels, they'd be living on the town. Not even Chris could appreciate his father and mother to the extent she did, Rhoda often assured him, for he had had them all his life.

Left alone, Nellie began to fill ten individual pudding molds with the cornstarch pudding cooked in the double boiler while she washed the dishes. She worked deftly, years of experience evident in her competent motions. A tall woman, large-boned, her figure a little thickened after thirty years of marriage, she still wore blue wash frocks because her husband continued to praise her blue eyes. Luther looked forward to dessert at every dinner; she had never been able to end a meal with the fresh fruit the nutrition experts so glibly recommended. With all the boys and their wives at home, however, she had been obliged to forego cakes and pies in favor of puddings and gelatin. Even so, the food bills were alarming.

She had shelved the hope of remodeling the kitchen, although she could not bring herself to throw away the collection of magazine clippings saved throughout the war. Luther had painted the walls and woodwork every year for her, had made the wall cabinets and a dresser for her bright-colored plates. A modern stove and refrigerator, magnificent as the Alps and about as unattainable on their present budget, could wait; but she did not think it unreasonable, Nellie argued in her low moments, to consider replacing the linoleum after fifteen years. The money, she admitted sensibly, always seemed to be urgently needed for something else.

The telephone rang, and she answered it, delighted to hear her sister Lou. Certainly she meant to go to the hospital today, Nellie said. She would have gone the second day, except for the rules. "I saw Lucy's babies the second day. So did Luther. And they seem to have survived."

"Oh, it's to spare the mother," Lou explained. "The modern idea doesn't encourage too many visitors. And the rest has done Patience a lot of good. She looks wonderful."

Nellie said unexpectedly, "Lou, are you worried about anything? The baby's all right, isn't he?"

"Of course. He's fine. And I'm *not* worried. What have I to worry about?" Lou's soft, low voice did not quicken.

Nellie sighed. "You don't have to have anything to worry about. You just worry. Is it the apartment?"

"Pauline and I are going to scrub the whole place today," Lou answered. "Jesse can do the painting at night, and I'll run up white curtains. But it's to be a surprise for Patience—don't tell her."

"And you're happy as a lark?" Nellie, two years the younger, had always been the protective one of the sisters.

Lou hesitated. "Well, I would feel better if they had stayed with us another year. I wanted them to have more money saved, before they set up housekeeping on their own." She never mentioned it to Hugh, Lou insisted, and she wouldn't dream of interfering. "If I do worry, I keep it to myself."

Nellie agreed half absently, listened to Lou's good-by, and cradled the handset. Strange, she thought, that Lou could be so blind to the consequences of her nervous fear. The most loving of wives and mothers, both Hugh, her husband, and Patience, her child, felt the tension she created without recognizing the source. Lou regretted her weakness, believed that she suffered alone, and refused to accept Nellie's warning that Patience especially was harmed.

"I don't exactly worry, but I always expect something to happen," Lou had once confided. "I never get a letter that I don't hesitate to open it—I have the feeling that it is bad news. I must have been born apprehensive."

She had been plagued all through her children's young years by her husband's business reverses, Nellie realized, and anxiety for their welfare had bred in her a fear of the future that never left her. Even a comfortable legacy to her husband had not enabled her to feel secure. She kept a rigid control over her distrust of life and would have been shocked by Nellie's accusation that she had infected either of her daughters, except that she honestly believed her sister to be mistaken.

Nellie turned from the phone to smile at Rhoda halfway down the stairs. "You look very nice, dear," she said.

Rhoda wore her winter coat, for the March sunshine, as Luther had remarked at breakfast, was more for looks than for warmth. The scarlet chesterfield—Rhoda loved red—lent a tinge of color to the pale face, and a small, tilted black hat was faced with red-and-white silk. That the thin young face under the smart little hat showed a spark of animation suddenly seemed to Nellie a pathetic admission of the dreary outline of each passing day. If a trip to see the doctor promised a break in routine, how weary of an invalid's discipline Rhoda must be!

"Take a cab and don't hurry." Nellie's warm, deliberate tone conveyed a pleasant approval. "Get yourself a new book at the circulating library on your way back. And go to bed as soon as you come back. I don't expect to be very late."

She watched Rhoda from the front doorway, saw her step into a cab at the corner stand. The postman, a sturdy old man, happily anticipating his pension in another year, paused at the foot of the steps, and Nellie went down to him to save him the short climb. He handed her two letters, reminded her as he always did, that she had met him halfway up the block in the mornings during the war. "You have no worries now," he chuckled and, shifting his heavy bag, crossed the street in a diagonal line.

One of the letters was addressed to Mrs. Barry Lake and had been mailed in England. Nellie hoped it might be from the mother of her oldest son's wife—poor Vi was so desperately homesick and unhappy in spite of all they could do for her.

The other envelope, addressed to Luther, carried the return address of a lumber firm. A quick breeze ruffled the gray hair that framed Nellie's kind, middle-aged face in a double ring of silky iron-gray spools. She looked at Midnight, the cat, sitting in the doorway, and she did not see him. "You have no worries now," the postman had said.

She went into the house, pushing Midnight gently before her, and closed the door. Everyone turned to the hall table for letters, and she dropped the two in the painted wooden tray Luther had made to hold the mail.

Luther's absorbing interest was working with woods. He had made himself an authority on his favorite subject, learning the different varieties of woods, their grains, and how to identify them even under commercial veneers. With the simplest tools he had taught himself to make beautiful things of his own design. The carved wooden chain and pendant and the exquisitely turned box into which it fitted were gifts for Patience to be delivered by Nellie today.

There had never been any extra money for him to spend on his hobby, but he had been able, because of his knowledge, to pick up handsome specimens of the hardwoods he coveted in old houses wrecked from time to time in various sections of the city to make way for more modern buildings. When the lumber shortage developed during the war, secondhand lumber began to interest even lumber dealers, and occasionally they had asked him to appraise the wood to be salvaged from old property. A trickle of such requests still came to him, and Nellie had recognized a familiar firm name on the letter addressed to Luther.

"My dish towels!"

She hurried to the kitchen, momentarily irritated at being caught off guard. The exclamation meant a five-cent fine, a punishment she had devised in an effort to cure the habit of talking to herself. The sincere horror of the girls had been, she supposed, the stimulus for her reform: to her sons' wives there seemed to be something almost repulsive in the practice.

"You're not an *old* woman," Rhoda had protested, and Vi, and yes, Jerry had looked at her as if she had been guilty of one of old age's obscenities.

"We must keep out of their sight when we finally collapse," Nellie said that night to Luther, and he laughed and retorted that their problem was likely to be how to dodge the company of their critics.

She was uneasy about Luther. Her hands busy in the rinse

water, she considered Luther's fresh cold and the puddings that ought to be put into the refrigerator, simultaneously but without confusion. Luther worried, of course, in spite of his belief that life had a design and plan even though no man could see it whole. "We must leave something to God," Luther said whenever Nellie, distressed by their inability to provide for a future old age because of the insistent demands of their children's youthful present, momentarily lost hope.

Working swiftly, she put the puddings into the refrigerator to chill, buttoned a heavy sweater over her cotton dress, and carried the towels out into the yard to be dried in the wind and sun. They had the house and a nice deep lot, she reminded herself, and if the taxes mounted every year, why, rents were increased too.

A woman in the next yard had finished wiping her clothesline with a clean cloth. "Wind gets you, doesn't it?" she called. "I always say March is a treacherous month."

Nellie pinned a towel straight, smiled. "I like it," she said.

You began to look toward the sun in March, she thought; courage, worn thin in the dead of winter, revived. She was glad that Patience's baby had been born in March—a brave, bright month that covenanted with the hopeful.

"Rhoda was showing me the afghan you knitted and the bunting you made for the baby." The neighbor had straddled a border of struggling green spears to reach the fence. "I always say you ought to sell the thing you turn out—you and Mr. Lake, too. Such beautiful work."

Nellie's blue eyes were amused. "I try to give the first baby things that will be useful for the second one. He, poor child, never gets the loot the first baby draws. And the third—don't I know!—is lucky if he can count on new diapers."

"My heavens, no one has three!" The neighbor, remembering Nellie's sons, amended hastily, "That is, not any more."

The distant ringing of her telephone called her indoors, and Nellie, turning toward her own back steps, reminded herself that the house would have to be painted this spring. Seen from the rear it looked hopelessly grimy and battered. Luther, after an evening at the movies where a tropical film featured pink and blue plaster houses, had suggested that they paint it black with red trim, to match the city's smoke and soot. But he acknowledged, when cornered, that they couldn't afford to paint the house any color at all.

Nor were they likely to realize the dream of opening a shop in the living room, Nellie mused, using a handy clothespin to comb dead leaves from the trellis set at the side of the steps. She and Luther had the shop planned down to the exact location of every item in the showcases and on the shelves. They had talked about the shop night after night, in the evenings when they were alone, or after they were in bed.

"We must get it going before we're old, and then it will carry us through," Luther liked to say. "How much more do we have to save, Mother, before we can ask Pancke for an estimate?"

A big window was to take up most of one wall, transforming the conservative living room into a shop. Monk's-cloth curtains and hooked rugs, and turquoise enameled chests for Nellie's sewing, knitting, and crocheting, waxed cherry cabinets and shelves for Luther's woodwork.

It would take money to start the shop, not a great deal but enough to finance the first six critical months. Nellie knew that she and Luther could sell whatever they were able to get ready for Christmas. It was a family joke that everything in the Lake household must be kept under lock and key at holiday time or some avid shopper would seize the entire collection for Christmas gifts.

"You haven't talked so much about opening a shop since the boys came out of service," Lou, speaking frankly as a sister can, had once or twice reminded Nellie. "I suppose the twins' tonsil operation took the money once; then you've had to help Chris with Rhoda's doctor bills, too. And I remember Vi and Barry wanted a lot of new furniture, and you probably helped them. If you and Luther don't look out for yourselves, no one else will do it."

Lou could sit at the phone and talk like that with Patience and Jesse occupying the first floor (Patience must be saved stairs) and filling the house night after night with young people who were always politely astonished to discover that they had turned the radio up too loud.

"Well, naturally you do what you can for your children," Lou defended herself, when discrepancies between her opinions and her performance were called to her wandering attention. "It doesn't seem like a normal world to me any more—does it to you, Nellie? I think postwar marriages carry almost as heavy a load as those made during the war. Someone has to help, and mostly it's the parents."

You did what you could for your children, Nellie thought, looking up at the blank windows of her shabby house without seeing the scaling paint now or the two cracked panes that each of the three boys in turn had promised to replace.

Barry, the oldest, had married an English girl, Violet, who after a year and a half in the United States was still violently homesick and refused all friends except those like herself exiled from England. The home Barry had so eagerly furnished for Vi, borrowing money from his parents because his bride had definite and expensive tastes, had not made her happy; when Barry lost his job and found another at a lower salary, the smart little apartment had been lost, too. Barry had brought Violet home for a few days to recover from the shock. The days had lengthened into weeks, but the English girl had begun, they all thought, to act more as if she felt herself at home.

A noise, faint, undefinable, within the house, focused Nellie's attention sharply on the present. Midnight had a habit of hurling himself from the kitchen-cabinet top to the floor, as if he hoped to shake the walls. He might be trying to compel her notice by this trick, and in any case she must go in and change her dress.

"Why, Jerry!" There in the cheerful coral-and-cream kitchen stood her daughter-in-law.

Nellie hoped she did not show surprise, but Jerry should have been at her office an hour ago. The slim, tall girl with the shining dark eyes and hair, married to Seth, her youngest son, was Nellie's daughter in spirit and in love. She had known Jerry to be the girl child she had never borne, from their first meeting—the hurts that Seth dealt her, his mother, mattered little, but his careless indifference or definite unkindness to Jerry kindled her quick resentment.

"Are you ill, dear? Did you have to come back?" Nellie searched her memory to discover whether Jerry had looked pale at the breakfast table, had refused hot muffins, or had been snubbed by Seth.

The girl's pointed forefinger traced an imaginary design on the porcelain-topped table. "I waited for everyone to go. I thought Rhoda never would get off."

Then it was Seth. Nellie sat down a little suddenly in one of the two straight chairs. Jerry had amazing patience for one so young, but even a wife's patience has its limitations. A lovely girl, this pretty creature, gentle, soft-spoken, willing to put love before pride, but with enough strength to guard her self-respect.

Jerry looked up from her tracing. She could force her lips to smile, but her brown eyes were troubled. "Seth's leaving," she said.

"Leaving?" Nellie felt as she did when her foot missed a step on the stairs. "Why, he lives here," she insisted stupidly. Her body sagged, but she denied the great weariness that weighted her bones and made her conscious of a new clumsiness. She couldn't be so exhausted in the morning, just after a good breakfast. "Did Seth say he wants to leave?" she tried again.

"Yes," Jerry said. "He's going. Tonight, I think. You know how he is when he's made up his mind."

Nellie had persuaded herself that it was the war. No one returned from war unaltered, and Luther had warned her that none of the boys could be as they had been.

Seth had been slow to shake off the restlessness that had at first possessed them all. He seemed selfishly unwilling to share his leisure, his plans for the future, or his uncertain income with his wife, and he had lost the boyish friendliness that had been his distinguishing charm.

"He wasn't like that before he went into the Army," Luther insisted when Seth's brothers criticized him. "I've never thought that war brings out the best in any of us."

Jerry had blamed the war, too, for her husband's moodiness. She never questioned him or attempted to pry into his mind; she suspected that he was as confused by his actions as his family was, and if she could not help him at least she could spare him reproach. No man ever had a more loyal wife, Nellie thought; she would not have been half so surprised had Jerry announced that she wanted a separation.

"Has he—has he asked for a *divorce?*" Her involuntary emphasis of the word vexed Nellie as much as the hushed tone in which she uttered it.

To her relief Jerry burst into laughter, crinkling her brown eyes and showing a flash of her very white teeth.

"Darling, you've heard about divorces, haven't you? Mrs. Moore across the street got one—and it was all in the paper—last week."

Jerry stepped lightly around the table and dropped a quick kiss on Nellie's cheek. "Of course when it's your family, that's different."

Well, it was, mused Nellie, suddenly conscious of overpowering exhaustion that made it an effort even to breathe. Jerry and Seth had been married during the last year of the war, no, in 1944—why, they had been married four years! Seth had been restless, true, but a man could be restless without breaking up his marriage. And he loved Jerry—they had been in school together, although Seth was three years older than his wife.

"He hasn't said that he wants a divorce." Jerry was the restless one now, walking from table to stove and from the stove to the window, where she stood tall enough to look over the cottage curtains but obviously seeing nothing in the yard beyond.

"I think he's tired of being married." Jerry's young voice

sounded bewildered. "Other men are free, he says, they can go and come. There isn't anyone else, he tells me, but he hates his job. He's going off by himself to—to rest."

Midnight stretched in the rocking chair, and his features assumed a sardonic leer intended to be a yawn. He meowed derisively and resettled his tail.

"What about you, Jerry?" Nellie asked.

The slim shoulders shrugged. "I'll wait till he comes back."

She would speak to Luther, Nellie promised, Seth must be out of his mind, but his father could bring him round. Quiet as he was, Luther had the respect of his sons, and they had a wholesome dread of rousing his just anger. "Seth is acting abominably. His father will know what to say to him." It was a confession, Nellie thought, that his mother didn't, but let that pass.

Jerry came back to the table, folded her pretty, smooth hands together, and let them rest lightly on the white surface. The full sleeves of her pink linen blouse gave her a mid-Victorian air, currently quaint. "Don't tell Dad. Seth would only resent it. And he'd hate me. I'd be a millstone then, instead of just a mistake."

There must be something she could do, Nellie reflected; it was absurd to be middle-aged and still feel confused. Young people today were different; their passionate determination to consider themselves first in every situation could not be altogether explained by the war and the aftermath of war. Luther had served in the First World War, and he had shown no inclination to please himself at the expense of those who loved him. As far as she knew, Luther had never longed to desert her or the children, but how could she be sure? Perhaps he had disciplined himself to silence where his son would think it cowardly not to speak.

"We have to let him go." Jerry broke the strange quiet in which the clearing of one's throat or the sudden creaking of a chair startled taut nerves.

Nellie waited, dismayed by the chaos in her own mind.

"You see"—Jerry spoke slowly as if she felt her way—"Seth thinks we're all watching him, that we want to run his life for him.

He has an idea that Dad wants him to take any job, whether it interests him or not." Seth had told her that she had what she wanted but that he wasn't satisfied. "He says all the women in this house believe that the success of a marriage depends upon a man's willingness to sacrifice his personal ambitions."

He had talked half the night, and Jerry had been sick at the resentments he had uncovered. He wanted to take the car and start out with no destination and no goal. He might write home and he might not. The thing was he must not be bound in any way.

"The car," Nellie said dully, "is really yours. You paid for it."

Jerry bit her lip. She had paid for more than the small coupe that Seth coveted. Maybe she had paid too much for love. She could not add up her accounts. No one could. In the end the answer might be that love was worth whatever you paid for it.

Someone passed the house whistling, and the shrill, swift notes stirred the thick silence of the room.

"He is so dreadfully unhappy," Jerry sighed. "Perhaps he thought that after the war he would never be unhappy again. We all believed that, didn't we?"

Nellie remembered the postman's remark, but she merely nodded agreement.

"So much was promised." Jerry's voice, grave now, held a faintly accusing note. "Sometimes I think Seth has only believed too much."

He couldn't expect to contribute nothing, Nellie protested. The world would never right itself unless everyone took hold and did his part. "Seth asks a great deal, but he doesn't *give*."

"He gave." Jerry's dark eyes flamed suddenly in her quiet face. "He saw things he can't talk of. Some boys have forgotten, because it was expected of them—Seth is the odd one. He can't take up where he left off, for he was young when he left off and he isn't young any more."

Nellie said again, "What about you, Jerry?"

"I'm all right." The dark head came up proudly. "I know I love him and always will. It's Seth who doubts."

She had her plans, she said, and she was so patently anxious to prove herself in control of her emotions that Nellie could do no less than assume an equally capable air. She wanted to continue to live with Nellie, Jerry began bravely, but only if she might pay board.

Seth had said at first that his father and mother understood that a young couple must get on their feet. Now that she was to have her pay envelope for herself, she was firmly resolved to contribute to the household expenses. "You and Dad have carried us all too long," she urged.

She forestalled Nellie's objections neatly. "Otherwise I'll have to go to my mother's. And—I'd rather stay here."

Her mother, and to a lesser extent her father, would bring pressure on her to divorce Seth. They thought she didn't know how to handle him, and they felt that she would be well rid of him. There would be no peace for Jerry under her mother's roof; she would have no chance to listen to her heart, to make her own decisions, or to see Seth in the light of whatever her future convictions might be. Once she was separated from her husband and had returned to her parents, Jerry's only role in their eyes would be that of the injured wife.

"It will be better if you stay here," Nellie acknowledged and, having made a definite decision, felt a measure of relief. But the heaviness still weighted her body, and she knew a fear that touched all her children since she had cause to be uneasy for one.

Jerry put a strong, slender arm across her shoulders and kissed her gently. "I have a little shopping to do for Seth—he needs some things. Want to come? I'm taking the day off."

Patience and her baby and the hospital assumed a place again in Nellie's unquiet mind. The presents were wrapped; she had only to change her dress and perhaps put on a little lipstick—

"I'm due at St. Luke's this morning, dear," she smiled at Jerry.

But she did not mention Nicholas, because she remembered that Jerry, when she had consented to buy the car, had said that she would much rather have a child.

Chapter Two

THE nurse's aide, a pretty woman with smartly waved white hair and gold hoop earrings, said that Mrs. Garrison was in No. 33 and ready for visitors. "She looks lovely, too," the aide twinkled at Nellie.

Patience, propped high on her pillows, a sky-blue hand-knit bed jacket over her gown and a matching ribbon threaded through her cap of gold hair, might have been twelve, rather than twenty-one. The warmth of her kiss surprised and pleased Nellie, who could remember when the baby in the family had been this gray-eyed girl.

"Well, my dear!" Nellie put her packages on the bed, began to unbutton her heavy coat. "No need to ask you how you feel—you've got the sun and the moon and the stars in your pocket, and you look it."

Patience laughed a little uneasily. "Auntie, half the time I don't believe it. Last night I dreamed that Doctor Guye explained to me that Nicholas was only a doll and he'd given it to me to keep me from crying. He said I'd have to give it back, too, because it was so expensive."

The shadowed eyes were intent on the ribboned parcels, the pretty mouth curved in a smile, but how could one be sure that apprehension vanished with a dream? Heaven help the young, Nellie thought, folding her coat on the chair, automatically straightening the few articles on the dresser, and noting that the vase of yellow tulips needed more water; the less experience one had of living, the stronger one's imaginary fears.

"Oh, Auntie, how lovely!" Patience had unwrapped the carved chain and pendant. "It's Uncle Luther's beautiful work—I'd know it anywhere."

She put it on at once, so that everyone who came in would see it, and asked for the hand mirror in which to admire it. "I'll wear it with my blue tweed suit when I go home," she planned. "And I can hand it down to my grandchildren." This suddenly discovered interest in heirlooms rather surprised her.

The bunting and the afghan were for Nicholas, Nellie said; he must make a good impression; the Garrisons would have to meet inspection from their new neighbors. "You in your tweeds and himself in his eiderdown," she suggested.

The bunting and afghan admired, Nellie proceeded to fold up paper and string, rescued the collection of magazines cascading off the foot of the bed, and straightened the throw rug that the doctor invariably kicked aside. Every movement of her capable hands furthered the effect of neatness and space. There would never be enough aides, she thought; perhaps if she made an extra effort she could find the time to give a half day a week at St. Luke's; during the war she had served six afternoons regularly.

"Tell me about the baby, Patience." She seated herself beside the bed. "He's quite a young man, I hear. Your mother will be disappointed not to have a chance to spoil him."

As if she had been waiting a signal, Patience squared her shoulders, took a deep breath. "Auntie, he's wonderful! Really extra. Even the nurses say so. The little babies I've seen have all been shriveled and ugly, but Nicholas looks as bright as a button, and so compact. I mean he doesn't dangle. He's perfectly put together."

"You do feel relieved when you find they're arrived all in one piece," Nellie recollected. "The shouting and the tumult usually fosters doubts."

There had been shouting and tumult, Patience admitted with a fleeting smile. "Auntie, don't think it's my imagination, but he knows me already. He looks at me in a certain way."

All babies, decided Nellie, absently smoothing the counterpane, should have young and beautiful mothers to reconcile them to entering a cold, strange world. Nicholas, already subject to the hospital's discipline and routine, must turn gratefully to one serene face to be reassured of tenderness and love.

For a moment the small, neat room, freshly aired and bright with light reflected from the court, seemed far away from the busy life of the hospital and the still busier world beyond. But a bell rang in the corridor, and a subdued murmur of voices instantly followed.

"You can see him now!" Patience quickened to excitement and delight. "Don't let anyone hurry you, Auntie. Make the nurse hold him up for you to get a good look at him."

The nursery at the far end of the corridor already had its queue of eager spectators, although not so many as would line up for the inspection that night. Nellie, waiting her turn, saw only two young women in the group. Middle-aged matrons and frankly old ladies, as grandmothers, held almost a monopoly of the visiting privileges.

"The only way I'll ever have one will be through adoption." The slender, red-haired girl standing before Nellie spoke to anyone who might listen.

A proud grandmother began to coo proudly to the bundle the nurse held up behind the glass door. "The first girl in our family in forty years," the grandmother confided.

"My husband won't hear of adopting a baby." The second young woman, a handsomely dressed tall girl, stared moodily at the blanketed infant. "I tell him it's our duty to give some child a home, but he says it's our own or none."

The nurse continued to shift babies in rapid succession, and the red-haired girl admired her sister's child and went away. Nellie said "Garrison" through the glass and beamed upon Nicholas, a child who slept with such concentrated determination that his tiny hands clenched and his eyelids puckered into rosettes.

"He's just grand, isn't he?" Nellie turned aside to find the tall girl watching her with unhappy eyes.

The girl shrugged impatiently. Her silver fox jacket smelled of violets, and her beautifully tailored wool frock, the color of violets, was fastened at the throat with an amethyst pin. "Babies all look alike to me," she said.

The visitors were dispersing, chattering gaily and eager to report to the proud mothers. Nellie put a kind hand on the silky fur of the sleeve nearest her. "Did you come to see a special baby?"

"My best friend's. She—the mother—died. And everyone told her that modern science has made maternity perfectly safe." Fear overlaid the scorn in the girl's repressed voice. "I've made up my mind never to go through with it."

Nellie, walking beside her, said nothing.

"Grace was only twenty-two. And her husband will marry again and be happy. It isn't fair." She halted her long strides because Nellie had stopped opposite a door marked "33." "I suppose you think I'm an awful coward," she said.

The door, a quick glance assured Nellie, was closed.

"You can't do much of anything with your life as long as you're afraid," she warned. "Any fear is always worse than the thing itself."

The girl gestured toward the closed door. "Your daughter wasn't afraid to have a baby, then?"

"My niece." Nellie smiled at a passing nurse. "Oh, no, she wasn't afraid to have a child, but she has other assorted fears. We all do."

"What's she afraid of?"

Nellie did not know. "Perhaps I can help her, perhaps not. Sometimes it's difficult, and I don't like to pry."

"You probably think I ought to have a baby. Everyone does." The girl twisted her long, soft gloves nervously.

"Not necessarily. But I think you ought not to be afraid to have one," Nellie said and hoped that she did not sound virtuous or stiff. Patience must be wondering what detained her, but she couldn't be brusque.

The girl turned as if to go, swung round again. "My husband wouldn't care if I died," she said.

"It's all because you're undecided about the baby," Nellie assured her. "You may be saving your life, or you think you are, but it isn't much use to you, is it?"

"No," said the girl. "No, it isn't." She nodded a sober little good-by and started down the corridor toward the elevator, her heels striking sharply on the tile floor.

Patience greeted Nellie with suppressed eagerness. "Well?"

"He's a beautiful baby." Nellie spoke authoritatively as became the mother of three sons. "Solid like a pink velvet pincushion and able to sleep without rocking, as your grandmother would say. You needn't worry about his formula either—he has a fine start."

The nurse's aide interrupted them to bring a pitcher of fresh water for the tulips. "Your sister and your grandmother telephoned, Mrs. Garrison. They're going to try to come this afternoon. Is there anything I can get for you?"

Mrs. Landley had kept her figure, Nellie admitted wistfully, as Patience introduced her. A middle-aged woman who wore a size twelve probably lived on lettuce and tea. For a moment Nellie pictured Luther's reaction if she made her dinner of lettuce and tea.

"Your baby's perfectly lovely, Mrs. Garrison," the slender, beige-frocked aide said. "I tell my husband the babies get nicer every year—it's partly because they improve the feeding, I think."

She went away smiling, and Patience remarked that she was a rich woman who with her husband had endowed a bed in memory of her only son killed in the war. "She has two married daughters and five grandchildren," Patience said.

"A hospital is a complete world, isn't it, Auntie?" she went on. "Sometimes I lie here and think of all the people—Nicholas and the other new little babies beginning their lives; the mothers, young like me, and the patients in the surgical and accident wards, who may be old. And probably every night somebody dies."

Nellie believed in letting people talk. Lou, she suspected, tried resolutely to direct Patience's thoughts into approved and cheerful channels. The danger of attempting to direct thoughts was that you could not be sure whether you helped or harmed. Poor Lou, who hid her own anxieties behind reassuring phrases, could strangely enough find comfort in the same empty words paid back to her.

"What else do you think about?" Nellie asked.

Patience twisted a lock of her yellow hair, a gesture carried over from childhood. Nellie had seen her evening after evening doing her homework and tugging at a strand. Incredible that the years had passed so quickly and that you must begin to remember almost before you realized how far you had come.

"I think about the apartment, of course," Patience said. "Has Mother told you that we have the top floor in a remodeled house? All the way through, and wonderful rooms with a little porch at the back—a balcony, really, but just right for Nicholas. The rent is paralyzing, but Jesse says someone has to send the landlord's children to college."

"Save on something else," Nellie advised, thankful that young and untried housekeepers never asked what.

Patience thought it would be fun to have a housewarming. "I'll have all the cousins. Auntie, I didn't ask you—how is everyone?"

Nellie accounted for her brood, shielding Jerry without difficulty because Patience, politely attentive, was still incurious about lives that did not have a direct impact upon her own. In many ways it was a shattering experience to have a baby, Nellie conceded, and Nature probably protected a young mother by invisible restrictions.

"I like to look at you, Auntie." Patience might not have been listening at all. "You look as if you had everything all thought out."

"You mean smug?" Nellie turned to the dresser mirror in some alarm.

Patience, too much in earnest to laugh, tried to be explicit. "I think I mean you look—secure. As if you knew the way out."

"The way out?" prompted Nellie, instantly economical of words.

She would never be able to forget the squirrels, Patience decided. As clearly as if she had been there the picture of the gnawed window frames and the trapped, lifeless, small, furred creatures had stamped itself upon her brain. A second picture, equally detailed, was that of the frantic animals hurling themselves against the glass and outside the tall pine trees and a carpet of snow. Sun on the snow in the morning and the moon at night—how many days and nights could a squirrel live without water or food? *If you don't know there is a way out, it might as well not be there.*

"I never thought much about what I was doing to Nicholas. But now I feel so responsible," Patience confessed. "Do you suppose he'll blame me? When he's old enough to blame anyone?"

She spoke half to herself, and the withdrawn, listening look deepened in her eyes.

"Why should he blame you at all?" This was Lou's daughter all right, thought Nellie, wondering if it had been a mistake to assign Patience a single room.

The carved chain and pendant swung forward as Patience propped herself higher, and the line of her full breasts showed sharply under the blue jacket. "He might have to go to war," she said.

There had been generations of women who bore their children without memories of wars past or fears of wars to come, Nellie thought wearily. How long must it be before mothers could believe in peace again and hold their sons in their arms without remembering that armies needed men?

"Suppose Nicholas grows up and must go to war—like Jesse and your Chris and Barry and Seth and all the boys we know," Patience said. "He might be eighteen, or twenty, with all he wants to do planned. And instead he is dragged through horrible suffering. Perhaps he's wounded and dies. While he is still so young. Would it be so strange if he blamed me, his mother, for having brought him into the world before we've made it a—a fit place to live in?"

The gray eyes had darkened, and the shadows that swept in under them seemed to have darkened too.

Nellie stood up, reassurance in every line of her comfortable, solid figure. She put one firm, warm hand over the slim, white fingers that fumbled with the pendant, and her voice was steady and sweet.

"Lamb, you've been turning things over so much in your mind that you've missed the answer plain before you: the men who have been to war and have come back are eager to have children. Chris has the twins. Barry was thrilled at the idea of a baby, until Vi's miscarriage. Have you forgotten the veterans and their husky families? Perhaps they feel that children are needed to help shape a better world."

Patience felt the tension throughout her body slacken as if every small, quivering nerve had been relieved of strain. Perhaps Aunt Nellie had healing power—certainly when, as now she removed her hand, she left a sense of tranquillity as light and lovely as a happy dream. She had been right to ask Aunt Nellie, Patience thought: her own mother had never had a son, and Jesse's mother had died years ago. His stepmother, married late and childless, always seemed a trifle self-conscious in her maternal role.

A lassitude so delicious that she sought to prolong its luxury assailed Patience. She stifled a yawn. "What do you think, Auntie? About having children, I mean. When things are as they are."

"Sleep, darling," Nellie spoke softly. She began to space her words almost in rhythm. "Having children is part of the pattern of life. There is a pattern. I don't believe that any child is born who wasn't meant to enter this world. Or who hasn't a place here." She stepped away from the bed, moved toward the door. "Life isn't haphazard, it has a pattern," she repeated.

A student nurse peered in, nodded, and retreated as Nellie put a finger to her lips.

"Maybe she'll sleep till her lunch comes up," the youngster whispered eagerly when Nellie reached the hall. "The doctor was in early this morning, so nothing will disturb her."

Nellie surveyed her appreciatively, noting how the blue-and-white striped uniform set off the clear skin and chestnut-brown hair combed smoothly back and netted in a large bun. Girls that age had so much vitality some of it must spill over into the rooms and wards they tended, although it must be admitted that they sometimes spilled the contents of the trays instead.

"Are you Mrs. Lake?" The student nurse was breathless, as if perpetually excited by the duties of her profession.

"Yes," Nellie said.

"Well, the switchboard operator has a number for you to call. She was afraid you might go out without her seeing you. The elevator lets you off right in front of the switchboard in the main hall."

Nellie thanked her, shut herself into the self-service car. She hoped that Rhoda would rest quietly in bed—if she reached home first—and not try to get her own lunch. Probably Rhoda would be better off in a first-class hospital, but few hospitals had space for patients not in need of surgery. There seemed to be no provision made for the woman of ordinary means whose health might depend on a respite from accumulative pressures. Long ago women like Nellie's mother had looked upon their confinements as periods of well-earned relaxation, when they could expect to have two full weeks in bed without household responsibility. Now even this brief release had been cut to conform to shortages in beds and nurses, so that the average maternity case was discharged in less than ten days. Patience's doctor had insisted that she remain a fortnight, a ruling that, she had told her mother, made her a marked woman throughout St. Luke's.

The main hall of the hospital, dark and clean—it was the oldest part of the group of buildings—stretched an indeterminate length to the right and the left of the open offices. Benches set in niches broke the straight lines of the corridor, and huddled figures sat on each bench. Although it was nearly noon of a sunny day, the dome lights burned in the ceiling and flickered on the columns of polished wood. The only signs of life the various figures displayed were slight movements of the hands or feet or the turning of a head when a step sounded on the tiled floor.

"You have a message for me?" Nellie smiled at the switchboard operator, a middle-aged woman with a hairdo that resembled a gray stone castle set on a cliff.

The castle lurched perceptibly as the operator held out a paper slip. "You Mrs. Lake? They want you should call that number. There's a pay station down the hall."

Nellie recognized the number as that of Lucy Gray's office. Lucy was the sister of Patience. She was sixteen years older than Patience, and her two children, a girl of fifteen and a boy of seventeen, could offer the small Nicholas no companionship. There was such a thing as spacing your children too widely, the gossips sometimes commented, ignorant of the series of miscarriages that Lou kept a secret.

The two phone booths, both in use, faced a bench. Nellie seated herself beside a round-shouldered, stocky man zippered into a leather windbreaker. He held his cap between his knees, his elbows resting on his thighs and his chin on his hands.

"Do you know how long an operation takes?" he asked, not looking up from the floor.

There was no set time, Nellie tried to explain. "Some require a longer time than others. If you're waiting to hear, someone will let you know."

"I been here two hours." The man's gaze came up to rest on the laughing face of a girl in the phone booth. "My daughter—"

Nellie's sympathetic, "I'm sorry. I know how you feel—I have children, too," apparently stirred his apathy.

"She was out with a fellow last night—the cops chased them, and there was a smashup. But she didn't know the car was stolen. She told me she didn't know."

The girl in the phone booth put in another nickel. Nellie, eager to get home to Rhoda, sighed. In the second booth a man talked placidly, making notes on a pad as he spoke.

"We didn't want to keep her in too much," the man said, the doubt that was to haunt him forever heavy in his tormented eyes. "You have to let a girl go out with boys—her mother and I talked it over. We were both brought up too strict."

Nellie thought of similar conferences. You must not be too strict, Luther had reminded her. They must learn to stand on their own feet, he had said.

"You do what you can for your children," the dull, bewildered voice beside her muttered. "And then it comes to this."

You do what you can for your children. Lou had said that. Nellie could not know how or where this man had failed. Had she and Luther failed with Seth? There was no room for smugness in any parent's summing up, and the responsibility ended only at death.

The girl in the phone booth began to fumble with the door, still speaking into the mouthpiece. Nellie rose, looked down at the huddled figure.

"She is young. You can still help her," she comforted. "When you know what you must do, the important thing is not to give up."

Not to give up was the important thing for all of them, she thought, stumbling a little as she wedged herself into the vacated phone booth, which smelled of cigarette smoke, perfume, and disinfectant. Through the glass as she dialed she watched the man on the bench, his shoulders hunched, his gaze fixed on the old cap between his knees.

"Mrs. Gray, please," she said into the phone. "Lucy? This is Aunt Nellie. I'm at the hospital."

Lucy's light, clear voice had the pleasant pitch of the habitual telephone speaker. "Auntie, I'm trying to get away to see Patience. It's my afternoon off, but everything hinders me. I phoned Mother to ask if it would be all right to go up to St. Luke's, but no one answered."

Nellie explained her sister's absence, wondering how Lucy had known where to reach her. "Did you call me at home, dear?"

"Yes, and Jerry told me you'd just left. Will this afternoon be all right? I don't want to have Doctor Guye lecture me, if Patience is supposed to lie low."

The doctor had approved visitors, and Patience seemed thoroughly rested, Nellie answered. "Mother is going to drop in this afternoon, I hear. But, Lucy, I've been meaning to ask you—have you heard anything about Ross Garrison's wife? She and Patience are such friends, but Patience didn't say anything about expecting her."

"Heather's home from the hospital—I know that," Lucy said. "But she still has a nurse. I've phoned several times, but the dragon says no visitors yet. No one seems to know *what* the trouble is."

Nellie talked a few more minutes, asking about Lucy's children and husband, answering questions in return. As she hung up the receiver, she saw a nurse's aide stop beside the man still on the bench.

"Come down to the coffee shop and have something hot to drink," the aide urged, glancing absently at Nellie involved with the phone-booth door. "You'll get word just as quickly down there."

The man did not speak, but he got to his feet, and they walked toward the stairway that led to the basement coffee shop. Nellie thought of the girl in the accident ward—no, the operating room—and of the parents who had done what they could. For a moment she felt, like Patience, awed and mystified by the world within a world that was this busy hospital, where human beings lived and died, their stories never completely told.

Outside in the street the wind stirred the winter's accumulation of dust and trash, sweeping it purposelessly from one corner to another, and the lemon-colored sunshine seemed diluted even at noon. But the window of the florist shop opposite the hospital offered tulips and daffodils and a forest of pussy-willow branches, the catkins faintly tipped with rose.

Nellie, waiting for the bus, heard the clatter of dishes in the drugstore, the inevitable neighbor of the flower shop in a hospital zone. The odor of boiled coffee, frying bacon, and soft-drink sirups drifted through the door left open for ventilation. The passion for eating at soda fountains alternately amused and irritated her.

Seth, when he had the money, ate three times a day in any convenient drugstore, and Jerry believed that the habit carried over from his Army days.

"The boys were so crazy to get away from camp food, they went into town every chance they could get and flocked to the soda fountains," she told Nellie. "Seth must have eaten hundreds of toasted sandwiches."

But Violet, Barry's English wife, considered drugstore meals, breakfasts especially, the refuge of selfish males and lazy housewives.

"Jerry, I see these men having their nice little quiet breakfasts, with the hot toast and the paper cup of marmalade and eggs and bacon and coffee, served to them just as they order—the toast not too brown, the egg fried or boiled just so." Violet with one expressive gesture of her long white hands made you see the neatly arranged club breakfasts.

"It's all cheerful and quiet, each man reads his paper," Violet went on. "He doesn't have to wait on the children or speak to his wife. She's home, struggling with babies and bottles and doorbells. And probably there isn't enough money, but he must have his breakfast out—it costs money, even a small breakfast for one."

With surprise Nellie realized that the brisk young man on the curb had stepped back to allow her to enter the bus first. Nothing made her feel so old, she had once confided to Luther, as to have a young man offer her his seat in a bus. "Unless it's the feeling that I'd drop from fatigue, if he didn't," she added.

The need to be alone, to quiet the uneasiness that had weighted her heart since morning, to strengthen the faith that she must pass on to others made her leave the bus two blocks from the house. Here was the beautiful silent old Church of the Ascension, a familiar sanctuary to Nellie, who always slipped into the last pew, where the amethyst and purple and gray shadows closed around her like a curtain and healing was in the very air.

Kneeling, it seemed to Nellie that she had been praying all her life for her children. For the boys and for Rhoda, Vi, and Jerry, who had become her children, too. Everyone had prayed during the war, the churches had been filled at all services, and now with the war ended the pews were empty again. As if, thought Nellie, conscious of an aching bone, for the faded green velvet kneelers were thin, they preferred to depend on God only in a crisis.

"Do you think we prayed too hard?" she had asked Luther a few days ago when they had admitted to each other that the safe return of their sons had not absolved them of anxiety and stress.

Luther's quick smile assured her he understood. "Well, we did storm Heaven, but you don't suggest that the Lord rebukes prayer?"

Her eyes on the ivory and gold altar, Nellie said her prayers as simply and sweetly as she had prayed from childhood. The idea that she might ask too much did not trouble her, nor did she hesitate to make her petitions detailed. As a child she had had so much to ask God that, night after night, she had fallen asleep saying her prayers, and she still slept often, kneeling beside her bed, because she loved so many and their needs were great.

A lovely peace warm in her breast, she waited quietly for a moment, when she had finished. A half-dozen supplicants knelt, widely scattered, in the old box pews. The altar was without flowers since it was Lent, but the carpet glowed ruby red in a shaft of sunlight. On a side wall the service flag studded with stars hung, a mute record to be incorporated in the church history. The light picked out six gold stars.

"There is a pattern." Nellie whispered to herself the assurance she had given Patience. . . .

The house was too warm when she reached it, and the hot, dry blast of air reminded her forcibly of the winter's coal bill on which the last ton must still be paid. Vi and Rhoda bickered constantly about the heat, and the English girl condemned central heating as unhealthy and a wicked waste; but Vi habitually forgot to turn off the lights, and the electricity bills mounted. The boys, Seth especially, resented the slightest hint from either parent that current might be saved, and Nellie suspected that all the young people privately confused extravagance with generosity and distrusted thrift as a mean and parsimonious gesture.

Nellie, relieved to find Rhoda asleep, exchanged her black crepe dress—no one ever expected her to wear anything else, there must be millions of middle-aged women in black crepe uniforms—for her favorite blue cotton and went down to the cellar to fix the furnace drafts. She answered the doorbell, convinced the huckster that she needed no bargain in cauliflower, and hurried upstairs to quiet the awakened Rhoda.

"It's all right, dear—I heard the bell." Nellie once would have automatically straightened the room as she talked, folding up the garments strewn on chairs, picking up the shoes and gloves dropped on the rug, closing the closet door on the accumulation too hopeless to be put right. Now acquired tact enabled her to say only, "I'll bring your lunch up right away, Rhoda. You look much better—the doctor is doing you good."

She broiled the liver, made toast, arranged an attractive tray. If Rhoda spent the greater part of the day in bed, she usually felt able to come down to dinner, and that encouraged Chris, as Vi said, "no end." The twins, too, persuaded themselves that Mommy was well again if she sat at the table with them.

"Stay and talk a minute," Rhoda urged, when Nellie brought her the food. "Tell me about Patience and her baby."

Nellie took Rhoda's coat and a woolen skirt from a small chair and sat down near the bed. Patience looked wonderfully well and happy, she said. "The baby's just fine, too. I kept remembering how Patience looked when she was two days old."

"They have an apartment, haven't they? Patience and Jesse?" Rhoda was elaborately casual. "How did they ever find it?"

It was probably the only vacant apartment in the city, Nellie answered lightly. "One of those Birch Street houses remodeled, one apartment to each floor. Patience didn't say, but I think Jesse's stepmother knew the people who moved out."

"I hope they'll get ahead," said Rhoda. "Mother, if you could have foreseen what your married life was to be—would you have married Dad?"

Nellie's blue eyes met the dark ones squarely. "Why, my dear, I'm afraid that if we could foresee what our lives were to be, married or not, none of us would have the courage to accept life. That's the reason we don't see the entire pattern—it isn't for us *to* see."

Rhoda sighed. "Well, I often think it would help in planning our lives, if we could see what's coming. Vi and I were talking about that this morning. We'd know at least what to avoid."

"If you girls think you would have avoided marriage, or married someone else, that's only another example of the misery a forecast of life might mean to you." Nellie laughed as she stood up to remove the tray. "You'd be so cautious that you'd be afraid to live at all." She patted Rhoda's thin cheek, rescued the slipping blanket from sliding to the floor. "You and Vi and Jerry have the future, and that's all anyone should ask."

She was halfway down the stairs when Rhoda called after her to ask if she had had her lunch. "Dad says you go without food, unless you see the family at the table to remind you it's customary to eat."

Nellie promised to have a sandwich and a cup of tea, and she had barely finished when the sound of a key in the front-door lock startled her. If Luther's cold had taken a turn for the worse—

"Mother Lake?"

"Why, Vi! My dear, I couldn't guess who it was." Nellie stepped into the back hall as the front door closed with a bang that shook the house.

Vi and Barry, her husband, always closed doors by the simple expedient of slamming them. Nellie, who had spent years trying to train her son to move more quietly, had found herself sympathizing with Vi's English mother, whose efforts, presumably directed toward her daughter, had been equally unsuccessful.

"There's a letter for you, dear," Nellie said.

She heard Midnight crying to come in and hurried to open the kitchen window, where he crouched on the sill. Rhoda liked to have the cat on her bed, and Nellie picked him up, intending to carry him upstairs to keep the invalid company. Perhaps Vi could be persuaded to read aloud for an hour or so—her clipped English voice fascinated Rhoda, as indeed it did all of them. Her search for a job could not have been decisive, Nellie thought uneasily, or she would have sounded more cheerful.

"You can read signs better than the Indians," Luther had once said in affectionate exasperation, and Nellie had reminded him that most parents were forced to cultivate a sixth sense.

Had Vi gone up to her room? The child might not have had lunch, and although she usually frankly declared herself starved, she might have some idea of waiting until she had the kitchen to herself for afternoon tea. Nellie had intended to ask Patience if she had ever used the tea cozy Vi had quilted for her after learning that the young Garrisons were pitiably ignorant of the advantages of teapots as compared with the horrid little tea bags on which they relied. Vi had made tea for them in her own careful fashion, and when Patience had admired the elaborate yellow tea cozy, shaped like a fat mother hen, Vi had offered to make one for her.

"Barry never cared for tea, until he tasted it at our house one Sunday afternoon," Vi had said.

At twenty-seven she looked seventeen, with a round, childish face and soft, tumbled yellow hair. Less than five feet tall, she had a slim figure and wore sweaters and suits. She had been so bitterly homesick that Barry had suggested she ask her parents to move to the United States. The idea, impractical, even fantastic, had set Vi to daydreaming for weeks at a time. Her parents had nothing saved, neither Vi nor Barry had money beyond their immediate needs, and their friends, like themselves, were struggling to keep afloat. Yet evening after evening Vi wrote long letters and Barry worked on the plans of a house that should combine the best of English and American architecture.

"I suppose you expect Vi's father to bring the land over with him," Seth had derided. "You haven't a lot on which to build, let alone money enough to dig a cellar."

At such moments even Luther admitted that the house wasn't large enough for four families. He had a daydream of his own, which he shared only with his wife. "It's crazy, the sort of thing that would ruin the children, but there's no danger that it will ever be fulfilled," he said.

He worked on it nights when he couldn't sleep, he had once told Nellie. Like a painting on which the finishing touches would never be completed. Luther, the artist, cherished the patriarchal motif: five hundred acres of rich fields, one hundred acres and a house set aside for each son, with two hundred acres and the manor house reserved for Nellie and himself. He could design a new house every night, if he chose, landscape the grounds, and replant the fields. Barry came honestly by his foolishness, Luther said; as he grew older, he would learn that dreams last longer if kept for the night.

The clock in the kitchen ticked so loudly that Nellie realized that for a moment she had been deaf to all sound. The cat in her arms waited passively, his body fluidly adjusted, green eyes heavy with wisdom.

"No wonder Barry wanted to rename you 'Placid Lake,' " Nellie told him, smiling at the recollection and at the memory of Barry's difficulty in explaining the joke to Vi.

She started for the front stairs and halted at the sight of the little figure huddled on the lowest step.

"Vi, darling! Whatever happened?" Nellie tumbled the cat from her arms, leaned over the sobbing girl. The crumpled envelope on the hall rug offered a clue. "Vi, is something wrong at home?"

The blue eyes—the color of the sky, Barry said—that Vi lifted to the kind, worried face above her overflowed with tears. They streamed unchecked, with an alarming calmness that suggested complete despair. It was this absence of noisy grief that frightened Nellie: as a rule Vi, whether happy or depressed, could be depended upon to act out her moods.

"My mother!" she whispered. "My mother is dying!"

"Oh, no!" Nellie sat down on the step and gathered Vi, heavy gray coat and all, into her arms. "No one has a right to send you word like that. Why, darling, she may be better by now. When was that letter mailed?"

Vi, almost strangled by sobs, fought to answer. "It's an operation. She's needed it for years, but she didn't want me to know."

"Has she had the operation?" Nellie told herself that Vi might have been spared some of the shock had her father—presumably her father had known—thought to write her in advance.

"They're building her up—so they can kill her. She's in the hospital. They want to operate next week." Vi pulled herself free, twisted the letter in her hand. "I ought not to have left her, she's been sick for years. I was young, I could have waited. And now I'll never see her again." She rocked herself back and forth, like an old woman tuned to the rhythm of a hopeless grief.

Nellie hoped that Rhoda's door was closed and that she was asleep. There was always more than the one to be considered; the needs of the individual must be related to the larger problem in which they all shared. Nothing short of a trip home would comfort Vi, Nellie conceded, stroking the bowed yellow head, but where was the money to come from?

"Has Barry anything saved? Have you?" Nellie said.

Vi gulped. "Anything saved?" she echoed. "Barry hasn't a cent, three days after payday. And I haven't a job, so how would I save? At home I saved something every week. Over here, it's spend, spend, spend. We cashed the last war bond two months ago."

Savings bonds—war bonds, as Barry and Vi still called them! Nellie decided to avoid the subject, heard herself asking if Barry didn't pay something on bonds every week out of his salary. "Not that I'm prying, dear, but the only way you can get to England by next week is to fly. And that's expensive."

"Barry thought we couldn't afford to buy any more bonds," Vi said dully. "And he's borrowed on his life insurance. We still owed on the furniture when he lost his good job."

She looked like such a child, and she might have been reciting a lesson in her clear, clipped English—a lesson in arithmetic in which the answers came out wrong.

"Well"—Nellie picked up the envelope from the rug, stuffed it into Vi's coat pocket—"we'll talk things over tonight, and perhaps we can work out a plan. Write your mother an air-mail letter, and try to encourage her. Patients are constantly surprising their doctors by getting well."

Vi put up a hand to smooth her hair, an unconscious, familiar gesture. She seldom wore a hat but as a concession to snow and rain might tie a scarf over her long bob. Luther had once declared that if Helen of Troy had tied her head up in a "handkerchief" the history of the world would have been changed, but he admitted that the fashion was kinder to Vi than to most.

"Mother told Daddy that she wouldn't care how the operation turns out, if she could see me once more." Vi's small weary voice held a defeated note. "I guess money can fix almost everything, and if you haven't it you might as well give up."

She didn't want anything to eat, she said, answering Nellie's question, and if she did lie down she couldn't sleep. "I'll write Mother, and then I'll just wait for Barry to come home. Perhaps he can think of some way to borrow the money."

At the top of the stairs she turned to ask if Nellie thought it would be "all right" to make the trip. "I mean if Barry can get the money. I wouldn't stay away long. You tell him, Mother Lake, that he needn't be afraid I'd deceive him and not come back."

Nellie soothed her with the assurance that she would support her in any controversy, but after Vi had shut herself into her room, without slamming the door, she lingered beside the table in the hall. The letter addressed to Luther was the only one in the tray now, and it was past time for the second delivery. Nellie fingered the envelope idly, let it drop.

Why, she thought in mounting exasperation, had Vi brought up the subject of cashing war bonds? The child could not possibly know—or could she? *Our last line of defense, our only secret hoard, the one small cloak to cover us, if we are ill or in need.*

She would, Nellie resolved, be sensible. There was a limit, even for parents. Undoubtedly it was heartbreaking for Vi and her mother to be separated by an ocean at a time like this, but Vi was young, she had her life before her. She and Barry, like the others, had a tendency to assume that life owed them whatever they chose to ask; perhaps a first real sorrow might serve to jolt Vi out of her chronic homesickness and enable her to value happiness more highly.

"I sound positively revolting, as Jerry would say," Nellie admitted with a wry smile for the sober middle-aged woman she saw in the mirror on the wall.

The doorbell rang, and she jumped. Turning to answer it, she stumbled over Midnight, who always responded to telephone or doorbells, eager to satisfy his shameless curiosity.

"Do you need any pot holders? Single or sets? They make nice gifts." A stout, white-haired woman with anxious, dark eyes spoke rapidly.

Nellie shook her head. "No-o, not really. I'm sorry." She had made dozens of pot holders herself, quilted, crocheted, and tied, cut in every variety of design.

"Perhaps if you just looked? I'm not selling, just taking orders from samples." The desperate pleading in the dark eyes flared into fear. So many doors had been firmly closed before she could open the small box she carried.

No human being ought to look at another like that! Nellie stepped back, beckoned hospitably. "Come in for a moment and rest. I'll be glad to see what you have, even if I can't buy."

Seated on the living-room couch the woman's massive figure relaxed wearily. She jumped a little when Midnight leaped to a cushion beside her but protested when Nellie would have pulled him away.

"I haven't had a cat sit in my lap and purr for years—not since I had my own house. When my husband was living, we always kept a cat." The wrinkled fingers stroked the black fur expertly, and Midnight obligingly produced a baritone purr.

Nellie thought how few words were required to tell a widow's story. If one day she should be left alone—

"You have to have a license to sell, but not if you take orders first and then deliver," the woman said. Her hands fumbled with the pink string tied around a flat white box. "There—they're all handmade."

Women had made gingham pot holders for generations, Nellie reflected, examining the pathetic collection so painstakingly stitched, so neatly arranged. If she only had her shop in running order, she could give work to women like this, too old and slow to compete in factories, but able, if unhurried, to do excellent needlework.

"My niece is starting to keep house—she's just found an apartment," Nellie heard herself saying. "I think I'll give her a set like this—four, and the matching rack. How much is the set?"

The dark eyes mirrored anxiety again. "I ask a dollar for the four, but you get the little rack with the screws and all. And the material is new and strong. I buy remnants." Old hands fumbled nervously with the tissue paper, brushing an imaginary fleck of dust from pink-and-white gingham.

"We don't have piece bags any more, do we?" Nellie forced herself to smile. "You look so tired I'm going to make you a cup of tea, and you can take down my name and address. Patience—my niece—will feel like an experienced housewife with these in her kitchen."

The hot, strong tea put new life into her, the old woman declared gratefully, but although she did not say so the luxury of having someone willing to listen did even more for her. She lived with a married daughter and had, as the family frequently reminded her, enough to eat and a roof over her head.

"But there's nothing for me to do, the apartment's so small, and I have to sleep on the living-room couch. When they have company, I go out to the library but it closes up early. Sometimes I sit in the bus station."

She made pot holders because she had to have a little money and because she liked to sew. Her sewing machine had been sold with her other household effects, after her husband's death.

"It's dreadful to be a burden on your children."

Nellie, pouring a second cup of tea, told herself that the Lord had sent her a sign. She would bury the few remaining bonds six fathoms deep in the sea before she would cash them for the needs of anyone. The children would be the first to be ashamed if their mother should be reduced to selling pot holders from door to door.

"You have to know when to be selfish," Nellie said.

Chapter Three

LUCY Gray, the third consultation for the morning crossed off on her desk memorandum, reached the penciled line underscored in red.

"Patience. Phone Mother or Aunt Nellie; Bus 27, St. Luke's." She read aloud, smiling at the waiting young stenographer. "My sister's in the hospital with her first baby. I hope to get up to see her this afternoon. Let's try to get those letters done before lunch, shall we?"

First, though, Lucy must call her mother. The doctor had refused to permit anyone but her parents to visit Patience for the first ten days. If he thought a maternity patient required hospitalization for two full weeks instead of the nine or eleven days the overtaxed staff insisted was a safe margin, Dr. Guye's ultimatum stood but he served notice that no patient of his need expect to fill in the extra time by holding a reception for her friends.

"Try to get Otto to fix the lock on that old wooden file while I'm off this afternoon, Sadie." Lucy began to dial her mother's number. "And make an appointment for me with the cafeteria manager. Any day next week—" She broke off to listen to the steady, measured tone of the ringing bell. Her mother might be in the cellar or upstairs—the extension phone had been removed during the war and had not been replaced. Stairs, her mother said, were less of a shock to her nervous system than the phone bills.

Sadie's plucked eyebrows perpetually questioned, so that her young, round face always suggested curiosity. "Don't they answer?"

"Not yet." Lucy tried to recall her aunt's number—Aunt Nellie had planned to go to the hospital this morning, but she must still be at home. With that houseful of nonpaying boarders, you'd think someone might offer to do the breakfast dishes and make the beds to give Aunt Nellie an early start. That they didn't was partly her fault, of course; subconsciously, the kids waited for her to lay down the law, would feel safer if checked.

"She must have gone out," Lucy said. "I'll call my aunt in a few minutes. Let's see to the mail now."

They worked together smoothly, Lucy a thin, dark woman in her middle thirties and Sadie Elland, blonde and nineteen. Lucy's name on the glass panel of her office door carried the title "Personnel Director."

The manufacturing firm of Estey and Bates, stressing the cleanliness of the work involved in the production of radio tubes, attracted hundreds of young girls touchingly conscious of the importance of guarding their good looks. Light benchwork did not ruin the hair or skin or nails. An excellent cafeteria supplied lunches at cost, music piped to the various departments lightened the monotony, and a doctor and nurse were always available in the fully equipped infirmary.

Lucy Gray's chief duty, as personnel director, was to listen. Women employees brought their problems to work with them or, worse yet, created their own as they worked. Lucy had soon discovered that light benchwork, so replete with advantages in comparison with the exactions of heavy machines, offered no protection against emotional tensions. Romance, tragedy, anguish, and despair flowed in deep currents through the lives, mostly young, of these women whose pay envelopes could not buy them immunity from their common inheritance.

"I don't know which is harder," Lucy had once told her mother, "for a working woman to be forced to stay on the job with worry and fear haunting her, or for the woman at home to have to stay shut up with her anxieties within four walls."

"Did the doctor give you something for your cold, Sadie?" Lucy, her dictation finished, fancied that the stenographer's slight hoarseness had increased.

She had a gargle, Sadie said. "Are you coming back after lunch, Mrs. Gray? Or do you want to sign these tomorrow morning?"

"I'm not coming back." Lucy glanced at her wrist watch. "The letters can go out tomorrow morning—but get them typed today, Sadie. And *please* write out any phone calls that come."

The blond girl grinned, aware that her preference for verbal messages usually involved important omissions. She looked forward to a slack afternoon with Mrs. Gray out of the office and no appointments to be clocked. Mrs. Gray, who refused to have a wall or desk clock, arranged to be reminded of the time on the half hour or hour, as she might direct, when conducting interviews.

"I hope you'll find your sister all right," Sadie said politely, gathering up her notebooks and pencils. From the door she added over her shoulder, "I like babies when they get old enough to be cute."

Left alone, Lucy looked with pleasure at her blank appointment pad. Presently she must call Aunt Nellie, but for an instant, precious and fleeting, she need not even think. It might not happen again, she doubted that it had happened before, this cessation of all demand, rare and absolute.

The office, decorated to her specifications, sustained an atmosphere of spaciousness and peace. A rather small, square room, the absence of distracting objects added to its size. The walls were a soft, light green, and darker green cotton string rugs lay on the waxed surface of the black linoleum floor. Lucy had curtained the two windows with sheer white voile, made straight and full, and dark shades controlled the light. Her plain walnut desk, rubbed to a dull finish, faced the door, and the chairs had been slipcovered in green-and-white chintz.

"Nothing will encourage the girls to talk to me," Lucy had assured her employers, who found the room too plain, "as much as a comfortable chair and a shaded light. They're not on the witness stand—I don't want them to be blinded by a glare. And neither do

I want their attention to wander about among pictures and vases and other odds and ends. Why make concentration difficult?"

She must call Aunt Nellie, Lucy reminded herself; there were a dozen things to be done. How had she ever deluded herself into thinking that there could be a gap in the relentless march of hours? She would take Patience ice cream; the stretch between lunch and supper seemed interminable in a hospital. Lucy remembered that she had practically starved during her two confinements at St. Luke's, and she would have traded flowers for extra meals any day.

Patience had been brought to see her when Ronnie had been born and again when Cinda came. Such a beautiful little sister, Patience, with her gray eyes and her hair, not the tow color of so many children, but bright, shining gold. The nurses liked to take her to see the babies, and Patience wept because she could not take one or two home. She thought it unreasonable and selfish for a hospital to have so many babies and be unwilling to give any away.

Well, Patience had a baby of her own now, and Lucy, when first the news had been telephoned her, suddenly felt old. Like a grandmother, she decided, for the relationship between her and the sister sixteen years younger had always been protective and maternal on her part. You grew up and married and bore children, were happy and worried, learned what could be bettered and what must be endured, but it was always a shock to discover that the footsteps following close behind you were those of the youngsters you thought were still learning how to walk.

"You were only twenty when Ronnie was born," Patience argued when Lucy had remonstrated. "Doctors don't think I'm too young."

Doctors! Lucy had capitulated, remembering the sober, bearded specialist who had outraged her husband's sister by informing her that the degenerative diseases set in at thirty-five. If you listened to doctors, the span of life had no elasticity.

The desk phone buzzed. Lucy heard her husband's quick, eager voice as she lifted the handset.

"Lutie? The switchboard girl said you weren't in conference."

Lucy's thin, dark face smiled, warming her eyes and voice. "It's all right. But I can't make a lunch date. I'm due at St. Luke's this afternoon—Patience is receiving."

"Swell. Give her my love." Mel liked Patience; he liked all his wife's relatives. "And Lutie, I'm not asking you out to lunch. It's dinner. I thought you and the kids might like to go to that sea-food place on Bell Street for a shore dinner."

"How can you get hold of the children? Never mind, I'll have time after leaving the hospital. I'll go home and round up Ronnie and Cinda."

"Do you like the idea?" Mel, conscious of something missing, was disappointed. "This is on me. If there's anything in the ice-box, it will keep, won't it?"

Lucy hastened to supply the omission. "It will be lovely to have dinner out, dear. The children are crazy about steamed clams. It will be wonderful not to have any arguments about washing the dishes, either. Shall we meet you at six?"

"Make it quarter of." Mel, satisfied, sounded eager again. "Be seeing you, Lutie—we'll go to the movies afterward. I'll get reserved seats."

He had, of course, made a good sale and was spending the commission, as usual, in advance. Money slipped through his fingers, burned holes in his pockets—there wasn't a spendthrift proverb that didn't apply to Mel. Lucy, after seventeen years of marriage, had schooled herself to the acceptance of his generosity that made no provision for his family's future but delighted to embroider the present. Mel spent his drawing account and commissions for the extras—in effect he supplied the desserts and his wife the bread and butter—but he had no thought of scattering largess beyond the boundaries of his home fireside, and if he lacked ambition, he was also free from envy and bitterness, its thorny fruits.

"Mel doesn't worry, does he?" One of Lucy's friends, a woman married to a man who had begun selling office appliances simultaneously with Melvin Gray and who had two years later been made manager of a branch office, had commented wistfully when her husband received his second large increase in salary. "It must be wonderful to be married to a man who doesn't worry."

It merely meant, Lucy forebore to point out, that the wife assumed the burden of anxiety. Most of the wives she knew who worked, whether in the white-collar occupations or in the factories, carried the heavy end of married responsibility. In the main they were philosophical, readily acknowledging that someone had to worry, grateful for the lovable traits that in many instances they were honestly able to rely on in their men. You couldn't judge a marriage by the money a husband brought in, these women testified with simple candor in the interminable confidences poured out to Lucy in her role of counselor. The test was whether a man was easy to live with.

"My sister's married to the nervous, high-strung ulcer type," one of the private secretaries told Lucy at a company luncheon. "She has her mink coat, but if she drops a pin when he's home he's ready to divorce her."

Mel would provide no mink coats, Lucy knew in the first year of her marriage, but by the time they had been married ten years he surprised her by admitting that he knew it, too.

"I haven't got what it takes to roll up a bank account," he said quietly when he had presented her with the anniversary corsage he always remembered. "If I had a big opportunity, I'd muff it. If you expected me to be a big shot, I'm sorry, Lutie. You're married to a pretty limp guy."

Later, when the children began to take a practical interest in household finances, Mel listened good-naturedly to their reports of school friends bountifully supplied with spending money by indulgent—and solvent—fathers. If he saw that he was something less than a hero to his son, he accepted Ronnie's attitude as a temporary adolescent judgment.

"You are the only one in the world who has never tried to make me over," he confided to Lucy in one of his rare moments of self-revelation. "You're a lovely person and a wonderful wife. I'll bet nine out of ten men I know are being melted down and cast into improved molds by their conscientious wives."

She had no conscience, Lucy assured him. Nor power to change him, she confessed in her heart. Whether, had she been a more clever woman, or more fascinating, or perhaps more helpless or less loving, she might have fired him with the fighting drive he lacked, she could not decide. Their marriage had endured.

"Mrs. Gray?" Sadie knocked, entered, and closed the door behind her apparently in one neat movement. "Mrs. Gray, Nola Hall wants to know if you'll see her for a minute."

Lucy said, "Yes, of course. Let me make one phone call. I'll ring for you to send her in."

She dialed the Lake house, and Jerry, her cousin Seth's young wife, answered.

"How come you're home?" Lucy spoke impulsively; if Jerry, who worked, was at home, it didn't necessarily mean that she had lost her job, but it would have been more tactful to ask if she were ill—or something.

Jerry murmured that she had the day off. "There were—things I had to do."

Her mother-in-law, she explained, had gone to the hospital to see Patience Garrison and her baby. "At least Mother was headed for St. Luke's. She had an awful time getting out of the house, and if she meets anyone on the way who wants her to do him a favor, she'll be held up again. I never saw such a woman for wanting to help."

"Maternal," said Lucy into the phone. "She should have had twenty-five children, but of course it isn't done. Well, if you're all right, Jerry—"

"I'm fine!" Jerry seemed to think she had been challenged.

Vaguely surprised, Lucy left a message that she would call her aunt at the hospital. Aunt Nellie was devoted to Jerry, but even a devoted mother-in-law must find it difficult at times to have three daughters-in-law as permanent guests. Lucy, pressing the buzzer, wondered what trials might be in store for her when she should be a mother-in-law in her turn.

"Yes, Nola? Come in and sit down." She turned to smile at the girl who waited hesitantly in the doorway. Because of this interview with Nora, the hospital trip would have to be delayed.

Lucy pulled the desk phone to her and dialed. "May I speak to Mrs. Toller? Yes, I'll be patient."

Her grandmother, Lucy explained to Nola, lived in a home for the aged, and although there was a phone on each floor, an old lady couldn't be hurried when called. "She's past eighty and as spry as a cricket. She— Yes, Grandmother. How are you, dear?"

Would her grandmother go to St. Luke's to see Patience early in the afternoon? Lucy asked. She herself would drop in, but later. "I don't want Patience looking for me and imagining all sorts of things. Take a taxi, Grandma, and be elegant. I'll pay for it."

After Nola had left, Lucy decided she might as well look at dresses for Cinda, who had, according to her own report, nothing to wear to the spring prom. It was too early to go to the hospital, since Grandma Toller would be there and Doctor Guye was firm about limiting visitors to one at a time.

"I wouldn't let a sick dog be subject to the cross fire of two friends with a patient in the middle," Lucy had often heard him say.

As she expertly evaluated materials and examined price tags of the gay "formals" on the hangers in the department store's glass cases, Lucy considered the ever-present problem of Cinda's college education.

"They'll both have to go," Mel argued in the evenings when the children were upstairs with their homework or out with their friends. "A kid stands no chance at all these days, unless he has his college degree. Competition's fierce."

Ronnie, their son, had no aptitude for books. He learned slowly, and although he remembered what he learned, the work he had to do to get passing grades appalled his mother. A year older than Cinda, who had lost a year of school as a youngster because of a complicated measles attack, Ronnie barely managed to keep up with his sister. His skill lay in his hands, and there was nothing, his shop teacher said, he couldn't do with tools.

"He's got to be something better than a greasy mechanic," Mel protested. "Sure, left to himself, he'd putter his life away among automobiles and airplane engines. It's up to us to see that he does better."

Behind Lucy a modulated voice asked with mechanical politeness, "May I help you?"

"Is there anything less expensive?" Lucy had mortified Cinda by asking the familiar question on their last shopping trip together. Cinda felt it was humiliating enough to be obliged to count every cent, without having to tell the world about it.

She loved to shop with her father. Mel had good taste, he liked his womenfolk to be well dressed, and if asked to decide between two price tags, he invariably voted for the higher figure.

"We have nothing lower priced on this floor, Madam," the salesclerk said.

Cinda was too young for an evening gown, anyway, Lucy thought wearily. Just as Nola was too young to have faced such a crisis, and Ronnie to expect to be judged fairly, since he could not prove his case. *People without children live longer.* Lucy in the crowded elevator tried to make room for an angry, red-faced woman who slapped the small girl she had in tow. *Children must hate us sometimes, too.*

Mel dreamed of college for his two, but if only one could go it should be the boy, he said. That Cinda was a brilliant student and a social success—she had Mel's personal charm, his friendliness and sunny optimism—demonstrated, he said, that she would get along. The one who needed the backing of a college diploma was Ronnie. Besides, to send a girl to college and not a boy was a topsy-turvy procedure that couldn't be explained.

"You can't get good material unless you pay for it," the clerk in the second shop told Lucy. "Of course, you could make up a dress for less, if you can sew."

She had no time for sewing. The doctor had suggested that she spare her eyes evening work—women who worked all day should relax after office hours as men of good sense had done for years.

"Your husband doesn't do housework at night, and neither should you," the doctor had pronounced. "Rest your eyes, enjoy your leisure—you owe it to yourself."

"I'll look a little longer," Lucy appeased the clerk, whose expression immediately dismissed her as a potential buyer.

The trouble, of course, was that she didn't dare to spend the money. Mel resented any suggestion that he save his commissions; he feared penury more than poverty. He wanted to be carefree, to live in the present, and he trusted his wife to deal with the unpleasant facts and anticipate the unforeseen.

He had, perhaps, attempted a warning or explanation, in the early days of their marriage. "In a crisis I shall not know what to do," he had said. "Unlike other men, I let go instead of taking hold."

She wouldn't buy any dress, the styles were ridiculous for a fifteen-year-old girl, Lucy decided. The sensible thing to do was to get one of the new books to take to Patience and then walk all the way to the hospital. That ought to cure the dull headache that had developed from bad air and shopping nerves.

Afternoon

Chapter Four

LUNCH, always served promptly at twelve o'clock in the Carberry Memorial Home for the Aged, was over, and Emmeline Toller had returned to her room to dress for her visit to St. Luke's Hospital. A definite appointment pleased her, for the peaceful routine of her days provided few variations.

"Lucy Gray, my granddaughter, asked me to go in her place to see my younger granddaughter, Patience," Emmeline had reported to all the old ladies and gentlemen within hearing distance at luncheon. "I'm anxious to make the acquaintance of my new great-grandson."

No relationship was too complicated for the Carberry Home folk to follow. They knew each other's family trees to the remote twigs and were on intimate terms, conversationally, with children and grandchildren, aunts, uncles, cousins, and in-laws in this world and the next, the great majority of whom they were unlikely to meet on earth.

Every man or woman in the Home knew that Emmeline Toller, the widow of Simon, had two devoted daughters, Nellie and Lou. Grandchildren, as counted on wrinkled fingers, numbered Nellie's three boys—Barry and Chris and Seth—and Lou's two girls—Lucy and Patience. Great-grandchildren yielded the respectable total of four: Chris had twin girls and Lucy a daughter and a son.

"Nicholas makes my fifth great-grandchild," Emmeline had boasted shamelessly when Lou had phoned her the wonderful news. "Great-grandchildren give you the feeling of being a matriarch, even if you have nothing to rule."

It was sometimes a little appalling, she thought now, exchanging her house slippers for the arch-supporting black oxfords she had adopted reluctantly two years before as a concession to her eightieth birthday, to contemplate the descendants of all the old men and women in the Home. Children's children's children, they spread till, like the waters in the Bible, they bid fair to cover the face of the earth.

"I'd like to see my great-great-grandchildren, but that's probably asking too much," she said aloud, rubbing her shoes with a lamb's-wool pad as her husband had taught her to do—Simon detested dusty shoes.

The room seemed a little chilly, and she turned on more heat. The Carberry Home never stinted on heat. In fact, Emmeline reminded herself, she had always been comfortable since she and Simon had become residents more than seven years ago. The girls had been so humiliated. What would people think?

"The question is, what will you and your husbands think when your mother and I become dependent upon you?" Simon said. "We're thinking of you, as well as ourselves. Into a home we go, and we pay our way with the last of our savings. I've always taken care of your mother, and I'll make sure to take care of her to the end."

Residents of "The Carberry" were proud, even smug, about the conditions governing the admission of guests. A board of directors passed on the desirability of applicants, and only married couples were accepted. The death of a husband or wife did not affect the standing of the surviving mate, once admitted. The entrance fee of five thousand dollars guaranteed perpetual care ("like a cemetery lot," Simon told his shocked daughters) and a scale of comfort possible only because of the Home's substantial endowment. Once "in," the old people regarded themselves as fortunate and displayed a tendency to patronize friends who remained on the waiting list or entered institutions with lower ratings.

"I wouldn't live in a home for indigent and respectable aged,"

Emmeline vigorously instructed her daughters. "Nor one where they give card parties and teas to buy linoleum for the bedrooms. We have carpets, and nobody gives card parties to raise money for us. Your father and I will never be objects of charity."

Simon had been dead four years next month, his widow reflected, taking up her silver-backed comb and running it through her soft, abundant pompadour. She was vain of her hair, and the girls at the Florence Beauty Shop always admired its dazzling whiteness, its texture and length. Most of the old ladies in the Home patronized the Florence shop. They took great interest in their personal appearance and expected the old men to notice how they looked and what they wore. The presence of "gentlemen" was considered an asset, not only by the Carberry residents, but by their envious friends who lived segregated lives either in institutional homes restricted to females or with their children, who assumed that the sexes ceased to be interesting to each other after they became grandparents.

As a matter of fact, Emmeline was frequently surprised to remember that she was a grandmother and great-grandmother. None of her experiences, she admitted a little sadly, had prepared her to be old. Whatever she had expected—she was not sure what she had expected—it had not been this outward change that so far transcended the inner response.

"I haven't even trained myself to feel old," she once confided to Mrs. Palmer, who had the room next to hers. "Knitted bedroom slippers still are a shock, and I've exchanged six lavender scarves for rose and blue and red. The time has gone so quickly that I haven't caught up with the years."

Mrs. Palmer agreed that the body aged before the spirit and the heart. "Life is so short," she said. At eighty-six she had left so much undone.

Emmeline stood before the mirror one moment tidying her white hair and the next seeing herself as a girl of nineteen. She had been two years younger than Patience when Andrew, her first child, had been born.

"He's my present to you, on your twenty-first birthday," she said to Simon, such a young, bewildered, proud father.

("Isn't it lovely," the mother of Patience had telephoned, "Nicholas was born last night, on Patience's twenty-first birthday.")

Simon's father had no telephone; but his first grandchild, and named for him, had set him to making wonderful plans. His grandson should go to the best schools, to college, perhaps for a year or two abroad. Andrew's place in the firm would be assured, and his son's after him.

"I think I'm nervous," Emmeline said. "There's a touch of *Dombey and Son* in your father's dreaming. If the baby had been a girl, would he have forgiven me?"

But she had turned to the grandfather when, two months before his first birthday, the rosy, smiling, adored little Andrew had died. His grandfather had idolized the child, the family said, and Emmeline knew then that she had worshiped her son, too. She wanted nothing of Simon in her anguish—perhaps she realized subconsciously that he would give her another child to comfort her. No other child should still her longing or have her love.

"You are the only one who understands," she told her father-in-law. "I will not bear another child. This is the beginning and the end of life for me."

He had helped her, Simon's father had helped her, to shut Simon out. Together she and the old man—he had not been old before—had kept vigil for three nights beside the tiny white coffin.

"Hasn't closed her eyes for a week," the neighbor women said, plying her with hot coffee and bringing in fresh white roses to replace the ones that withered in the summer heat.

Simon, thin and tired, scarcely spoke, but when his father protested that anything a minister might say would only insult the bereaved, Simon insisted quietly that prayers should be read.

"What can a minister tell a woman who's lost her baby?" the grandfather demanded bitterly. "Look at your wife—you going to ask her to listen to a mealymouthed hypocrite tell her that everything is for the best? If you have no consideration for my feelings, look at your wife."

Emmeline, exhausted, lay on the couch, the coffin at its foot. Her thin black dress clung in close folds to her slim body; the loosened knot of her hair, as black as her dress, allowed two heavy coils to curl over her shoulders. The scent of roses lay heavy on the room, dusted and scrubbed by willing neighbors, whose kindness found expression in familiar, homely tasks. They were gathered in the dining room now, counting the silver to make sure there would be "enough."

"People coming from a distance have to be fed," one explained to Emmeline, disturbed by the rustling, whispered conferences. "I'm baking a chocolate cake, and Mrs. Williams is boiling a ham. We can serve it sliced cold."

The thought of anyone sitting down to enjoy boiled ham and chocolate cake, after the burial of that tiny white coffin, sickened Emmeline. She wanted to order the women from the house, but Simon, to whose authority she appealed, explained that they acted in kindness.

"Some of the aunts and cousins are driving twenty miles," he reminded her. "It will be late at night before they reach home. You are spared all the work of cooking and serving by these good friends—the least we can do is to be grateful for their kindness."

"Look at your wife," Simon's father repeated.

Simon said, "I am looking at her," and touched her inert hand with his long, gentle fingers.

"I won't listen to a minister." Emmeline spoke without unclosing her eyes. "I don't believe in God any more."

Simon did not raise his voice, but he had no need to shout. "I believe—in sorrow as in joy, I believe. The Christian burial service will be read for our son."

When Simon talked like that, no one, not even his father, disputed him. He didn't show his feelings, they said of Simon, but standing beside him at the grave—a baby's grave took up so little space!—Emmeline saw such stark anguish in the tense, still face that sudden fear iced her heart. She touched his sleeve, and instantly Simon tried to smile, a pathetic effort that released her tears in a fresh flood. But this time she wept for her husband, not for her son.

"For heaven's sake! I thought you'd gone." Mrs. Palmer, tiny and almost as thin as a paper doll, slipped into the room, closed the door behind her. "I knocked, but you didn't answer—then I heard something drop, so I knew you must be here."

They smiled at each other, sharing the secret of failing ears and eyes.

"I'm almost ready," Emmeline said, glancing at the bed where she had laid out her hat, gloves, and purse. "Thinking of Patience and her son reminded me of bygone days and set me dreaming."

Mrs. Palmer knew Patience Garrison—had tatted her a set of hot-plate mats for a wedding gift—and hoped she might bring the baby for a visit to the Home later in the spring.

"She always comes to see you," Mrs. Palmer, whose own family were remiss in their attentions, observed.

Emmeline, pinning on a black hat with a smart veil, murmured that she didn't expect to see much of Patience now that she had a child. "She has an apartment to look after, too. She'll find housework difficult at first—after living with her mother for all her married life."

"Before you go," Mrs. Palmer said, "I want to tell you about Nina. We're all so worried about her."

They all worried about someone, although one or two old men, bereft of all relatives and close friends, worried about the world and the atom bomb. Mrs. Palmer counted herself fortunate to have Nina, the daughter of a distant cousin, about whom to be concerned. She couldn't, Mrs. Palmer frequently informed the circle that formed around the fireplace in the evenings, teach herself to worry about foreigners or strangers; but she cared a great deal about the happiness of her own kith and kin.

"You can tell me about Nina while I mend this rip in my glove," Emmeline said.

Mrs. Palmer rocked gently as she talked. "You have such beautiful hair," she began, because she had always envied Em Toller her heavy hair and because her mind was so crowded with thoughts that they contended with her words.

"Nina's been married seven years, and the doctors say she'll never have a child. She and her husband consulted the last specialist a week or so ago, and he told her there's no hope. I was married three years myself before my first, and I remember I was half sick with worry for fear I'd never have a child," Mrs. Palmer recollected.

"Nina won't take an interest in anything, she doesn't eat, they can't get her to go out. Her husband was dead set against adopting a baby, but now he says if Nina will rouse up and get well, they'll put in an application for adoption."

Even that didn't bring Nina out of her black mood, Mrs. Palmer went on; she was in such a state that the doctors warned her family not to leave her alone. "No one in our family has ever committed suicide, but there's no telling what a high-strung young woman might do, given opportunity. Her husband's terribly worried about her, and yet he doesn't know what to do."

"Then he might try letting her alone." Emmeline examined her stitching with satisfaction. She couldn't see to sew in the evenings now, but she still did fine work by daylight. "If I knew people were watching me to see how I felt and what I did, I'd commit suicide myself, just to escape them."

Mrs. Palmer conceded that it made her nervous to be watched, too. "Be sure to give Patience my love. Nicholas is such a nice name, but I suppose he'll be called 'Nicky.'"

Emmeline glanced at the open-faced gold watch lying on the bureau top, as the door closed. The watch was Simon's, and its plain, easily read face was like that of a friend. On her fiftieth wedding anniversary the girls had given her a wrist watch, but she had not been able to see the tiny numerals even with her glasses, and they had later exchanged it for a handsome gold pin.

"I wish I had asked Hetty Palmer what would be nice to take to Patience," Emmeline said aloud. She talked to herself and to Simon a great deal, perhaps because, even after four years, she had not become accustomed to being alone.

Hospital rooms were always smothered in flowers, she reflected, and she had already sent the baby a knitted carriage robe. She could not, however, go to see Patience empty-handed; a grandmother didn't do that, no matter if lollipops no longer were fitting.

"I do believe it's a treasure chest occasion," Emmeline announced to the photograph of Simon that hung in a velvet frame beside the bureau.

She dragged her rocking chair over to the dark mahogany chest that fitted into the space beneath the south window. All the furniture in the room had been hers since her wedding day, and when she lay awake at night she could feel herself surrounded by familiar objects. Her father had given her the bedroom "set," and she had not been one to do over her house when styles changed. Nellie and Lou had vexed her sometimes with their willingness to discard their tables and chairs and beds.

"We won't move into any old folks' home unless they let us bring our bedroom set," Emmeline told Simon. "I haven't waxed and rubbed those pieces all these years only to sell them or give them away, now."

Emmeline raised the lid of her chest and sniffed the good, clean smell of dried lavender. Here were the things too precious to be used, priceless and irreplaceable, the heirlooms which she had not yet distributed and which, she supposed, the girls would have to apportion after her death. In spite of the most careful planning, there were always things left, in bureau drawers, in chests, on the closet shelves, when one died. It was because you could not bring yourself to give everything away, because you dreaded the sense of loneliness and empty spaces, and yes, because you knew that, until your children were old themselves, they would not have your capacity for caring.

Everything in the chest represented a link with the line of shadowy women who had preceded Emmeline. Her mother, her grandmother, her great-grandmother had handled the thin silver teaspoons, had worn the brocade scarf and carried the tiny handkerchief of real lace. Great-grandmother had played with the carved doll's furniture and worked the sampler; her daughter had cherished the string of amber beads and the silver tray; and in turn Emmeline's mother had added amethyst earrings, sandalwood boxes, and china and glass.

Things lasted for generations, but bodies so soon dissolved to dust, Emmeline thought, turning over the neatly labeled packages. She still found it incredible that a silver spoon, surely not so valuable as human life, should remain in excellent serviceable condition for more than a hundred years and a man or woman collapse when merely seventy or eighty.

"There's no comparison between a hundred-year-old teaspoon and a hundred-year-old man," she had argued with Simon. "The teaspoon is practically as good as new, and the man is a—a ruin."

"Everything outlasts people," Emmeline complained. "Sometimes I wonder, when I remember all the old things that are in museums, and the men who made them dead this long time past, whether God really thinks we're important."

Yes, she admitted, she had an immortal soul. No, she didn't really believe that teaspoons and clocks and old houses would outlast Eternity. And, of course, if a house burned down, that was the end of its two-hundred-year career, while a man, according to Christian doctrine, continued to live after his earthly existence had been destroyed.

"But all these things make the span of life seem mighty short," she added firmly. "You must confess that life is short, Simon."

"For the happy," Simon said and kissed her.

Emmeline smiled, remembering that kiss.

"I do believe I'll give Patience the little tureen," Emmeline said, turning to speak to Simon's photograph over her shoulder.

The little tureen she knew to be coveted by both Nellie and Lou.

Not that they would ever ask for it, but they talked of it as a "collector's item." Emmeline had worried about the tureen, because it could not be divided and she had made it a rule since the girls were born to divide her gifts evenly between them. There would be no question of division if she gave the tureen to Patience. Obviously it should descend to a girl, and Nellie had no daughter. A glow of satisfaction flushed Emmeline's cheeks, the color of wrinkled cream. She had found the perfect present!

Her grandmother had been proud of the little tureen, too, brought to her from England by a young uncle who knew that she collected blue china. It must be nearly one hundred and fifty years old, a rich dark-blue oval, with a matching ladle and tray. It stood about four inches high, shining and smooth, without a nick or chip to mar its glaze.

"My grandmother lived her life, and my mother lived her life," Emmeline told Simon's photograph. "My own life is far gone. But, barring an accident, this china tureen will outlast Nellie's life and Lou's and the life of Patience and her children. I tell you, Simon, the indestructibility of *things* startles me."

She had only to slip the tureen into her capacious knitting bag, for it was kept swathed in tissue paper, to pull down her veil and pull on her gloves, and she was ready to go. Her decent black coat had been the subject of some criticism from Nellie and Lou, who complained that all the old ladies in the Home looked alike in their winter coats.

"You wear smart hats, Mother," Lou conceded, "but your coat looks like the Home uniform. When you can be individual, why don't you be? If it's a question of money—"

It wasn't a question of money, Emmeline interposed hastily. "It's just that a black coat looks like a black coat on any woman past seventy, and black coats are practically immortal. Hetty Palmer's had hers for fourteen years, and I've worn mine for ten."

"And they wear them from September through June," Lou confided to Nellie. "The winter season for old people is ten months long."

Emmeline, taking a final glance at herself in the mirror, thought she looked very well. The bow on her hat brought out the blue in her eyes, her white hair set off her still nice skin and the pale rose lipstick—her granddaughter Lucy had chosen the lipstick—and not even the black coat could make her figure quite shapeless. She had begun to shrink, Emmeline admitted, but when she remembered to stand erect she still could be called tall. For years and years the old ladies in the Home had worn a bunch of artificial flowers on their black coats every spring, but word had gone about that children and grandchildren condemned the custom this year as quite out of the fashion picture.

"I think a neat bunch of artificial flowers is much prettier than poor, little spiked gardenias pinned on with a silver ribbon bow," Emmeline militantly proclaimed to the after-dinner forum in the living room.

But she had put her make-believe flowers away, and so had the other old ladies, except for a few who had no children to be critical of them.

The self-service elevator, descending slowly and smoothly, carried Emmeline from the fourth to the first floor. Mr. Dale, at the desk, smiled pleasantly as she turned in her key. He was only sixty and vain of his youth.

The first floor of the Carberry resembled the lobby of a well-conducted residential hotel. Each resident had a mailbox, and a switchboard clerk took messages for them in their absence. They were asked to leave their keys at the desk because they lost them at an appalling rate; keys were the articles most often listed in the lost and found notices posted on the bulletin board.

At this hour in the afternoon the lounge was deserted, for naps were as routine as the southern siesta. A little later the chairs by the front windows would be occupied, and the three o'clock delivery of mail would increase Mr. Dale's bustling importance.

"I'm going to visit my great-grandchild," Emmeline volunteered, realizing that no matter how often she repeated the words they must still sound incredible to her own ears.

Mr. Dale's wife, who was the matron, had told him of Nicholas's arrival because she told him everything that furnished current news in the collective Home family. He murmured politely now, unable to recall the baby's name or to remember whether Emmeline had other great-grandchildren. How did his wife manage to keep everything straight!

"Boy or girl?" Mr. Dale decided the question was suitable and safe.

"Oh, a boy. They've named him Nicholas. You've met my granddaughter, Patience Garrison, and her husband, Jesse. They had dinner here one night soon after they were married." Emmeline remembered that Mr. Dale had grandchildren, too. "How are Albert and Christine, Mr. Dale?" she asked.

But when he would have recounted their prowess in kindergarten, she gently but firmly retreated. If she didn't get to St. Luke's soon, she might lose her chance to visit with Patience.

At the hospital a nurse's aide at the reception desk said that it was quite all right to see Mrs. Garrison and that the self-service elevator was the third door on the right in the back hall.

"Can you operate it?" the aide asked, a little doubtfully.

"I have one," Emmeline assured her, "in my home." Which was the truth, she quieted her conscience.

On the third floor, at the end of a maze of corridors and turnings, a sturdy, square nurse, with a self-absorbed expression, charged out of No. 33 and, grazing Emmeline and her parcels, skidded to a halt.

"You want Mrs. Garrison? Would you mind? I'm busy with her at the minute, but I won't be long. There's a bench out near the elevator where you can wait."

She would wait, Emmeline said, and moved dreamily toward the elevator. The hospital atmosphere always weakened her knees, but it wasn't, as Nellie and Lou tried to teach her, the drugs and the antiseptics, but the intangible weight of life and death, hope and despair that the heavy silence distilled. Emmeline, walking as if in her sleep, glanced from side to side at the closed blank doors—

behind each door there would be a woman in a standardized hospital bed, but no two women's stories would be the same.

Emmeline sniffed—the odor had changed, the air smelled heavier and more acrid. She saw that she had crossed the bridge into the surgical section and that the doors of these private rooms were, most of them, standing open. Not so young these patients, as in the maternity building—the internal organs of women, Emmeline admitted with a sudden flash of humor, were standardized, after all.

"Come in and talk to me?" A woman, propped high on an elevated bed, beckoned, a frightened note in her thin voice.

Neither nurse nor aide was in sight to be consulted. Emmeline crossed the sill, went up to the bed. "Can I get you something?" she asked.

"Stay a minute. Don't go away. I'm afraid when I'm alone." The woman was perhaps fifty, with gray hair and dark eyes red-rimmed from weeping. No, she admitted, she wasn't in pain. Nor did she need the nurse. "That cold-blooded fish has no more heart than a lump of iron. She chirps at me."

The only thing Emmeline could think of to say sounded like a burlesque of several radio programs, but her effort was sincere. "And what is your trouble?" she asked.

"They're going to operate!" The woman's fingers closed on Emmeline's arm. "I heard them talking. Tomorrow morning. I know I'll never come out of it alive."

Emmeline surveyed her with calm disapproval. "You don't know any such thing. No one knows. Except God." She gently freed her sleeve, wondered if she could back out—Patience might be waiting for her.

"I'm scared to die," the woman whispered. "You don't know what it is to lie here and imagine that it may be your last day. I can't face death—maybe it's different when you're old."

She was probably Nellie's age or Lou's, Emmeline decided, a woman finished with childbearing and prepared to enjoy her middle years—the leather-framed photograph on the bureau top must be that of her husband—and her rings and elaborate bed jacket placed her in comfortable circumstances. The room was stuffed with flowers in tin and pottery and glass containers, the rather pathetic evidence that her friends were not individually able to help her.

"People say they're not afraid of death, only of illness and pain." The woman stirred restlessly in the bed. Her counterpane was littered with magazines and books. "I'm afraid of death. There's so much I wanted to do, and I kept putting it off, to look after Paul and the children. Besides"—she laughed a little strangely and her eyes, lifted to Emmeline, were clear and young—"it sounds queer, but I was just beginning to get used to life."

You did get used to living, somewhere along the way, Emmeline reflected. The loss of youth was compensated for, in a measure, by a hard-won perspective that enabled you to care less for many things and more for a precious few. You tested your courage and your love, and the mysterious fear of life, perhaps not recognized but an unseen force to be reckoned with, gradually faded. Not that in the beginning the fear was altogether foolish, Emmeline admitted, suddenly conscious of the weight of her parcels. She hooked a chair rung neatly with her heel, jerked it to her, and sat down, smiling at the woman in the bed—poor dear, who had so slowly begun to "get used" to life.

"You're a lot older than I am," the patient said. "I ought to live longer. It isn't fair." She hesitated. "I haven't much religion—have you? I've always had a feeling that death is the end, and now all of a sudden I don't want it to be like that."

Emmeline fumbled in her knitting bag. "Well, when you reach my age, you don't need an operation to start you thinking. I've thought about death very seriously—and my feeling is that I shall live longer than a soup tureen."

"A what?" The woman in the bed glanced involuntarily at the buzzer attached to the headboard.

But Emmeline had found what she searched for and was lifting a paper-swathed package from her capacious bag.

"There!" She unwound the tissue and disclosed the little blue tureen. "I'm taking it to my granddaughter, who's just had her first baby," she explained. "It's a hundred and fifty years old—maybe more. My grandmother left it to my mother, my mother left it to me."

"What *are* you trying to say?" The woman, eyeing the tureen, coveted the exquisite bit of perfection. She had always wanted to collect china, and this would make a beautiful start. If, she suddenly recollected, she had any time left in which to start to collect china. "I don't suppose you'd sell that?" she suggested.

Emmeline declined to sell. "What I started to tell you," she went on composedly, "was this: If a bit of china can go on for one hundred and fifty years, or maybe four thousand, supposing no one breaks it, isn't it reasonable to expect that a human life will last even longer?"

"We—ell," the woman pondered. "Perhaps. But of course your china tureen has never been alive."

That only strengthened her argument, Emmeline retorted. Life, mysterious, intricate, far more wonderful than anything man-made, must transcend mere pottery. "Doesn't it seem reasonable to you that we should be more precious to God than our china or silver is to us?"

"Yes," the woman said. But she added quickly that she had never thought much about her soul. "And as soon as you go away I'll be scared again. Besides, so many dreadful things happen that I can't understand why God permits them to be. Things we pray for we don't get—how do you account for that?"

Emmeline wrapped her tureen in the great folds of tissue paper, replaced it in her bag.

"I don't account for anything." She smiled, her voice confident, her eyes serene. "The universe is beyond me. You go to doctors about your body, why should you hesitate to see a minister about your soul? He can answer questions I can't."

"But if you were facing death, what would you believe?" The afternoon sun flashed on a diamond wedding band as she raised her hand to push back a lock of hair.

"I am facing death—at eighty-two you have time to think," Emmeline explained. "And I believe in love."

Chapter Five

SUPPOSE she had stayed too long, Emmeline chided herself, retracing her steps across the bridge, into the maternity wing. Suppose Patience had gone to sleep, or the nurse had told her no one had asked for her—

"Well, there you are—talk about timing!" The square-built nurse beamed from the doorway, which gave a glimpse of a linen room. "Mrs. Garrison is all set for company, and she'll be more than glad to see you. Go right in."

Emmeline knocked on the half-closed door of No. 33, pushed it open.

"Oh, Grandmother! How lovely!" Patience, on the high bed, held out her arms. "You look wonderful, darling."

Patience had always made her feel younger than her own daughters did, Emmeline remembered, her delighted smile blessing her favorite grandchild. Nellie and Lou were solicitous, they grieved to see her carry a bundle, their concern was for her health and limited strength. Patience, however, treated her as a contemporary, assumed they shared the same interests, and apparently did not watch her every movement in fear that she might fall apart. Christmas and birthday presents from Patience did not include lamb's-wool bedroom slippers or lavender scarves.

"I brought you a special package," Emmeline said.

She put the tureen down beside Patience and kissed her, noting that the young face was thinner and the deep-set gray eyes more shadowed than before. This having a baby wasn't quite the automatic gesture the realists would have you believe.

Emmeline, unfastening her coat and folding it carefully across the back of the chair, recollected the cheerful young manager of the drugstore near the Home, whose pride in his three handsome youngsters was second only to his love for his pretty young wife. He carried the four photographs with him and was quick to explain that the likeness of his wife did not do her justice.

"Each time she has a child, the mother gives it something of herself," he said once to Emmeline. "She doesn't get it back. Childbearing takes a bit of the mother's life—I have seen it with Annie."

Few young husbands spoke like that, Emmeline had commented to Hetty Palmer to whom she had repeated the manager's words, but probably more husbands were aware of the gradual alteration in the women they married than was popularly supposed.

"But it must be nice to be married to a man who can understand and say that he does," Hetty Palmer observed wistfully. "I don't know of anything else that would make having babies as near a pleasure."

Patience, untying string, murmured, "I hope you see I'm wearing your bed jacket, dear. It's been admired by everyone who's seen it."

"The color becomes you," Emmeline conceded, but secretly she admired her handiwork, too. She must make the baby a sweater soon.

"Grandmother—you shouldn't!" Patience had finished unwrapping the tureen. "Your pet heirloom. Mother and Aunt Nellie will perish. Wait till I tell Nicholas."

Emmeline held up a warning finger. "It isn't for Nicholas, but for you. The women in the family have handed it down. I skipped a generation because I couldn't divide a piece of china, but it mustn't go to a boy."

"Nicholas is very sweet—he wouldn't dream of taking it away from me," Patience assured her. "And I suppose you'll make it up to Lucy in some way."

They both laughed because Emmeline had said that since the days when Patience had been a little girl and Lucy, serious and maternal, had encouraged Grandma to give the presents to Patience.

"Lucy's coming this afternoon—let me put it on the bureau. There!" Emmeline deposited the tureen safely between a framed photograph of Jesse and a fan-shaped crystal vase filled with giant sweet peas. "Florists don't have to bother about seasons," she commented.

"The sweet peas came just after Aunt Nellie left," Patience said. "Mother's bridge club sent them, vase and all. Don't you want to take some to Mrs. Palmer, Grandmother? There are too many of them for that vase."

"Maybe I will." Emmeline had removed her hat because she couldn't acquire the habit of wearing a hat indoors, and now she took out her crochet work and seated herself near the bed. "Tell me about the baby, dear," she smiled.

"Grandma, you're deliberately leading me on!" Patience tried to look reproachful, failed. "I've been to see my friends who have had babies, and I resolved I would provide myself with at least one other topic of conversation when my turn came."

Emmeline twitched her thread composedly. "There's nothing like your first baby," she murmured. "Your mother admits, under pressure, that there's a hint of the Garrisons in one eyebrow, but the rest of him she swears is all our side of the house."

"He's going to look exactly like Jesse." Patience fell into the trap so neatly prepared. "And Jesse is the best-looking man I've ever seen." If the babies were not displayed that afternoon, her grandmother must come again, she insisted, before Patience left the hospital. "Because we're going to live in a walk-up and the stairs will be hard for you. I'll get Jesse to build me a wall cabinet for the tureen, Grandma. It will be the perfect accent for our living room."

The silver crochet hook went in and out, in and out, and a lacy border followed in its magic train. Emmeline's thoughts, as busy as her needle, pondered the wisdom of mentioning her trip into the surgical division, decided against it. Better to ask about the photograph on the bureau top—that reminded her the scarf was crooked, and she got up and straightened it.

"Mother brought the runner," Patience explained. "She said the top needs to be refinished. She would have painted it, I'm sure, if I hadn't balked at having to smell paint."

Emmeline inserted a finger in a vase, touched water. "Fresh?"

"Aunt Nellie worried about the tulips this morning." Patience laughed softly. "Mrs. Landley, the nurse's aide, gave them water. Heather sent them, Grandma. You know—Ross's wife."

Emmeline sat down again, resumed her work, scarcely conscious of the even movement of her hand. "Didn't I hear that Heather's been ill?" she asked. "In the hospital, your mother said. Is she here?"

"Thatcher Memorial." Patience named the medical center downtown. "I never did hear exactly what the operation was for—Ross hates to be questioned. When I see Heather, I'll find out. I think perhaps she had something done so she could have a baby."

Sometimes you could, and sometimes you couldn't, Emmeline observed sententiously. Hetty Palmer's niece, Nina, had had everything done, and that was that. The doctors told her now she could never have a child.

"I never knew that Heather Garrison wanted a baby," Emmeline said.

She didn't know, either, Patience admitted, but the operation could easily have been for that. "They've been married over three years, Grandma. On the other hand, I may be simply baby-minded."

"Perhaps." Emmeline found her gaze returning to the framed photograph. An old-fashioned custom, one's husband's picture on the bureau top, but not out of style, at least not at St. Luke's. Nor at the Carberry Home.

"Is that a new picture of Jesse?" she asked.

Fainter than a flush, a tinge of color brushed the smooth white skin, crept toward the inscrutable gray eyes. "Do you like it, Grandmother? I made him have it taken for the baby. And I had mine. In case Nicholas should be an orphan."

Emmeline blinked. "An orphan?"

"Oh, laugh if you want to—Daddy almost choked. But I'm sure you read of dozens of babies whose parents get killed in automobile accidents and are burned up in fires. How could a baby, left like that, remember his parents, if they didn't leave him photographs of themselves?" Patience tugged at a lock of her hair. "I might have died when he was born, too," she said.

Well, she hadn't died, Emmeline reminded her briskly, and Jesse was a live and handsome papa, so Nicholas could enjoy the photographs without associating sadness with them. "I must say photography has improved, along with everything else. The photographs of your grandfather and myself, taken when we were young parents, would give any intelligent baby a convulsion."

Patience said gravely, "I think Jesse will be a wonderful father. He was so unhappy as a child that he'll know what a little boy needs to make him happy."

She had planned her son's entire future before he was a week old, Emmeline recalled; it was almost the only free time a young mother could snatch for daydreams. But she had taken it for granted that he was to be happy, because her generation had assumed that childhood was a period of sheer delight. Now people seemed to have gone to the other extreme and to believe that no child ever knew a happy moment. "The truth," remarked Emmeline aloud, "is probably somewhere in the middle."

"What did you say, Grandmother?"

"Nothing, dear—just thinking. Why was Jesse an unhappy little boy?"

"Well—his mother died." Patience watched the crochet hook, finding something mesmerizing in the rhythmic silver flashes.

Jesse's mother had died, not when he was a baby and might have been comforted by another's physical care, but when he was seven years old, and her image was stamped indelibly upon his mind and heart.

"Ross is more like her than I," Jesse always said, speaking of his brother, three years his senior. "Ross has her capacity for love."

He meant, Patience had learned, that Ross was like his mother in his protective tenderness. Jesse had become his responsibility when the mother died, for the big, handsome father, warped by anguish, sickened by guilt, had made no further effort to conceal his heavy drinking.

"Wouldn't you think he'd skip a night?" Ross, trying to serve the cold supper, would abandon his efforts to prop the sorry figure upright in a chair at the table. "I'll have to get him to bed. You eat while I help him upstairs, Jesse."

But Jesse, half repelled, half fascinated, insisted on helping, and if Dad didn't happen to be in a quarrelsome mood, the two boys could push and prod him up the stairway and tumble him on his bed, where he would make spasmodic attempts to help them undress him.

Other nights he would turn on them belligerently, ordering them to keep their hands off him, accusing them of trying to take his money, to poison him, to handcuff him—no suspicion was too fantastic for him to entertain.

"He misses Mother." Ross tried to excuse him to Jesse with some dim idea that the younger brother should not be completely disillusioned. "Maybe if we fix the house up nice, he'll stay home more."

The family finances were in as deplorable confusion as the once pleasantly ordered house, and sometimes the boys were weeks without money. They could charge food, but not domestic help, and the woman by the day who had done the cleaning said she wouldn't work for a drunk anyway.

"The police ought to be notified, the condition things are in," Cousin Belle, an energetic middle-aged woman, scolded the boys several months after their mother's death. "Your father is neglecting you, and I've a good mind to have the law on him."

After that the boys wouldn't let Cousin Belle in when she rang the bell, and lest the neighbors criticize their father, they refused entrance to the friends of their mother who timed their calls—they learned later—for the hours when Dad might be expected to be downtown.

Ross wasn't very successful in making the house attractive, but he did manage to hold himself and Jesse to a semblance of routine with a perseverance unusual in a ten-year-old boy. The two lads went regularly to school; they got their own meals and parried the bill collectors. Their clothes were shabby and often in need of buttons, but since it was known that their father earned a good salary they were not regarded precisely as uncared for. There were women, of course, who would have gladly fussed over the boys, from motives not of charity alone, but the youngsters were unapproachable.

"It's a dreadful thing to say of Avis Garrison's husband," one neighborhood matron told another in Jesse's hearing, "but he's degenerated into the kind of man you're afraid to be in a room alone with."

Even to Jesse it seemed that she took a peculiar enjoyment in her statement, and without understanding her he doubted that she meant what she said.

"You know, Jesse, there ought to be a closed season for widowers," his father confided a year or two later. "No man knows what it's like until the women are after him."

He was drunk, of course, when he said it, his heavy body lurching beside his small son's, as they set out for the movies together. Dad would go to sleep, no matter how exciting the picture, and his heavy breathing would anger or disgust the person who sat on one side of him.

Perhaps six months later Jesse, surprised in the back yard by Cousin Belle and retreat cut off, resigned himself to answering questions about the lady Dad had brought to the house the evening before.

"What did she say?" demanded Cousin Belle, and before he could answer she added that it was a wonder his mother's furniture hadn't knocked her flat. "Your father certainly has a gall," Cousin Belle hissed.

Jesse had no special liking for, or antipathy to, the lady. She had gushed over him and Ross, but all women did that. His father had been fairly sober and had wanted to take them all to a restaurant for dinner, but Jesse and Ross were worried about their dog, sick with distemper, and were unwilling to leave him.

"You're not old enough to understand now, but some day you'll remember what I'm telling you," Cousin Belle said. "That woman made your mother terribly unhappy. Don't forget that. For all I know, she might be alive yet, if your father had been true to her. Everyone in the neighborhood says the same thing."

Ross listened gravely when Jesse repeated Cousin Belle's waspish sentences. He knew what she meant, he admitted; the woman next door had told him the same thing.

"Dad was in love with Miss Ley, before Mother died," Ross explained. "Mother knew about it."

But if the gossips who had carried the sorry tale to two small boys had hoped to punish the man through them, their scheming went for nought. Ross and Jesse wanted their father to be happy, and if Miss Ley was part of that plan, they had nothing against her. Their attitude was one of indifference even when she helped them to bury their dog in the pet cemetery and paid for the lot and a headstone.

Jesse knew that Ross worried lest Dad be picked up for drunken driving, and although Miss Ley's driving was erratic it was a relief when she took the wheel of the car. She was a brusque woman, with a rasping voice and abrupt, jerky movements. Her severely tailored suits and clipped hair emphasized her lack of femininity, and her prowess in athletics dismayed Cousin Belle, who thought that sports made women "stringy."

"We're going to the shore for the summer," Ross told Jesse, the second summer after their mother's death. "Miss Ley likes to swim and play golf and tennis. She says she'll teach us to swim."

They always spoke of her as Miss Ley, even when she begged them to call her Billie. She shared a cottage with two woman friends at the shore resort, and at first they made some attempt to get meals for the two boys and keep the Garrison bungalow in some kind of order. But Ross, gentle, obstinate, and tight-lipped, discouraged their attentions, and gradually the women desisted.

"We can take care of Dad ourselves," Ross told Jesse.

His drinking continued, and once Ross and Jesse spent the night under the boardwalk, where they had found Dad after a search that lasted past midnight. During the next few years a bad fall from a train and a serious illness seemed to serve as caution signals, and he began to straighten out. By the time Ross was fifteen and Jesse twelve, Miss Ley had dropped out of the picture, replaced by a fussy, bustling, younger woman who continually demanded praise for her homemaking qualities.

"Vera will look after us all and be a mother to you boys," Dad said when he announced that he and Vera were to be married.

He drank very little then, but he had formed the habit of talking to his sons as if they were contemporaries in those long, lonely years, and now he confided to Jesse that he felt it unfair to Vera to make her a stepmother.

"She's a young woman, she ought not to be tied down at the start," Dad worried. "Maybe I ought to marry someone who has been married before. An older woman."

Jesse, accustomed to responsibility, furrowed his brow in contemplation of this problem. "I guess Vera wouldn't want you to marry anyone but her," he ventured.

The marriage made life easier for the boys in many ways. With no capacity for mothering, Vera did know how to keep a house in order and how to cook and serve delicious meals. She was indefatigably industrious and saw to it that her menfolk did not lack clean laundry with every button in place.

"I'll look after your father—you two enjoy yourselves," she said to the boys, and she saw to it that they were left free to play or study or read, after school hours.

Vera managed the finances, too. Dad, old and sober and strangely quiet after years of bluster, left everything to her. Ross, a junior at college, finished before the Army took him, but Jesse enlisted in the Navy at eighteen. Vera had conscientiously put aside the money for his college course in his absence, and her thrift had enabled him to marry Patience at the end of the war and get his diploma in three years, instead of four.

"She says she loves us as if we were her own sons," Jesse repeated to his wife, "but she isn't maternal. Contrast her with your Aunt Nellie, and you'll see what I mean. Vera is a good little soul, and she makes Dad comfortable. If she gives the impression of being dried up along the edges, it's nothing she can help."

Vera did seem brittle and dry, Patience admitted upon reflection; she had a quick, nervous manner that was hardly restful. And in spite of all she did for Dad Garrison and the boys, her labor remained impersonal, unmotivated by affection.

"Jesse knows how much a child needs to be loved," Patience said. "He will be a wonderful father." She turned her head on the pillow. "Grandmother, did I go to sleep? Such manners!"

Emmeline rescued her crocheting from her lap. "We both dozed off," she decided. "Shows how quiet this floor is. I suppose the babies are in a soundproof section."

"Down the hall." Patience looked suddenly radiant. "I want you to see Nicholas, Grandmother—Aunt Nellie did. She said—"

A light, quick tap on the door interrupted her, and the nurse followed.

"Oh! I forgot you had company, Mrs. Garrison—I just wanted to leave some towels."

Patience detected the hand of Providence, but no one could read the expression in her gray eyes. "Grandmother, this is Miss Coburn," she said. "Miss Coburn, my grandmother, Mrs. Toller. Are they going to show the babies this afternoon, Miss Coburn?"

"We're shorthanded—three nurses are laid up with the grippe." Miss Coburn gave the impression of being practically indestructible herself. "But I'll show your grandmother Butch, if you like—a baby's great-grandmother ought to have a pass, seems to me."

"I knew you would!" Patience had a lovely smile. "Look at him carefully, Grandmother, and tell me if he resembles anyone in the family. Mother has all his features traced to his relatives, but I'm not so sure, and Jesse thinks it's just funny."

In the corridor Miss Coburn patted Emmeline's arm and confided that she was glad to see Mrs. Garrison having visitors. "I think the doctor made a mistake keeping her quiet so long, but of course it isn't my place to say so. She's the type that thinks along gloomy lines, if left alone too much."

"But she seems very well," Emmeline protested. "And I know she's delighted about the baby. Has she said that she's worried about anything?"

Miss Coburn paused, her hand on the knob of the nursery door. "Said anything? That's the trouble, she doesn't say anything. I never worry about women who chatter or complain or cry; Mrs. Garrison lies there with those shadowy eyes of hers and that still face, and you hope she's asleep and you know she isn't."

"What makes you think she may be worried?" Emmeline told herself that Miss Coburn was active and probably regarded any tendency to dream as suspicious.

"She's the type to worry," Miss Coburn repeated firmly and let herself into the nursery.

Through the glass door Emmeline watched her speak to the nurse in charge, and a moment later she had brought a bundled baby over to be displayed. Her great-grandson Nicholas gazed placidly at Emmeline, and she regarded him with something of his own serenity. He would undoubtedly find life wonderful and difficult, as she had, and as his children and grandchildren would in their turn. *Unless the chain breaks,* Emmeline thought, and dismissed the possibility as morbid.

"Isn't it strange," she said to Miss Coburn when the nurse rejoined her, "how a baby suggests a long line of descendants to come? Looking at Nicholas I could see my great-great-great-grandson smiling at me."

The nurse shrugged. "If there's any world then," she said.

At the door of No. 33 she stopped, made sure that it was closed, and spoke hurriedly in a low voice. "It wouldn't surprise me if that's what Mrs. Garrison has on her mind. She's brought a child into a world that's a good deal less than perfect. Mostly it isn't even pleasant. She might even blame herself for having a baby. She's the type that would."

"Yes," Emmeline admitted to the nurse, "she might think of that."

Miss Coburn betrayed some embarrassment. "As a matter of fact, I overheard her talking to her aunt this morning—something about having children who might grow up and have to go to war. She oughtn't to hear anything but cheerful talk in her condition."

Emmeline agreed to be cheerful, and Miss Coburn—who had long ago forgotten her story of the squirrels—departed to refresh herself with a coke, convinced that she had advanced her patient's welfare.

"A beautiful baby," Emmeline pronounced. "And beautifully cared for—you don't nurse him, your mother said."

"I tried to, but I couldn't. The doctor says it's all right." Patience sounded apologetic. "And to think of all the quarts of milk I drank while I was pregnant!"

They had not been wasted, Emmeline remarked dryly; you had only to look at Nicholas to know he had benefited. "Babies get better every generation. Doctors have more sense."

Patience smiled, her eyes on the flashing, weaving motion of the crochet hook. Grandmother's generation, she reflected, had been brought up not to sit with idle hands. She sat there so quietly, a serene picture of placid old age. Past all the hard places in the long road and with only one uncertainty before her. If she had ever been bewildered, had ever found herself in a room with sealed windows and locked door, she had found her way out.

"Grandmother, didn't your first baby die?" Patience said.

Emmeline's busy fingers hesitated an imperceptible moment; then the scallop continued to take form. "Sixty-three years ago. His name was Andrew. Why, dear?"

"Oh, I'm probably morbid, but I remember Mother telling us years ago that your first baby was a boy and that he died." Patience's shadowed eyes might be picturing another young mother of another day. "I don't see how you could go on living. I don't see how any woman could go on living."

"My dearie!" Emmeline checked herself. Perhaps that square-faced nurse had been right; perhaps Patience had been left too much to herself. Not, Emmeline reflected, that she would willingly be a party to any conspiracy that might be formed to invade the girl's privacy or control her thoughts. There was something indecent in the efforts of the well-meaning to force lightheartedness.

"If Nicholas died, I should want to die, too. I'd never be the same again. You don't believe that silly platitude that Time heals all wounds, do you, Grandmother?" Patience, twisting a lock of her hair, moved her body restlessly.

Emmeline felt suddenly empty of wisdom or even common sense, but she said evenly, "All wounds heal, but they leave scars. Now Andrew has become my one child who never gave me a moment's worry. Life was never the same afterward—I will not lie to you—but most of it was good."

"Do you mind if I tell you something, Grandmother?"

"What is it, dear?" Emmeline thought of herself as a kind of receptacle for confidences. A grandmother was safer with secrets than a mother.

Patience spoke slowly, as if selecting her words. "I used to think a lot about dying. When I was a little girl. I think it was the Sunday school lessons. Anyway, I'd wake up in the night and wonder if I might not be going to die."

"Why didn't you tell someone?" As if a child would, Emmeline reflected.

"Lucy was married, and I couldn't tell Mother or Daddy. I used to take a blanket off my bed and creep downstairs and lie outside their door, where I could hear them breathing. As long as I could hear them breathing, I felt safe." Patience drew a deep breath. "I outgrew it, of course, but now I keep thinking about your baby who died and what I should do if Nicholas died, too."

Emmeline resisted the temptation to feel of the slender wrist lying on the coverlet. Patience had no fever, at least none that could be detected.

"It sounds to me as if you might be more afraid of living than of dying," Emmeline said. "Nicholas is growing like a weed, and the real question is what you're going to do with his life and yours." She removed her glasses to polish them with her handkerchief, and without them her face looked unfamiliar and strained. "Maybe I'd better tell you what it's taken me eighty years to learn," she suggested.

"Please, Grandmother."

The glasses slipped back into place, and a wise, shrewd, old lady peered out. "You might write it down and hang it in your new apartment, where you'll see it every morning," Emmeline said. "It's only five words long, but each one counts: *Don't let life scare you*—that's all."

Patience laughed, a young, relieved sound. Miss Coburn, bringing in a glass of milk, glanced approvingly at the old lady industriously crocheting.

"You must be what the doctor ordered," she grinned. "I wish I'd come in time to hear the joke."

"If there's any joke, it's that milk." Patience eyed the glass distrustfully. "It must be for my next child—Nicholas won't get its benefits."

Miss Coburn said that Nature was funny. "Down in the ward there's a girl with enough milk for two babies—and it's her bad luck that she has one."

"Gossip?" suggested Patience hopefully, but the buzzer sounded in the corridor, and the nurse frowned.

"If that's Her Royal Highness, I swear I'll paint her face green—she's made up three times since breakfast. Don't let me come back and find any milk in that glass, either." She trotted off, the square lines of her back managing to express vivid irritation.

Emmeline took the glass Patience handed her presently but said nothing. As she expected, in a few moments the light, easy breathing changed, altering to that mysterious rhythm that betrays one who sleeps. Why should the child be so apprehensive, Emmeline thought, rolling up her crochet work. Lou had been careful to give the girls a secure home life—at least she had not burdened them with her worries. Emmeline gently subtracted enough of the sweet peas to make a small bouquet for Hetty Palmer. Why should

Patience be cherishing a bagful of troubles to plague her in secret?

"She's asleep," Emmeline told Miss Coburn outside the room. "I got my things on without waking her. It's most time for her sister Lucy—Mrs. Gray—to come. They'll have a good visit together."

The elevator was in use when Emmeline reached it, and the wide, dark steps of the stairway tempted her to walk down.

Holding her flowers carefully, she progressed slowly to the next floor, where she found herself in a square hall with an open double doorway on her right.

"Go right in!" A young probationer hurrying past glanced at the sweet peas. "It's visiting day, you know."

Rows of beds, all occupied, stretched from the doorway to the windows on the far outer wall. Groups of visitors stood around the beds, most of them in dark clothes and cheerfully indifferent to antiseptic precautions.

"Have you come to see your daughter?" Another probationer in stiffly starched blue and white spoke politely. "Do you know her name?" The girl enunciated each syllable so distinctly that Emmeline stared at her in startled fascination.

"Has she had her baby?" The little student nurse rounded each word.

Emmeline began to understand.

"My dear child, I speak English," she announced clearly. "I've been visiting upstairs."

"Oh!" The girl blushed, the color staining her fine, clear skin up to the roots of her braided red hair. "Well, you see I can't always tell —did you want to see anyone in the ward?"

Emmeline, who had been surveying the rows of beds, nodded. "I've come to see that girl in the corner—if you don't mind I'll go right in."

"Miss Kesnick?" The student nurse opened copper-brown eyes very wide. "Well—you can stay till four o'clock."

She had never been one to talk to strangers, Emmeline admitted, wondering what she should do if Miss Coburn chose this moment to pay one of her visits to the ward. An old woman could talk to anyone without being criticized, and perhaps that was a compensation of sorts. The reason why, too, so many old persons—men and women—became garrulous. Their disciplined tongues were celebrating the removal of restraints.

"Well, my dear—" Emmeline had reached the corner bed. "I'm very glad to see you," she assured the occupant and looked around for a chair.

If it was Miss Kesnick in the bed, Miss Kesnick might be eighteen, or sixteen, or twenty at the most. A pretty girl, with fluffy, dark hair, a pale oval face, and eyes that matched her hair.

"Mayme!" A stout woman who with a companion sat visiting with the patient in the next bed jabbed an elbow into her friend's ribs. "Mayme, look!"

Emmeline pretended to be oblivious to the nudge and the concentrated stares of the group of three. She placed her chair so that she faced the room across Miss Kesnick's bed, a device that forced the young woman to face her, thus shielding her from the nearest knot of spectators.

"You're probably surprised to see me," Emmeline chattered. If she had only thought to bring reinforcements in the person of Hetty Palmer! The woman in the next bed had two visitors, and one could talk and the other listen, an arrangement manifestly unfair.

Miss Kesnick's dark eyes widened, and she drew the covers up to her throat. "Are you a new doctor?" she whispered.

"Just a friend," Emmeline assured her. It might be funny to be taken for a doctor at eighty-two, but it wasn't funny to think that only a doctor or a nurse stopped beside this bed.

A low buzz came from the next bed, where patient and visitors had their heads close together. Emmeline caught a glance from Mayme, who held her body rigid and twisted her neck like an expert listener.

"I'm a neighbor of your grandmother's," Emmeline said in a clear voice. "She knew I would be visiting my granddaughter today, and she asked me to drop in and speak to you. Here, let me pin these on your gown."

As Emmeline leaned over the girl to fasten the sweet peas to her hospital shirt, she felt the tremor of her body and when her hands touched the thin fingers clutching the coverlet and sheets the flesh was cold.

"Your grandmother sent her love," Emmeline reported, stepping back to view the effect of the flowers. "There, you look very nice. Now I'll get you some ice cream. What kind do you like?"

Nearly every patient in the room held a paper cup of ice cream, and the visitors were consuming their share, too. Mayme, Emmeline perceived, was outfitted with a cup, and her companion was feeding the woman in the bed.

"If they have strawberry, would you like that?" Emmeline patted the top sheet. Miss Kesnick's bed was smooth and uncluttered, without wrinkles, magazines, or any of the cheerful clutter of paper and string that might be left in the wake of gifts.

Miss Kesnick's lips moved, but no words came. She moistened them with her tongue. "Yes, please," she murmured.

"I'll get strawberry," Emmeline promised. "I remember your Aunt Sally always liked strawberry."

She would be back in a few moments, but the canteen was in the basement and Miss Kesnick was not to worry if she should be delayed, Emmeline explained, vastly pleased with herself for having created a grandmother and an aunt for a supposedly friendless girl.

Of course Miss Kesnick probably thought her an escaped mental case, Emmeline admitted, backing out into the shining space of the broad central aisle. There ought to be a soundproof curtain made for ward beds, transparent perhaps to promote cheerfulness, but treated to ensure the individual patient's privacy. Some, of course, would prefer noise—Emmeline passed a half-dozen young women holding a "shower" for a young, laughing mother who looked as if she belonged in high school.

"The canteen?" The woman at the information desk on the first floor was briskly competent. "Take the elevator to the basement, and follow the red arrows on the wall. It's too late for lunch now."

She wanted ice cream for a patient, Emmeline answered, thankful that she had no vigil ahead of her and need wait for no verdict. She had spent so many hours waiting in the course of her life—for the sick to get well, for time to heal grief, for her children to learn wisdom, and for Simon to forgive himself. Now perhaps women were less passive, they believed in forcing issues, but she doubted that they were any more successful in solving their problems. They were too restless to wait and too hurried to discover whether their decisions had value.

The red arrows on the green-painted wall led down one corridor, up the next, in the clean, light basement. A rattle of dishes advertised the canteen more effectively than the signs. Emmeline, rounding a corner, found herself facing a soda fountain with two girls in green- and white-striped cotton uniforms busily drying glasses.

"Ice cream?" the short blond one repeated Emmeline's question. "Could you wait just a minute? The porter's bringing in some—he's getting it off the truck now."

The tall brunet one said, "We sold out at lunch. People sure do like ice cream for dessert."

Emmeline perched rather precariously on a stool and ordered a coke. She belonged to the generation that had asked for a lemon or orange phosphate. No one drank phosphates any more, Emmeline mused, but the very name brought back to her the lovely drugstore smell that had been part of the charm of the soda fountains she remembered.

"Are you a nurse's aide?" she asked the blond girl, who served her deftly, providing a paper doily, napkin, and straw, with a small glass.

The girl smiled and wiped up an invisible spot on the counter, flourishing her cloth professionally. "We're volunteers. Mrs. Parker, who runs the canteen, is a member of our church, and she signed us up."

"We give two afternoons a week." The brunette twitched her green chambray apron straight. "For three months."

They had learned to mix sodas and make sandwiches, the girls said, pleased to have an appreciative listener. They made excellent coffee, and the interns and nurses practically lived on coffee or cokes.

"It's a lot of fun," the blonde testified. "Honestly, we don't even mind the dishes any more."

Emmeline took a deep gulp, sighed for the vanished lemon phosphate. "Do you ever work directly with the patients?" she inquired.

Quick headshakes answered her.

"The nurses and the aides are always going round in circles, and when you add the patients, you have a free-for-all." The blonde mopped the counter again. "Down here, we work in pairs, and we see the interns too, and—well, it's easier even if you do have to be on your feet more."

The other agreed. "You can sign up to work with your girl friend, so you know there'll be fair play," she said. "And if there's ice cream left at five o'clock, when the canteen closes, Mrs. Parker doesn't mind if we eat it. Mostly there isn't any left, though."

Emmeline finished her drink and found that the shadowy plan revolving in her mind had taken definite shape. "Could you take a cup of ice cream up to a friend of mine in the maternity ward, if I paid you in advance? I'd like her to have it once a day for a week, if she's here that long."

"Sure." Both promised. "After rush hours. What's your friend's name?"

The blonde wrote it on a slip of paper as Emmeline spelled it, counted the money needed on her fingers, and murmured that her friend was better at working the cash register than she. "Here comes the ice cream now," she said, identifying the rattle of an approaching hand truck.

The porter, a muscular, middle-aged man, transferred two heavy drums of ice cream to the proper compartments, conscious of the admiration of his feminine audience and perhaps aware that he was safe from their competition.

"Did you bring strawberry?" Emmeline asked, shrinking back from the shower of crushed ice.

"Strawberry *and* chocolate." The porter crunched ice under his large, flat feet, like a man conscious of his power. "There! Now you can start up again," he told the girls and trundled away with his truck.

One began to fill a container, and one mopped up water and ice.

"Sometimes I think Ben likes to make a mess, so we'll have to clean up after him," grumbled the brunette. "He's always cleaning up after people himself, so maybe he likes the idea of someone doing it for him."

The idea that the porter might like to be waited on amused Emmeline. She paid for the cup of ice cream, said good-by, and began to follow the arrows that led back to the elevator. It was human nature to sidestep the dirty work, if the chance presented. Emmeline remembered a friend whose daughter had married into a wealthy household where the servants outnumbered the family. The higher paid servants had each his assistant, and when the family spent the winter in Nassau, the staff had been left intact in the town house, to wait upon each other.

"Blessed be nothing," Emmeline quoted aloud to the amazement of the nurse who left the elevator as she stepped in.

The dark eyes of Miss Kesnick had been watching the doorway for her return. Emmeline decided that the friends of the patient in the next bed had been watching, too.

"I ran into two girls," Emmeline said, in her clearest tone. "They'll probably be up to see you tomorrow. You ought to let your friends know where you are."

What on earth was the girl's first name, Emmeline puzzled. You couldn't say "Miss Kesnick" within hearing of those eavesdropping pussycats. They were not entirely convinced yet; the smallest slip would undo all the careful planning.

"Let me fix your napkin." Emmeline spread out the tissue square. "Here's the spoon—there, now enjoy it. I saw the porter bring it in, so it must be nice and firm."

Miss Kesnick smiled, and the proverbial ten years fell away. She couldn't be nine years old, Emmeline reasoned; she might be nineteen.

"Eat it slowly, I'll work on my crochet," she said. "Your grandmother"—this time she raised her voice unconsciously—"tells me you knit and crochet as well as she does."

"I like to crochet better than to knit," Miss Kesnick said.

Emmeline caught her crochet hook before it fell to the floor. That came from inventing relatives for a friendless girl.

"I'll send you some of my patterns," she promised.

"Here?" Miss Kesnick could not be called loquacious.

Well, that depended upon how long she expected to be in St. Luke's, Emmeline countered. "If you'd like me to get you some thread and a crochet hook, I'll send those right away."

She took a pad and pencil from her bag, wrote quickly, "Put down your name and home address," and handed the pad to the girl.

"Jot down the number of the thread and the size crochet hook, dear," she commanded, hoping that her voice carried. "My memory's so poor I have to make a memorandum of every little thing."

Miss Kesnick understood. Her attentive dark eyes swung toward the group at the next bed and then back to Emmeline. She took up the pad and pencil, began to write slowly, like a child anxious to do his best.

She could not be more than seventeen, Emmeline decided, watching the fan of dark lashes on the smooth cheek. There should be an adoring mother and a proud husband in her background; her planning should be all for a baby's rosy future. Why, Lucy's daughter, Cinda, was fifteen. Just beginning to go out with the boys and confidently expecting marriage and children to be her ultimate portion.

"Amy Kesnick, 89 Ivy Street," Emmeline read on the pad the girl returned a little shyly. In the lower corner of the paper, in smaller, cramped letters, another line: "I have a baby—a girl."

Emmeline reached over to pat the slim arm. "I know." She slipped the pad and pencil into her bag. "Well, I never! Here's an extra hook and a ball of number twenty cotton. You can start a motif now."

"Excuse me!" Mayme had risen ponderously and now stood looking down on Emmeline, the width of the bed between them. "Are you from the Social Service?" she asked.

Emmeline's "Mercy, no!" sounded abrupt, even to her own ears. "I'm just a friend." Nothing, she assured herself, would induce her to use the name of "Miss Kesnick" to call attention to the girl.

"Well, I told my sister you were probably from the Social Service." Mayme was obviously disappointed. "They come in the ward quite a lot. My sister's just had her third boy. Her husband's crazy for a girl. It's always like that. I have two girls myself, and my husband says he won't have another baby unless we can be sure it will be a son."

Miss Kesnick, crocheting a chain swiftly, smoothly, scarcely listened. The Social Service worker had visited her three times, and the woman in the next bed had nearly fallen on her face trying to hear every word that was said. The social worker had been anxious to explain that the only thing that mattered was the welfare of the child.

"You naturally want the best for her." She had a rather unfortunate manner of talking as if she stood on a platform, making a speech. "If you'll give her for adoption, she will be secure and you can start life again."

Miss Kesnick had intended to sign the baby away for adoption. She had no illusions about her earning capacity. If she never had any money, living with a girl friend in two rooms, how could she expect to support a baby, too? The girl friend would not welcome a baby in their cramped quarters; the child wouldn't be properly fed.

But the case worker somehow rubbed her the wrong way, Miss Kesnick discovered at their first meeting. Perhaps it was that the case worker was so plainly a good woman. Perhaps her habit of classifying human beings as problems irked a younger woman lacking all ability to solve hers. Miss Kesnick had declined to discuss adoption.

"But you can't get a job, unless it's doing housework buried in the country," she had been reminded. "And even there you might not have time to give the baby proper care. Earning a living and looking after a baby at the same time is more than a young girl should undertake."

The prospect of undertaking it frightened Miss Kesnick, but a strange, foolish obstinacy forced her to repeat her "No." If the case worker had displayed any interest in her, Amy Kesnick, as a person, if she had been less intent on asking questions and writing down the answers, and more sympathetic toward the physical suffering of Miss Kesnick, who still felt miserable, she might have been more successful. There was the baby, Miss Kesnick thought resentfully, nice and warm and comfortable, and she, its mother, alone and headachy and worried, in a big ward filled with women who whispered.

"I love my children so much it makes me sick," the woman in the next bed had announced complacently, when the nurse had brought Miss Kesnick her baby for "mothering."

That, the affectionate mother had explained, was something new. "My first two babies you'd have thought they'd die if I touched them. The new way is to have a mother love them."

Miss Kesnick, to the disgust of mother and nurse, failed to display any emotion. She thought her baby homely, with its screwed-up features and fringe of reddish hair. Homely babies made pretty brides, the old saying ran. "I don't want her adopted," Miss Kesnick said.

She remained obdurate through two more calls from the social worker, who promised her that her case would be followed up and help extended after she left the hospital. Miss Kesnick considered the entire Social Service created to pester unfortunates. It was to blame that she had placed herself on record as refusing to permit adoption of her child when she had hoped that solution might end her troubles.

"If the Social Service couldn't find Rob for me, how can it take care of the baby?" Miss Kesnick asked the night nurse, who, with a dozen things to do every minute, had rubbed her aching back and resettled her pillows one especially dreary stretch of sleepless hours.

The night nurse said that men who deserted the girls they got into trouble had a special gift for dropping out of sight. "And of course there are so many of them, it would take the F.B.I. to catch them all. If a girl has a father or a brother who will take over the hunt, there's a better chance of success. You got anyone who can go around hunting?"

Miss Kesnick thought, with some justice, that people asked her a great many foolish questions.

"If I had anyone to go hunting him," she said, "I wouldn't have listened to him, in the first place. I wanted someone to care about me."

The night nurse, a good little soul, admitted that she often felt that way, too. "You get so tired of knowing you don't matter to anyone. My married sister's fond of me, but she has her husband and children."

At that a sister must mean more than a girl friend, Miss Kesnick thought, when the nurse had skillfully tucked a pillow in the small of her back and hurried away. A sister could remember you as a little girl.

"No one remembers me," she had once complained to Virgie, her girl friend. "I went to a couple of the day nurseries where they used to leave me when I was a kid; at one they had changed matrons, and the other didn't know the first thing about me."

Virgie insisted that no good ever came from raking up the past. "The present is what counts. Your mother left your father, and your father left you—why do you expect a day nursery matron to make a fuss over you?"

Miss Kesnick, in the hospital with a baby and no husband, realized that her desire for love and attention had cost her dear. Rob Brewer had made a fuss over her, and she had been fool enough to believe him. He had no family, he had told her, over the cafeteria breakfast where she had met him, and he had fetched her a glass of water as if he handed a goblet of wine to a queen.

They had gone to the movies that night, and the next Sunday he took her to an amusement park. Virgie later professed to have distrusted him from the beginning, but she went willingly enough on square dates, when Rob brought a friend.

"I will say for Rob that he can't see another girl when you're around," Virgie commented after one of their Sunday excursions.

But when in July Miss Kesnick found herself pregnant beyond a doubt, Virgie furiously condemned Rob for his smooth technique.

"You're probably one of a dozen," she suggested. "He doesn't look right or left, till he's got what he wants. A girl who wants to be first with someone falls for that line."

Virgie had been practical and reasonably loyal and at least had not deserted Miss Kesnick in her extremity. It had been Virgie who arranged for prenatal care, had insisted that a complaint be lodged against Rob Brewer—who had so successfully dropped out of sight that his previous experience was generally conceded—and who helped Miss Kesnick to keep her job in the department store until the last possible moment.

"You can come back here, afterward, but don't bring the baby," Virgie had pronounced as her final warning.

And she had not visited the hospital. She said when she died in one that would be time enough.

Miss Kesnick manipulated her thread expertly, glanced at the woman in the next bed. She had identified herself as Mrs. Gresser, a devoted wife and mother, and her manner implied that Miss Kesnick was none of those things. Mrs. Gresser was critical of the hospital ruling that children under twelve could not be admitted to the maternity ward, but she kept her two children's photographs under her pillow, and Mr. Gresser's likeness was in the locket that rested on her ample bosom.

"My husband is an angel from heaven when I'm pregnant," Mrs. Gresser had told the woman in the bed beyond hers, because Miss Kesnick, friendless and alone, was being punished for her sins. No one came to see her, and that *proved* she had transgressed.

"When I go home, he'll have the place all cleaned and always something new in the way of furniture or curtains," Mrs. Gresser continued. "He tells me he worships me, for all I've gone through."

Miss Kesnick had not been impressed by Mr. Gresser's personal appearance when he visited his wife, but at least he had come to see her. At that moment Miss Kesnick would have been grateful for a store dummy to stand beside her bed.

She finished another scallop, delighted to discover that she had not forgotten the teaching of the knitting and crochet instructor at the store. That good-natured woman had laughed at her enthusiasm for crocheting but had encouraged her by suggesting that with study and practice Miss Kesnick might be able to teach needlework classes or to find work with some of the pattern firms.

"You ought to do work you enjoy," the instructor had said.

Miss Kesnick had remained in cosmetics because it was too much effort to make plans. But now she thought that after she was over this and free to return to the store she would ask the needlework instructor to tell her how to use her special skill.

Of course she would have to let someone adopt the baby—why, Miss Kesnick realized with a sudden feeling of comfort, she had someone to advise her at last. Like the other women in the ward, she had a visitor. This quiet, unhurried old lady in the pretty hat would help her. Miss Kesnick, now that she thought of it, had been helped from the moment she had been endowed with a grandmother and shielded from the curiosity of the women who listened.

"I'll have to be going." Emmeline, rising, leaned down to pat Miss Kesnick's thin young cheek. "Why, how fast you work! You must come and see me as soon as you can, when you've left the hospital. And I'll write to you and send you more thread."

Watching the girl, she saw that she understood—the door was not closing, she would have a chance to say all the things she had left unsaid. Mayme, who had fussily been gathering up gloves, purse, and fur scarf, glanced over her shoulder, and Emmeline stooped impulsively and kissed Miss Kesnick good-by.

In the hall Emmeline hesitated a moment, wondering whether Lucy might be upstairs with Patience and debating the wisdom of returning; the pause allowed Mayme to overtake her.

"It's always a pity when a girl messes up her life like that, isn't it?" Mayme fell into step companionably as Emmeline started for the elevator. "Such a contrast between her and my friend who's a lovely woman with three children besides the new baby."

Emmeline allowed herself to be herded into the elevator, and the car started down. "You couldn't expect a young girl to have four children," she objected.

"She could have a husband, though," Mayme snapped as the car jarred to a stop at the main floor. "I think there ought to be a separate ward for illegitimate births. They're depressing."

That was all the unwed mother needed, Emmeline told herself, undecided whether to laugh or cry. Put her in a ward with a sign over the door to warn the upright and good of the plague within. Or leave the doorway unscreened and put up a rope, so that the curious could peer in without personal risk.

Mayme opened the elevator gate but blocked the exit with her heavy frame. "Honestly, did you ever see that girl before?" she demanded.

The question caught Emmeline off guard, but she controlled her impulse to snap at her tormentor. Anger could only betray her.

"I'd never seen her before, but she's no stranger to me," she said. "I am not in the habit of calling on strangers. I know her, through my own friends."

Everyone knew Miss Kesnick. Emmeline, finally free of Mayme, found a seat in the bus that would take her home. She was no stranger to anyone who had heard her story, and what woman had not? Each generation assumed itself to be more liberal and open-minded and, when tested, proved to be uncharitable and given to persecution still. Except for the lapse in time, Miss Kesnick might have been the Miss Fanning Emmeline's mind retraced seventy years to recall.

"You know Miss Fanning who has the real-estate office down by the railroad station?" the hired girl had asked Emmeline's mother as the family, newly moved to town, worked busily to put the house in order.

Emmeline's mother, her head in a barrel of china, signified that she was not acquainted with Miss Fanning.

"Well, she ain't married." Allie, the hired girl, sounded triumphant.

"But she has that little girl." Emmeline's mother raised a vaguely alarmed face from the dusty straw lining the barrel. "A pretty little thing, about Emmeline's age."

Allie, eager to orient the new family, explained that Lydia was Miss Fanning's daughter. "Born twelve years ago. And Miss Fanning wouldn't tell her own mother who the man was. That real-estate business was her brother's—he died and left it to her, and she runs it to support her mother, herself, and the child. They say she's a fine businesswoman but as cold as ice."

Emmeline, enrolled in school, found herself sitting behind Lydia Fanning. They walked home together the first afternoon, and the next day Lydia said quietly, "My mother says I must tell you that I have no father. If you don't want to play with me, it will be all right."

The pathos of that statement impressed even a child who could not understand the implications behind it. Emmeline and Lydia were to be lifelong friends, but Emmeline never succeeded in her overtures to Miss Fanning. No one in the town knew her, except in her role of businesswoman. She enlarged her office and became the leading realtor in the county, attending conventions, serving on boards, and accumulating considerable property. But she refused to attend church, accepted no social invitations, and gave nothing to charity.

"She was only eighteen when the child was born," Allie told Emmeline's mother. "Her family wanted her to move away, put 'Mrs.' in front of her name, and bring up the girl as if her husband had died. She said no, she would stay here and live it down. And I guess she will."

Emmeline could not be sure that she had. True, Miss Fanning had the respect, if not the affection, of her fellow townsmen when she died in her sleep, aged forty-eight. But Lydia, who continued to live in the town and kept up the office, scoffed at marriage and, once out of school, deliberately neglected her friends.

"It's as if she is determined to remind people that she was born out of wedlock," Emmeline protested to Simon. "I was actually afraid she would refuse to be my maid of honor, unless I promised to tell every guest that her mother was unmarried."

Lydia had died before she was fifty, and her money had gone to the state, since she left no will. Emmeline suspected that she wanted no trace left of a Miss Fanning.

"Don't you usually get off here, Ma'am?" the bus driver signaled respectfully. He knew most of the Carberry Home residents by sight. "I don't want to take you past your corner."

Emmeline thanked him, backed carefully down the step, and consoled herself that skirts concealed her stiff joints. Old men hobbled much more noticeably than old women.

"Hetty!" She tapped on the door of Mrs. Palmer's room a few moments later and turned the knob. "Hetty, I've found a baby for your niece to adopt."

The Home doctor, they decided, talking it over while Emmeline rested her aching feet on a fat hassock, could be persuaded to attend to the details. Mrs. Palmer was confident that Nina had only to see the baby to desire it.

"Talking to her about a baby doesn't mean a thing to her, but when she holds an actual child—"

Emmeline had no doubt about Miss Kesnick's willingness to give her baby for adoption, if she trusted those who made her promises. "I don't think she'd care if she never had another child," Emmeline said. "I gave her your sweet peas," she added belatedly. "I didn't think you'd mind."

Doctor Connor, they agreed, once interested in Miss Kesnick's case, would see that she had a week in St. Luke's Convalescent Home, before she went back to her job.

"I think I'll knit her a bed jacket," Emmeline declared. "Pink, because she's dark. And you can make her a pair of slippers to match. Patience looked lovely in the blue jacket I knitted for her. And wait until I tell you about my great-grandson, Nicholas."

Chapter Six

"WELL, for pity's sake!" Lucy Gray peered around the screen set up in the doorway of No. 33 and stared at her sister propped in bed. "So this is what goes on."

Patience gazed dreamily over her son's fuzzy head, her shadowed gray eyes inscrutable, but her red lips smiling. "Hi, Lutie! Come in and meet your nephew. He's nicer than anything you've seen in a long time."

"I was gypped," Lucy complained, divesting herself of hat, coat, and gloves in practically one movement. "I had my babies when it was considered fatal to let the mother—poor, ignorant menace—touch them." She kissed Patience, touched the baby's cheek with a careful forefinger. "How long has this been going on?"

"Well, it's the newest idea," Patience admitted. "They want the baby and his mother to get acquainted, so they bring them—the babies—in for mothering. Heather told me that at Thatcher Memorial they keep the baby's crib in the same room with the mother."

Lucy suggested that the medical profession consult an architect, when doctors prepared to reverse their ultimatums. "You couldn't keep a baby in this room unless you moved the bureau, the washbasin, and the chair out. How long do they let you keep him?"

The nurse might let Nicholas stay twenty minutes, half an hour—the arrival of a visitor was the signal for Miss Coburn to whisk him away. "Even Jesse has been here only twice when I had Nicholas with me. Want to hold him, Lucy?"

"You *do* love me," gibed Lucy, but she was touched. Patience, she thought, looked well—everyone said she looked wonderful—but she had changed. It might be maturity, or it might be a deepening of her capacity for secret worry. Lucy believed she had developed a sixth sense for identifying the victims of hidden anxieties.

She would take the baby while Patience ate her ice cream, she said, and they effected the transfer quickly, with the efficient Miss Coburn in mind. She hadn't forgotten how to hold a baby, Lucy said, pleased with her own remembered dexterity.

"He's gorgeous," she assured her sister. "They get better all the time. Some of the theories must be good."

Patience waved her spoon instructively. "*Everybody*—Mother, Aunt Nellie, Grandma—thinks babies are healthier now. I'd like four," she added, "if I could be sure."

"Sure of what?" Lucy was examining the perfection of miniature hands and feet.

"Oh—sure of security. Of a fair chance for them. If I could reach out ahead and safeguard Nicholas—"

Someone rapped sharply, folded back the screen. "Ah, there he is! Time for all good babies to have afternoon tea." Miss Coburn eyed the visitor critically.

"This is my sister, Mrs. Gray, Miss Coburn." Patience watched with envy the nonchalant, easy approach of the nurse to the precious bundle and her expert handling of the tiny body.

Lucy surrendered the sleeping child, tenderness softening the angles of her thin, dark face. "They never let me touch my babies in the hospital," she confided.

"Ten years from now it will be something else," the nurse assured her. "Theories are just dandy as long as they last. In the end a mother does well to rely on her own common sense."

She turned on her capable heels and marched out, Nicholas still sleeping in the concentrated fury that appeared to be his answer to theories old and new.

"I suppose I'll be trotting to St. Luke's to see my first grandchild in a few more years," Lucy sighed, removing the paper plate and napkins and murmuring, "You're welcome, dear," to Patience's words of thanks. "Cinda's social life is getting to be serious in spots."

"How is the clothes situation?" Patience asked. "It was an awful blow to her when I had to wear maternity styles."

They both laughed. Fifteen-year-old Cinda frankly coveted the wardrobe of Patience and her sister-in-law Heather Garrison. Lucy had constantly to interfere, or the child would have borrowed furs, suits, and shoes with indiscriminate freedom. Heather, as the "dressy" member of the family, was an especially magnificent source of evening gowns, and Cinda, tall and slim, could wear tweeds or lace with equal success.

"Heather's still ill, you know," Lucy said. "No one seems to know exactly what the trouble is. I've been to see her twice, and the nurse is a devoted dragon who stands at the door and says that Mrs. Garrison is doing all right but isn't up to seeing visitors yet. She's been reciting that for nearly a month. What does Jesse say?"

He said nothing, Patience declared. "Honestly, Lucy, there are times when I wonder if I'll find anything as I left it. According to everyone I've seen, this is the best of all possible worlds, there isn't a worry in it, and every human being is lying in the sun with not a wish unfulfilled."

"My lamb, you're a maternity case, and the new mother is protected from the bumps until such time as she shall go forth," Lucy explained. "It's always that way."

Patience drew a deep breath. It was such a relief to talk to Lucy. A sister, even a much older sister, could be trusted to be on your side. "Sometimes I imagine that Jesse has lost his job, that we haven't the apartment at all, and that he's forgotten to pay the fire insurance and doesn't tell me. Did you feel that way, too?"

"That and more." Lucy smiled wryly. "Wait until you have your second child. The efforts made to convince you that the first is supremely happy in your absence will be enough to drive you wild."

She would be the last one to tell Patience not to lie there and worry, Lucy reflected. Any woman with imagination, once hospitalized, must think of many things and inspect many fears. Her mother had taken Ronnie to stay with her when Cinda had been born. Rules forbade the two-year-old Ronnie to visit the hospital, and it seemed to Lucy that Mel became more aggressively cheerful each visit he made.

"How's Ronnie?" Lucy put the stock question casually, tried to read the answer in Mel's face rather than in his words.

Mel invariably said, "He's fine." No, he didn't cry, no, he didn't ask for his mother. "Patience plays with him. She's too good to him—lets him bully her."

"You sure he hasn't fallen downstairs?" Lucy, awake the night before, had fancied she heard a child crying. Not the wailing of newborn babies, but the sobbing of an older baby, one perhaps two years old, like Ronnie.

Certainly Ronnie hadn't fallen downstairs, Mel said. "He hasn't carved himself, and he isn't drowned. Ask your mother, if you don't believe me."

"Well, you don't act like yourself," Lucy, driven to defending her anxiety, protested. "I never go two weeks at home without something happening, and now when I'm flat on my back suddenly everything is fine."

Her father and mother were as persistently sunny as Mel. It was wonderful to see Patience with Ronnie, her mother said. "You'd think she was twenty, instead of four. I'm sure she'd give him his bath, if I'd let her."

"Mother, you didn't have to worry about me when Patience was born; I was sixteen. But I worry about Ronnie—he must wonder what's become of me. Are you sure he's happy?"

Her mother scolded that she was a born worrier. "Here your father and I are taking all the responsibility of Ronnie. What could happen to him in our house? The doctor says all you have to do is to relax."

It had taken her years to realize that her mother never relaxed, Lucy admitted, wondering what fancies troubled Patience so anxious for security for her son. "What's on your mind, Patty?" Lucy said.

"Why do I always expect something to happen?" Patience demanded. "Why can't I just take it for granted that everything will be all right? Other girls do."

Lucy sighed. She sat in the one chair facing the half-closed door and felt hemmed in between dresser and bed. Even the cheaper hospital rooms might be designed with more discernment, she thought. "Don't you bring up your baby the way we were brought up," she said.

"Mother never worries. She told me so." Patience pulled the bed jacket more closely around her, although the room was evenly warm. "Jesse thinks I worry when I look ahead. He has more confidence in the future than I have, he says."

Jesse's good sense would pull the Garrison family through, Lucy prophesied. "And let me tell you, if you want Nicholas to feel secure—which is more important than to work for his financial security—you'll have to feel secure yourself."

"Do you?" Patience flashed.

The quick retort, so unlike her sister, startled Lucy, but she managed a nod and a gulp and then found words. "You bet I do. My formula may not be yours, but you can work out your own." She laughed a little, her thin, dark face alight with earnestness. "I've found that I can do anything I have to do. Anything. The things I can't do fade into unimportance."

If you could do anything you had to do, she went on, there was no reason for fear or dread. "It's wonderful to know that you're equipped to meet a crisis at any turn. That's why I take what comes in marriage more successfully than Mother did, although she doesn't know it and wouldn't admit it, if she did."

The family thought Lucy worked far too hard and felt that Mel Gray might, with a little more effort, be a better provider, Patience recollected; usually they qualified criticism with the admission that the sun rose and set on Lucy, as far as he was concerned. Grandmother Toller had always defended him, asserting that lack of ambition made a man easy to live with.

"Maybe it's easier for Lucy to earn half their living and have a husband who thinks this world is a pleasant place, than for her to be married to a go-getter who would make her a nervous wreck," Grandmother Toller argued when the family conversation centered on "poor Lucy."

It was difficult to decide, Patience told herself, whether Lucy was happy or merely busy. Perhaps the difference was slight. She looked like a person who could do anything she had to do—not capable, she had once said that to call a woman capable meant you couldn't think of anything nice to say about her—but confident and prepared. As if—Patience suddenly remembered Miss Coburn's story of the squirrels—she could always find the way out!

"Why is it hospital bouquets always look so infernally stiff?" demanded Lucy, suddenly rising to pull a vase out of line. "Every room I passed had a row of vases backed against the dresser mirror, each vase crammed to choking with helpless flowers—there!" She had succeeded in loosening an arrangement of tiny pink rosebuds and lilies of the valley. "Good gracious, Grandmother did break down and give you the tureen!" Her voice betrayed her surprise.

Patience explained. "She said she couldn't very well divide it between Mother and Aunt Nellie, and she knew you'd think it was all right for me to have it—you always think it's all right for me to have everything."

"Well, I'm fond of you." Lucy, busily working with the flowers, laughed. "I'm glad Grandmother finally made up her mind—I've been afraid that she might give the lid and the ladle to Mother and the tureen to Aunt Nellie, to save disappointment. Now it's settled. Who sent all these?"

"The pink sweet peas came from Mother's bridge club, the tulips from Jesse's office, and the roses and valley lilies are Heather's—they came just before you did. It's the third box from her. I said to Jesse that we ought to be sending her flowers, but Ross told him she won't have any in her room." Patience sounded vaguely worried.

Lucy, tugging gently at a spray of green, remarked that plenty of ill people developed a dislike for flowers. "What does Ross think?"

"He's coming tonight, and I can ask him. Nurses don't like flowers, either, but your friends want to send something. Miss Coburn says that in the next building there's a diabetic—an old gentleman—and he has six baskets of fruit on his dresser. He can't eat as much as an apple." Patience laughed. "The only thing you can be sure is right is a card with 'Best Wishes' on it."

"Or 'With Love,'" Lucy amended. "Well, I think your conservatory looks less repressed now. That nurse or the next nurse's aide will probably cram everything back into the vases as soon as my back is turned, but at least I've tried to rescue the posies. It would be nice if I could rescue you, too."

"Me? I?" Patience's inscrutable look deepened. "I am trying to improve my grammar so I won't be a shock to Nicholas," she explained. "Why should I be rescued, Lucy?"

She didn't know why, Lucy retorted, but she would be interested to know from what. "There's something sticking out from under your pillow—your shorthand book."

"Well—" Patience resentfully thrust the telltale notebook out of sight—"you didn't hear that Mel had lost his job until you left the hospital."

A pencil-slim, black-haired, black-eyed nurse, who looked twelve and might be twice that, floated in at the door, thermometer in hand. She smiled, inserted the tube in Patience's mouth and took the pulse count, then withdrew as noiselessly as she had come.

Lucy pictured her going down the corridor sowing little thermometers as she might sow seeds, gathering them up on her return trip, and writing the harvest in her little notebook. If all the patients waited as quietly as Patience, how much did the nurse know in the end? A neat and orderly routine, flowers arranged upright, not a vase out of line—it would save much trouble if human lives could be as easily arranged. Unfortunately she had learned from experience, Lucy thought a little grimly, that the unexpected was untidy and that misfortune refused to follow a straight line.

Mel had lost his job the day his son was born. Lucy had never been sure whether the shock would have been greater or less, had she been told before she left the hospital. She suspected that the family had forced Mel to promise he would not tell her until she came home with Ronnie and that her mother's efforts to have her bring the baby to her parents' home were a further attempt to shield her.

"Ronnie has to get used to the flat," Lucy had said lightly, but she had been glad to be relieved of housekeeping until she should have mastered the intricate details of baby care. It was only for a week or two at the longest and then she would be ready to return to their flat in the four-family house. They had the top flat, and the stairs, Mel said the morning after she had left the hospital, would be too much for her.

"The stairs are nothing, compared with the light and air we get," Lucy argued. "Besides, I can take Ronnie up on the roof for sun baths. We can't expect to do better for the rent we pay."

Mel, returned from shaving in the bathroom, took a clean but faded khaki shirt from the chiffonier drawer. "Your mother certainly is swell, fixing up the sewing room for the baby." He produced his favorite pair of corduroy pants from the depths of the closet. "I told her we could keep the crib in here, but she says babies should have their own rooms."

"You can't go to the office in those clothes!" Lucy, who had been instructed to stay in bed for breakfast but who had been awake since Mel had given the baby his six o'clock bottle, looked distressed. "Are you out of good shirts, Mel?"

He came over to her and sat on the side of the bed. She smelled soap and shaving lotion and remembered that her mother had once said he was the neatest man she had ever known.

"I'm going to build your mother a set of shelves down cellar—for canned goods." Mel's clear hazel eyes were happy. "I know where I can get the lumber, and she says she's wanted them for years."

Lucy noticed how brown his hands were on the white counterpane. "But your job—don't you have to go to the office, Mel?"

"Well, as a matter of fact, they let me out." One of the brown hands gently patted her cheek. "Didn't want to upset you, Lutie, while you were in the hospital. I had a number of leads, and I thought I'd have something before you were ready to come home. There's nothing to worry about—you're not going to let yourself get nervous, are you?"

She assured him that she wouldn't be nervous, and later in the day her mother confided that losing a job didn't mean much to a man like Mel. He was sure to get something better, and until he did Lucy and the baby would be comfortable where they were.

"Patience will be heartbroken if you take Ronnie away—I never saw a child so enraptured with a baby. She told me this morning that she thinks she will have a baby next week and she's going to name it Lily." Lucy's mother chuckled. "Boy or girl, she says the name will be Lily."

The pencil-slim nurse floated in, removed the thermometer, and read it in one expert glance.

"That's a trick I'll have to learn," Patience said as the crisp white silhouette vanished. "I never can tell anything about a thermometer, but with Nicholas facing life and germs I must be able to read his temperature. You can show me, Lutie."

Mothers didn't take a child's temperature as often as they had when her babies were young, Lucy remarked. "In fact, baby care has a whole new set of rules since I was leaning over cribs. I'm probably as archaic as Mother."

Far away the distant scream of sirens began, a wailing, winding stream of sound that even as they listened rose to flood tide and swept past the hospital, the whistles of the traffic police punctuating the thunderous rumble and rattle of the fire apparatus. The scream of the sirens faded into unfathomable distance, died away.

"There was a girl in one of the wards whose husband was killed," Patience said. "She has a baby, but no family to help her."

Lucy brought her straight, dark eyebrows together in a ferocious frown. "Nice, cheerful little item to relay to you. I thought Doctor Guye screened your visitors to eliminate the Calamity Janes. Whose idea of cheerful conversation was that?"

"Oh—it doesn't matter. You have to think about your future." Patience began to tug at a lock of hair. "Didn't you worry, Lutie?"

Her sister's puzzled expression matched her voice. "What are you talking about, Patty? Didn't I worry when?"

"When you found out Mel had lost his job. The time you came home from the hospital with Ronnie." Patience's shadowed eyes turned to the perplexed face watching her. "Before you learned that you can do anything you have to do."

Lucy bit her lip, laughed. "I had that coming to me. It's the fruit of my experience I've offered you, but I admit I was several years in training. Did I worry when Mel lost his job the first time? Yes, I suppose I did. But none of us perished, and a little of my terror dissolved. If I hadn't had Mother, it would have been more difficult but I still think we would have managed."

"Well, I think I could get my job back." Patience pulled the frayed book from under her pillow. "I've been brushing up on my shorthand, but I don't want Jesse to know." Jesse would not listen to any talk of her going back to work, she said, but Temple and Springler had told her that they'd have a place for her whenever she wanted to come back to them.

"Of course, that offer wouldn't hold forever." Patience turned the pages aimlessly, and Lucy saw that the wedding band hung loosely on her finger.

It was a mistake to let any skill rust, Lucy said briskly. "But for pity's sake don't lie there wondering if you and Jesse could manage if he lost his job. You could, if you had to. And if you don't have to, that's even better. So either way you're on solid ground."

She had left a six-weeks-old baby to return to work, Lucy remembered, and after that she had made no more plans to stay home. Her mother had fretted, but her mother's married life had been without financial security all during Lucy's girlhood and until Patience had been half grown.

"But I never left you," her mother had argued, aghast that Lucy could plan a long-range schedule as a businesswoman when she had so recently resigned that role. "You always knew where I was. I think a young child needs to know where his mother is."

Lucy said, "Ronnie will know. I'll tell him."

"Suppose you have another child?"

She hoped for three at least, Lucy answered. "I'd love to have twins. That would be economical."

"How about the effect on Mel of your working?" Her mother was not to be deflected. "He'll lose his ambition and be perfectly content to let you carry more than your share."

A young wife could not explain to her mother that she had married a man without ambition or, worse still, that she had discounted the flaw. If a man had no talent for making money, he could at least kill himself trying to be a success, women like her mother reasoned.

"Mel will be a wonderful father," Lucy said. "He's lovely with the baby, and he never grumbles about having to get up and feed him."

The birth of Cinda, two years later, complicated Lucy's double career for a brief period, but she remembered clearly Mel's unfailing good temper and devotion. She had learned then that Mel instinctively knew his limitations, and she had a wholesome horror of developing into a managing wife. Their marriage adjusted to the measure of its success—something less than she had hoped for and something more than she had been able to foresee.

Lucy suspected that her friends and her family alternately

blamed her for Mel's easy contentment and pitied her for his acceptance of her earning power. The employed wife should, theoretically at least, feel free to walk out of her job whenever she decided that she preferred to stay at home. "You work too long, and you'll find you can't bear to give up your own pay envelope," one of Patience's contemporaries, married two years, had confided to Lucy. "If you stay at home, you might as well make up your mind not to have any money for yourself."

Why should she attempt to make this youngster understand that her goal was not to have money for herself, Lucy thought, exasperated and yet amused. She spent her earnings for the children and Mel, just as he spent his. Not quite as he spent his—Mel's slogan was that you couldn't take it with you, and his favorite quotation, "Consider the lilies of the field. . . ."

In the bed Patience stirred. She and Lucy could share a silence without anxiety and without trying to read each other's mind.

"We can live on Jesse's salary—that doesn't worry me," Patience said. "Even poverty—supposing Jesse's salary stopped—wouldn't dismay me, for us. But Nicholas—he mustn't be handicapped. I want him to grow up well and strong and intelligent. And that will take money. Lutie, you know it will take money."

Practically everything took money, Lucy agreed, her dark eyes smiling. "But fortunately you don't have to have the entire huge sum in hand at once. You and Jesse can wrestle with the milk bills and the drugstore bills for the present, and as Nicholas expands, the family income will, too."

"Let us hope," inserted Patience.

"One or the other of you will attend to that." Lucy stood up, the movement bringing her closer to the bed. "I'll bet on Jesse being the bread- and cake winner in your life, Patty, but it won't really matter to the baby which parent is the go-getter. He has what he needs—a father and mother who mutually respect and love each other."

She crossed to the door and opened it wider. "I thought I heard a knock. Why, Grace Andrews! How nice—"

A tall, smartly slender young woman stepped into the room, patted Lucy's shoulder affectionately, and slipped past her to reach the bed.

"Don't kiss me through my veil—it's bad luck." She raised the heavy mesh and dropped a light kiss on Patience's smooth forehead. "You look blooming, my pet. I hear you've produced your first-born."

Patience said dryly, "He's a boy—Nicholas." Grace, she remembered, was famous for her ability to carry on a conversation without any specific knowledge of what she was talking about. An inveterate chatterer, she relied on her friends to supply the key words if she really faltered.

"I've been up to see Wal's sister." Grace took the only chair, unhooked her mink jacket. "She's just had a girl."

Lucy, from the foot of the bed, surveyed the visitor appreciatively. Grace, nee Andrews, twice married and twice divorced, was still under thirty, a striking-looking woman with dark hair, blue eyes, and the gift for wearing clothes. Her fur jacket topped an almond-green wool frock, and her wide-brimmed violet-wreathed hat tipped at an angle contrived to show the beautifully arranged waves of her hair.

"Anything less like a maternity outfit I have not seen," Patience proclaimed. "You're a vision to rouse envy in the breasts of women who have forgotten how to look slim."

Grace removed her butter-soft beige gloves to reveal an amethyst and diamond ring on her left hand. "Think nothing of it," she instructed, conscious of unspoken questions in the air. "Wal's sister was all agog, too—she thought we might be going to patch things up."

With some difficulty Lucy recalled that Walter Pierce had been Grace's first husband. How you patched up a divorce from your first husband, after marriage to and divorce from a second, presented something of a problem. The word "patch" was ineffective, Lucy thought.

"Patience," she said aloud, "I ought to be on my way. If Miss Coburn finds you with two visitors—"

"Wait till I tell you about the ring." Grace, rummaging in her beige suède bag, had found a green enameled lipstick. "I picked it out myself—as a birthday present from an awfully nice man. I'd marry him in a minute if I thought I'd be willing to settle down and have a family."

Lucy glanced toward Patience, who lay motionless, her thoughts on guard behind her shadowed eyes.

"Well, what's the matter with having a family?" challenged Lucy briskly. "Unfortunately time is of the essence in this business—even with all the modern improvements."

Grace touched up the corners of her lovely mouth. "Well, I've never felt that I had enough to offer a child—Wal's income was uncertain, and Steve Frisch lived up to every cent of his. And of course, if I marry again, I'd want to wait five years—and then it might not be so safe for me. Do you know that doctors think a woman of thirty-five is downright elderly, when it comes to her having a child?"

"You can have 'em at twenty-one," suggested Patience smugly.

"Yes, you should see my two," Lucy chimed in.

She wasn't the irresponsible type, Grace informed them. "Any healthy cat can have a batch of kittens as soon as she's old enough to have boy friends; but I'd feel a terrible sense of responsibility if I brought a life into this world."

"There's no other place to bring it," Lucy reminded her. "What's the idea of waiting five years after your third marriage?"

Grace dropped the lipstick into her bag, took out an eyebrow pencil. "I set five years as the trial period," she explained. "I certainly wouldn't marry a man, have a child by him, and then be saddled with a youngster, if I found it necessary to divorce him."

Patience was silent. Lucy told herself that Grace Andrews had always made other women feel frowzy and awkward when confronted by her detailed perfection. It wasn't fair to resent her philosophy when in reality you envied her her clothes and furs.

"Then you have to practically live at child guidance centers." Grace apparently decided that her eyebrows would do, replaced the eyebrow pencil in her cosmetic kit. "Wal's sister spends all her spare time attending lectures and reading books. And then she gets off on the wrong foot. When her second child was born two years ago, she almost wrecked the first one for life, she said."

"Probably she didn't prepare him." Patience had a matronly air. "You're supposed to talk things over with the first child, to save him from developing jealousy."

Wal's sister had spent months preparing her first child, a boy, for the event of a sister or brother, Grace insisted. "I thought she overdid it myself. Bertie told the news all over the neighborhood, but his mother said she didn't care as long as he was ready to welcome the new baby with open arms."

"What happened?" Patience demanded.

Grace regarded her long line of skirt with satisfaction. "Do you like the new styles? Thank heaven, I've always had a small waist. Well, Herta said she went to the hospital sure that Bertie was looking forward to the baby's arrival and that she had prepared him for everything.

"She didn't see him for eleven days, and when she brought the baby home with her—it was another boy—Bertie flew into the most awful rage. Screamed and kicked and bit them all—out of his mind, you might say. Of course, Herta hustled him to the child-guidance center, and they finally got the truth out of him. He had expected his little brother they all talked so much about to come marching up to the house beating a drum and blowing a horn. No one told him he'd have to wait two years for a baby to grow to playmate size."

They laughed, and suddenly Grace's eyes were shrewd as she glanced up at Lucy. "You have two, haven't you?"

"Ronnie and Cinda." Lucy looked proud. "A nice couple, if I do say so."

Grace twisted her lovely ring. "But can you give them everything they ought to have? I mean it's such a struggle for existence now—children have to be perfect physically and specially educated, which means a large outlay of cash. It isn't fair to ask them to go without, when they see that others have so much."

"Well, of course the population can't be confined to millionaires' families," Patience interposed. "The rest of us have to have children."

That was just what she meant, Grace retorted; no one had to have children. "If you can't do the right thing by them, at least you can refrain from condemning them to disappointment and bitterness."

The familiar, discontented phrasing, thought Lucy, with just enough truth in it to make you uneasy. Cinda wanted to have the luxuries; the older she grew, the more likely she would be to covet the easy existence of the well to do. But for the sake of Patience she must be honest in her answer, Lucy resolved, and yes, for the sake of Grace, too; she, poor thing, couldn't decide on the flavor she wanted, so, like a child in a candy store, she was feverishly intent on trying them all.

"What I hope, girls," Lucy said slowly, "is that my children will discover what I've learned—that the experience of living can be very sweet. Now and then—not always—I find myself being sorry for the souls that are not to be born."

Patience shifted her position and sighed. "But so much can happen—to your children, or to you. Good things and bad. Not," she added with a quick glance at Grace, "that money guarantees protection."

"I'll give you a motto, Patty, to embroider in your spare time." Lucy glimpsed the approach of the square-built nurse in the dresser mirror. "You don't have to live your life all at once. That's what makes it endurable."

She and Grace left together, to the obvious relief of Miss Coburn, who wanted her patient to have a nap. Grace had her luxurious coupe parked a block from the hospital, and she offered Lucy a lift before she herself should drive "down the line" to pick up Crale and attend a cocktail party.

Presumably Crale was the man who had given her the amethyst and diamonds, Lucy concluded, thankful to be dropped at Dutchard's department store, famous for its "yard goods" and pattern section.

"I want to get material to make my daughter a dress," she said to Grace, and Grace had remembered her teen-age ambition to be a dressmaker.

"Funny, the notions you get. I used to make all my clothes, draft my own patterns, too." Grace, driving with effortless precision, added that she supposed sewing could be called a creative outlet. "The trouble is we outgrow the simple panaceas."

It had upset her a little, she confessed, to learn that Patience had a baby. "One of the girls" had told her, and they had agreed that motherhood was worth while if you had a son.

"I get positively silly over the little boys with tousled light hair who walk into you, if you go through the park," Grace said. "And then I think how it would seem to have a son old enough to be protective when I'm middle-aged. But they say there's positively no way to guarantee the sex, and I'm certainly not going to run the risk of having a girl. A daughter makes you old as soon as she's past the baby stage."

The trouble with women, Lucy reflected when Grace had let her out at the store and driven away, was that they insisted on trying to arrange their lives. As the night watchman at the plant had once observed, "Too many of 'em have the idea they're Mrs. God."

It was difficult to be a woman, Lucy admitted, but her sex had a tendency to make it more difficult than it need be. The majority were tone-deaf, she sometimes thought; they set themselves against the natural rhythm of the universe and in effect struggled at cross purposes with God. They either did not hear, or they disliked, the inexorable beat of their individual measure, and they stubbornly determined to alter the values to suit themselves. Then, like Grace, they assumed that the resulting discordant jangle was proof that life had nothing to offer them.

The pattern department on the fourth floor was always crowded. This afternoon, shoppers waited at the two long counters and four aisle tables to consult the heavy pattern books in turn. Lucy was fortunate enough to find a chair at one of the tables after a brief delay and began expertly to leaf through the brilliantly colored pages.

As she finished one book, she slid it across the table to another woman, who offered hers in exchange. Lucy's glance at the half dozen of them, all absorbed in the simpering illustrations, appraised the group as mothers with daughters to dress. Probably they were all trying to decide, as she was, whether it was cheaper to make a frock than to buy it—or whether a fifteen-year-old could be persuaded to dress her age.

"She's thirteen and she wants an off-the-shoulder dress," a stout young woman confided to her companion. "When I was her age, I kept teasing for a slinky black satin, with long black gloves."

Cinda wanted to wear extremes, too, perhaps merely to establish her independence. Yet Cinda relied on her father—Mel's opinion of her boy friends had considerable weight with her.

"It doesn't mean a thing," Mel laughed, disclaiming influence when Lucy spoke of Cinda's readiness to have him meet her dates. "Sure I'm good friends with my daughter. Why not? This is only the rehearsal, and she knows it.

"If she falls in love with a ne'er-do-well, she'll marry him, no matter what I say." Mel had no doubts on that score. "Once she makes up her mind about one of these kids who clutter up our living room, she won't even hear me, if I'm rash enough to express an opinion. Like her mother, if she happens to choose a poor stick, no one will be able to persuade her she's made a bad bargain."

The stout young woman murmured that thirteen was too young to go formal. "Honest, Joan, I dread the thought of her starting to go to dances. It means she'll set her heart on some boy and something will go wrong and she'll wind up crying night after night. I remember—if he's there or isn't there can wreck your whole evening."

Lucy, reading that three yards of thirty-nine-inch material was required for pattern number two-one-seven-six, remembered, too. At eighteen she had been engaged to Harry Bacher, and after six months of alternate ecstasy and despair he had told her that they would not be happy together and that he had made up his mind not to marry anyone unless he could be sure that they would both be happy.

"I have to be free," he had said vaguely, but his dark eyes filled with compassion for her. "If I have hurt you, I'm sorry."

In the weeks that followed it seemed to Lucy now that she had been panic-stricken in her efforts to hide her anguish from her parents and her friends. She had gone everywhere, to dances, to parties, conscious of a dull weight in her breast and steeling herself to meet Harry, always with a different girl. If she lived to be eighty, she thought, she would not forget those dances; the dull misery, buried in her subconsciousness, stirred to haunt her still, revived by inconsequential trifles against which she could have no guard. And at long intervals she dreamed and woke in the night with the old unhappiness pressing on her heart.

I never loved him that much, she reminded herself, frankly surprised.

Harry Bacher married a girl from another state and went into business with his wife's father. Lucy's mother, who read the local papers "with a fine-tooth comb," Grandma Toller said, reported various small items about him from time to time, probably in the hope of one day being able to report that misfortune had tripped him. Lou Allow had neither forgiven nor forgotten the broken engagement.

She had prepared Lucy for Harry's return for his father's funeral, twelve years later, but it had not occurred to Lucy that she would meet him. Yet she did, briefly, on a crowded street in her noon hour. That the steady gaze of his dark eyes, the light touch of his arm on her sleeve had the power to shake her so profoundly alarmed her, lest she betray an emotion she would have denied she felt. She was fine, she assured him in answer to his rapid questions, her husband and children were well, she had been sorry to hear of his bereavement. The restless, seeking look had not died out of Harry's face, and she remembered from her mother's gleanings that he had been divorced and remarried.

"I've got to make a train," he told her, but his eyes, compassionate and gentle, held hers. "Ah, Lutie, you can be thankful you didn't marry me."

Lucy decided that number two-one-seven-six would have to do and surrendered her chair to a pretty woman in an enormously full coat. At the counter two distracted clerks attempted to serve perhaps thirty women, and the delay was repeated among the fabrics, where Lucy debated the question of coral and ice-blue. Coral would be infinitely more becoming to Cinda, but ice-blue was approved by the high-school sophisticates. The least a mother who planned to make a dance frock could do would be to follow the color trend.

"You can make two dresses for the price of one, if you can sew," the middle-aged clerk approved, as she measured the crepe.

A harmless cliché, Lucy noted, and not any more out of line than dozens of other platitudes. As she waited for her package, she wondered if her father's attitude toward Patience had been influenced by Harry Bacher's treatment of her. Patience, in high school, had apparently not resented parental supervision, but Mel had called Lucy's attention to her father's possessiveness.

"He's always on hand when one of the boys might suggest a date with Patience," Mel said. "The kid stays away from class dances, and if she goes to a party, your father takes her in the car and calls for her. It's medieval."

Lucy thought he exaggerated, but she protested when at seventeen, a graduate with her first job, Patience had elected to spend her two weeks' vacation with her father and mother, who took a sedate automobile trip each summer.

"You didn't have to time your vacation with Dad's," Lucy scolded. "Why didn't you plan to go somewhere by yourself?" And to Mel she said that Patience was in danger of marrying the first man who was alone with her long enough to propose. "She ought to be having dates and comparing suitors, but Dad likes to keep her for himself."

Mel, who had a gift for shrewd analysis, said that he had placed his bets on Patience. "I worried about her when she was in school, because she couldn't very well assert herself. But now she has a job, she's no longer helpless. You get one good look at those deep-set eyes of hers, and you wonder if she ever was helpless."

Patience had known her own mind when Jesse Garrison found her, and as Mel had said, she had not been helpless in the sense of being unable to retreat from her father's efforts to hold her. Yet, Lucy suspected, she might still be bound in ways they none of them quite understood.

"Sometimes I think Mother has had a deeper influence on us than Dad," Lucy had suggested to Mel. "We heard him, but we felt her—children can feel and remember more than they actually see."

It would make everything so much simpler, she told herself when she had boarded the bus with her packages, if the frankness of children, which so often embarrassed their hapless parents, could be taken at its face value. No human being—she had decided years ago, struggling to be a good mother—was ever frank, least of all a child. Words were a screen, and a baby learning to talk learned simultaneously to keep the important things to himself.

Patience will discover this, too, now that she has Nicholas. Lucy pulled the cord for the next stop.

"Mother!" Cinda tumbled down the stairs at the sound of the key in the latch. "The most wonderful news—I've got the lead in the play! Miss Gorman says she knows I can do it."

She smiled delightedly at her pretty self in the hall mirror, already practicing for her part in the school play. A tall, slim girl, vivid, dark, with an enchanting smile.

"We're to meet Daddy downtown for dinner," Lucy announced, suddenly conscious of weariness. "Where's Ronnie?"

"He phoned. I mean Daddy did. He said if you don't mind, he'll be home for dinner. And Ronnie's over at Jack's, but he'll be back before six." Cinda noticed the packages next. "What did you buy, Mother?"

But she frowned when Lucy said that she had bought a pattern and material for the new dress.

"I hate having to stand for hours to have you fit me," she grumbled.

Lucy scarcely heard. She wondered whether Mel had lost the anticipated commission entirely or whether it might be paid him later.

Chapter Seven

"YES, it's a pretty color, I suppose." Cinda refused to look up from her salad. "But you'll have to sew on it at night, and it takes you so long. Dutchard's had a window full of formals last week—stunning ones!"

Ronnie, always critical of his sister, asked her why she didn't make her own dress. "You turned the house upside down for that sewing project of yours last winter. I thought you were going to be a dress designer."

"She's going to be an actress." Mel, whose daughter resembled him so closely, smiled across the table at Lucy. "Wonder how it will seem to see her name in lights on Broadway some day."

Cinda murmured, "Don't be silly, Dad," but she was pleased. For the moment she forgot the dress and thought only of the play. It was characteristic of her that she chattered as enthusiastically to her father as to any of her friends, and even Ronnie, skeptical of her histrionic talent, yielded to the charm of her bright interest.

They would have to rehearse at the house three or four times, Cinda was saying; so many of the kids lived in apartments and had to be careful about noise.

"What do you mean, noise?" Ronnie jeered. "Sam Larsen says a fellow in his apartment house belongs to a jazz band and they practice there two nights a week."

Lucy scarcely heard the ensuing argument. She had held on to the house in spite of Mel's complaints that an apartment would be cheaper and his insinuation that the care of the furnace was too much for him, for just such a purpose as this. Cinda and Ronnie might have to keep their hospitality simple, but at least they had the freedom a house afforded and the knowledge that they could always bring the crowd home. As the upholstery faded, Lucy slip-covered the pieces in chintz, she managed new curtains, and she and Mel learned how to paper and paint. The dining room where they sat tonight opened into the living room and would make an excellent improvised stage. Lucy began to calculate the cost of serving sandwiches and cokes to the cast—if the entire class came to watch the rehearsals, refreshments were out.

"Seems to me you're planning to lose more sleep than you can afford," Mel remonstrated. "When is this dance—before or after the play?"

Cinda said quickly, "Ronnie, it's your turn to clear the table and get the dessert. The dance is next week, Dad."

"Why can't we eat pie on these same plates?" Ronnie demanded. He didn't expect an answer to the question he asked whenever he cleared the table but got awkwardly to his feet and set to work.

"What on earth made you buy material, Mother?" Cinda's mouth drooped discontentedly. "No one else bothers to sew. Especially formals, because they don't cost much."

Lucy explained. "Dear, the frocks I saw were simply too expensive. Out of this world, you'd say. I can make you one for half the price."

"Oh, Mother!" Cinda flung down her napkin, pushed back her chair as the telephone rang with harsh impact. In the doorway she turned, her brows drawn together in a scolding frown. "Mother, *don't* be so tight with your money!"

In the kitchen Ronnie whistled as he cut the apple pie and made fresh drip coffee, an accomplishment in which he took great pride. Lucy looked across the table and tried to smile for Mel.

"It's my fault, I guess," he said. "I ought to make more money. That commission I thought I had sewed up would have bought her a couple of dresses. She shouldn't talk like that to you, though."

Lucy heard Ronnie's whistle diminish to a low hum, the signal that he had filled his tray. "Don't say anything, Mel," she begged. "She didn't mean it."

It wasn't the dress that had upset Cinda—that was only an outlet for hidden disappointment or resentment, Lucy told herself. Probably something connected with a boy—Cinda was talking to a boy now. Her voice, her laugh identified the partners of her interminable phone dialogues with unfailing accuracy.

"Why do the kids have to call up just at mealtime?" Mel asked that question every night and, like Ronnie, really expected no answer.

Ronnie kicked the swinging door back, brought the tray to Lucy who liked to pour the coffee for Mel and herself. The children still preferred milk.

"Swell pie, Mom," Ronnie complimented her, putting the glass pot on the tile he had decorated in the ceramics class. "I got a taste, because I had to trim a jagged piece to make it neat."

They both laughed at this family joke, and Ronnie returned to the kitchen to fetch the pie. Cinda's murmurs indicated that she might be preparing to finish her conversation.

"We have enough, really, Mel," Lucy hurriedly interposed. "The children have everything they need. They won't know it, perhaps, or understand us, until they reach middle age, but parents shouldn't expect to be understood."

Ronnie served the pie; Cinda came back, slipped into her seat. "I'm sorry, Mother," she said in a low voice.

Afterward she offered to help with the dishes, a practical act of contrition that Lucy appreciated. When a little girl, Cinda's remorse had taken such strange forms as denying herself cake, which she kept under her pillow to demonstrate her ability to withstand temptation.

"I went to the hospital this afternoon to see Patience and the baby," Lucy volunteered, scraping plates and clearing the drainboard with an economy of motion born of experience.

Cinda waited on the high stool, her slim, drooping body silhouetted against the pale green wall. "How's the baby?"

"Lovely. And Patience is fine. She had plenty of company today —Grandmother was there just before me, and Aunt Nellie went this morning."

She only hoped Patience wouldn't regret it, Cinda sighed portentously. She and Ronnie had never called Patience "Aunt," and the five or six years' difference in their ages had not impressed them.

"Why, Cinda, how you do talk!" Lucy tossed her daughter a green gingham apron. "What should Patience regret? You don't mean the baby?"

Some people thought only of themselves, Cinda grumbled, buttoning the green apron over her skirt and blouse. "I know how you feel, Mother, but I have to form my own opinions. I think it's terrible to have children when you can't afford them."

"The baby's paid for," Lucy assured her. "Patience had hospitalization; and she told me they had enough saved for the extras."

Cinda's face, flushed and lovely, set in stubborn lines. "Having a baby is only the beginning," she declared. "Suppose Nicholas grows up and wants the things other children have; suppose he can't go to nice schools or to college; suppose he wants to develop a special skill—how will he feel then?"

"Well—" Lucy let hot water run into the pan. "I must say you don't seem to have much faith in Jesse," she suggested. "What's to prevent him from earning all the money Nicholas is going to need to send him to college?"

"Not all fathers—" Cinda faltered.

"Are money-makers," Lucy completed the sentence for her. "But, Cinda, you can't make people over, especially parents. I'm not sure that you can do much with your children, either. Perhaps we all come ready-made."

A dish towel, Lucy thought, had a depressing effect on the young. Both Cinda and Ronnie positively drooped, whenever they found one in their hands.

"Dry the glasses, darling, while they're still hot," she urged.

Cinda said, "Don't you wish we had more money, Mother?" She began to dry a goblet almost tentatively.

"Of course I'd like to have more money," Lucy admitted. "Who wouldn't? But I'm not willing to give up the things I value most, in order to have it."

Upstairs the radio blared as Ronnie sought a program that should, as he had often explained, blend with his homework without distracting him. Lucy surmised that Mel was busy with the furnace in the cellar. He kept the basement combed and brushed, the children said, but they appreciated his fanatical neatness since he preferred to stoke the fire and remove the ashes himself.

"I don't think I'll bother going to the dance," Cinda announced, tackling a second glass.

No, it wasn't the dress, she disclaimed; the material was lovely, and probably better quality than in the teen-age shops. "It's just that I've lost interest, Mother. Maybe I've been to too many dances. The novelty has worn off."

"Be sure to dry the silver thoroughly," Lucy murmured. Looking at her daughter's smooth young face, the corners of the red lips turned down, the short, thick lashes curtaining dark rebellious eyes, Lucy felt as old as Time.

You loved the first few dances. Unless you were unhappily a wallflower, you danced every number and remembered the music, the lights and laughter, and your dress. Your partners were exciting only because they could dance, but one nice boy was like another, and a boy who couldn't dance simply didn't rate.

Soon, however, all too soon, your outlook imperceptibly altered; everything that hadn't mattered before became fearfully important. The best floor, the finest music, your loveliest frock—what were they, if all the boys asked you to dance except one? You might be asked to the Coronation Ball, and if you knew he would not be there, why should you bother to plan a dress? Those few brief first dances—before the novelty wore off—were more precious than a girl ever knew until she realized that for her daughter they had come and gone.

"Is Hal Locke going to the dance, dear?" Lucy examined a spoon. "I hate to see silver scratched," she said.

"Mother, it's perfectly foul! Maybe you don't think it's wrong to have children when you can't do anything for them, but look at the Locke family! They're all martyrs—at least the children are." Cinda waved her dish towel like a red flag. "Six children, all of them doomed!" she cried.

In spite of herself Lucy laughed. Hal Locke's father was a Presbyterian clergyman, and the six doomed youngsters seemed to her to be a remarkably healthy, energetic set. "Excuse me, dear," she apologized, "I didn't mean to laugh. But surely Hal isn't doomed—or is he worried about his finals?"

Cinda handed the damp towel to her mother. The gesture indicated that she must be free to express emotion. She tossed back her long bob, a studied movement from the movies.

"Mother, in all his four years in high school, Hal has hardly had a dollar to spend. He works like a dog weekday afternoons and Saturdays, but he can't keep what he earns. His father is determined all the kids shall go to college, so Hal's money is used for his clothes or his expenses or put in the bank for college." Cinda's eyes flashed. "He can't go to the dance, because he hasn't money for a ticket and he won't hold back what he collects through the week."

It had been Hal who telephoned then, Lucy reflected. A sturdy, cheerful lad, obviously attracted by Cinda's quick grace, always neatly dressed, and with nothing of the burden bearer in his friendly manner.

"Hal has missed out on an awful lot in school," Cinda was saying. "His older brother did, too. And the other four will have to kill themselves working so they can be decently educated. I don't think it's fair."

Lucy poured hot water over her china cups. "Well, dear, if you're hinting that Mr. Locke ought to have more money, I daresay he thinks so, too. But he wouldn't give up one of his six to get it. Do you think your father or I would ever part with you or

Ronnie, to—to reduce expenses? Once you're here, you're priceless."

"That's what is so exasperating, Mother." Cinda forgot to toss her head; the words tumbled off her pointed tongue. "The Lockes didn't have to have six children. They just did. We've talked a lot about it at school, and all of us think one child's enough, if you're poor. No one asks to be born."

Well, you could hardly expect them to have original thoughts at fifteen, Lucy conceded. Besides, she could remember longing passionately, as a little girl, to be an only child like a young neighbor whose well-to-do parents, so the gossip ran, granted her every wish. Lucy and her companions envied the fortunate Vivian who had so many more toys and clothes and good times than they did and whose wishes seemed scarcely to be expressed before an adoring father or mother rushed to make them come true.

"My mother says Vivian is an only child and can have everything for herself," a third-grader finally explained to Lucy. "It's always like that with an only child, my mother says."

And Lucy had confided to her parents that night that she wished she were an only child and could have a dollhouse like Vivian's. The laughter of her parents and the confusion into which she was plunged by their announcement that she *was* an only child had discouraged her from asking questions, and it was years before she understood that even the only child might be affected by economic limitations.

But as the third grade had reached the conclusion that an only child was to be envied, so Cinda and her group had decided that one child was enough, if more meant that there would be less to share.

"When I look at Hal, I think his parents are practically criminals." Cinda looked around vaguely for the towel, accepted it from her mother, apparently with no immediate thought of using it. "The idea of having six children, when they can hardly feed them, let alone give them a normal life."

Lucy sneezed and murmured, "God bless you!" with a gravity that provoked Cinda's smile. "It's the soap flakes," Lucy explained, "not your ideas."

"But, Mother, you're a sensible woman; I couldn't talk like this to Grandma, much less to Gran Toller. Old ladies won't admit a truth, if it's unpleasant, but you have a lot of guts, Mother. You can see how unfair life is to Hal—can't you?" Cinda polished a cup so energetically that her objective might have been to obliterate the pink sprays in the design.

If life was unfair to Hal, then she must be a little blind, Lucy said. "He has always looked brimful of good spirits and cheerfulness. I doubt if he resents his brothers and sisters—do you think he does?"

"How can he help it? But I suppose he wouldn't let himself complain."

Cinda added that Hal felt a keen sense of responsibility for his younger brothers. "His father and mother are perfectly willing to let him kill himself working and deny himself all pleasure. It doesn't seem to occur to them that they had no right to have six kids."

Lucy interposed. "Now there you're wrong, Cinda. *Please* be careful of the cups."

"Do you think people should have hundreds of children, when they can't afford to care for them decently?"

"Not hundreds." Lucy slipped a stack of plates into the water. "I think Hal's father and mother have a right to have as many children as they may decide is the proper number. That's for the parents to decide, dear. When you're married, you and your husband can settle it for yourselves."

Cinda's stormy young face slowly relaxed. She could follow this line of reasoning. At that moment she undoubtedly pledged herself to have one child, a girl, and to give her every luxury, specifically a new gown for each class dance.

"Well, you may be right," Cinda conceded, "but I still think

Hal ought to relax more. He ought to go to the dance, even if he has to spend some of the money he earned."

She raced up the back stairs to her own room when Lucy, according to the code, intimated that she could finish the pots and pans alone. Hal Locke must be a year or two older than Cinda, not more. Thank heaven he had four years of college before him and presumably a period of adjustment beyond that—well, say the boy wouldn't be ready to marry before six years at the earliest. In six years' time Cinda would be twenty-one. And Patience at twenty-one had been married two years and had just had her first baby.

"Need any help?" Mel stepped into the kitchen. He had thought Cinda was lending a hand, he said, until he had heard her radio upstairs. "She has one station and Ronnie has another, and they're both concentrating on French."

She was almost finished, Lucy assured him; one pan could be left to soak. "I want to save my hands, or they'll be too rough for sewing. Mel—did you mind very much about the commission?"

His hazel eyes met hers without faltering, and she read no regret in their clear depths. "Oh, no, you have to expect that sort of thing. I was mad for a minute, but I'm used to the gamble. Only thing is, I'd like to have given you a bit of rest and change by eating out."

He had a habit of following her about, from sink to stove, from stove to refrigerator—to be trailed by Ronnie, her good-looking, gangling son, irritated her, but she found the trait in Mel rather endearing. He had no talent for helping her, but he liked to be where she was, and he could carry on a conversation satisfactory to himself whether she spoke in monosyllables or not at all.

"You don't want to wear yourself out sewing nights," he grumbled, opening and closing the doors of the wall cabinets in a series of staccato clicks. "Cinda has enough clothes. If you have to make a dress, make it for yourself."

At fifteen you couldn't have too many clothes, Lucy said. "This will have to be an extra-lovely frock—I think I'll loop up the hem with black velvet bows."

"Dance? That affair next week? Cinda told me she didn't think she'd go." Mel observed that, left to themselves, the kids came to their senses. "Cinda is beginning to discover that she can't keep such late hours."

The school dance was Friday night, so the juniors and seniors could sleep late Saturday morning, Lucy countered. She began to rub a softening lotion into her hands. "Hal Locke isn't going to the dance," she said.

"Who's he?" But before she could answer, Mel had recollected. "Say, that's the kid who telephones so much. I don't see how his father stands the bills, and I'll bet if the old man wants to use the phone he has to go out to a pay station."

Lucy rested the soft, smooth back of one hand against his cheek. "Satin or tweed?" she challenged.

"Satin." He kissed her palm. "Nothing serious between Cinda and this boy, is there, honey?"

She shook her head. "But life was simpler when, according to Grandmother, girls didn't even think of boys until they were eighteen. Of course, Grandmother married at seventeen, but perhaps she just got married without thinking. Anyway, the boy problem is with us for the next few years."

Mel said that he must take another look at the furnace—you'd think Nature counted on a rake-off from the fuel dealers, the way the cold weather lasted every spring. "And of course you girls have to go around in point d'esprit, no matter what the temperature."

The children grumbled because a coal furnace dated the house. None of the other kids' fathers bothered with an old furnace—except Mr. Locke, and of course he had to take what the congregation allowed him.

Lucy suspected that, left to himself, Mel's natural inclination would have been to buy an oil burner "on time"; but the children had not known where to stop, and their constant complaints had stimulated Mel's stubbornness, so that the coal furnace became to him a symbol of personal independence. He murmured every month that the electricity and telephone bills would ruin him, but he did not discuss the totals of the coal bills, except to remind Lucy that she liked the house to be warm.

The phone bell rang as Lucy passed through the hall on her way upstairs. Before she could put out her hand to take the instrument, Cinda clattered down the steps, crying that the call was for her.

"Hello!" Her bright eyes surveyed Lucy without seeing her. "Oh, hello." A subtle change altered every feature. Even the firm young voice perceptibly softened. "No, I'm not busy. Tell me now."

The blue fabric spread out on her bed, Lucy wondered about Mrs. Locke. A woman with six children couldn't very well take a job downtown to eke out the family income. The Lockes managed, because they were willing to sacrifice the nonessentials, but a clergyman's family could more easily be independent than a household expected to conform to ordinary standards. The minister and his family, the community implied, set an example for others to follow: if they practiced plain living and high thinking, theirs were praiseworthy aims. . . . Ministers' children were usually well adjusted, though there could be little in their backgrounds to make them feel secure. Except, Lucy rebuked herself, their parents' faith.

Hal was the only one of the family who came to the house, and his father's church and parsonage was in another section of the city. But Dr. Locke had married Ross Garrison and Heather Allen, and Heather said that his wife was a wonderful woman and the children "live wires."

"You don't suppose Hal will be a minister like his father, do you?" Mel had asked Lucy when the handsome senior's calls could no longer be credited to a desire to help Cinda with her homework.

Lucy thought he might do worse. "I think he'd make a fine

clergyman. Young, progressive, in touch with reality. His father would probably be pleased."

"Well, I can't feel comfortable with ministers," Mel worried. "I'm self-conscious, always feel they think I'm headed for hell and it's their duty to save my soul."

To some extent she shared his uneasiness, Lucy admitted, but she insisted that the blame was the laity's.

"Religion is something that ought to be a part of our daily lives. Why should we be embarrassed if someone speaks of God on a Thursday, instead of Sunday? Suppose we said grace at meals and had family prayers—don't you suppose we'd be able to take a minister more for granted?"

Mel looked alarmed. "Perhaps. But I'm depending on you to get me into Heaven. I just don't feel comfortable around a minister."

"Hal can't be ordained for years, even if he decides to study for the ministry," Lucy protested. "You're not likely to see him then, anyway."

Their daughter, Mel said glumly, was likely to marry him. "The prospect of a minister in the family depresses me and affects my dreams."

Lucy had laughed at him, declaring that she couldn't picture Cinda married to a clergyman. Cinda who wanted so much, who one week decided to be an actress, another a dancer, and at other intervals fancied herself as a nurse. Cinda was the last person in the world to marry a struggling young minister, Lucy had assured her husband.

"She has no patience with economies, she's mad about clothes, and I simply can't see her submitting to the mandates of a church congregation," Lucy said. "Besides, the child is only fifteen."

But tonight, hearing Cinda's murmuring laughter—if Hal had called from a pay station, the poor boy wouldn't have a nickel left—Lucy could not be sure. She studied the pattern absently, placed it on the material. After all, was Cinda so poorly equipped to be a minister's wife? Youth and gaiety, vitality and charm drew people to her, and a clergyman needed friends for his church. Perhaps one reason why Mel was so ill at ease with the clergy was that they tended to be ponderous and grave. Hal and Cinda together would be the exponents of a joyous religion in which the depressed and fearful might find they could believe.

Lucy began to pin the pattern expertly. *Stop daydreaming, you ninny.* She had married off her daughter to a young minister who faced four years of college before he would be ready for the seminary. Cinda would undoubtedly have a successful career and wind up by marrying a millionaire. A millionaire, Lucy confessed, would make her as nervous as a minister did Mel.

"Mother! Oh, Mother, listen!" Cinda sped up the stairs, her voice like a bell ringing out good news. "Mother, where are you? The most wonderful thing has happened!"

She halted in the doorway, and ecstasy illuminated her, a radiant inner light. "Oh, Mother!" she breathed.

"Yes, dear?" Across the width of the bed Lucy smiled, too tactful to attempt to guess the tidings. Hal had in some way managed to get a ticket for the dance, of course. Not many girls had Cinda's fair skin with such dark hair, and her eyes were as black as sealskin and as soft.

Cinda felt the instinct to prolong the lovely sensation of happiness. "You'd never guess, Mother. I didn't dream it could happen. It's too, too perfect."

"Is—is it something about the dance, darling?"

"Oh—the dance." Cinda dismissed that in disdain. "I don't care anything about the dance. But Hal's going to have the male lead in the play—he phoned me. Isn't that the most marvelous thing that ever happened?"

"Kiss optional" the directions in the school play had read when her class had put on a three-act farce, Lucy recollected.

"You know, Mother," Cinda said, "Hal tried out for the part in the beginning. He was awfully good, but he told the coach he wouldn't be able to give up the time for rehearsals. Now he's got a job that pays more money and doesn't tie him down nearly as much. Hal's always been like that: when he wants something, he studies out how to get it."

Cinda loved the talk of a new dress now that she thought she could wear it the night of the play—there would be a party afterward, if someone's mother could be persuaded to ask the entire class to her house.

"Mother, you're sweet to make me this dress. I'll do the basting, if you'll pin it. And I can get dinner tomorrow night, if you want to start sewing as soon as you come in." There wasn't anything Cinda wouldn't do, with this great tide of happiness rising in her heart.

"Lutie?" Mel, who instructed his son not to scream for his mother but to go where he supposed her to be, shouted again, "Hi, Lutie!"

When she answered, he called that he was going after cigarettes and might drop in at the drugstore. Did she want anything?

Cinda smiled at her mother as the front door banged, a woman-to-woman smile that said, *Thank heaven, now we won't be interrupted.* She had homework, she murmured, but she made no movement to withdraw.

"Hal's mother was really the one who got him to change his mind," she confided, leaning against the doorjamb, her gaze fixed on the bed, but her thought evidently not with the pattern.

Lucy slashed a breadth with competent shears. "She wanted him to be in the play, then?"

"Oh, she thinks he ought to enjoy every school activity he can—there are so many he has to miss." Cinda's eager voice warmed to her subject. "Mother, would you believe it, I had to beg him to try for a part—he wasn't even going to go to the first meeting when Miss Gorman had us read."

This pattern allowed for seams, Lucy recollected; at the same time her thoughts touched on Ronnie, who had such difficulties with his Latin, and followed after Mel, who had been disappointed with apple sauce as an improvised dessert. Lucy could listen to Cinda, too, without losing the thread of her daughter's conversation and without consciously dividing her attention.

"His mother fixed it so George—that's the brother in my class—can take Hal's job until after we give the play." George, Cinda added, worked afternoons, too, but his were odd neighborhood jobs and didn't hold him to a schedule. "You see, Mother, the dance would cost money for tickets, for flowers, and a suit for himself—he'd positively have to have a new suit. But *The Shuttered Window* is a costume play, and we have money in the treasury to pay all expenses."

Lucy said, "I see. And is Hal really good in dramatics?"

"Mother, he's super. Honest, he's a knockout. Sometimes I think his father is afraid he might want to go on the stage—I don't think he was too crazy about having him in the play, but he didn't [illegible] fere. Are those panels, Mother?"

"The front and back." Lucy's shears outlined a yo[illegible] have great fun, darling. Amateur theatricals are fascina[illegible]

Cinda, hands in the pockets of her brown corduroy s[illegible] left theatricals behind. "You know there's the biggest differen[illegible] mothers," she announced. "Some are so stuffy. But Mrs. Locke is wonderful."

"Is she, dear?" Lucy straightened her aching back. The bed wasn't a good cutting table, but it was handy. "Have you met her?"

She didn't know Mrs. Locke, Cinda admitted, but one of the girls in her class attended the Fourth Presbyterian Church, and Anne said Mrs. Locke was sweet. "Besides, I've heard simply volumes about her from Hal. Mother, would it be all right if I went to their house for dinner some night?"

"If Mrs. Locke asks you." Lucy made a mental note not to put off buying the new sherbet glasses any longer. She must have Hal Locke for dinner some night soon.

Something worried her, Cinda confessed; supposing that Mrs. Locke invited her. "Do you have to do anything differently in a minister's house, Mother? I don't expect to be very comfortable."

"Oh, for pity's sake!" Lucy, rememberin[illegible] Mel's anxiety, struggled against laughter. "Just behave natur[illegible] don't feel that you're in church. The ministers and their families I have known have been pretty much like everyone else."

But Cinda demurred. "How well did you ever know a minister? Did you have dinner at one's house?"

No, and I didn't lie awake nights, wondering if I'd like to marry a minister's son, Lucy prompted herself.

"Darling, I'm only trying to persuade you not to imagine obstacles that don't exist. You and Hal are good friends—he'll be just as natural and jolly in his home. And you are never self-conscious or stiff with people."

She couldn't be sure, Cinda murmured. "But I know I'll get [illegible]h Hal's mother. She's a good sport, he says. Most of the [illegible]inks of everyone but herself, he says, tries to please [illegible]tion and help his father. But once in a while—I guess and [illegible]ts tired of not having much of anything for herself—[illegible]me she says, 'Nuts to the world!' and makes herself an [illegible] sandwich!"

A half hour later, alone in the living room where she had carried her sewing, Lucy still laughed over that gesture of independence. An onion sandwich probably represented wanton recklessness to Mrs. Locke, who attended so many meetings of church organizations that she dared not risk offending anyone.

Mel had not returned, which meant that he had lingered in the drugstore to talk with the amiable proprietor, who welcomed company in the evening when business was slack. Charlie Voegler, a rabid critic of chain stores, resisted modern innovations and ran his one-man shop precisely as his father had before him. Mel liked the atmosphere of leisure and said that Charlie treated each customer as if he were irreplaceable. No one could make money in such a place, but Charlie's father had also left him a trust fund, so that he could well afford to be old-fashioned and stubborn in his ways.

The phone rang, and Lucy put aside her basting to answer it.

"Why, [illegible]!" Like most mothers of teen-age children,

Lucy had not expected the call to be for her. "We're fine—all of us. The kids are studying, and Mel's gone to the drugstore. How are all your boys and girls?"

"Everyone's gone to the movies," Nellie accounted for her brood. "Except the twins, who are asleep, of course. And Jerry and Luther have gone miles uptown, to look at some old wood. I'm baby sitter."

Lucy thought that perhaps her aunt had Patience on her mind, for she rarely called, although she kept in close touch with Lucy's mother. "Nicholas is a prize winner, isn't he, Aunt Nellie?" Lucy said.

"A lovely baby," Nellie assented. "And Patience is coming along well, too. I think she lies there and worries a good deal—it will be better for her when she's up and around."

The trouble with Patience was that she conjured, Lucy suggested. "You remember Ollie, who used to wash and iron for Mother when Patience was a kid, Auntie? Ollie used to say that Patience could conjure up more worries than any child she had ever known. Once Mother was caught downtown in a traffic jam and was a couple of hours late. Patience would have it that the trolley car had plunged off a cliff, though where the cliff was in the shopping district she couldn't explain."

"I didn't know she worried like that when she was a little girl." Nellie was aghast. "Who told you about that?"

Lucy had a hazy idea that her mother had heard it from Ollie and had told her. "I laughed, I suppose, and forgot it—I'm so much older than Patty that I wasn't home long after she was born. Seeing her today must have reminded me."

"Probably." Nellie hesitated a moment. "Lucy, I don't suppose Seth is there? Or that you've seen him today?"

"Seth? Why no, Auntie. I—"

"Well, I thought he might have dropped in to talk to Mel. Or stopped in at your office—only you were at the hospital all afternoon, of course. He'll turn up all right; I merely asked because I thought—" Nellie's voice trailed into silence.

If Seth came in with Mel—he might meet him at Voegler's—she would phone at once, Lucy promised. That explained the call, she told herself, replacing the handset. Poor Aunt Nellie didn't know where Seth was—presumably he "had a mad on," as the children said, and had not been at home for dinner. There wasn't a chance in the world that he would wander into Voegler's drugstore—it must be at least three miles from the Lakes—but the thought might keep Aunt Nellie from wondering whether he would return at all.

"Who was it, Mother?" Cinda called down, a little surprised that the call had not been from one of her friends.

"Aunt Nellie." Lucy, who disliked long-distance communication, moved from the telephone stand in the hall to the foot of the stairs. "She's worried about Seth again."

The upstairs hall was dark, but the light from the first-floor globe faintly illuminated Cinda's oval-shaped face, framed by shining bangs, and the sweep of her long bob, like two soft, dark curtains.

"Oh, Seth's always acting up." Cinda felt no responsibility for a mere cousin. "Mother, don't you think gold ballet slippers would be pretty with my new dress?"

The vogue for ballet slippers—Mel thought them the ugliest footwear ever invented for the feminine foot—might be confined to evening wear, Lucy hoped, if she encouraged that outlet. Several of Cinda's friends wore them, in black suède, to class, but so far Cinda had remained loyal to loafers.

"If you can find what you want, not too expensive, get them tomorrow," Lucy said.

Mel had been persuaded to lend Charlie Voegler a hand with the primitive soda fountain, Lucy decided, returning to her sewing. Not that it required much persuasion—Mel adored getting behind the counter and experimenting with the sirups. Charlie refused to serve sandwiches or cakes and frowned upon the sundae concoction. But when Mel put on an apron and bustled about, the customers ventured to ask for banana splits and like fancy fare.

"I could make a good thing out of that fountain," Mel liked to declare. "All it needs is some new dishes and a sandwich toaster. I'll bet it would be a gold mine."

Lucy suspected that with a little encouragement he would offer to operate the fountain as a concession. Mel liked to meet people, and he enjoyed surprising them with his dexterity. "It's my versatile nature," he assured them.

When he came home tonight, he would bring her gumdrops; Lucy's fondness for that candy was a standing joke in the family, and she always insisted that they tasted better from a paper bag. She and Mel had been married eighteen years, and on his every trip to the drugstore he had brought gumdrops back to her. Even when the things the babies needed had been more than she could pay, Mel had remembered the gumdrops. They would be charged on her bill.

"We ought to run up a few bills, to establish our credit," Mel had argued. "No one knows whether you're a good risk if you've never asked for credit. Besides, Charlie Voegler would let me buy the store out and charge it—he knows we're not going to move away."

Charlie had implied that Mel's father would not move away and that some day Mel would have the house in which they lived and then he, too, would be a fixture in the neighborhood. Charlie had been shrewd in his prediction. When Mel's mother died, his father proposed that Mel and Lucy and the children come to live with him. Lucy reported to her mother, "He'd board with us, and Mel would take over the house."

The house would be a responsibility, her mother hinted; it was always more expensive to live in a house than in an apartment. "The coal bills are probably staggering," she said, "and the walks have to be shoveled in winter. Mel isn't used to doing that sort of work."

The spacious yard behind the house, the wide, deep closets, and the big windows that made all the rooms light more than compensated, Lucy decided, for the services of a janitor. She had longed for years to be able to hang a coat out on the line, she told her father-in-law.

She and Mel could gradually paint and repaper the rooms. Mel's mother had been a cheerful soul, but dark woodwork and drab wallpaper, somber, serviceable rugs, and heavy draperies had been her generation's fashion. The solid, comfortable furniture could be re-covered a piece at a time.

"We're going to need so much, I think I'd better keep on working," Lucy reassured Mel, when they had moved in. "If I can get a maid to look after the children, I can manage breakfast and dinner."

Her father-in-law reserved the large, second-floor back bedroom for himself. He had not married until late in life, and Mel had been born on his fifty-second birthday. Thaddeus Gray, determined not to be a burden to his only child, had arranged for an annuity, sufficient for his wife and himself upon his retirement. His only property was the house, and this would be all he could leave to his son.

"We mustn't impose on your father," Lucy anxiously reminded Mel in the days that followed their transplanting. "He's entitled to peace and rest at his age."

She had never known anyone so simply good, she told herself, when in the topsy-turvy household the old man alone remained gentle and serene. His wife had been a notable housekeeper, she had catered to his preferences, and the orderly routine of his days at home had functioned as smoothly as clockwork.

"Then we barge in, and the girl doesn't come in time to get breakfast, so we rush off to work, leaving him to feed himself and the children," Lucy confessed to her mother. "Or else I'm held up at the office, and we have dinner at eight, instead of six-thirty. I ask Mel to send out the laundry, and he forgets to tell his father, whose shirts are left out. The children sneak past the maid, when we have a maid, and play in his room, when he's trying to read. Honestly, Mother, the poor man hasn't had a comfortable day since he turned the house over to us."

The mishaps, the confusion, and the general turmoil were easily described, but of her father-in-law's gentle consideration, his wordless understanding, Lucy did not attempt to speak. From the first week she had been conscious of his complete grasp of the mold in which her marriage had set. He showed her that she and Mel were dear to him and that they were both above reproach. He made no complaint about the housekeeping, he served cheerfully as baby sitter (although he did not live to hear the term used), and he even learned to cook and serve the children's meals so that Lucy's unpredictable schedule might matter less.

That the house, as the years slid past, gradually became shabby, inside and out, hurt him deeply, Lucy knew.

"We must do something to the house this spring," she said endlessly. "We must do something to the house this fall," she repeated as often.

But if the children's tonsils were removed the wallpaper couldn't be; if Cinda had her teeth straightened, the old roof must be patched again and again; slip covers cost as much as a summer at camp for Ronnie, and a woman by the day to do the heavy cleaning meant that nothing could be set aside for new rugs.

"What do you suppose Dad does all the time he stays shut up in his room?" Mel pondered when he realized that his father spent the greater part of each day by himself.

Since the children had begun to attend the city-country school, where they spent the day until four o'clock in the afternoon, their grandfather had time to himself, Lucy pointed out.

"He likes to be among his own things, and I think he reads a great deal. If I didn't call him at noon, I don't believe he'd remember to go down and eat his lunch."

When, to the almost pathetic amazement of her family, a cousin of her father's willed Lucy the sum of one thousand dollars, she resisted all attempts and suggestions that she spend it on something besides the house.

"I know we've never seen the Grand Canyon," she admitted

patiently to Ronnie. "I know that Cinda would love a riding horse and your father could use a new car. But we've lived in this house for ten years, and I don't think we've spent twenty dollars on it for repairs. Before your grandfather dies, I want to have it painted at least."

So the money had gone into the house, and Mel's father had been pleased that they had cared enough about the house to put it in order. Not long afterward he had died peacefully at the old desk in his room, an open ledger before him.

No one had known of the existence of this ledger, but when she examined it, Lucy discovered it to be a quaint bookkeeping record. Her father-in-law, over a period of years, had posted every kindness shown him and had tried to balance each entry by a kindness paid in return. Wherever possible he had tried to repay the person who had been kind to him, but failing that it had been passed on in his name.

"It's a form of diary, too," Lucy decided, as she read it aloud to Mel. "See, here he writes that everyone meets with kindness in some form but that we forget it, often, unless we write it down. Mel, he remembered the smallest things—like Charlie Voegler trusting him for a postage stamp, when he found he'd left his little coin purse home."

Mel thought the ledger evidence that his father's mind had begun to fail. "Secretive old fellow, wasn't he? I suppose when you retire from active business your faculties go slack."

"There was nothing the matter with your father's mind," Lucy announced indignantly. "Of course, he didn't wander about showing his ledger to people. He was keeping a record of debts he repaid, and it would have sounded pretty conceited if he had called attention to his own kind deeds."

"He gives us an awful lot of credit, doesn't he?" Mel's lips brushed his wife's cheek in a swift caress. "You always understood him, Lutie."

He always understood me. Lucy thought of the last entry in the ledger, written the morning her father-in-law had died.

"I have always found what I looked for," he had noted in his clear handwriting that scorned flourishes or affectation. . . .

The front door banged, and Mel's cheerful "Hi, Lutie! Are you upstairs?" brushed the past aside.

"In here, dear." Lucy in a low chair under the floor lamp sat facing the deep old sofa strewn with basted sections of blue silk.

Mel smelled of fresh cold air and good tobacco smoke and very faintly of Charlie Voegler's mysterious drugs, when he bent to kiss her. "You'll ruin your eyes, Lutie. I brought you some gumdrops. Anyone phone?"

"Aunt Nellie." Lucy peered into the paper bag with anticipation undiminished after more than seventeen years. "He's put in plenty of licorice this time, Mel. Aunt Nellie asked if Seth was over here. Do you suppose he's staying away again just to be mean?"

Mel said, "Could be." He helped himself to a gumdrop from the bag she offered him, murmured, "Thanks," lighted a cigarette. "Guess who I ran into at the drugstore?"

"Who?"

"Ross Garrison. He was going up to St. Luke's to see Patience. Jesse has to work late at the office tonight."

Lucy remembered that she had intended to call Heather, who must think it strange not to have heard again from her. "I keep putting it off until I have time to be deliberate and slow, and that time never comes. Did Ross say how Heather is, Mel? She can't be too ill, or Mother would have told me."

"She's still in bed and has the same nurse. Ross seems to think she's getting along all right. He's a nice chap, awfully quiet, but friendly, isn't he?"

Ross was a grand person, Lucy agreed. After Mel had gone down to look at the furnace, she sat for a moment, before she should begin to gather up her sewing. Had Heather ever said exactly what the operation was for? They had all sent her flowers, but the nurse had said the doctor had forbidden visitors on the ground that the patient needed complete rest. You didn't associate nerves with Heather, but perhaps she ought to give up her job and stay at home. She must phone Ross tomorrow, Lucy decided, and ask him when Heather could have visitors.

I have found what I looked for. In odd, detached moments like this, her father-in-law's simple declaration of faith became hers, too. She heard Mel whistling in the cellar, the faint musical murmur of the radio in Ronnie's room. The comfortable old house, a little shabby but warm and bright, assured them a background familiar and kind. If you took the years one at a time, Lucy thought, the answer came out right. "You don't have to live your life all at once," she had said to Patience.

Chapter Eight

"WHAT I don't understand," Jerry had remarked wistfully at dinner that evening, "is how people get things together to set up a home. All the furniture and sheets and towels—and stair carpets."

Rhoda, down for dinner, had laughed. She liked to say that Jerry was better than the doctor's tonics for a fit of the blues. "Why stair carpets?"

"They're so kind of complete." Jerry laughed at herself. "I mean, there are so many things to buy, things you have to have, that it always seems to me carpet for the stairs would be left to the last. With a stair carpet I'd have nothing more to shop for."

Nellie Lake looked across the table, extended to accommodate the nine of them (she had not laid a place for Seth, and she hoped no one would notice), and smiled at Luther.

"It's a gradual accumulation, Jerry," she explained. "You don't start out with everything you need. Mostly you begin with the things you don't need."

Violet, whose eyes were swollen from prolonged crying and who had powdered her nose until it looked like a marshmallow, recalled that she and Barry had a dozen luncheon sets and not one dish towel when they married.

"Where's Uncle Seth?" Lydia, one of the blond twins, had been studying the arrangement of the table.

Carol, the other, chimed in. "Where's his knife and fork?"

Everyone, except Luther, turned expectantly to Jerry, who sat at Nellie's right hand, sheltered inadequately by two large casseroles.

"I thought maybe he was late," Barry rumbled. He had a deep voice, and he was the only one of the Lakes who sounded as if he might be able to sing.

Rhoda and Violet exchanged a swift glance. "Remember you children have to drink your milk, or you'll get no dessert," Rhoda warned.

Beside Nellie, Jerry made a little sound, half impatient, half pathetically tired. "Oh, you might all as well know: Seth is tired of his job. He's going to look for something else."

"What goes on—" Chris subsided at a glance from his wife.

Barry, never a quick thinker, eyed them all with evident exasperation. "Has he given up eating? Lots of guys come home to dinner, even when they're looking for something else."

Nellie decided that as a mother she must be a total failure. Surely no other woman had ever brought up a son as slow-witted as Barry. Then she saw the honest bewilderment in his honest gray eyes, and she remembered how lovely he was with his homesick wife.

"Seth is tired of everything." Jerry faced them all composedly, but her hands locked tightly in her lap. "He's tired of going downtown and coming home. Nothing is the way he thought it would be after the war. Most of all he's tired of me."

The children continued to eat, their silverware making a startling clatter in the sudden silence. They assumed that, like most adult conversation, the present dialogue must be above their comprehension. If they were patient and did not incur the displeasure of their elders, they might learn, before they were excused from the table, what had happened to their adored Uncle Seth.

"The trouble with that guy," Barry pronounced grimly, "is that he's rotten spoiled. Someone ought to shake him up."

Jerry lashed out furiously. "He's not spoiled! If he wants to look for another job, that's his right."

"And leave you flat?"

"I'm not flat." Jerry tried to laugh, but her voice broke.

Luther interposed. "Calling names won't help anyone, Barry.

I'll try to talk to Seth, but he's stubborn. Anyway, Jerry, Mother and I are proud as peacocks that you want to stay with us. If Mother's wondered how she's been making out as a mother-in-law, I guess you've reassured her."

"We're going to the cinema tonight, Jerry," Violet said. "You come with us—the feature's good."

Rhoda spoke with sudden animation. "Let's all go to the movies. You'll stay with the children, won't you, Dad? You can't be dragged to see a double feature."

The startled, half-alarmed expression in Jerry's eyes as they turned to hers grieved Nellie afresh. This humiliation was the first stab at her pride. Overkind, overeager, the well-meant attempts of her sisters-in-law to include her in their plans had succeeded only in impressing her with the knowledge that she was to be a solitary woman.

"Thanks a lot." Jerry's dark head came erect. "I've mending to do, and I can catch up on my reading while I darn. Mother, I'll stay with the twins, if you want to go out."

Dinner over, the usual controversy about the dishes followed, ending finally in Nellie's frank announcement that she intended to wash them and that she liked to do them alone because she could take her time.

"Deliver me from doing the dishes with anyone who is trying to get through in order to dash off to see *My Final Finish,*" she declared. "My china plates can't take such treatment, and neither can I."

Jerry offered to put the children to bed and read them one story each. Luther, called to the phone, was still talking when the two couples set out for the neighborhood movie house.

"Don't go to a weepy film," Nellie had said in a hurried aside to Barry. "Vi is trying to be cheerful, but she can't take any artificial tragedy. I wish we could promise her the trip to see her mother."

What did people do before they had the movies, Nellie mused, gazing in some dismay at the confusion of dishes in her kitchen.

The girls had insisted on clearing the table, and "Out of sight, out of mind" had evidently been the motto.

If she had had a daughter, would she have grown up to put the bread plate on a handy chair? Nellie, rescuing the gold-banded china tray, decided that she probably would. The mad rush for the movies might imperil the dishes, but it could also save strained nerves.

If a woman felt depressed, if her problems whirled like a merry-go-round in her aching head, if disappointment mocked her hopes and her family failed to measure up to her expectations—she could go to the movies and forget it all. She didn't even have to "dress up" for the neighborhood picture house. For a small sum she could escape from herself and indulge in dreams. It would be a terrible mistake, Nellie told herself, if the critics ever succeeded in reforming the movies so that the films appealed to the head instead of the heart.

"Good heavens, the place looks like something out of modern art!" Luther from the doorway surveyed the chaos with dismay. "How could the kids upset the whole place in fifteen minutes?"

Nellie retrieved a silver fork from the floor. "You're supposed to look at the dining room," she instructed. "Table all cleared, dishes out of sight. This is behind the scenes. But I'm glad Vi and Rhoda could go—it'll do them both good to get out of the house. Jerry, I think, is hoping that Seth will come back, if only to pack."

"I thought maybe she'd drive with me, out to the North End, to look at some wood." In the bright kitchen light Luther's face showed haggard. "Berger called just now, and he's had two loads of secondhand stuff come in."

"Do you think—" Nellie hesitated.

"If Seth's been gone since morning, I doubt if he turns up tonight. If he does, he won't listen to her or to us. He knows exactly what he's doing, though he may not know why." Luther sighed, brushed an impatient hand across his eyes. "God forgive him, his conscience is probably clear because he knows Jerry will be safe with us."

The sea of unwashed dishes, Luther's dark figure and troubled face, the ostentatiously neat outline of Midnight, withdrawn from traffic under the sink, stood out for a moment, distinct and detailed as a photograph. The smell of meat loaf—a meat loaf went further—still flavored the air, and the refrigerator, cumbersome and old, heaved a tremendous cough and chugged noisily through its stint.

She and Luther had planned their middle age so differently. They had expected a tranquil period to follow their release from the dependence of their children. How could they have foreseen that their serenity rested upon the welfare of their sons and their sons' wives and that happiness could not be based upon a cultivated detachment?

Apron strings, Nellie reflected scornfully, bound the child to the parent and were best cut, of course. But the invisible bonds that bound the parent to the child could not be destroyed in this life and perhaps not in the next. Patience would learn, Nellie thought, her mind touching swiftly on her visit to the hospital, that once you brought a child into the world you were responsible for him until you left it.

And, in turn, Nicholas will be obligated to his children. Nellie heard Jerry's heels clattering on the uncarpeted back stairs. *There is a pattern.*

"I can't bear to leave you with all these dishes." Jerry deliberately slanted her face up to catch the light, so that they should see she had not been crying. "The twins are asleep, Mother; let me help."

But she welcomed the suggestion that she drive to the far end of the city with Luther. He would be silent, if she wished, and in the darkness she need not wear her fixed smile.

"It must be my fault," Nellie confided to the cat, who liked to sit on the high stool to watch her work at the sink. "Everyone says that, if a child goes wrong, it's the parents' fault. Usually the mother's."

She still couldn't be sure that Seth had "gone wrong," despite his treatment of Jerry. There was the war. Barry and Chris had apparently suffered no mental or spiritual injury, but that did not guarantee Seth a similar escape. In their anxiety to forget, people constantly assured each other that the war seemed so long over; they tried to push their memories into the dim past. Perhaps for Seth and others like him, there could be no dim past, only a vivid and tormenting present.

"He has a sense of failure, too, I think," Nellie told the cat, lifting her voice above the sound of running water. "Perhaps a sense of failure is hardest to bear."

The boys had quarreled among themselves while growing up, of course, but there had also been a strong sense of solidarity among them. Perhaps if they had been able to set up their own homes, Nellie sometimes thought, they might more easily have recaptured their old comradeship.

Instead, after the war, they faced a responsibility without the fanfare of excitement and general acclaim that had been accorded them in their capacity of soldiers. Their wives expected more of them, and, in the case of Chris, children presented insistent demands. Public indifference, a brutal wall that reared itself with incredible swiftness following demobilization, toward jobs, the housing shortage, and mounting living costs, baffled the three brothers as it had thousands of other men.

"They have no feeling of permanence, living with us," Nellie mourned to Luther. "The girls can't even spread out their wedding presents. These are the precious years when they ought to be accumulating possessions and trying out their ideas in homes of their own. No wonder the boys get on each other's nerves—it's a constant irritation."

The question of entertaining their friends provided another point of friction. One living room, divided among four couples, yielded little more than a corner for each group. Nellie and Luther discovered that they were expected to disappear at frequent intervals, and often these diplomatic withdrawals interfered seriously with their own work. Gone were the evenings in which Nellie knitted and Luther carved, in silent contentment. For large parties the three young wives shared guests and expenses, but usually they preferred their own friends, and then the two couples not entertaining fled to the movies.

"What we ought to do," Luther suggested now and then, "is to go off by ourselves on a little spree. We could let the kids get dinner, and you meet me downtown. Have dinner at a good place and go to the theater. Remember we used to go to the theater once a month when we were first married?"

Nellie remembered. But they couldn't afford to dine out when so much must be spent on the food at home. "Whether we're here or eating out, there'll be eight people for dinner," she reminded Luther. "Those sad little stories written about the dining-room table that grows smaller with the passing years, until only Pa and Ma are left smiling wanly at each other, don't fit our household."

There was nothing that could be done about it, Nellie admitted, glancing at the mountain of clean dishes already dried. Her wedding china, "service for twelve," had seemed to her sufficient to supply a hotel when it was given to her, and many of the pieces had never been used until the mushroom growth of her family after the war. But in another year it might be necessary to buy another service for twelve, she conceded sadly, since the girls, always in a rush to finish kitchen tasks, broke so many dishes.

"Mostly by dropping them in the sink," Nellie explained to Midnight, now going to sleep in an upright position. "Rhoda dropped three cups this week, but then she should not be out in the kitchen at all."

Violet was the handiest around the house—poor Vi, with her mind filled by gloomy thoughts of her sick mother. Poor Rhoda, too, who would probably be in bed tomorrow as a result of sitting at the movies too long tonight. And poor Jerry, perhaps the one needing pity most of all.

Jerry had come in just before dinner, her arms filled with small parcels. "Socks for Seth and a few shirts. He needs them." She spoke to Nellie from the kitchen doorway. "How were Patience and the baby?"

"Lovely. You must go to see her as soon as she's home." Nellie bit her lip. She had not meant to remind Jerry that Patience had an apartment.

"Some people have everything," Jerry said with forced lightness. "But as Seth would say, it couldn't happen to a nicer girl. I don't suppose there were any phone calls, Mother? Or weren't you home?"

There had been no calls since she had been home, Nellie answered, and Rhoda had reported that the phone had not rung in her absence.

"Lucy called you—a minute after you'd started for the hospital," Jerry recollected belatedly. "She's another one who seems contented with life. Maybe mine isn't the cycle for happy marriages."

Patience and Jesse had been married only two years, Nellie noted dryly. "You might include her in your cycle. And Lucy's had enough ups and downs in her eighteen years of married life to discourage a less optimistic woman. Jerry, I think you'd understand her: if her marriage is happy, it's because she has accepted what it can give her and has refused to expect too much."

"But you don't want to compromise in your marriage," Jerry said. Her dark eyes, above the armful of packages she continued to hold, begged for comfort.

Nellie shut the gas off under the meat loaf and turned it on under the spinach. "My dear, life is a constant compromise. In marriage it isn't a question of settling for less than your dreams but of deciding between values. I think Lucy feels that what she has more than compensates for what she has had to forego. There's such a thing as asking too much of marriage, you know."

Not that Jerry asked too much, Nellie told herself when the girl turned away to go upstairs. Jerry was being shabbily treated. But a little later, when she could think clearly, she might be helped to make her decisions if she faced honestly the question of her ability to separate the unreal from the real.

The thick silence—she certainly enjoyed an evening without the radio, Nellie congratulated herself—cracked abruptly as the doorbell rang. Midnight unclosed his round green eyes and stared fixedly at Nellie, his gaze intimating that it might mean anything from adventure to a late delivery of laundry.

"Seth wouldn't ring—would he?" Nellie recognized the futility of consulting the cat, dried her hands.

She clicked on the porch light as she went through the hall. *Dear heavens, not a cable for Vi.*

"Mrs. Taylor?" The thin, dark lad's face expressed nothing.

"I'm Mrs. Lake. You must have the wrong house."

"You know a Mrs. Taylor?"

Nellie considered. "Not in this neighborhood. Why?"

"Well, you see it's like this—my brother got into a little trouble with his car tonight. He picked up a girl, and they had a few drinks, and of course they hit another car. Now my brother phones me to come down to the police station because they released the girl and he thinks she gave a phony address, see?"

She didn't see, but in the chilly March night air Nellie shivered.

"My brother's married, and he wants to know whether the girl is—she said she was Mrs. Edna Taylor and lived at 309 Ash Street. I've checked, and that's a vacant lot."

Nellie pointed out the numerals, 3-1-8, above the doorbell. She could offer no suggestions, nor did she recognize anyone from his description of the girl as "a good-looker, with lots of class and a scar back of one ear."

When she had closed the door and turned off the light, she stood for a moment undecided in the hall, an old fear stirring in her heart. Give Seth the car and let him go, Jerry had said. But Jerry had never lain awake in the long, dark hours at night, hoping for the sound of a son's car and praying for strength to feign sleep when he should finally come. She had worried for the careless, tumultuous Seth of eighteen or nineteen, and the reckless, resentful man he had become only increased her anxiety. The familiar combination of liquor, car, and women, as outlined in the dark boy's commonplace story, could so easily be tragic if the names involved should another night be changed.

The cat rubbed himself against her ankles, and Nellie automatically stepped over him. "I'll call Lucy," she said aloud. "Seth might just happen to be there."

But when, the call finished, she replaced the handset, she admitted that the subterfuge had been childish.

She went back to her kitchen and the waiting pots and pans and had almost scrubbed her way through the collection when the phone began to ring in a measured, even rhythm that bespoke unlimited endurance.

"Mom?"

She had known it would be Seth. "Where are you, dear?"

"At a pay station. Who's home?"

"No one, except me. And the twins, of course, but they're in bed." Did she only imagine that his voice sounded furtive?

"Where are they—movies?"

Nellie accounted for the household. No, Jerry had not taken the car. "Your father drove her."

"Well, if you're sure the coast's clear, I'll come up and pack. That all right with you, Mom?"

"Yes, dear. And I'll have something for you to eat." She thought as she turned away from the phone that Jerry had more courage—and perhaps more love—than she had.

Jerry had left the way open for Seth to come home, pack his belongings, and leave in her car without a painful final scene. Not pride but love motivated her self-effacement, and the pity of it was that Seth should be incapable of recognizing the depth of her devotion.

The front door banged.

"Mom?"

"Here, dear." Nellie stepped from the kitchen into the hall.

Seth kissed her, his cheek rough against hers, evidence that he needed to shave. "I see you have the same old cat," he grinned.

Nellie accepted the creaking joke as a warning that Seth would reject what he termed "moralizing," and indeed she had no real hope of persuading him to reconsider his plans. His quick, nervous manner distressed her, for, like the furtive tone of his voice, it indicated his desire to escape.

He ate the food she offered him, listening to her carefully edited conversation without comment. But when she mentioned Patience and the baby he muttered that the child would probably be drafted at sixteen.

"I'm going up to pack." He pushed back his plate, declining dessert.

The light, striking on his thick, sandy hair, intensified its rough waves. He had dark-blue, restless eyes and a fair skin that burned in sun or wind. His unhappiness had communicated itself to the tense outline of his tall, thin figure—perhaps, she thought, Seth no longer cared to conceal his misery.

"I'll get your bag for you," she said, although she knew that he hoped to be allowed to pack alone.

In the room he and Jerry occupied, the new socks and shirts and a supply of underclothing had been neatly laid out on the bed. Jerry had even added a new necktie. She had always been proud that Seth approved her taste in neckties.

"Seth, aren't you making a mistake?" Nellie, seated on the bed, tried not to wince as Seth tossed Jerry's purchases into the heavy suitcase. If he had ever learned neatness in the Army, the training had been superficial and quickly forgotten.

"Nope." The sandy eyebrows drew together in a quick frown. "I've got to get out of here, Mom. I said during the war that if I ever got home I'd never be regimented again. And I meant it."

Nellie cautioned, "Don't wake the twins. They—"

"See, Mom, that's what I mean. You can't draw a free breath in this house. The kids have to have this so you can't do that. You mustn't say anything about dear old England, or Vi will burst into tears. Chris crabs eternally that no one is considerate of Rhoda, and if I spend ten extra cents on myself, I'm accused of not appreciating my hard-working wife."

Anything she might say could only add to his resentment. Nellie kept still.

"I've never had much chance to do what I want to do, Mom." Seth tumbled a pair of shoes and a set of clean pajamas into the suitcase together. "There was the war, and then I got married. If I don't watch out, in a few years I'll be too old to get around. The time to go your own way is while you're young."

Nellie stirred. "Jerry is young, Seth. Three years younger than you. The war wasn't easy for her, either."

"It isn't as important for her to be free." Seth's stormy eyes had darkened. "Women take naturally to settling down, to being stodgy. My personal freedom's at stake—that's what no one seems to understand."

Well, she didn't understand him, Nellie reminded herself. It would be easy to label him selfish and cruel; or if she could believe his jargon about personal freedom, she might see him as martyred and misunderstood. Neither analysis would be just. Certainly he lacked personal discipline, but there again his army training might be held to blame.

"The Army keeps them up to standard," Luther had once argued with Rhoda, who had been distressed by what she called Chris's relapse from basic training. "But as soon as the rigid mold is knocked off, your young man is going to return to his natural outline."

It had been Luther, too, who had offered a breakfast monologue on selfishness one morning, when Vi had charged Barry with being "rotten selfish." Now that she thought of it, Nellie could not recall a complaint or criticism of Seth from Jerry, who had more cause for reproach than either of her sisters-in-law.

"Well, do you know, Vi, I find selfishness the easiest fault to forgive," Luther had said in his kind, deliberate voice. "It's such a human trait. We're all of us selfish, in varying degree. There are some vices only monsters have, and there are cold, mean traits that belong only to nasty, little natures. But selfishness—why, you find that in everyone's make-up. The good and great, and the ordinary, everyday citizen—we're all selfish more or less."

"What you're trying to say, Pop, is that I'm normal," Barry had grinned.

Seth's quick, angry motions ceased. He let the lid of the suitcase close. "That's about all, I guess."

"Aren't you going to wait until Jerry gets back? She won't try to stop you, Seth. But don't go without saying good-by to her." Nellie stood up.

He scrambled to his feet, his face turning an ugly brick red. "When's she coming back? I have to be out of here before she starts a scene. I told her I wanted to clear out in peace. She—"

"Seth Lake, I'm ashamed of you! Jerry's staying away purposely to make things easier for you, and you talk like a—guttersnipe." Nellie choked. "It must be my fault—I haven't brought you up right, and your wife is suffering for it."

For a moment they stared at each other, anger and grief searing Nellie's throat like a flame. Seth, momentarily startled, wanted only to get away.

"Well—I guess I'll be going." He stooped to buckle the bag straps. "I've got the garage and car keys."

"Where did you get them?" Even to herself Nellie sounded like a policewoman.

"Jerry gave them to me. This morning. I'll leave the garage key in the door."

Trailing down the stairs after Seth, who swung the heavy bag easily, Nellie watched him stop to pat Midnight, who sat decoratively on the newel post. People were kind to animals under the most unexpected circumstances, even a man who was deserting his wife would stop to speak to a pet cat—Nellie stifled a hysterical desire to laugh.

"Seth, what do you expect Jerry to *do?*"

"Why, she can go to her mother, can't she?" He picked up his topcoat from the chair where he had dropped it.

Nellie said, "No, she can't. No woman with any pride can go back to her mother and announce that her husband's left her. It's easier for her to stay with her mother-in-law, who's more ashamed than she is. Jerry is going to stay here."

"All right." His indifference, if feigned, was well done. "I'll drop you a card at my first stop, Mother. Don't worry—everything will come out all right."

He kissed her hastily, his body tense as if he expected her to cling to him. She let him go, and he breathed an unconscious sigh of relief. The next moment he had opened and closed the door and was dogtrotting down the walk and across the street, on his way to the garages two blocks off.

Nellie sat down on the stairs. She was still there fifteen minutes later when Vi and Barry, Rhoda and Chris returned from the movies.

"What's the matter?" Vi and Rhoda voiced instant alarm.

"Nothing. I just felt a little low." Nellie let them pull her upright. "Rhoda, you ought to go right to bed—what would the doctor say? Does your back ache?"

Only on the insistence of Chris could Rhoda be persuaded to lie on the living-room couch while the others made tea for her and hot chocolate for themselves. It did her good to get out, Rhoda declared; she could stay in bed late tomorrow morning to make up for tonight's spree.

"We had the bad luck to run into a deathbed scene in the second feature," she confided to Nellie when Vi had gone into the kitchen. "Poor Vi almost had hysterics. She used up all our handkerchiefs."

Steps outside announced the arrival of Jerry and Luther. They were just in time, Nellie greeted them, for the refreshments. The old-fashioned word was a family joke. Nellie as a little girl had been taken by her mother to spend a long, hot summer afternoon with a wealthy but stingy old lady. They had been entertained on the shady lawn, and Nellie, who had been given a book to read while her elders chatted and embroidered, had been delighted when a trim maid appeared, carrying a silver tray. The maid had solemnly passed around three heavy cut-glass goblets of ice water —and nothing more.

Nellie, however, had been carefully trained, and she had no intention of betraying her disappointment. When prompted by her mother to bid her hostess good-by, the small girl had shaken hands properly and said in her clear treble, "And thank you for the delicious refreshments."

Years later Nellie sometimes suspected that her sons had taken advantage of the story to persuade her to be reckless with her cooky supply when they brought their gangs home from school. But at least they had boasted of her hospitality.

"Was the wood any good?" she asked now as Luther pushed a chair to the couch and motioned Jerry to take it.

"Dad bought fourteen pieces." Jerry had glanced quickly around the room when she came in. "We left it in the car. Did—did anyone come, Mother?"

Nellie's eyes met Luther's. "Seth was here."

Rhoda sat up. "For heaven's sake! And we missed him."

"Didn't stay?" Luther was deliberately casual.

Jerry said nothing, but her silence would have been less noticeable had she moved, instead of sitting as if carved out of one of Luther's pieces of wood.

"He said he'd write. I couldn't persuade him to wait." Nellie stepped to the couch, gently pushed Rhoda flat again. "I haven't any influence with him any more."

In the kitchen someone dropped a dish, and Chris laughed, his short, husky laugh that the other boys called his bark. The odor of hot toast and melting cheese drifted to the living room; Vi's clipped, brisk voice held a note of irritation.

"The loose tea, Barry. Yes, it does make a difference to Rhoda. I hate tea bags, you know that. Rhoda needs a decent cup of tea to settle her nerves."

Nellie thought that if she had heard the argument about tea bags versus loose tea once, since Vi had lived with them, she had heard it a hundred times. Barry always bickered with her, convinced that it was his mission to convert her to American ways, including the use of tea bags. Luther usually laughed at the clatter, but then Luther laughed at all small sorrows, as he said.

The trouble was, Nellie mused, that she was sick and tired of her children and their incessant demands. They were leeches, nothing more. If she didn't go out to the kitchen now, the chances were that they would eat up the breakfast supplies and confidently expect her to produce bacon and eggs the next morning. Last week Chris had made waffles at midnight and used five eggs and half a pound of butter and all the cream, since he had made a pot of coffee, too.

They didn't eat downtown after the movies because they couldn't afford it, but they figured home meals cost nothing, Nellie raged. Vi and Rhoda and Jerry ought to know, if the boys didn't. The girls didn't go without clothes; even Jerry paid sixteen dollars for her shoes, and Vi had no money for her passage to England because she had been on a continual shopping spree ever since she had landed in the States. *I am mean and vindictive and unfair,* Nellie rebuked herself, *but, oh, I am so discouraged.*

There was something wrong with her, she worried. . . . She could stand here, looking at Jerry, whose heart was breaking, and at Rhoda, too pale by far against the blue cushion, and grieve to recall that she had planned to have the living room remodeled into a shop a year ago this spring. Instead she had made new slip covers for the old furniture, new curtains for the three plain windows, and she and Luther had papered the walls in an old-fashioned flower print, so that the children would have a place in which to spend their evenings. The electricity bills had tripled, and the heating bills had jumped, too, but you could not expect the three young couples to stay cooped up in their rooms.

"Tea for Madame!" Chris brought in the tray, so intent on not dropping it that he didn't see Jerry until he had almost reached the couch.

"Well, look who's here!" He let his mother take the tray, deposit it in Rhoda's lap. "Come out in the kitchen, Jerry, and have chocolate with us. Rhoda can't break training, the doctor says, so we keep temptation out of sight."

Vi was keeping out of sight, too, Nellie thought. Ordinarily she would have come in to talk with Rhoda while she waited for the kettle to boil. Poor Vi, homesick and heartsick, grieving for her mother. And Jerry, lonely for Seth and his lost love, and Rhoda, so conscious of imposing a heavy burden on her husband—and she, a selfish woman, Nellie berated herself, fretting because she couldn't set up a shop in the living room and bundle these poor creatures out.

"I thought I'd make a small bookcase for Patience." Luther, who had been filling his pipe as if he arranged the tobacco grain by grain, seemed finally to have accomplished the task to his satisfaction.

Jerry had not spoken since her one question, but she shook her head as Chris beckoned her to follow him to the kitchen.

"Some of that lumber we bought tonight is old mahogany," Luther's even tone was cheerfully matter-of-fact. "Patience likes hanging shelves, and I have an idea she could use a set in her new apartment."

Rhoda set down her cup. "Patience has a baby. She has everything," she said.

"You had two babies." Jerry spoke with unexpected energy.

"That was six years ago. I'd like to have four children." Rhoda looked at Jerry. "You have to have your own home, to have four children. And better health than I have, too."

Luther, who had been standing behind Jerry's chair, said, "I'll go down and look at the furnace. Jerry, you'd better get yourself a cheese sandwich while you're young. They're not for the old."

He grinned at Nellie, and she was sorry as always for women whose husbands did not have his kind brown eyes and thin, lined face. She loved every hair of his thick, rumpled pepper-and-salt thatch, and though he was shorter than his sons, she thought he moved with more grace.

"Luther is a good man," Nellie's mother had said of him years ago. "I mean through-and-through good. You see it in his face."

"I'll come down with you," Nellie decided. "You girls go up when you're ready."

In the doorway she turned, and in the glow of the lamplight Rhoda's coat, draped over a chair, made a splash of color as red as blood. Jerry had risen to take the tray, but as she lifted it, Rhoda put an arm around her neck and drew her face down to hers.

Nellie, following Luther through the kitchen, admonished the group at the porcelain-topped table.

"Remember you'll be hungry in the morning, and please don't raid my breakfast shelf," she warned. "If there isn't enough bread left for toast, I can make muffins, but bacon and eggs I must have."

Vi, her nose pink, her eyes swollen, nodded over the rim of her chocolate cup. "I broke the saucer—I'm sorry," she apologized. "I'll match it for you tomorrow."

The china couldn't be matched these days, but what was one saucer among the remnants of thirty years? In a charitable mood Nellie ascribed the appalling amount of breakage in her kitchen to war nerves and reminded herself that she was entitled to a new dinner set; when exasperation took possession of her, she grumbled to herself or the patient Luther that when the girls had china of their own it would undoubtedly be given loving care.

In the cellar she sat down on the lowest stairstep, where she could watch Luther attending to the furnace. The boys had offered to relieve him of the chore, but they burned too much coal and balked at having to sift the ashes. They also intimated that oil burners had practically replaced the coal furnace and that, failing to install such equipment, Luther owed it to himself and them to put in a stoker.

"Modern equipment pays for itself, in a saving of time and physical energy," Barry had assured his father.

Luther agreed. "But unfortunately modern equipment requires a substantial down payment first," he explained.

"Wouldn't you think," said Nellie, as Luther armed himself with the coal shovel, "that we might have an early spring just once?

There must be hundreds of people like us, hoping that the coal will last until warm weather and knowing darn well that it won't."

Luther opened the furnace door, and in the glow of the heat his face turned brick red, with deeply carved lines.

"I won't send up any more steam tonight, but we can't let the fire go out much before the middle of May," he murmured. "Can't let the place get chilled."

The house must be kept warm for Rhoda during the day and for everyone in the evenings. Nellie tried not to remember that when she and Luther had been alone they had managed economically with a banked fire during the day, and that only until April, when a portable electric heater had kept the living room comfortable at night.

Luther's figure, stooping to enable him to see into the firebox and spread the coal evenly, looked too thin to Nellie's anxious eyes. His cold was better, he had assured her; he had not coughed much during the day. But the few precious years remaining to them before they should be old and heavy with a weariness that discouraged effort were slipping away. The strength of the rebellion that rose in her at the thought in a measure reassured Nellie; she couldn't be aged while she still wanted so many things with such intensity. It was exasperating to read all the criticism of parents who clung to their children and never to come across an article acknowledging the dilemma of parents whose children clung to them. She and Luther wanted to be *alone.*

"I'll just make sure the side door's fastened." Luther spoke over his shoulder. "The kids forget."

He disappeared into the shadows beyond the swaying bulb that made a pool of light between the furnace and the stairs. Midnight came to sit with Nellie and to stare solemnly after Luther as she did. Overhead quick footsteps crossed and recrossed the kitchen floor. The girls must be doing the dishes. Their voices alternated with the deeper tones of the men—if Seth were there, he would have the radio on. Seth, his brothers said, didn't care what program he heard, he didn't even listen, but the undercurrent of noise seemed to fulfill some need. He had been furious with Jerry because she refused to have a radio in the car, and he had bought a portable to have on the seat beside him when he drove without her. Wherever he might be driving tonight, he must be tuned in to some station—perhaps, Nellie reflected sadly, he hoped to lose himself in a flood of sound.

"Mother!" Chris called. "We're going up."

"Good night, Mother Lake!" That was Vi. "Rhoda says good night, too."

Nellie twisted around to smile at the group in the doorway above her. "We'll be right up—good night. Tell Rhoda she's to sleep in the morning, Chris. Put out all the lights except in the hall, won't you, Barry?"

"Ready?" Luther blinked as he stepped out of the shadows.

Nellie said, "Luther, if we cashed our bonds, Vi could take a plane to England," and was surprised at her own words. She had not been thinking of Vi at all.

"I thought you wanted them for a kind of last anchor." Luther, leaning against the rough handrail, was not surprised, only contemplative. "What's changed your mind?"

Nellie reached up to take his hand and hold it against her cheek. "Jerry. We can't help her. But Vi is one child we can do something for. The misery that has to work itself out—that's the hardest. If we can *buy* happiness, in heaven's name let's do it."

"All right, we will." Luther's smile wiped out the last of her doubts. "Tell her before you go to bed, so she won't cry all night and keep Barry awake."

"Barry!" Nellie laughed with him, for Barry's inability to remain awake under the most trying circumstances exasperated Vi and amazed his family. He was not likely to be kept awake by his wife's weeping, Nellie reflected, as she made her way up the cellar steps, but she hoped he would forego his sleep long enough to sympathize with Vi's excitement and relief. An unresponsive husband was such a cross, and Vi was too young to know that the trait was human.

"Thought the kids had gone up." Behind Nellie Luther dexterously closed the door before Midnight could slip into the kitchen. "There's a light in the living room."

Jerry sat alone in the chair near the couch, and Nellie wondered uneasily if she had moved at all. "Tired, Jerry?" she asked.

"Not very. I think it's going to be a little hard at first not to be one of a pair." Jerry looked up at her husband's parents. "Do you suppose it would have been better if I had had a baby?"

Nellie sat down on the couch, but Luther remained standing, resting his arms on the back of his favorite chair.

"Seth might have felt responsible and stayed here," Jerry said.

She didn't know, how could anyone know, Nellie asked. "When I saw Patience this morning, she was worrying about future wars and the possibility that her son will blame her for bearing him. What are the limits of responsibility, Jerry?"

"I wanted a baby." Jerry's dark eyes seemed enormous in the shaded light. "I never envied anyone in my life as much as I did Patience when I heard she had a son. I couldn't be sure that Seth would be a good father, and yet if I'd had confidence in him . . . Perhaps I had no right to judge."

Nellie spoke briskly. "You had the patience of Job. I won't have you blaming yourself. I'm Seth's mother, and there may be justification for his treatment of me—mothers are natural handicaps, I believe. But nothing will excuse what Seth has done to you. You're young, you have your life to live, and he thinks of no one but himself. I'm ashamed of my son, Jerry."

"I don't know what to do," Jerry said.

Luther cleared his throat. "If I may be permitted to advise—"

They laughed a little, turning to meet his gaze, quizzical and kind.

"The trouble with good women like yourselves is that you assume too much," Luther informed them. "You struggle to load yourselves down with imaginary burdens and go out of your way to find roads blocked by imaginary obstacles."

Nellie glanced at Jerry, whose face had come alive again.

"For instance," Luther went on, "you seem to feel that Jerry's love has been wasted and her life spoiled. That isn't true. She and Seth had everything to learn about life—all young people have. Seth had more to learn, so he's having the harder time, but he'll catch up with Jerry. If she has the patience to wait."

Jerry's eyes glowed; her voice had regained its warmth. "I'll have all the patience in the world," she said.

"You've done the best you could," Luther said. "So has Mother. You've both prayed, and your prayers have been heard. They've been heard even if not yet answered, even if never answered exactly as you hope."

Luther believed in the pattern, too, Nellie realized. His very quietness was convincing; his naturalness inspired confidence. If anyone could stabilize Jerry's rocking world, it would be this gentle, serene man whom she trusted.

"Good women make the mistake of trying to be omnipotent," Luther was saying. "The hardest lesson they have to learn seems to be to leave something to God. They forget that He's in charge."

She forgot, Nellie admitted silently, and Jerry forgot, and Patience. They substituted fear for love; they left nothing to God.

"I think"—Jerry released a long sigh—"that I feel better."

Upstairs in the hall she halted at the door of her lonely bedroom to kiss Nellie. "There's a light under Vi's door. She must be writing to her mother."

"I'll stop a moment and speak to her—there's something I want to tell her to put in her letter," Nellie said.

Evening

Chapter Nine

PATIENCE, turning a page of her book, glanced toward the clock on the dresser. Seven o'clock, and the tide of evening visitors had set in. Outside in the corridor, footsteps sounded, and people whispered shrilly, asking to be directed to a numbered room.

"That good-looking husband of yours is late, isn't he?" Miss Coburn paused in the doorway, adjusted the screen.

One of the nurses had brought her the phone message, Patience said. "Mr. Garrison can't get here until after eight. But his brother is coming."

"I suppose he's married, too?" Miss Coburn laughed, because the probationers always asked, "Is he married?" whenever they saw a new man.

Patience admitted that Ross Garrison was married. "He has a lovely wife. They were married a year before us."

Miss Coburn went away, and Patience picked up her book. Sheer luxury to be able to read in bed, comfortably isolated and yet not cut off from reality. The shuffling feet outside her door, the murmur of voices, and the more distant clang of the elevator gates—all the small, familiar sounds assured her that she was not alone. But she reveled in the quiet of her room like this, with the ceiling fixture turned off and the shadows concealing the cluttered effect of too much furniture. The lamp fastened to the headboard of her bed shed a golden pool of light on her book and the small table, spreading to take in Jesse's picture and the lilies of the valley on the dresser.

"Thank you—" Footsteps halted on the other side of the screen; a pleasant masculine voice had spoken. "She's expecting me."

Patience looked up delightedly. "Ross! You don't know how glad I am to see you."

"Lovely as ever." Ross Garrison, taller than Jesse, heavier than Jesse, older, but with the family resemblance so marked that anyone would know him to be Jesse's brother, stooped to kiss her.

"You smell of nice fresh air," she told him. "Is it cold out? Put your things in the closet— I think there's a hanger—"

He disposed of his topcoat and hat, took the chair beside the bed. A man not yet thirty, with dark, cropped hair and friendly hazel eyes. "I brought you a book, but I see you have a book—" He put a package down beside her. "Open it tomorrow—it's just one of the new novels; Heather thought you wouldn't have it yet."

"Ross, you mustn't! I've had so many presents. Heather sent me a house coat and the baby beautiful clothes and a silver cup. I wrote to her as soon as I could." Patience remembered her duties as hostess. "Don't you want to smoke, Ross? It's all right."

He shook his head. "Heather got a kick out of your notes. She loves to send things. So you have a son, Patty—how does it feel, when you and Jesse talk it over?"

"Wonderful!" Patience smiled. "Oh, Ross, don't get me started —he's so little and helpless, and yet he's a person, too. I think Jesse is rather in awe of him, and we're both scared of him—that is, of having him grow up and decide that we don't rate as parents."

Ross growled. "Let *me* hear him making any such remarks and I'll attend to him," he promised. "The ungrateful cub!"

"You'll be a great comfort to Jesse and me, and we'll grow old gracefully together," Patience told him. "I'm not slipping yet," she hastened to admit, answering her visitor's upraised eyebrow, "but when you have a baby you begin to count up generations. My grandmother was here today, and she's eighty-two years older than Nicholas."

Ross had a deep, mirthful laugh that provoked Patience to laughter in turn. She had decided already that he would be her son's favorite uncle, for Lucy's husband, Mel Gray, was years older, and the list of uncles numbered only two.

"What do you think about, when you are so still and I can't see your eyes?" Ross asked.

He sat easily in the straight chair, facing Patience, one elbow propped on the bed and his brown fingers twisting the ribbon she had been using as a bookmark.

"I was wishing that Nicholas could have dozens of uncles and aunts and cousins," Patience said slowly. "There's Lucy and Mel and you and Heather—and that's all. He'll have only Cinda and Ronnie for cousins, unless—unless—"

Ross completed the sentence. "Unless we have children. You approve of big families, Patty?"

"I never thought much about it before," Patience acknowledged, "but now it seems to me that a child with plenty of relatives must feel more—well, more secure. The more people who love him and are willing to look after him, if anything should happen to his parents, the less he is apt to feel at the mercy of the world. Don't you think so, Ross?"

He looked at her gravely. "You're assuming, I take it, that this large family is loyal and devoted? That they all get on together and foster no grudges?"

"My dream family is ideal," Patience declared with firmness. "There are enough of them to make one of those handsome drawings you see in the back of books that are family chronicles. And all of them, grandparents, parents, sons and daughters, uncles and aunts and cousins, are knit together by the closest ties of respect and love."

Ross said, "My dear little Patty, I'd like to belong to your large family myself. As one of Nicholas's handful of relatives, I'm sorry not to be able to muster a dozen stalwart uncles for his approval."

""You're worth a dozen yourself. Jesse would say so." Patience touched the busy brown fingers lightly.

Jesse's pathetic, weak father had not been able to spoil his life, because Ross, protective, tender, and wise beyond his years, had been his brother. Ross had the same attitude toward Heather, the lovely, vivid girl he had married at the close of the war. There wasn't anything in the world too good for Heather, his little, fussy stepmother, Vera, frequently observed.

"You would think, as long as she works, that she'd try to save a few cents," Vera protested to anyone who would listen. "I never knew a girl so clothes crazy—not a payday goes by she doesn't buy herself a dress. And always something too gay. She has enough costume jewelry to stock a shop—you'd think Ross would put his foot down."

Whatever Heather did was approved by Ross. He went where she suggested they go, he welcomed the crowd she asked in for Sunday night suppers, he took her to the shore as often as she expressed a desire to spend a week end at one of the good hotels.

"Can't be saving a cent," their critics grumbled. "Money goes out as fast as it comes in."

Patience suspected that even Jesse, who thought his brother almost perfect, sometimes wondered at the haphazard household in which he and Heather lived and entertained. Not that Jesse would ever say one word against Ross, and he often declared that his brother's married life was ideal. Heather liked people, liked to fill the apartment with friends, dispensed the type of hospitality that put them at their ease and emphasized their several specialties.

"Didn't we have fun!" Patience had said one evening when she and Jesse had come home from one of Heather's Sunday night suppers. "Everyone had a good time. When we have our own place, we must have that kind of a party, too."

She and Jesse recognized that her mother's orderly kitchen and pleasant dining room did not suggest the easy informality that Heather's entertaining achieved. Her mother had never been able to have even a very simple party without being to some degree anxious about its success—Patience had realized that when she saw Heather, a natural hostess.

"Mother worried about the sandwiches, or the cake, or whether she ought to have waited until she could afford new curtains," Patience recollected once as Lucy helped her to mix sandwich fillings for an evening's bridge. "And she never seemed to be sure whether her guests were enjoying themselves or not. Heather takes everything for granted, so nothing upsets her. If something falls apart or gives out, or someone doesn't come, she does a little re-shuffling and it all comes out right."

Lucy pronounced Heather a genius. "She has a gift for putting people at their ease. No wonder her firm practically had hysterics when she suggested she resign when she married."

Heather, for all her gay chatter, her love for bright colors and earrings that jingled, was right-hand assistant in a firm of busy lawyers. Her familiarity with legal papers awed Patience, who had no talent for statistics, but an even greater asset to Heather was her skill in handling clients. She remembered names and faces, kept confidences, took a warm, personal interest in each person's welfare, and made him feel himself an important individual.

"We've decided that I might as well stay on for a year," she had told Patience a week or so before the wedding. "Ross has to get on his feet after the war, and we need so many things. But not more than a year—we both agree on that. I'm not going to go through life without children."

She had been married to Ross for three years now, and she still kept her job. After one miscarriage, there had been no more talk of children. Heather herself said that she couldn't cram another thing into their apartment and she might as well spend her money on clothes. She had furniture and dishes and linens and glass—and more dresses and hats and shoes than any of her friends.

"She's very generous. She gives Cinda a lot of her clothes," Lucy said, "but I can't help wondering if she hasn't a mania for just buying. She ought to put something aside, in case she has a family. Ross is worse than she is—he positively eggs her to go on these spending sprees."

Heather, Lucy added, had once said that she had twenty pairs of earrings, no matter how many she gave away.

"Ross brings me a new pair whenever he sees an odd design. Mostly from the five-and-ten," Heather explained. "Flowers are special, but earrings are for every day, he says."

Why hadn't Heather been to see her? Patience wondered. True, today was the first on which the doctor's strict rules had been relaxed, but Heather had not asked when she might come. She loved to visit new mamas and their babies, she had proclaimed before she had gone to the hospital. Heavens! With something like a shock, Patience remembered that Heather had entered the hospital at least six weeks ago. But she must be home—yes, Lucy had said she was at home, with a nurse.

"Ross, how is Heather? Lucy told me she's in bed and has a nurse. Didn't she like Thatcher Hospital?"

The long silence had become a part of the room to Ross, who found even the straight chair restful. He had shifted his position and now rested one shoulder against the mattress edge.

"The hospital was all right, I guess," he answered. "But the doctor said she'd do as well at home. And of course she'd rather be in her own room."

Patience hesitated. It wasn't like Ross to be reticent where Heather was the topic. "Lucy told me she has a nurse—and no visitors—so—"

"She has so many friends—the stream would be constant." Ross was matter-of-fact. "Later, perhaps, when her strength is regained, company will be good for her. But the doctor and nurse both agree that you can't sift and select—if one comes, then all would have to."

"But you're sure she's all right? I just can't think of Heather being ill," Patience protested. "I wish she could see Nicholas, but of course he'll be improving steadily."

Ross laughed. "He was perfect at the start, wasn't he?" he teased. "Heather's heard all about him—your mother wrote a long letter, and of course Jesse backed me into a corner and contributed his incoherent bit."

She wouldn't worry then, Patience thought; Ross didn't seem to be upset. As soon as she had the apartment in order and her schedule planned, she would go to see Heather and they'd have one of their long talks to bring each other up to date. Her mother would stay with Nicholas—Patience must consider every suggestion now with the welfare of Nicholas in mind.

"Isn't it funny?" she said to Ross. "Not so long ago I was saying unkind things about mothers who dragged their babies to grocery stores with them or into restaurants at noon when office workers can never get waited on quickly. And here I am, positively humbled—I may be doing the same thing myself, soon. If you haven't anyone to stay with your baby, you have to take him with you. Your viewpoint changes, doesn't it?"

Ross grinned. "I've heard that babies are educational."

"But I won't take Nicholas to a restaurant. Not until he's at least five years old," Patience interposed. "I may have to shop for groceries, but I will not have to eat downtown."

He thought she was quite right, Ross gravely encouraged her, just as footsteps halted at the door.

"Someone for you? Shall I see?" Ross raised an inquiring eyebrow, rose to look behind the screen.

"Mrs. Comerford?" a woman's voice asked. "They told me her room's No. 33."

Patience prompted Ross. "This is 33. But there must be some mistake."

"She's about fifty years old, with gray hair and a limp, and she's had an operation for gallstones," the voice recited.

Ross dodged back, a smile tugging at his lips. "Ever met her, Patty?" he said.

"She's a surgical case," Patience directed, as a hospital veteran of ten days. "Her room must be in the other building. You show her, Ross—go down the corridor and cross the glassed-in bridge. Help her find the room. The nurses are always so busy."

Left alone, Patience absently fingered the wrapped book Ross had given her. She would open it tomorrow at breakfast and be surprised. Dear Ross, who laughed at her weakness for surprises, who laughed, perhaps, at all her weaknesses, but never at her. Next to Jesse, she thought Ross understood her most completely. She suspected that he understood anyone who was timid, uncertain, or afraid. Ross had begun at ten years old to protect those he loved from unhappiness and fear.

Miss Coburn peered around the screen, glanced at the shadowed eyes and the motionless figure of the girl on the bed, and started to retreat. A button on her cuff struck against the frame of the screen.

"I'm not asleep," Patience said.

"Well, I never saw anyone so still as you are." Miss Coburn, immaculate in a clean uniform, bustled forward. "I just wanted my box of talcum. I must have left it on your basin."

"Are you still on duty?" Patience wondered if she could have that much vitality left at the end of a twelve-hour day.

Miss Coburn retrieved her talcum box, nodded her neatly waved head. "Overtime. One of the nurses had a death in her family, and another had an appendicitis attack. So I said I'd fill in." She hesitated. "I thought you expected your brother-in-law?"

"He's here—he's taking a lost visitor to the other wing." Patience accounted for Ross. "Miss Coburn, you know what you said this morning—about squirrels—"

"Squirrels?" The nurse looked blank.

"Squirrels that got trapped in your sister's country house and starved to death," Patience reminded her. "They gnawed the window frames."

Miss Coburn frowned. "Good heavens, why do you think about them? They were too stupid to go up the chimney, the way they came down. Too stupid to rescue themselves, that's all."

"There was a way out, but they couldn't find it," Patience murmured. "How long does it take a squirrel to starve to death?"

She didn't know, Miss Coburn retorted. "And I wish you'd put that silly story out of your mind. Your brother-in-law ought to be here telling you something cheerful."

"I'm cheerful," Patience assured her with some dignity. "I'm only thinking."

"Well, don't think," Miss Coburn instructed. "I'm busy on a case now, but if I see your brother-in-law, I'll hurry him along. You ought to have a little radio to keep you company."

She patted the counterpane, in unconscious imitation of her highly starched supervisor, reiterated her advice not to think, and went off to give comfort and support to some prospective mother with her ordeal close at hand.

Patience wondered if Miss Coburn's patient might be young, expecting the birth of her first child. Or an older woman with perhaps two or three youngsters, to whom she had promised a brother or sister, at home. Everyone said the second baby arrived with far less trouble than the first, Patience mused, but she doubted that it could be quite so blithe an experience as some implied. And of course, as her mother had once said, the second pregnancy was nine months long; a woman saved no time.

She had wondered whether she might die in childbirth, Patience remembered suddenly, a little amused at the thought, since she had survived. One of the girls with whom she had gone to school had died with her first child—Patience had not known her well and had lost track of her following graduation. But she had read the obituary, and the name "Elinor Payne, nee Burbage" had identified her friend. Elinor had died, leaving a son a few hours old.

"She was a big, husky girl," Patience told Lucy, who said that that had nothing to do with it and that only old ladies read the obituary notices.

Patience, beyond a passing pity, did not brood over Elinor's death and was quite honestly unprepared for the panic that seized her without warning one evening when she and Ross Garrison played gin rummy in her mother's living room.

Ross had dined with them, for Heather, on her day off, had gone upstate to visit a school friend and see her new baby and would not be home until nearly midnight. After dinner, Jesse had left to represent his employer at a civic meeting, and Patience's father and mother had gone to the theater. A neighbor had been unable to use the tickets, and Patience had bullied her parents into accepting them. Ross would stay with her, she told them; it was positively indecent the watch they kept upon her.

"Mother's been wanting to see this play ever since it opened two months ago," she scolded, "and nothing is going to happen if she goes. Nicholas isn't due for five weeks, but to hear her you'd think he'd sent word to expect him directly after dinner tonight."

Then, while she waited for Ross to add up the score, the conviction that she was to die when the baby was born smote Patience with suffocating force. The terror that had choked her when, as a child, she had crept down at night to lie outside the door of her parents' bedroom gripped her throat again. A damp coldness numbed her body, and when she looked up, the familiar objects in the room were only dark and fuzzy outlines.

This, she told herself in silent despair, must be the premonition people talked about. She would die and never see her baby, and Jesse would be left alone to bring up a motherless child. Patience thought of the little clothes ready for the baby, of the carriage her father had bought and the chest of drawers that Jesse had painted. Her share was to be only the preparation, not the beautiful realization.

Patience picked up the cards, and the pack fell from her shaking fingers and cascaded smoothly to the floor.

"You're getting too good—" Ross looked up from the score pad. "Why, Patty! What's the matter—don't you feel well, dear?"

Her voice sounded faint in her own ears. "I'm afraid!" Patience said.

She saw Ross spring up, and his long legs toppled his chair to the floor. He was beside her in a moment, his hands, warm and firm, pressed upon hers, shaking and cold.

"What is it, Patty? What are you afraid of?" Ross had an arm around her now, the rough surface of his coat sleeve grazed her cheek. "You're all right," he assured her, his calmness communicating itself to her taut nerves. "You're all right, dear."

The fuzzy, dark outlines sharpened; the room slipped into focus again. Patience drew a deep breath. "Suppose I died?" she questioned. "I have a premonition, Ross—and I want to live. It wouldn't be fair if I died, just when life is at its best."

"But—" Ross saw that she had not finished, waited for her to continue. Only he took both her hands in one of his, and Patience leaned against him gratefully.

"Women do die in childbirth. And my baby would live, perhaps, and not have me to take care of him. I'm not thinking just of myself," she hastened to disclaim. "There's Jesse, too. He'd be so alone. I've got to live, Ross, I've got to!"

Ross said matter-of-factly, "Well, then, you will, darling."

"Don't laugh," Patience implored, although she knew he was not laughing. "Premonitions come true, plenty of times. I had the strangest conviction, Ross, that I'll never come back from the hospital. It's probably a sign."

He released her hands, came around to stand before her. "Patty, look at me. Have you had premonitions before?"

"Well—yes." She considered. "I suppose you'd call them premonitions."

"Any of them ever come true?"

An unwilling smile curled the corners of her mouth. "No-o. Not that I remember. But this is different, Ross."

"Just the same," he grinned companionably. "Only difference is Nature is taking advantage of you right now. It won't last—as a soothsayer you're a frost, Patty."

The terror had lifted, but Patience still did not feel quite secure. "If anything did—did happen to me, Ross, you'd help Jesse, wouldn't you?" She looked up at him, dear Ross, who never seemed to stand in need of comfort himself but who always had strength to give to the unhappy.

She didn't remember what Ross had said, beyond that his words satisfied her, but tonight, recalling the incident, she knew why it returned so clearly to her mind.

"Yes?" She answered the light tap at the door.

Ross stepped around the screen. "Think twice before you

delegate me to escort wandering females to their destinations," he said good-naturedly. "Her name is Mrs. Flickering; she has two children by her first husband and three by her second. Mrs. Comerford is her husband's sister, and this is her third operation. She practically lives in hospitals, her husband's borrowed on his life insurance to pay the bills, but she's never had an operation to compare with Mrs. Flickering's. She was on the table for three hours, and they took out—"

"You're making it up!" Patience's first startled look gave way to laughter. "She never told you all that stuff!"

That was only a small portion of Mrs. Flickering's confidences, Ross declared. "She buttonholed me outside the door of No. 33, after I'd got her that far, and I would have been there yet if a nurse hadn't rescued me. She came up, ready to give us 'Hail Columbia' for disturbing the other patients, but when she sized up the situation she gently detached me and towed Mrs. Flickering into port."

"You've done your good deed for the day," Patience told him. "Probably no one listens to the poor soul at home. It's pathetic, when a woman wants to talk and there's no one handy to listen."

Ross agreed that it was a calamity. "However, I came to listen to you. What's on your mind, Patty?"

She felt no need to dissemble with Ross and said quietly that she had been remembering the "premonition" which had terrified her during pregnancy. "I was so sure I was going to die, and you were so sweet to me, Ross. I was silly, of course, but the panic was real."

"Now what made you think of that?" Ross took his chair again, smiled at the girl in the bed.

The shadowed gray eyes regarded him intently. "Do you mind if I talk, Ross?" Patience said.

"Worried?" His tone acquiesced.

Patience stirred restlessly. "There's so much to think about. Last time I was afraid I might die and leave Jesse alone, and now I'm wondering what I'd do if he died and left me. There's a girl in the hospital whose husband was killed yesterday. Her baby was born the same day as Nicholas."

"But Jesse's alive and husky," Ross suggested.

He mustn't expect her to make sense, Patience said, but she could not forget the other man, who must have been so proud of his first child. "And Ross, since I've had Nicholas, Jesse is twice as dear to me. Before, I took everything for granted. Perhaps I thought he loved me more than I loved him. Not any more. I love him so much that if something happened to him—if he died—I know I wouldn't want to go on living."

It wasn't a premonition, she added hurriedly; she didn't have the feeling that danger threatened Jesse. It was only that she realized tragedy existed and that, facing it in imagination, she measured the depth of her pain.

"I can't tell Jesse. But I can tell you. Such terrible things happen —like that girl's husband being killed. Why should she be a widow, Ross?" Patience wondered if she had been allowed to cry in peace or if the well-meant efforts of the ward patients and nurses to sympathize had left her no privacy.

Ross was speaking. . . . "Patty, listen to me. This is important, so try to believe I am telling you the truth. You're still not completely your old self. It takes time to snap back, after childbirth. These ideas and worries that beset you have physical causes. Temporarily you're depressed. Jesse is all right, and you know it. Because one young mother is widowed is no reason for supposing that you'll lose Jesse; the accident ward is filled with patients, but that doesn't mean you'll break a leg or fracture your skull."

"Yes, I know." And she did know, Patience admitted to herself in a clear, uncluttered corner of her mind. But she still wanted to cry, and the pressure of anxiety did not yield. "But, Ross, we love each other more every day. If he died I couldn't stand it, and if I died what would he do? People do die, no matter how much they love each other."

Something flashed into his face that she had not seen before. It passed so quickly that she could not be sure what it revealed except that for the instant his haggard expression set in carved lines which made him old. Then, familiar, gentle, his smile replaced that strained, anguished mask, and the Ross she knew took up the task of dispelling her fears.

"I think, my dear, that if either of you died the one remaining would set about living for your Nicholas." Ross's quiet, sincere voice neither protested nor denied. "You would go on for his sake. Or if Jesse had to, he would put his son's needs above his own."

Ross, suddenly aware that his hands gripped his knees, deliberately loosened the pressure.

"Jesse has probably told you about our father," he said. "When Mother died, he went all to pieces. That isn't a bromide—you can go to pieces in a crisis. He forgot his children."

Patience murmured. Jesse had told her. Vera, the stepmother, remembered, too. "It must have been awful for you boys, Ross. But Jesse had you. He says you brought him up."

"Poor Dad!" Ross's present concern was not for Jesse. "He made every possible mistake, but he taught us one valuable lesson: we learned from his wasted years that the only way to endure grief is to live with it and face it."

He was silent for a moment, and Patience, relaxed, wondered if he might be thinking of his boyhood and of the nightmare years that had followed his mother's death.

"Things weren't right for a couple of years before that," Jesse had said once, when he had been answering Patience's insatiable questions about his life at home. "Mother did her best to keep us kids from knowing what was wrong, but once or twice she broke down and of course, as Dad stayed away more and more, she found it difficult to make plausible excuses."

"Did she find out about him?" Patience, a bride, could not visualize her slow, ponderous father-in-law as an unfaithful husband. Her experience with infidelity had been confined to the screen, and it did not occur to her that old age sets a trap.

Cousin Belle had made it her business to tell his mother, Jesse admitted. "But I suppose she would have learned it sooner or later. She took us away for six months—we spent a winter in Maine and nearly froze, because none of us knew too much about stoves."

The old farmhouse belonged to a friend of his mother's, Jesse believed, and was equipped only for summer living. He had never known the exact reason for the six months' exile, but years later he and Ross had decided that their mother had probably suggested a trial separation.

"And I think, too, she was trying to pull our finances out of the red," Jesse added. "We were in a bad way, with bills piling up and Dad drinking and staging tantrums, if money was mentioned to him. We could live cheaply in the country."

His father had come up once, during their stay. He reached the farm too late for Christmas and returned to the city the same day.

"Christmas that year wasn't much of a success," Jesse commented.

Patience shivered slightly. If a woman lost her husband before death . . .

"Death doesn't matter so terribly, Patty," Ross said, as if he had been following her thoughts. "That is, not if two people are in love. Then the separation isn't real. The greatest sorrow is when the death of love separates us. That happens every day."

Ross, Jesse had once said, was absolutely free of self-consciousness. He could say what he had in his mind and not be uneasy about any possible misinterpretation of his words. Other men, Patience reflected, shied away from talk about love, skirting the subject awkwardly, fearful, after courtship, of being accused of sentimentality. Jesse had Ross's serene self-control, too, and his freedom from regimented pressures. She and Heather were lucky women to be married to men who believed in love and could say so clearly.

But was Heather happy? Something was not as it should be, something had been wrong, for how long? Patience tried to remember when she had last seen Heather. Before Nicholas had been born—her calendar would be divided now into the years which preceded and those which followed his birth—and before Heather's birthday early in February.

It had been Sunday afternoon, a snowy Sunday, and Heather and Ross had stopped in because Patience and Jesse had people in every Sunday afternoon—"to make the time go faster," Patience said.

Their crowd was more mixed than usual, for Vera, stepmother of Ross and Jesse, and her husband had been there. Patience found her father-in-law vaguely pathetic, although Vera, brisk, decisive, would have been quick to resent the implication. Vera, her critics said, told old Mr. Garrison when to come in and go out. It was the invariable use of the word "old" that roused the sympathy of Patience. No one called her father "old Mr. Allow," and yet Jesse's father couldn't be much his senior.

"I declare, Heather must buy herself a new dress every payday—I've yet to see her wear the same dress twice." Vera's whisper, like everything else about her, was neat and precise.

That meant only that Vera was a little envious of Heather's clothes, not that she criticized her. Vera and old Mr. Garrison loved her because she was bright and gay and took as much pains to make them happy when she invited them to dinner as when she asked friends of her own age.

At twenty-five Heather sparkled with the fun of living. Her black eyes glowed; her pretty face reflected every merry mood. She wore her black hair parted and drawn back severely from her wide, smooth forehead, but once past the restraining combs it tumbled in wide waves to her shoulder. Heather was always on the verge of having it cut or trained into an "upsweep," but Ross's loud outcries deterred her.

"First thing you know I'll have wrinkles and here I'll be, with my hair still in a long bob," she warned him. "You know what the fashion mags say about women who can't be their age."

"You," Ross assured her, "are different."

She was different. Patience sometimes wondered how Heather

could use so much rouge, such vivid lipstick, and paint her nails bright scarlet and yet look only lovely and young.

This Sunday afternoon she wore a soft red wool dress with a wide gold belt and heavy gold choker, bracelets, and earrings. She was mad about color, she said, and she had a barbaric fondness for jewelry. It was a part of her joyous nature, and wherever she was in a room people turned to her with the expectation of being cheered.

"Do I imagine it, or is Heather quieter than usual?" Lou Allow asked her daughter when she brought in more sandwiches.

Patience thought not. "It's only that she's listening to Dad Garrison, Mother. You know how he talks."

"Well, I hope that's it." Mrs. Allow still stared anxiously at Heather on the couch, flanked by her in-laws. "I thought she might be coming down with Virus X."

That was the popular complaint that winter; "intestinal grippe" was out. Patience studied Heather covertly, and her respect for her mother's judgment went up a notch. Heather might not be harboring the germs of Virus X, but she didn't act like herself. Speaking, she was animated enough, but in the brief intervals when no one made demands upon her attention the bright face assumed a listless look, disquieting and strange.

She might be pregnant, Patience decided, her own condition accounting for the suggestion. For a long time Heather had expressed no longing for babies, but presumably she intended to have a child or two. For that matter Heather had no great love for her job; she did not regard it as a career, and Jesse had seemed surprised that she did not give up her office work when she had been married a year.

"I was sure Ross and she planned to have her stop after one year," Jesse said. "It isn't as if she were a specialist and couldn't be happy without her desk. Ross makes enough, too—but it's none of my business."

Vera, who made everything her business, had asked Heather

point-blank for the reason behind the change in their announced plans.

"You said you'd work a year and then stop," Vera reminded Heather. "You don't like your new boss, and you know you don't have to go to business. Why do you keep the job?"

Heather said, "I keep it because I like the money," and to Vera's objection that she didn't save a penny Heather replied that Ross bought enough bonds for two.

Patience, trying to listen to a girl who wanted advice on how to persuade a fiancé that it was silly to wait for the housing shortage to be ended, decided that being pregnant wouldn't make Heather look like that. She'd be as gay as a lark and regard it as a new and delightful kind of circus. What could depress Heather except—well, where was Ross?

"I told him to look at you and Jesse—you didn't wait until you could lease an apartment," the girl said. "The thing to do is to get married and trust to luck."

You had to live somewhere, Patience pointed out. "Your parents are out in Ohio, and Cal's live in the South. If Mother didn't have this house, Jesse and I would have had to wait, too."

"Married people are so darn smug," the girl complained bitterly. "Once they're settled they tell everyone else to wait. I'm going to ask Heather how she and Ross got their apartment."

As she stalked away, Patience caught a glimpse of Ross, leaning over the back of the couch, his hands on Heather's shoulders. So then there was nothing wrong between them, and if Heather was unhappy it must be something else.

Then, a week or two before Patience expected Nicholas, Heather had phoned that she was entering the hospital.

"I was afraid you might be upset if I didn't tell you myself," she said cheerfully. "It's nothing, really. Mostly for observation. I thought it would be fun to go to St. Luke's and greet you when you arrived, but my doctor's on the staff of Thatcher Memorial."

Patience promised that her mother and Lucy would visit Heather, if visitors were allowed. To her very real surprise,

Heather said she gathered from the doctor's instructions that she was to be interned.

"At least I'm not supposed to write letters or have phone calls, so I doubt if he'll be cordial to callers," she reported.

"It's probably your nerves," Patience said. "He thinks you ought to slow down."

Heather laughed and agreed that might be the doctor's idea. She would at least have time to finish the sewing she was doing for Patience's baby; surely she would be allowed to sew.

After that first week Jesse had called Ross, who was indefinite about the time Heather would be hospitalized. There was some talk about an operation, he admitted, but the doctor wanted an observation period and also an opportunity to build up her strength.

"She sends her love and says Patience isn't to worry—and she hopes the baby will be a boy," Ross told Jesse.

How long had Heather been in the hospital? Patience, plunged into her own ordeal, had lost the count of days. She thought it to be two weeks, but it might have been three. Beautiful gifts had come for Nicholas and for herself—Heather loved to make presents, always wrapped them lavishly, and stressed the details. Patience wondered who had wrapped these packages, since Ross couldn't tie a decent knot and Heather, marooned in the hospital, had no opportunity to revel in pink and blue papers and satin ribbons.

Now Heather was home, and no one seemed to know how ill she had been or whether the operation had been performed. You did not fire questions point-blank at Ross, because if he did not wish to answer them he would let them fall into a silence as deep as a well. She would have to be tactful, Patience reminded herself, but she must find out if anything was amiss.

"Ross, you said the greatest tragedy is the death of love—or rather, when the death of love separates us—didn't you?" she asked.

"Thought you were asleep." Ross in the small straight chair had not stirred. "I've been planning to sneak away without waking you."

"You did say that, didn't you?" Patience persisted.

He said, "You've the gist of it."

"Well, do you know anyone to whom it's happened?"

Ross stretched his long legs as if cramped. "My mother, I think."

"Oh!" Patience sounded disappointed. "I—I mean recently."

He laughed then and leaned forward to persuade her to look at him. "Could you, by chance, be asking if Heather and I have come to the parting of the ways?" he suggested.

"Well, you don't tell me about Heather. And I thought she seemed unlike herself one Sunday at our house." Patience recited her grievances doggedly. "And you talked about people being separated by the death of love—"

Ross could understand, he said. "But you forget—I said, too, that there can be no real separation when two people are in love. Heather believes that, and so do I."

"Tell me about Heather," Patience begged.

"Well—" Ross hesitated only an instant. "She's in bed, you know, but she still likes to look pretty. I'll have to describe that redingote you're wearing to her in detail."

Patience, twisting a lock of her hair, corrected him. "Not a redingote, Ross. This is a bed jacket."

"O.K., bed jacket. Heather has a lot of 'em, wears a different color every day. She wouldn't think of breakfasting without her earrings, and the nurse gives her a manicure." Ross smiled, as if he saw his pretty young wife clearly. "Her bed is usually strewn with fashion magazines, and she has her screen filled with letters and cards."

She had taken hers down, Patience confessed. "The more I looked at them, the more I remembered that I have so many letters to write. I still have, of course, but I can put them out of my mind."

"Heather never was a good correspondent, so none of her friends expect to hear from her," Ross said. "She's strictly oral.

If she can't see someone she phones, and if she can't phone she goes into the silence. When we were engaged, I wrote three letters to her one."

In fact, he went on, as if glad to talk about Heather, if he wanted to be at all sure of a letter from Heather during their engagement, he had had to send her a charm for her bracelet.

"She loves her bracelet," Patience agreed.

All the girls envied Heather her bracelet, even the ones who sniffed disdainfully at her fondness for what they termed "costume junk." But the bracelet, a link design, was gold and a gift from someone who had known Heather's mother. It had come to Heather with four exquisite, tiny gold charms, ranging from a water wheel, incrusted with diamond dewdrops and turning with smooth precision, to a tiny box that opened on a hinged lid and was designed to hold one aspirin.

"And to think that up to the present I've had to worry along with a bracelet that cost two dollars and charms that cost less," Heather, dazed by her good fortune, telephoned Patience. "In fact, if I bought 'em, the charms were less than fifty cents, although I do have some given me that cost a dollar."

In wartime the jewelers made no intricate, expensive, tiny baubles for a collector's chain, but Ross, a man in love, searched the shops in every city where he might have leave. He succeeded in supplying a charm at odd intervals, careful always to make sure that his gift was gold and that it "worked." Heather had explained that the attraction lay in the workmanship and that wheels must move, keys must turn, hinges give, to make her happy. The sole exception was the tiny ring, perhaps half an inch in circumference, engraved with the date they had set for their wedding. Ross sent her this to help her remember, he wrote.

After the war they had needed so many things for their apartment—as all the young couples did—that few new charms had been added. Also, Heather had seemed to care more for clothes and for entertainment than for extending her collection. The bracelet, she said from time to time, was to be her oldest daughter's dowry, but she remained vague on the question of the daughter herself.

It would be like Heather to have a baby and keep it a secret until she sent out announcement cards. Patience, considering this possibility, felt sure that she had solved the puzzle. Some women could carry a child and show almost no alteration in their figures —her mother knew a Mrs. Nelson who went everywhere and fooled everyone and triumphantly produced a child at the appointed time to surprise and mystify her unsuspecting friends.

Well, then, suppose that Heather knew she would be like that. Never mind how she knew it, since she had never borne a child, but say she knew that she could keep her figure. Certainly the full skirts and the swing-back coats were a godsend to pregnant women. Patience's own mother had modestly remarked that the New Look could conceal triplets and no one be the wiser.

Heather, pregnant, would love to steal a march on everyone and telephone her friends casually one day that she had had a baby and would they like to come and see little John or Susan that afternoon.

Patience doubted, however, that such an announcement was imminent. Rather, with Heather in and out of the hospital and a nurse in attendance at home, the situation must be that the danger of a miscarriage had been discovered. The doctor was probably keeping Heather flat on her back, and quiet, until he had everything under control.

Of course, she could ask Ross point-blank, but that didn't seem the sporting thing to do. If Heather wanted to surprise people, that was her privilege. Only, poor dear, if she had to spend most of her pregnancy in bed, the surprise might fall flat, after all. Still, when she wanted her friends to know, she would tell them, and later Patience could reveal that she had been clever enough to guess in advance.

Heather adored surprises. She liked Ross to take her out and not say what play they were to see or where they were to dine. He bought her foolish trifles from street vendors and wrapped them in huge boxes, and she afterward tied the toys to strings and swung them from her seventh-floor apartment window gently into the hands of children on their way to school.

"I hope Heather has half a dozen babies, when she decides to have a family," Emmeline Toller remarked to Patience's mother. "She'll laugh at their antics and take everything easily. And she'll get enough surprises then."

Ross had been inclined to take a dim view of his fiancée's weakness when, motivated by a desire to please her, he had heroically refrained from letting her know that he had unexpectedly been granted leave for a precious week end from the camp where he served as instructor. He had made the long, hot trip north only to discover upon his arrival that Heather had planned to surprise *him* and had presumably passed him en route to his camp.

"But that happens all the time," she protested when he complained. "Of course, I still love to be surprised. Just one mix-up doesn't mean anything."

It meant that he was cured of trying to surprise anyone and he hoped never to be surprised again, Ross scolded.

Not that he had any real hope of convincing Heather, Patience suspected. Grandmother Toller liked to say that the man who tried to make his wife over usually spoiled the original model and had no improvement to show for his pains. No one could say a word against Heather to Grandmother, and she had been indignant when Vera had characterized Heather as "flighty."

"What do you mean by flighty?" Really, if Grandmother had not recollected her duties as hostess at the Carberry Memorial Home tea, she might have tossed her cup at Vera, whose worst fault was her unfortunate choice of words.

"I only meant that she doesn't take anything seriously. I'm sure you agree, Mrs. Toller, that a well-balanced person can't go through life without encountering some serious problems," Vera said.

Patience, who had been asked to "pour," could see Heather if she leaned forward to look around the enormous silver urn.

Heather, this Saturday afternoon, wore beige velvet and a pink hat, and her charm bracelet had captivated a circle of the old people, who forgot to drink their tea as they examined the trinkets.

"If you want to know what I think about Heather Garrison," Patience heard Grandmother say, although, of course, Vera had not said that she wanted to know, "I'll tell you. That girl, for all her easy laughter and her good spirits and her love for clothes, has got spunk. You can't lick her. I don't care what serious problems she may come up against, I'll back her to tackle them and work them out and not ask for help, either. She has something that'll see her through the darkest forest and that she'll never lose—her bright spirit. Not too many people in this world have a bright spirit, Vera," Grandmother sighed.

Patience must have sighed too, for now Ross with a glance at his wrist watch said that he must be on his way.

"I didn't intend to stay so long, but I half hoped to wait for Jesse. The nurse expects me to relieve her tonight. You'll be all right, if Jesse doesn't come right away, dear?"

Patience reassured him. "Ross, I've been thinking of something I heard Grandma say, oh, years ago—during the war when you and Jesse were in the city on leave and we all went over to the Home because it was their annual tea and Grandmother wanted to show off you two in uniform. Remember?"

"That was the place where Jesse fell down the back stairs and I distinguished myself by knocking over the Boston fern—and all on nothing stronger than orange pekoe?" Ross asked. "Alas, I do remember."

She had forgotten that the place was a jungle of Boston ferns, Patience said. "Well, Grandmother happened to be talking to Vera, and I overheard. It was about Heather—Grandmother said she had a bright spirit and would never lose it. I think she meant that nothing would ever dim it—that's a lovely thing to have said about oneself, isn't it, Ross?"

He said nothing, but stood half turned from her, his eyes on the framed picture of his brother Jesse.

"Heather is so happy-hearted; she doesn't brood or worry," Patience murmured wistfully. "A bright spirit—that's a lovelier charm than any on her bracelet."

Ross swung round to face the bed, his smile a mixture of tenderness and pride. "Nothing dims her spirit—you're right. She's wonderful—I've always known it," he said.

The light from the table lamp threw his features into relief, and with a shock Patience saw for the first time that he must have lost a great deal of weight. The bones in his face had sharpened; his collar was too loose. Had Jesse seen him lately and not noticed the change?

"Ross, you're not ill, are you?" She caught hold of his hand, and that, too, was thin. How long had they all been blind? "Don't you think you should have a checkup, just to make sure, Ross?"

He insisted that his health was perfect, that if he had lost some weight it was to his advantage. "You don't want me to develop a bay window, do you, Patty? Heather likes 'em thin, too."

He leaned down to kiss her, asked her to give Jesse his love. "And put in a word for me with Nicholas. I'm really keen to make his acquaintance."

"Ross darling—" Patience clung to him for a moment. "I hope you and Heather have a son," she said.

• • • • •••••••

Chapter Ten

OUTSIDE the hospital, Ross Garrison stopped to light a cigarette. A wide terrace, paved with brick and bordered by a brick wall with a limestone coping, spread to the shallow set of steps connecting with the street. The indefinite figures of men and women huddled at intervals against the wall and a few children sat on its broad top. Ross glanced over his shoulder at the huge, dark building, its roof and chimneys towering above the evenly spaced windows ablaze with light.

"The nurse says she had a bad night—" A woman's voice spoke in the shadows. "They want to try something else, but it's so expensive. . . ."

An intern, walking easily in his white rubber-soled shoes, passed Ross, glanced at him impersonally. The siren wailed as the ambulance answered a call, gliding out from the back entrance that opened on the next street. A man who had been sitting on the wall, holding a child in his arms, muttered something and hurried away.

God help all those who waited for news of the sick, Ross thought, hearing the rustle of winter's dried, dead leaves blown across the terrace by the winds of early spring. The scratchy sound annoyed him—his nerves must be in a hell of a state if he couldn't stand to hear leaves rattle. He must get a grip on himself before he went back to Heather. Then he remembered that he had had no dinner and hoped that coffee might settle his nerves.

A dislike for hospitals that extended to their immediate environs forced him to walk three blocks before he found a small place with a lunch counter and a few tables, evidently utilized for the overflow. Three men, perched on the rickety stools, read newspapers over their doughnuts and coffee, and a girl with a mane of blond hair giggled appreciatively as the counterman demonstrated a coin trick.

Ross ordered black coffee and a hamburger bun and savored relief almost as tangible as the flavor of food. How could he have guessed that the sight of Patience would have the power to twist his heart? So young, so vital, so strong in the knowledge of returning strength—so like, he bade himself admit, Heather as she had been. So unlike her now.

It had been Heather's insistence that had taken him to see Patience, though he had tried to beg off until such time as she and the baby should have left St. Luke's.

"Why, Ross Garrison, I *am* surprised," Heather had reproached him. "Jesse is your only brother, and Nicholas is your first nephew, and Patience is my sweetest relative. As long as I can't go to see her, you certainly should. Why don't you want to go?"

Ross submitted that he didn't know anything about babies. "Patience might expect me to hold him—or something."

"Ten-day-old babies aren't brought out at night to be exhibited," Heather said. "So no one will ask you to hold Nicholas. I want to know how Patience looks and what she says—please, Ross."

She didn't guess—he hoped she never would—how he felt about hospitals—any hospital. Unreasoning, of course, because the modern hospital was one of the world's wonders, and its staff performed daily miracles. Ross, stirring his scalding-hot coffee, reflected that his mother might still have been alive if her doctors had been as advanced as those who practiced today. The fault wasn't with hospitals, Ross meticulously confessed to himself, but with him. Nevertheless, it had been an ordeal to drag his feet up the steps of St. Luke's, and even then he hadn't been prepared for Patience.

Heather had looked at him from a background of white pillows for weeks, and she never failed to smile. But Patience, also propped high in bed, her hair a close golden cap, her gray eyes shadowed and calm, radiated a sense of kinship to a new and radiant world. She had just begun to examine the experience of motherhood and apparently found it good. And yet Ross's most poignant impression was that of her resemblance to Heather, who had never borne a child. *It is the lovely undercurrent of eagerness that is gone,* Ross thought heavily. *Like a light put out.*

"Anything else?" The counterman had a sixth sense that enabled him to turn just as a customer decided to leave. "Choc'late cake?"

Ross declined the single section of cake and also the one cut of pie that remained unsold. He paid his check, bought a pack of cigarettes, and stepped again into the windy darkness, perforated at intervals by the street lights.

He stopped in a doorway to light a cigarette and realized that his conscience faintly suggested that he should have waited to see Jesse. Patience might have been disappointed. But Patience couldn't possibly imagine what he had endured or what his thoughts had been. That woman asking for someone had been a godsend in her own chattering way, for he had let her run on and on until he had himself in hand. If he was going to have the chronic jitters, he'd better ask Heather's doctor to give him something to take. Vitamins perhaps. You took vitamins for everything.

No great rush about getting home tonight, either. Heather would forgive him, if she knew the circumstances. He stepped clear of the doorway, and a boy, running for a bus, drove a sharp elbow into his side. Ross debated whether to ride home or walk—decided to walk. He had sold the car—no one needed a car in the city, he had told his friends—and in time expected to be reconciled to the inconvenience of city transportation. When you couldn't afford a car, the sane thing to do was to get rid of it. Vera would approve when she heard the news—his stepmother tried to conceal her disapproval of his and Heather's elastic budget, but the set of her lips usually betrayed her.

"I could come in and take care of Heather for you during the day, Ross," Vera had said when she learned that a nurse had been engaged to accompany Heather home from the hospital. "You could look after her nights. She won't need much at night, and I don't suppose she'll be in bed very long anyway."

Vera had taken a course in home nursing; she meant to be kind. Ross persuaded her that she ought not to leave his father alone; if for any reason the nurse engaged for Heather should fail her, they might call on Vera, Ross said.

To himself he added that he would have to be careful—very careful. Vera was nobody's fool; she prided herself on putting two and two together, and the answer always came out four. She had looked at him speculatively when she had suggested for the second time that Heather ought to have visitors during her hospital stay and he had answered her negatively.

"You act so kind of funny, Ross." Vera had a mildly plaintive voice. "Sometimes I think you're trying to keep Heather away from people, instead of keeping people away from Heather."

Ross watched a red light turn green, crossed the intersection because everyone moved forward. He had no clear idea of being carried with the crowd but acted automatically. Vera's interest in nursing worried him still, although Heather had been home a couple of weeks—or was it longer?—and Mrs. Warren, the nurse, had shown no signs of collapsing.

Vera took an almost proprietary interest in Heather, Ross knew, because the young people had met in her lawyer's office. There was something about a consultation with her lawyer that affected Vera like a tonic, and whenever she felt low she was apt to feel the need of legal advice.

"Your father thinks I can do everything alone," Vera complained to Ross one bright June morning when he was home on leave. "Why don't you come with me to Mr. Kennedy's office? You look so lovely in your uniform, it's a pity not to go out and show yourself."

Ross winced but could not regret his Navy whites when he saw himself mirrored in the big, dark eyes of Mr. Kennedy's secretary. They had half an hour to themselves while Vera discussed her grievances with the lawyer and managed the time so well that Lieutenant Garrison and Heather Allen lunched together every day for the next week. He took her dancing evenings and asked Vera to have her at the house for dinner.

"She's an orphan, and she and the girls who share her apartment eat frankfurters and tomatoes, because they don't like to cook," Ross said.

"I lived alone for years, and I cooked two good, appetizing meals a day, whether I had guests or not," Vera retorted. "And when I married your father, you were all glad enough to have decent food prepared for you. I don't see anything cute or smart in a girl not knowing how to cook."

His father always said to let Vera run down and you would discover she had intended to do whatever it was you asked, all along. Ross waited patiently, thinking how much she reminded him of a fussy hen, disturbed so easily and yet subsiding, when she had had her say, with every feather neatly back in place.

"I suppose, if you're going to have her, it might as well be tomorrow night," Vera decided, after a few more observations on the lapses in modern education. "The butcher's expected to have some kind of meat today."

The dinner proved a success, and even Vera conceded that Heather had more to do with it than the pot roast. Heather looked so alive, from her shining hair and eyes to her tinted finger tips, that Ross's father forgot his habitual dull heaviness and laughed until Vera privately decided that the California sauterne must be stronger than the imported. But she laughed too, and Ross felt a new and deep affection for her since she had led him to Heather, who was—he had known from the first day—to be his wife.

"But why do you love her?" Vera had been surprised and strangely hurt, when on his next leave Ross told her this wonderful news. "Oh, I grant you she's a nice little girl. I haven't a thing against her; in fact, I like her—but I always thought you'd marry someone with more—more background. With your commission and all, you could marry a girl who could do more for you."

Ross, ready with a quick retort, caught his father's eye. Well, in a way Vera had done a great deal for her husband. Nothing spectacular and certainly nothing to further his social standing. But she had helped him to sober up; she had saved his money for him, taken the responsibility for his welfare from the shoulders of his sons, and stayed sturdily beside him as nurse and companion by turns.

If she unconsciously permitted his father to see that she regarded her task as salvage, why, she was not to blame. Ross, remembering the comfort and order Vera had brought into the house where he and Jesse had been so bewildered and ashamed, could afford to try to understand her point of view.

"I'm in love with a girl who is in love with life," Ross said, and to the two dull, middle-aged people who stared at him he seemed to fling them a challenge. "Heather has the most gallant spirit of anyone I've ever met; she—she's warm and quick like sunlight. Invincible—that's what I mean."

He could never explain Heather, but he discovered that the girls in her apartment had far more understanding of her qualities than his father or stepmother had. The flat, which was the top floor of an old house, sheltered the four girls, all engaged and all, like the heroines of the old song, "waiting for the war to cease." They rationed the living room so that each couple had the use of it one night a week. Two nights they all clubbed together and entertained, and one night the girls reserved for themselves when they were not at home to anyone—unless a beau had unexpected leave.

"It's the darnedest setup, but lots of fun," Ross confided to Jesse, who took a lively interest in his brother's engagement. "Technically you put in a bid for the living room on a certain night, and get it; but the way the place is laid out you have to go through the living room to reach the kitchen, or the bathroom, or any other girl's room. So the traffic is constant, even if the girls plan to leave you alone. And if I can take Heather out, we don't dare come in until she thinks the couple entitled to the living room are gone—the man at least. We've seen a lot of pictures twice, because she didn't want to run the risk of infringing on a friend's date."

Jesse, fascinated, asked what Heather had done before she and Ross were engaged.

"She had dates with someone else," Ross admitted sadly.

Heather, whose only living relative was an almost mythical uncle far in the West, had nevertheless managed a beautiful wedding with a quiet church ceremony, followed by a reception in the apartment. All the girls felt responsible for the reception, and what it lacked in formality it more than made up in hospitality and affectionate gaiety.

"Did you see the silver bowl Mr. Kennedy gave Heather?" Vera, awe-struck, compared notes with another wedding guest. "It's sterling— I looked. And heavy— I noticed it when I lifted it. She has some beautiful things. I understand she's going to keep her job."

Only until the war should be over and he established in the main office of the grocery chain where they were keeping a place for him, Ross reminded himself. Heather wanted to save some money. She had never been thrifty; but as she said, most people saw no reason to save until they married.

"Mr. Kennedy wants me to stay, the work is pleasant, and my hours are positively luxurious," she assured Ross. "But I'll drop it all as soon as you're home for good."

Like so many only children, Heather dreamed of a family that should protect a child from loneliness. Five babies, or at least four, she thought would be "about right," and she did not think it too much to ask that the first two should be boys.

"Older brothers are so lovely to little sisters," she instructed Ross. "They look after them. But when the girls are older, the boys expect to have everything done for them."

Heather, in her letters written to Ross at camp, liked to select the names for her children and was apt to change the list every week. Of course, one of the boys would be Ross, but with the addition of a middle name, to eliminate the complications associated with "Junior."

"The other boy let's name for Jesse," she wrote. "He is such a dear brother. I'd like to name one of the girls Avis for your mother, your own mother, I mean. And perhaps the other we'll call Alma for my mother."

She was born lucky, Heather believed happily, and she was not too surprised when she and Ross found an apartment at the end of the war. Her employer numbered among his clients several who owned large parcels of real estate, and largely through his efforts Heather secured an attractive, modern three-room apartment with a huge living room and fireplace. It was perfect, she said; it would be wonderful until they were ready to buy a house in the suburbs, where the children could have space to play.

People loved to come to the Ross Garrisons' for Sunday supper, for dinner, for an evening of bridge. Heather, home from the office by half-past-five, still did not pretend to be a cook. But she could, as she said, get the food into the refrigerator, and someone among her guests was always able to cook it.

"They like to cook," she told Vera, who was faintly scandalized and couldn't reason why. "They love to use my beautiful, new, shiny pots and pans. I set the table and make things look pretty, and we eat in front of the fireplace, and Ross says he has never been so well fed in his life."

She didn't save much money, Heather admitted to Patience, who came more and more frequently with Jesse, but other brides had confided to her that the first year of married life was apt to be expensive. You had to entertain your employer and his wife. And your husband's employer and *his* wife. And of course, all the relatives on both sides of the family, and your friends and those of your husband.

Heather had no relatives to invite, but she made Ross's kin welcome with such sparkling enthusiasm that even Cousin Belle said Ross's wife was lovely. To Ross, Heather's eagerness to offer hospitality had a tinge of pathos—she so patently hungered for family ties. She envied Patience her relationships that numbered father, mother, and grandmother, as well as a sister and an aunt, uncle, and cousins.

"Everything but a brother," Heather pronounced one night after apparently analyzing Patience's family tree. "I'm going to be adopted by Grandma Toller—she said it would be all right. Grandmothers are lovely."

They celebrated their wedding anniversary once a month because Heather declared the date had been engraved on her heart. Unlike Queen Elizabeth, she remembered only happy days, and the simplest party pleased her as much as the most elaborate affair.

For the observance of the day when they had been married a year and six months, Heather made stacks of sandwiches to be served with coffee after the evening's bridge. She liked to have three tables, and this night she asked those whom she termed hers and Ross's favorite people.

"She looks prettier every time I see her," Patience said to Jesse. "I think she's a little thinner, though—don't you?"

Heather overheard and thanked Patience for the compliment. Certainly she wanted to lose weight. Didn't everyone? No woman, not even a thin one, liked to be told that she was putting on weight.

"You're slim all right," Lucy Gray commented. "No one can wear a pink wool dress and look like a reed unless she is positively thin. Cinda will drool when I tell her you have another new dress."

Afterward, when they gathered around the fire to eat, the flames had cast a rosy glow on Heather, deepening the color of her frock, flushing her cheeks, and accenting the flash of her engagement ring. Ross, noting the mane of black hair and her great, soft, dark eyes, thought her very beautiful.

It was after one o'clock before they went to bed, and when he woke, an hour or two later, to find Heather crying silently into her pillow, some confused childhood memory suggested to him that she might have a toothache.

"Darling!" He raised himself, intending to turn on the table lamp.

"No!" Heather caught at his arm.

"Don't you want the light? What's the matter?" Ross, his arm around her, felt her warm tears on his hands. "Are you sick, dear?"

She burrowed against him, murmuring that she wasn't ill.

"Then why are you crying? Something's wrong." Ross remembered the party. "Anything go wrong tonight, Heather? I thought you were having a wonderful time."

The convulsive catch of her breath hurt him intolerably. His happy Heather to be crying in the dark—how long had she been weeping in secret?

"What's troubling you, honey?" he urged. "Tell your old man—" And he added, because up to this moment he had believed it to be true, "You know we tell each other everything."

Heather felt for his hand, guided it up to her breast, and pressed it against the soft flesh. "Feel it?" she whispered.

"Huh?" Bewildered, he did not know what to say.

"There's a lump."

"A lump?" Still he did not understand. But as his fingers gently explored, a small, hard thing, like a stone, seemed to lie there.

"Feel it?" Heather's whisper implored him to say "No."

"Well, maybe I do feel something."

In the dark the fragrance of his wife's hair, the warmth of her body reassured him against the fear that was black and strange.

"Do you—what do you suppose?" Heather, turning, slipped her smooth, bare arms about his neck with the gesture of the swimmer who seeks to be rescued.

Ross, who had had no experience with ill-health, hoped that he concealed his sense of panic. Now, if ever, he needed wisdom and tenderness, if he failed Heather in this crisis she might forgive him but his heart must break. *God,* he prayed, *Oh, God!*

"I'll tell you what I think, darling," he said. "It probably has something to do with the way you were lying in bed. You go to sleep, and chances are in the morning you won't feel it at all. But if you should, we'll go to the doctor's. I'll go with you."

Either comforted or exhausted, she slept in his arms; and because he was young and able to hope, he slept, too.

In the morning when he woke, Heather, dressed for the office, had breakfast nearly ready. She did not mention the lump, and he knew that it had not disappeared.

"Won't tomorrow do?" she asked him, when he said that he would telephone the doctor. "I can tell Mr. Kennedy I won't be in tomorrow."

But she did not protest when he made the appointment for nine o'clock and she faced the doctor with more courage than Ross.

"Is it cancer?" she asked shakily after the examination, when she had dressed and returned to the desk where Dr. Beach waited, Ross silent in the chair near him.

"We'll hope not," the doctor said, his voice matter-of-fact and very kind. "We're taking it in time. You're very wise to have come to me when the lump is so small. And I'll make all the hospital arrangements—"

At that Heather said, "No," the impact of her refusal arresting because she spoke so quietly.

"But, Mrs. Garrison, surgery is the quickest, the surest—"

"It's the only way, darling." Ross felt as if he had been knocked out and must struggle for breath.

Heather, her soft lips drawn back against her teeth, desperation a fever in her dark eyes, said, "It isn't the only way, is it, Doctor?"

"I think it is the best way. The best by far."

"But you do use X rays? If it isn't cancer?"

The phone at the doctor's elbow rang, a muffled signal that spared taut nerves. He said, "Yes, Miss MacDonald?" and listened to his office nurse, replying in monosyllables.

Heather put a cold little hand on Ross's wrist. "Not all lumps are cancer. Please, Ross, tell him you want him to try the X ray."

What did Heather know about X rays? Ross glanced around the pleasant office, saw nothing but the blond wood furniture and soft green walls. Dr. Beach kept his instruments and machines in the examining room, of course, safely out of sight of his patients.

"Mrs. Garrison, the X ray will be tedious and painful. And you may have to have the operation in the end. Wouldn't you rather—"

Again Heather interrupted. "No." She appealed to Ross. "I can't stand the knife. I want to try the X ray—first."

They began the treatments, and Heather extracted a promise from Ross that no one should be told.

"Dr. Beach doesn't understand. I don't think any doctor understands," Heather said. "He is always telling me there is nothing shameful in having cancer and that it is wrong to be so hush-hush about it. There's nothing to conceal, he says, every time he sees me. Nothing to conceal even if—"

She sat beside Ross in the car, her shoulder pressed against his. He drove her to the doctor's office during her noon hour, and she returned to her work after every treatment, adamant in her refusal to let her condition be revealed.

"What the doctor can't understand is the whole ghastly business I'd have to take—the watching, the whispering, the pity." Heather's gaze was on the traffic ahead. "I will not be pitied, Ross. Not ever. That's why women with cancer don't tell. They don't want to be whispered about or to—to be a shadow on other people's lives."

Ross held her arm for a moment, when she was ready to leave the car at the Lawyers' Building.

"Don't shut yourself away from me, darling, will you?" he implored. "I'll keep your secret, I promise you. But you must let me walk the same road that you do."

She kissed him for answer and stepped lightly from the car. He watched her cross the walk and at the door turn to wave her hand. No one, looking at her, would think her a haunted woman.

The doctor consulted had advised Ross that habit and routine tended to steady patients and that if Heather preferred to keep her job her decision should be respected.

"She's always been active; you can't coop her up at home now and leave her to her thoughts," the doctor said. "Her determination to lead a normal life is in her favor."

But when Heather suggested that they give a Thanksgiving dinner for "the family," Ross at first vetoed the plan.

"You're crazy," he urged with husbandly frankness. "Why should you kill yourself, getting up a meal for eight people? You and I can go out to a good restaurant and have a bang-up dinner, without taxing your strength."

Of course Heather had won the argument. She had pretty things she had not had a chance to use, everyone had been so sweet to her, she was tired of informal, helter-skelter parties—she marshaled a dozen reasons why they should have an old-fashioned Thanksgiving dinner for Ross's stepmother and his father, Patience and Jesse, recently engaged, and Patience's father and mother.

"I had set my heart on having Grandmother Toller," Heather confided, "but she was snapped up by Aunt Nellie. Next year I'll ask her earlier."

Heather revealed that Lucy, Patience's sister, had been snapped up, too—by her husband's sister. Ross privately considered this an act of mercy, since, left without competition, Heather would undoubtedly borrow relatives right and left.

"I think she's so cute, the way she goes after accumulating relations," Patience told Ross. "She takes on Aunt Nellie and Grandmother and my mother and father and Lucy and her family—it's fun to hear her."

The Thanksgiving dinner absorbed Heather's attention for a week. A woman in the apartment house, who made a specialty of cooking and charged well for it, agreed to stuff the turkey and make the pies. She made the cranberry jelly, too, and coached Heather in the preparation of vegetables and salad.

Heather put three leaves in her drop-leaf table and draped its extended length with the Irish linen damask cloth the girls with whom she had shared the apartment had given her. She and Ross polished silver at night and rubbed up the brass andirons in the fireplace. They debated whether to have flowers or fruit for the table centerpiece, decided to have chrysanthemums and oak leaves, but the day before Heather saw an arrangement of purple grapes and a lighter shade of purple asters and said she must have that.

Then, after all the work and anticipation, after the guests had arrived and Heather, in a new frock the color of bittersweet, had taken them to the kitchen to see the turkey through the glass door of the oven, after Ross had served the punch and everyone had admired the beautiful, festive table that dominated the living room, dwarfing in interest even the snapping fire—then Ross found Heather in the pantry almost in a state of collapse.

"Don't let them know—maybe it will stop." Her rouge stood out in two vivid patches where the blood had drained from her cheeks. "Oh, Ross, it's worse than usual; what shall I do? What shall I do?"

His first duty was to relieve her anxiety. No one would know, he said. Everything he and Heather had done for the last two months had been keyed to that refrain, he thought.

"You go to bed, and I'll tell them you've been fighting a cold and it's caught up with you. The dinner will go off all right—I'll see to everything. Don't be upset, Heather—you can't drag yourself around in such pain as that."

Heather in bed, Vera took hold. She could make gravy, certainly; cranberry jelly that stuck to its mold held no terrors for her. She knew just what to do and how to do it, and Ross thankfully yielded the responsibility to her. He suspected that the opportunity to be of importance pleased the little, drab woman, whose humble talents were apt to be taken for granted.

"Women never know when to give up," Patience's father had declared, thus unconsciously setting a stamp of veracity on Ross's explanation of his wife's illness. "They seem to think as long as they can put one foot before the other they're doing fine. You keep Heather in bed for a week, and see if she doesn't bounce right back."

How Heather managed to conceal her agony and keep her head

when she returned from a treatment at noon to a busy, exacting afternoon in the office Ross did not know. She tried to conceal her pain from him, but he learned to read it in her face and the way she held her body, and when the doctor refused to use the machine again but insisted on an immediate operation, Ross wondered if Heather might not be secretly relieved.

"I'll be—lopsided, you know." She looked at him, laughter on her lips but none in her eyes. "Dr. Beach says he can fix me up, but you'll always know. Do you care? Or can't you tell until you actually see me?"

If that was her only worry—Ross held her tightly, cursing silently his imagination and her own.

Heather arranged for a winter vacation and accepted placidly the envious comments of her friends. No, she had no intention of telling where she was going, a week was such a short time, and she didn't plan to write to anyone.

"I'll bet you're going skiing," Patience cried triumphantly. "If you are, I think it's mean not to tell us. Jesse and I could come up for the week end at least. I look so nice in ski pants."

She looked nice in ski pants, too, Heather retorted. "Perhaps we can arrange a week end after I am back. Only you and Jesse ought to be saving your money to get married."

"Look who's talking!" Jesse jeered. "You and Ross are two spendthrifts if I ever saw two. But at that maybe you need a vacation. You're losing too much weight even if the skinny ones do fit better into ski pants."

Heather's most persistent fear was that Ross might tell his brother or in some way betray himself to him.

"You won't tell Jesse, Ross?" she begged. "He couldn't help telling Patience. They're so happy, I love to look at them. We were happy when we were engaged, too—let's not spoil it for them."

Ross had not expected the ruse to be successful, and that Heather could drop out of her world for a week and not be discovered startled him in spite of her elaborate network of preparation. Everyone was alone, when you admitted it honestly; life was a flood that rushed on whether you sank from sight in the current or continued to swim.

"Now am I all right?" she asked the nurse when she recovered consciousness, and the nurse told Ross that she knew exactly what she meant.

"Now you're all right," the nurse answered.

Modern surgery, a great many people—none of whom was aware that Heather was hospitalized—explained to Ross, was wonderful. You take an operation, they said; it used to be that the simplest operation kept the patient in the hospital for two weeks at least, and usually he was advised to take another two weeks' rest at home. Now, appendicitis cases were sitting up the second day, and plenty of them were out of bed on the third.

"Why, heavens, my mother-in-law had her breast removed, and she was home within a week," one acquaintance, lunching at the same table with Ross, informed him. "Think of it—and women used to die under the knife like flies."

Heather—home within the week, too—looked rested, her friends agreed. She hadn't gained weight, but putting on weight was always a risky business. Nine times out of ten, you plumped out in the wrong spots. Even though Heather seemed actually thin, no one could doubt that she was rested. She laughed more; she never seemed to be tired.

"I want to do everything," she said to Ross. "It's so wonderful to be alive. Let's go skiing, even if we can't afford it."

The hospital and surgery bills had been heavy, in spite of health insurance. Ross, reluctant to sell his car, would have liked to economize in the household expenses. But Heather, with a new restlessness that puzzled him, spent more freely than ever.

Patience and Jesse, looking forward to their marriage, must either refuse invitations or be obligated to an embarrassing degree. Jesse, rather soberly, declined the ski trip, on the grounds that he couldn't afford winter sports.

"Playing in the snow costs as much now as a set of bedroom furniture," he observed. "Besides, I have to save for a honeymoon trip. I'm not made of money like you two."

Heather confided to Ross that "everybody" considered them extravagant. As long as they owed no bills, she added, she didn't care.

"We're happy, aren't we? And we have such beautiful times together. When we're old and too tired to run around, we can sit in the chimney corner and remember all the fun we've had."

They went skiing nearly every week end during the winter, and Heather in her scarlet outfit was a gay and joyous figure on the slopes. She loved to dance in the evenings, and her energy seemed to be inexhaustible.

"Don't you ever get mad, Mrs. Garrison?" Ross heard a waitress ask her one morning when they went in for an early breakfast. "I never saw you get mad."

She didn't mean exactly losing her temper and storming about, the girl amplified when Heather looked bewildered. Although plenty of guests did that when things didn't go to suit them.

"But you're never cross or in the dumps. I never saw anyone as cheerful as you are—always laughing," the waitress said. "My girl friend says the same thing. I guess you're happy."

When they didn't go skiing, Heather usually planned a Sunday night supper party and she and Ross went to the theater Saturday night. She spent her Saturdays in the city shopping, and her collection of clothes dazzled Cinda, Lucy Gray's young daughter.

"When I am old enough to go to business, Heather, I'm going to do just as you do," Cinda declared, elevated to cloud height by the gift of a hand-knitted sweater and matching wool skirt. "I'll have just tons of beautiful clothes and get my hair done every week. My mother isn't interested enough in clothes, but I adore 'em."

Heather smiled at the pretty young face bent absorbedly over a box of frilly neckwear. "Your mother has you and Ronnie. You're expensive."

"Well, I won't have children," Cinda announced. "There'll be just my husband and I. And I'll earn my own money."

Ross wondered if Heather remembered Jesse and Avis and Alma and the boy who was to have been named for him. By tacit consent they did not speak of having children any more, but he was sure that Heather did not realize the alteration in her face and voice, whenever she came in contact with a child.

Sometimes it would be in a crowded elevator when he accompanied her shopping. Let there be a baby in his mother's arms or a toddler lost in the crush of adult legs and knees, and tenderness flooded Heather's mobile face, yearning filled her eyes. She would smile at the youngsters and say something friendly and gay, in a voice rich with a warmth like a caress.

"Oh, Ross, look!" Heather would call his attention to a small person bundled into a snow suit. "Isn't he a darling—and he can hardly walk! How old do you suppose he is?"

Shopping bored Ross, but he knew that Heather liked to have him with her, and he sat patiently while she tried on garments, offered his opinion when asked, carried bundles without protest, and saw to it that she ate a substantial lunch.

"If you want to do something else, go ahead, Ross," Heather urged him at intervals. "I like to prowl around the shops, but you probably get sick of it. I'll be all right—I won't skimp on lunch, I promise you."

But he still had the feeling that she liked him to be with her.

They went to the movies three or four nights a week, a neighborhood show so that they need not be up too late. If they stayed at home, invariably someone dropped in or phoned to ask if it would be all right to drop in. Several families in the building had acquired television sets, and Heather tried to discover whether Ross would like a set for his birthday in the spring. The last thing on earth he wanted was a television set, he told her in some alarm, and she confessed to relief because on fight nights, one of the owners of a set had told her, the home living room became a haven for characters who would otherwise have been driven to a tavern.

"Do you know where I want to go for my vacation?" Heather challenged him one warm May night. "I know it sounds corny, but I'd love to go to Atlantic City. Just you and me."

Ross demurred. "But not in July, honey? The crowds are terrific; people walk all over you on the beach. Early in spring or in the fall, yes. But you wouldn't like it in midsummer."

Oddly enough, Heather's heart was set on Atlantic City. In spite of her gregariousness she had never cared for crowds, and the noise and glitter of a large resort at the peak of the season ordinarily held no attraction for her.

"But if she really wants to go, I'll make reservations, of course," Ross said to Jesse. "It sounds off key to me, but Heather usually knows what she wants. And I may be able to get in a little golf."

They spent two weeks in Atlantic City, staying at one of the boardwalk hotels. The salt water would be beneficial for Heather, Dr. Beach advised her, if she avoided a heavy surf and did not overtax her strength. Ross helped her with the padding for her bathing suit, adjusting it skillfully before and after she bathed. Her dependence upon him touched him deeply, and as he studied her eagerness to be with the crowds and yet not of them, he thought he understood why she craved glitter and noise.

A phrase from *A Tale of Two Cities* stirred in his mind one afternoon as they lay in the sand. They had their rug but no umbrellas since to secure privacy they had had to walk a mile up the beach, far past the chair and cabana concessions. A group of dilapidated pilings cast a grateful shadow where they lay, and a gentle, steady wind blew off the sea.

The tide was out and the beach deserted, save for the figures of two women walking close to the water's edge, too far away for their faces to be distinguishable, although their voices carried with startling distinctness.

Heather, in a white bathing suit, lay flat on her back, her head pillowed on her folded arms. She had removed her rubber cap, and her hair spread fanwise, a damp line at the edges. Her skin had tanned evenly, a golden shade that contrasted effectively with the white of her one-piece suit and the brown of the blanket. Her breast line, high and softly rounded, betrayed no hint of mutilation.

Recalled to life. Ross had been trying to remember the words ever since he and Heather had set out to walk up the beach after lunch. He had watched Heather, her head high, her black hair streaming in the breeze, and some vague memory of the words as he had read them—a boy in his teens, reading Dickens—had tantalized him by evading the proper sequence.

"Let's go in and then come out and run till we dry ourselves!" Heather suddenly set off for the creamy, lazy waves that lapped the glistening sand to their right.

As she ran, she bundled her hair into a rubber cap and her laughing face turned to challenge Ross over her shoulder.

Afterward they ran races until Heather quieted and suggested that they walk until they found some shade.

"Having a good time, aren't you?" Ross, his hand on her smooth, bare arm, was tall enough to look down into the glowing golden face upturned to his.

"Heavenly."

A gull screamed derisively overhead as they kissed, but they had the vast expanse of sand and water to themselves, except for him. They had outdistanced the amusement piers and boardwalk shops, and few vacationists strolled past the stores. Ross, still fumbling in his mind for the quotation that eluded him, saw ahead of them the silver-gray piling that offered an oasis of shade.

Recalled to life. That was it. Heather was like someone recalled to life, and her joy in living was because her reprieve had come while she was young. The old doctor what's-his-name, in the Dickens book, had been too old to take up his life again with enthusiasm and hope.

"I think you were right to come down here," Ross said, as if he confessed that he had been wrong. "The place has been fine for you, darling."

The slender body beside his on the thin brown blanket lay

quite still. "Ross, do you suppose I'd be as—as I am now, if it hadn't been for the operation?" Heather asked him.

Not sure of her meaning, he waited, feeling that steady current of cold air off the water against his tanned face. He saw the two women stooping, and the idle part of his mind knew that they were picking up shells. Middle-aged, he thought without conscious thinking, reserved women from some inland area, the type who thought it too much trouble to dress and undress for "a dip," but who wanted some tangible remembrance of their vacation to carry home.

"I mean, I think I appreciate being well more because I have had an escape." Heather stumbled a little on the last word but let it stand.

Well, that was natural, Ross assured her. If you never lost anything or never were in danger of losing it, obviously you'd take it for granted. "That's what old people tell us about youth—we don't realize its value until we've lost it." He smiled at her. "Do you appreciate your youth, my spouse?"

"A perfectly disgusting word," Heather said as she always did, because it rhymed with mouse and louse and, she added, if she remembered it, souse. "I don't feel exactly young," she murmured today.

Ross raised himself on one elbow, so that he could look down into her eyes. "You don't feel exactly old, do you?"

"No-o. But older than I used to be. And wiser. But I can't prove that I am. It's only a feeling."

She went to sleep a few moments later, losing consciousness with the childlike suddenness that had at first dismayed him and could startle him after three years. It was almost as if she fainted, he told himself, lying flat again and closing his eyes in the hope of sleeping, too.

The wind blew, measured, undeviating, and Ross pondered how well he knew his wife. She had regained her old high spirits; her bright joy in living was again undimmed. But, perhaps unknown to herself, a strange look flickered in her face at intervals, a secret look that had not been there before. She was older, she was wiser, Ross admitted, but how could it be otherwise?

When they reached home from the shore, Heather learned that Patience was pregnant and that the baby was expected to arrive in March.

"Isn't it wonderful for Patience and Jesse!" she exclaimed to Ross. "We can be the godparents—Patience said so. Lucy is so much older that Patience thinks I'm better for a sponsor."

Headlong in generosity as in other traits, Heather bought recklessly for the expected child. He had to have a trousseau, she argued; besides, statistics said that twins were increasing.

"I'm buying only from the stores that guarantee to duplicate everything, if you do have twins," she informed Patience.

Patience said that she planned to be X-rayed.

"X-rayed?" Heather sounded alarmed.

"To show whether Nicholas is twins or not," Patience explained.

Heather said, "Oh!" and glanced uncertainly at Ross.

"It must have been awful, before they could take pictures of your insides," Patience said. "Imagine the feelings of a poor mother who hasn't been warned, when she sees two babies instead of one. The X ray is certainly one grand invention."

The long, mild fall and the brief nostalgic Indian summer blended into winter, and Heather plunged into Thanksgiving and Christmas festivities with an ardor that left him, Ross complained, hanging on the ropes. And when, late in January, Heather herself admitted to exhaustion, he was not surprised or unduly alarmed.

"I'll go to bed early every night for a week, and that will fix me up," Heather planned confidently. "All I ever need is sleep."

She did go to bed at eleven o'clock instead of twelve and even took a nap before dinner on one or two occasions. But when one morning she found herself unable to rise, she consented to have Dr. Beach with a docility that revealed the truth of her statement that she was too tired to move.

"I've been tearing around too much," she told the doctor, "and besides there is always a letdown after the holidays."

He wanted her in the hospital, he said, for observation. She couldn't rest at home, he pointed out to her; the apartment was practically a Grand Central Station for her friends. A week in the hospital, to relieve nervous tension and build her up, and then they'd see. . . .

Visitors were to be barred, he warned Ross; absolute quiet was to be the goal. "An operation may be indicated, but we can't tell yet." They couldn't tell anything yet, he amplified a little irritably when Ross asked a single question.

Heather accepted the hospital edict tranquilly. Her nerves needed oiling, and she rather liked the idea of having her meals served in bed. No one could visit her, she told her friends, but she hoped they would write. And to Patience she said that the main reason she yielded to the doctor's whims so gracefully was to enable him to put her in shape for the baby's christening.

"I'll be home long before you have to go to the hospital," she promised.

At the end of the week, the doctor called Ross on the phone, asked him to drop around to the office. "We've got to operate," he announced with a bluntness that was studiedly kind.

"Does my wife know?" Ross thought that he was not surprised, thought that he had been expecting this for the past year. The past happy year.

Dr. Beach told him that Heather had asked no questions. She seemed to believe she had some sort of intestinal trouble, but even after the final consultation she had not seemed curious.

"It doesn't look too good," the doctor admitted, anticipating the second question. "But of course we can't be sure."

The operation had banished all doubt and with it all hope. A question of weeks, the doctor said then. "We can control the pain pretty well and she'll be comfortable for a while longer, anyway."

Heather did not know. Ross, allowed to see her briefly, the

first day, found that she expected to be up the next. "You don't stay in bed after an operation, any more," she whispered.

The young nurse in charge, standing at the head of the bed, shook her white-capped head in negation. A few days later she told Ross that she thought his wife assumed her operation had been for ovarian trouble.

"The first thing she asked was could she still have a baby," the nurse reported.

At the end of the week Heather grew restless. Other surgical patients sat up in armchairs or even walked the length of the corridor. "It takes me so long to get well," she sighed.

"Better slow and sure than rush and slip," Ross comforted her. "You know that old lady across the hall—she went home three days after her operation, and now she's back for a six weeks' stay. You'll be in good shape when you come home, and beyond the danger of a relapse."

To the doctor he suggested that Heather would be as well off in her own pleasant bedroom. With a nurse during the day. "I can take care of her at night," Ross said.

"You may have trouble getting a nurse—they fight shy of these cases—" But he would do his best, the doctor said.

His best proved to be a middle-aged, competent, motherly woman, a registered nurse, who promised to stay with Heather as long as she should be needed.

"My wife doesn't know what her trouble is," Ross explained in the preliminary interview. "She had one operation for cancer and believes herself cured. I am not willing, under any circumstances, to have anyone learn what her true illness is."

He thought of Heather's endurance of pain, her unwavering courage, her determination not to "cast a shadow on other people's lives," her brief period of reassurance—"I swear I'll kill anyone who dares to tell her," he heard himself saying.

"I understand, Mr. Garrison," The nurse spoke evenly. "Do her friends know?"

The danger was that they might suspect, Ross admitted. "My idea is never to allow anyone to see her alone. I want you to be on guard throughout the day, and I'll take over as soon as I get home. So help me, no one is to get to her and put ideas into her head. For instance, I've got a Cousin Belle who is a Calamity Jane, if there ever was one. She'd like to drop in and pick, pick, pick, until she started my wife wondering."

"No one will tell her while I'm there," the nurse said. . . .

Ross stopped, wiped his forehead with his handkerchief, although in March he did not ordinarily perspire. He had been walking as if the devil were after him, and Heather would be surprised if he arrived breathless and hot. With only two more blocks to go, he'd better slow down, get himself in hand.

Thank God for Mrs. Warren, the perfect nurse. Patient, tranquil, physically strong and spiritually serene, she had proved a bulwark against the rising tide that but for her might have engulfed Heather, in spite of Ross's passionate love and care.

The problem of visitors had been less insistent than they had expected. Heather, plagued by weakness, remained indifferent to those who called, although she delighted in her mail and liked to see her cards pinned to the panels of her Chinese screen. Some days she declined to see anyone, leaving Mrs. Warren to make a tactful explanation. Other days the nurse herself turned callers away, saying that when Mrs. Garrison regained her strength—

Usually Mrs. Warren's day ended at half-past-five, when Ross reached home. But she stayed willingly on occasions when, as tonight, he felt that he must be delayed. He insisted on paying for overtime although she would stay as late as she might be needed, without that, she assured him.

"And if she should be taken worse in the night sometime, don't hesitate to call me," she said. "I'm only half a mile away, and I'll come gladly, any time you need me."

The night nursing had been simple so far. Ross had lost some sleep, not too much, and he was, Heather praised him, an excellent nurse with magic in his finger tips when he rubbed her headaches away. She asked him once or twice about money, whether they had enough, because, if not, they could let Mrs. Warren go.

"It's terrible, to have a trained nurse for—how long have I been home?—almost six weeks, Ross. I thought maybe I was extravagant when we went skiing last year, but nurses and doctors cost even more." Heather tried to raise herself on her pillows. "I don't actually need a nurse," she said.

She didn't have to worry over finances, Ross declared. He put his arms around her thin body, lifted her into a more comfortable position. "We are solvent, honey. Remember we haven't had a steak supper for twelve for a long time."

They saved on entertaining, Ross convinced her, but he did not tell her that he had sold the car. Its upkeep ran too high to balance even the very real convenience. He had worried lest Heather ask questions about the car, but it was Mrs. Warren who pointed out to him that she asked no questions at all. Heather, the nurse said, only listened.

Ross stopped at the cigar store on the corner, bought a new fashion magazine. The last time he had taken ice cream to Heather she had not eaten it. There was so little he could do, except to save her from fear.

"I haven't told even my brother," he said once to Mrs. Warren. "It's my wife's secret."

If it killed him, Ross thought, pulling out his latchkey as he turned in at the apartment-house entrance, the end of Heather's bright life should be as quiet as the end of a song. So, he realized with a slight frown, he admitted for the first time that it could end.

Chapter Eleven

THE phone rang, and Heather listened as Mrs. Warren answered it. The nurse always spoke clearly and refused to muffle her voice. There was nothing more maddening than to be forced to lie in bed and hear someone trying to carry on a telephone conversation in whispers. You imagined that the whispers were alarming and that they concerned you.

"No, Mr. Garrison isn't home yet. Oh, you're Jesse Garrison? Yes, he did go to St. Luke's—he said something about meeting you there. Yes, of course. Yes, I'll tell him. Oh, she's fine! I will, thank you. Good-by."

Mrs. Warren, substantial yet not bulky in her white uniform, appeared in the doorway of Heather's room.

"Mr. Jesse phoned. He can't get to the hospital until the last minute tonight. He wants you to tell his brother he's sorry. And he asked how you were and sent his love to you."

Heather in the hospital bed, rented, Ross told her carefully, only for the period of her illness, said it was too bad the brothers had to miss each other. "They've both been so busy, lately. Ross won't leave me in the evenings, and Jesse has been spending all his spare time at St. Luke's with Patience and the baby."

Anyone could tell the two brothers were fond of one another, Mrs. Warren commented. She knew families where brothers and sisters scarcely spoke and might as well have been strangers. "I'm old-fashioned, relatives to me represent a real tie. Your husband and his brother mean a lot to each other."

"Ross must be walking home." Heather spoke as if to herself.

"He needs exercise and fresh air, poor boy." She put up one thin hand to the gold hoop earring that swung against her cheek as she turned her head. "They're getting heavy—will you take them, please, Mrs. Warren? I can look pretty tomorrow night. Ross won't care."

Mrs. Warren took the earrings, hung them in a groove of the lucite rack on the dressing table. "You rest a little, while I finish up some things in the kitchen," she suggested. "Your bell's right here, if you want to call me."

She was probably finishing the ironing, Heather reflected. Dear Mrs. Warren, she did a thousand things that had no connection with her nursing job. Her excuse was that she had to keep busy, but another woman would have settled down to read when her patient dozed or have taken cat naps herself.

Ross got his breakfast at the drugstore and his dinner before he came home at night, but Mrs. Warren prepared Heather's trays and kept the apartment in speckless order. She did as much of the laundry work as she could manage in the small kitchen, for she would not leave Heather to go down to the new electric washer set up for the tenants in the basement. Mrs. Warren mended for Ross, too, and when she thought the glass curtains looked dingy, she washed and ironed them in a single afternoon.

"I don't want you lying there wondering how your house looks," she told Heather. "Your beautiful living room is always going to be ready for anyone to step into. I keep everything just the way you like it."

An excellent cook, it grieved her when Heather could not eat, but she forbore to press her. She didn't believe in forcing patients to eat, she said; if Nature didn't urge them, who was a nurse to stuff their rebellious stomachs? "It drives me wild to see a mother trying to pour nourishment into a poor little tyke, without trying to find out first why he isn't eating her out of house and home," she said.

"I have to look pretty," Heather confided to her, the first day, sure that Mrs. Warren would understand.

And Mrs. Warren, helping at first by bringing Heather's make-up kit to the bed and standing by with the brush and comb, had gradually taken over the entire routine, so important she believed, to a sick woman's morale.

"I could get into a beauty parlor, I guess," she congratulated herself when she held the hand mirror for Heather to admire the results of her acquired skill. "You look good enough to eat—your husband will say the same thing."

Heather's heavy, dark hair was regularly brushed, and the shampoos were cleverly suggested on the days when she had the most energy; her increasing pallor yielded to applications of make-up, rouge, and powder, and her pretty lips kept their scarlet outlines. She looked like herself, when she glanced into the dressing-table mirror, and the thought that Ross would see no signs of haggard weariness pleased her.

She lay quietly, looking at the familiar furnishings of her room, yet not seeing them. The bed dominated the room, for it had been placed in the center to give her air and to make it easier for Mrs. Warren to move around her. Ross slept on the couch in the living room now, but the walnut chest-on-chest still held his shirts and pajamas, collars and ties. He had moved his favorite lounge chair—the one she had given him for his birthday—into the bedroom, and sometimes he spent half the night in that, although Heather assured him that staying awake didn't mean she had had a relapse.

The closet door was closed—Mrs. Warren closed doors and drawers—but Heather knew exactly how her gay garment bags, her matching hat- and shoe boxes, and the shelves, covered in peppermint-striped paper, looked. The one wide, deep closet was scrupulously divided so that Ross had an exact half. Heather had done her side in red and his in green, and the bags and boxes and fittings had cost more than either of them had expected. Only, of course, as Heather pointed out, you didn't do a clothes closet over every year—if they didn't move or have a fire, the closet should last them a lifetime.

Heather began to think what she would wear tomorrow. Ross liked her to be interested in clothes; he brought her fashion magazines, suggested that she clip the newspaper advertisements of dresses that she liked.

"You'll probably go on a shopping spree that will last a month, once you get downtown again," he told her. "You mustn't get out of touch with what they're wearing."

About the only change you could introduce into nightgowns and bed jackets was color, but earrings could be obtained in an inexhaustible range of material, color, and design. Ross never failed to notice her earrings, encouraged her to shop by phone for vivid silk and wool jackets and "throws," and said that he thought all invalids should have buttercup-yellow blankets on their beds.

The girls in the apartment had laughed at her before her marriage, saying that Heather must be descended from savage tribes who had bequeathed her their love of color and barbaric ornament.

"Heather, did you ever get enough color to satisfy you?" Tiny asked as they lingered over their festive ice cream and coffee.

"Once." Heather did not have to temporize. "When I was eighteen, a cousin died and left me four hundred dollars. I spent it all on a trip to Bermuda."

There had been only Aunt Dosia to advise her to be thrifty, and if there had been anyone else she would not have listened. Heather, who had just finished her secretarial course and had yet to get her first job, had been reading the travel sections in her favorite magazines, collecting the literature of the various vacation bureaus, and dreaming of "trips," throughout her high-school years. She had been orphaned at the age of ten; the courts had appointed a sister of her father to serve as guardian. Aunt Dosia, scrupulously honest in her administration of the life insurance that was Heather's only inheritance, was unfortunately so confused in her judgments that she considered beauty in any form to be a temptation and a snare.

"Aunt Dosia belongs to the school that believes if you're neat and clean you've done all you should to yourself," her nephew, Cordy Grasse, told Heather on one of his rare visits.

The scrubbed, immaculate rooms in Aunt Dosia's house were further testimony to her neatness and her distrust of what she termed "display." Steel gray and chocolate brown, durable shades, were Aunt Dosia's selections for walls and rugs and for clothes, too. She regarded make-up as "paint" and prided herself on never having used face powder in her life.

"Show me a woman who boasts that she never uses cosmetics and I'll bet you a hundred dollars she looks as if she never did," Cordy said. "Aunt Dosia avoids beauty parlors as if they were gin mills and for similar reasons—she regards them all as sinks of iniquity."

It was Cordy who gave Heather her first lipstick, and she used it during the day, after she left the house in the morning, removing all traces of it before she went home in the afternoon. She earned small sums by taking care of neighborhood youngsters—although the baby-sitter industry might be said to be in its infancy before the war—but her clothing purchases were supervised by Aunt Dosia, who frowned upon gay colors and expressed an especial aversion for red.

"If you'd happened to have red hair, she would have dyed it, sure," Cordy grinned. "Probably she figures black hair and eyes are a sober combination."

Cordy was an artist, and as such Aunt Dosia sighed for his mis-spent life. She had never seen his studio, but she imagined it to be a large, lofty place in which Cordy sat all day and half the night, painting naked women. Aunt Dosia knew of no reason why an artist couldn't paint as well at night as during the day, and for a woman who refused to set foot in a studio she was remarkably well informed as to an artist's way of life.

In one respect Cordy bore out her theories—he seldom had any money. Heather gradually learned that he did what he called "commercial" work to earn his living expenses, but his pictures, on which he lavished his real devotion and the bulk of his time, sold infrequently. He had a passion for painting water and, had Aunt Dosia only known it, used no models except the few he required for his poster work.

"The most fascinating subject I've ever found is water," he confided to Heather, whose admiration for anyone who could paint was boundless. "Rivers, lakes, brooks, and pools and of course the sea—a fellow can spend a lifetime trying to put the feeling of them on canvas."

He never painted a picture without water in it somewhere, and when he went to Bermuda for a summer—since the rates were cheaper than in the winter—he wrote Heather a series of charming letters illustrated in water colors that enchanted her.

"The English have a looser moral code than ours," Aunt Dosia warned her, as if the letters might undermine Heather's character. "They don't look at things the way we do."

Whatever the moral code of the English was, or Aunt Dosia supposed it to be, it could not weaken Heather's secret determination to visit Bermuda as soon as she should save enough money to pay for the trip. Her opportunity came suddenly and not as she would have chosen it, for Cordy, thirty years her senior, died unexpectedly from a heart attack.

His estate when settled amounted to four hundred dollars in cash, which the terms of his will gave to Heather. Aunt Dosia insisted that she keep the money for a nest egg and pointed out, sensibly enough, that the insurance money had "run out."

"You've finished your secretarial course, and the school is obligated to place you," Aunt Dosia said. "If you rush off on this crazy trip, it will look as if you didn't take an interest in finding a job."

She could get a job after she returned, Heather argued. "This may be the only chance I'll ever have to see Bermuda. Cordy would like me to go, I know he would."

"Well, then, the least you can do, it seems to me, is to wear black for him," Aunt Dosia suggested. "It shows shockingly bad taste, I think, to be buying yourself those fantastic red shoes."

Heather, in Bermuda, reveled in sunshine and beauty to her heart's content, wore her gay frocks, and danced in her red shoes. A letter from Aunt Dosia proved to contain the astonishing news that she planned to be married and to sell the house, left to her by her parents.

"Mr. Snyder is a widower with a well-furnished home of his own," Aunt Dosia wrote. "I have made arrangements for you to board at the excellent home conducted by our church for working girls—the only requirement being that you are employed."

The efforts of Heather to endow Aunt Dosia's engagement and marriage with a romantic aura failed completely. Mr. Snyder, middle-aged and morose, owned an upholstery shop, and apparently Aunt Dosia's selection of a dark-gray rep for the sofa she wished re-covered had attracted his attention to her durable qualities. Two people who took life more seriously it would be difficult to find, Heather decided, and wished that Cordy could have known.

As a beginner without experience, she could not hope to earn much at the start, and for a year and a half the residence club, which furnished two meals a day and a room for two girls at rates impossible to a self-supporting organization, provided her with shelter. Then she met Tiny Bailey in an employment agency and, simultaneously, obtained the position of secretary to the lawyer, Anson Kennedy.

"If we could get two other girls, we could swing an apartment," Tiny suggested. "I'm fed up with furnished rooms."

Heather, too, was fed up with the residence club and its restrictions designed for the greatest good of the greatest number. The idea of reducing the number to four appealed to her irresistibly. She thought she could find two congenial girls among the club members, and a little tactful investigation verified her impressions. Olive Moore and Rita Malone had, for years, been hoping for just such an opportunity, they said.

After that the war put their beaux into uniform and altered many of their plans, but the girls stayed together through their engagements, until one by one they married. Aunt Dosia died quietly in the second year of her marriage, and Heather, more shaken than she would have thought possible, puzzled over the question of what flowers to send. Aunt Dosia, who thought flowers were more trouble than they were worth, either to grow or to arrange for the house, might nevertheless be hurt if she had nothing for her funeral except potted palms.

"When I die, I want red roses," Heather declared to Tiny, who had stopped at the florist's shop with her. "I can't think of any dark flowers, can you?"

Tiny offered hopefully that some tulips were nearly black. But this was November, and even florists who delighted to anticipate the calendar had nothing so springlike as tulips yet.

"Asters are middle-aged, I think." Heather finally approved. "I'll send a spray of all purple asters, tied with purple ribbon."

But Mr. Snyder had not sent flowers at all, apparently relying on the potted palms.

It was strange, Heather reflected, opening her eyes as the shrill blast of a motor horn in the street recalled her to the present, that she no longer coveted flowers herself. If you could be said to lose your taste for flowers, she had lost hers. Mislaid it only, Ross insisted, and it was his theory that she had seen and smelled too many during her stay in the hospital.

"You'll be asking me to bring you red roses again, once you've had a respite," he prophesied.

Dear Ross, who was so determined that she should get well and who yet refused to let her feel that her convalescence was delayed. He had seen too many cases, he assured her, of swift recovery followed by a relapse.

"When you gain, if only a little every day, you'll keep it," he said. "Ill people shouldn't measure themselves by other ill people, for every individual case is different. You know doctors warn mothers not to measure the growth of their babies with other babies, even the same age; each baby is different."

His theory was comforting, Heather acknowledged, when, as tonight, she could not eat the attractive supper Mrs. Warren had prepared. Food, like flowers, distressed her, but perhaps that was temporary, too. As a child she remembered the awe and envy with which she and the neighborhood children heard the news that a small boy of their acquaintance was served ice cream every day during an illness. They would all be willing, they agreed, to be in bed for a week if they could have ice cream every day.

Ice cream did not tempt her now, but Heather could smile at the recollection. As a matter of fact, pretty clothes and jewelry didn't interest her either, except that they helped her to look attractive when Ross came home. She sometimes wondered how she looked at night when he waited on her so patiently and pretended that he had reached the age when he needed less sleep.

"You'd be sweet about getting up to fetch the baby his bottle," Heather whispered one night. "And you wouldn't swear, no matter how much he cried."

She wondered what he would say about Patience and her baby and how much he would conceal. Because Ross was strongly paternal—his protective care of his younger brother had always shown that. Ross would be eager to help take care of a little son or daughter, from the start would not ignore a baby, as some men did, until the child was old enough to run about and be interesting.

To her own astonishment Heather, shopping for baby clothes for Patience, barely saved herself from bursting into tears when she first entered the section in her favorite department store. She supposed that she must have passed the arched doorway dozens of times, but she had never passed through until she went prepared to buy something for Patience's expected baby.

"Childless women ought to keep out of such places," she confided to Grandma Toller the next day. "It breaks your heart to see the tiny things—dresses and bootees and bibs and blankets, everything blue and pink and white. And the faces of the mothers, the young ones I mean, as they handle the white kid moccasins or stop to examine a frilly bassinet—it makes you feel as if there is nothing in life for those who don't have babies."

Even the clerks were different, Heather fancied; perhaps if you folded and unfolded little sweaters all day or unpacked tiny embroidered sacques or straightened piles of pastel-colored carriage robes, you felt yourself a part of this terribly important business of having babies. Heather wondered if the younger clerks hoped to have babies of their own and if the gray-haired, middle-aged women without wedding rings found in their work some compensation for their lost dreams.

"I love buying for babies," Heather said when Patience remonstrated at the flow of packages. "It's a special kind of shopping that I wouldn't have missed for anything."

She and Ross would borrow the baby, Heather planned in the months when she waited almost as eagerly as Patience. There would be week ends, perhaps, when Patience and Jesse would want to take short trips or have guests and they would be glad to have the baby taken off their hands. Of course, Patience's father and mother might stand ready to act as substitute parents, but Heather comforted herself with the reminder that modern ideas tended to discount grandparents in favor of younger counselors.

"We're young," Heather informed Ross with a touch of smugness that made him grin. "We ought to be the ones to have the baby when Patience needs a rest. We can feed him and dress him and give him a bath, and he'll get so used to us that he'll want to come often."

It had been a little difficult to parry Patience's curiosity as to why Heather had resigned herself to a barren state.

"That's a ghastly word, isn't it?" Patience, having just uttered it, paused to consider. "I remember Grandmother telling my mother once that her father despised a barren woman. Which even then struck me as a little snooty on his part and more than a little outside his limits."

But Heather, Patience continued, should not be too sure that she would never have a child. Doctors did marvelous things, there were specialists to consult, and there was always a chance.

"I've noticed that, in spite of everything, babies do surprise everyone now and then," Patience observed.

She mentioned adoption, too, but was too honest to assume that Heather could bring herself to consider that, except as a last resort. "Perhaps if you didn't tear around so much, you'd be all right," she suggested. "I didn't know you really wanted a baby, Heather —you and Ross have so many interests, I thought you'd dread being tied down."

Heather had kept the question of adoption dormant in the secret places of her mind, reluctant to bring it out for Ross's inspection and equally reluctant to examine the shadowy warning that imposed the caution upon her. There was plenty of time, she told herself; a year or two hence might be better for the baby and for them.

An invalid couldn't hope to be allowed to adopt a child. Heather, hospitalized a few weeks before Patience expected to be confined, recognized the justice of that in the long night hours when she could not sleep. To her surprise she discovered that lassitude and indifference replaced her eagerness and that the hunger in her dulled. Illness, she dimly realized, narrowed her world, and at the same time she understood the absorption that had subtly altered Patience in the months of her pregnancy. You cared less, somehow, and in caring less you also cared more. There were days in which no one existed for Heather or had claim on her love, except Ross.

"I would rather rest a little more, before I see people," she said, when he brought her home from the hospital and installed Mrs. Warren as combination nurse and dragon.

But the strange indifference to the friends who had thronged the apartment in the three years of her marriage did not change. They wrote to her and sent her flowers—until they learned that she could not bear to have them in her room—and they called. Mrs.

Warren met them, told them something kindly and firmly (Heather thought it did not matter what she said), and turned them away.

Tonight the knowledge that Ross had gone to St. Luke's to see Patience and the baby had directed the flow of Heather's thoughts toward her sister-in-law. Patience, she mused, had everything. A husband, a baby, youth and health—

"But I have more." Heather opened her eyes at the sound of her whisper. In the subdued light the narrow, orderly room seemed to receive her as a traveler returned from a journey. How long had she been away? The faint ring of metal from the kitchen must be Mrs. Warren at the ironing—the poor woman had been on her feet every minute of the day.

Heather suddenly felt quieted and very wise. She lay motionless, wrapped in a new, abiding peace. Patience had so much, but she, Heather, had gone farther and had learned what every woman would like to know and is afraid to discover: whether love is to fail her in her greatest need.

She knew now, beyond the shadow of any doubt, with the beautiful, bright certainty of a fixed star, that nothing was ever to tarnish love for her or for Ross. Women could never be sure until some powerful test, merciless and cruel and imposed without their consent, furnished the incontrovertible proof. The fortunate ones, like Heather Garrison, were ever after anointed and secure.

Rich and warm and sweet, the heavenly feeling that she had come out upon the mountaintop possessed Heather. Ross had set himself the task of protecting her from knowledge she already shared, but he need never suspect that she knew. To spare each other, that was a motif worthy of their love.

I mustn't cling to him, not even when I am afraid. Heather said a small prayer for courage to face loneliness and fear. *I'll wear my pretty things and have people come in, so he'll see I believe I'm better.*

She must think only of Ross as he thought only of her. Instinctively she assumed that he had made no admissions to anyone, not even to his brother. Ross would protect her with almost fanatical care. Well, she could be loyal, too; her lips should remain sealed.

Far, far away the sirens began wailing, a lonely, urgent sound. A dog barked down in the street, a shower of sharp, staccato yelps cut off abruptly by the rumbling of a truck large enough to shake the apartment building. Heather wondered about the time, but the exact hour did not matter. The days shaded into nights and the nights slipped into days with confusing smoothness. She felt around on the sheet for the fashion book she wanted to look as if just put aside, and her fingers closed on the glossy surface of its cover—when Mrs. Warren came in, she would ask for the earrings again. Ross always remembered that she had once said she felt naked without earrings.

"Have you been asleep, dear?" Mrs. Warren spoke softly from the doorway. "I've brought you an eggnog—you ate so little for supper."

She came into the room, walking lightly but firmly, a small tray in her hands. In spite of her long day her uniform was still crisp and her face unwearied. Her heavy black hair, streaked with silver, was cut short and waved; her compact figure suggested strength. You couldn't be a bean pole and stand up to nursing, she had once told Heather.

"You don't have to drink it all," she said now, slipping an expert arm around Heather's shoulders and holding the glass to her lips. "Just try a few swallows, and it may all slip down."

Heather drank slowly and with difficulty but managed to finish half the liquid. Mrs. Warren did not urge her to drink more but removed the glass, bestowed a touch on the pillows that magically reshaped them for comfort, and seated herself near the bed.

"Mr. Garrison should be along any minute," she smiled. "I've a piece of apple pie saved for him when he does come."

"He's walking home." Heather spoke with confidence. "He always walks when he—when he is hurt or upset."

Mrs. Warren was that rare woman who could sit quietly with

hands folded in her lap and not fidget or twist. She could also wait in silence.

"He would be upset, seeing Patience and her baby, don't you think?" Heather appealed.

The nurse said gently, "Would he?"

"Well, he'd at least be shaken," Heather submitted. "You see, I know how he feels about me and, to some extent, how he thinks about—things. When he looked at Patience (I guess they wouldn't let him see Nicholas at night), I think he saw me in her place. With so much happiness in my arms and so much of life to plan for."

Heather ruffled the leaves of her magazine without glancing at it.

"So of course he'd be upset." She laughed a little. "That's such a silly word—it makes Ross sound as if he were in the gutter somewhere, flat on his back. My Aunt Dosia was always getting upset; in fact, it was one of her favorite phrases. I've thought a lot about Aunt Dosia lately—she never had a child, and perhaps she cared very much and I didn't know it."

She's trying to tell me something. Mrs. Warren, uncertain how to be helpful, simply kept still.

"I didn't understand her and she didn't understand me, because we didn't love each other. I'm afraid we didn't even like each other." Heather thought about that a few moments. Aunt Dosia's entire life had been a sealed book to her; now years later she couldn't explain a single action or analyze one decision, because Aunt Dosia must remain a stranger forever.

You misjudged people without intending to be unkind, and you hurt them without meaning to be cruel. Husbands and wives failed each other the most disastrously, of course, because their exactions and demands were based on love. They hoped, all of them, the men and women who loved, to be understood, even if they did not understand themselves, certainly if they did not understand themselves. And even if there were failures, they forgave each other in the knowledge that each had tried.

Heather remembered the earrings, swung the gaze of her dark eyes to the little rack of baubles on the dresser top.

"Will you get me the gold hoops, Mrs. Warren?" she asked. "I'll put them on again. And in the top drawer you'll find my charm bracelet. I haven't worn that in ages. Cinda, Mrs. Gray's daughter, has borrowed it several times, but she's very good about bringing it back."

The pretty gold hoops Heather screwed in place herself, but the bracelet had a trick catch that bothered her. "It's the safety—can you see it?" She held out her arm, and she could almost have doubled the chain around the thin wrist.

"I'll brush your hair a bit, too." Mrs. Warren snapped the catch. "How about another touch of lipstick? I'll fetch the mirror."

She did not move away but remained standing, looking down into Heather's face. The two pairs of dark eyes communicated wordlessly.

She knows that I know. Panic, despair, a weariness that terrified her choked Heather's heart. She had supposed her task to be only to keep Ross in ignorance and that if she accepted the wall he built around her he would believe he had not failed.

She had not counted on the perspicacity of another woman. One word from Mrs. Warren and the memories that were to comfort Ross when he should need comforting would be destroyed. A thousand questions to which there could be no answer must rise up to torment him. Nurses were like doctors, they knew all the secrets; all subterfuge, every pitiful little device was an old story to them.

But if she admitted her part, a sense of disloyalty to Ross must haunt her. Heather felt beads of perspiration dampen her forehead. She could not confess to a third person, when she could not confess to him. There was nothing to be said. Her hands fumbled with the magazine—she had intended to have it open, as if reading it, when Ross came home.

"Mrs. Garrison?"

Heather discovered that she had closed her eyes. She forced them wide—tired dark eyes, discouraged and sad.

"I heard the elevator." Mrs. Warren picked up the magazine, arranged it to show a double spread of photographs. "Your husband is coming. I want to tell you this—never forget it: I will *never* tell him. I swear it. Never."

A key turned in the lock; quick steps came down the hall. "Well, look who's wide-awake and all dressed up," Ross said.

Later, when the nurse had gone home, Heather could ask questions about Patience. For Heather this was the happiest time of her day, although she often tried to persuade Ross to go to bed early, he so plainly needed more sleep. But he refused to listen; so after she was prepared for the night, they turned the lights off, except for a night lamp, and talked, sometimes until well after midnight. Ross declared that he relaxed in the comfortable lounge chair that had a footrest; if he wasn't sleepy, what was the sense in his going to bed?

"How did Patience look?" Heather demanded.

"Lovely." Ross's chair faced the bed, and he could see Heather as he talked. "She's a little thinner, I suppose, and I'd forgotten how deep set her eyes are. But she's very sweet—asked me over and over to thank you for everything."

Heather stirred, and the charm bracelet gleamed for a moment in the dim light. "Is she happy?"

"Well—what a question!" Ross pretended indignation. "Here's a girl who has her first baby—and an apartment, don't forget the apartment—and you ask if she's happy. Of course she's happy."

Then there was something not quite right, Heather observed placidly. "You wouldn't be so vehement about it, if Patience was as blissful as you are trying to paint her. Is she worried, Ross?"

"Women!" Ross sighed. In addition to a sixth sense, they had a seventh and an eighth, he grumbled. "Patience hasn't a thing to worry about. She's well, the baby's fine, and Jesse is willing to be a good provider."

He might as well tell her, Heather said. "What did Patience say?"

"Oh, she fretted a little about the future—maybe that's natural. The future is so carefully concealed." Ross shifted his slippered feet on the ottoman. "You warm enough, Heather?"

The apartment heat dropped at eleven o'clock, and even in March the rooms chilled before morning. Ross had bought featherweight wool blankets for Heather, to replace those she had found too heavy.

"I'm plenty warm." Heather held fast to her conversational thread. "I always felt that Patience worries. She keeps things too much to herself. And she has imagination—combined with apprehension, that's bad."

Ross gulped. "Good grief, you sound like a psychologist."

"Well, if you prefer, I'll say she is a female. Women always have premonitions. But mostly they don't come true. You feel there's something looking over your shoulder or lying in wait ahead."

"You don't feel like that!" Ross's voice sharpened.

"I'm not the worrying type," Heather assured him. Then she added casually, "What really is on Patience's mind?"

"Oh—Jesse." Ross walked into the trap. "She used to be afraid she might die and leave him—remember I told you about the night she was so frightened, before the baby was born? Well, now she's nervous about Jesse—if he should die and leave her. Things like that. It's because she hasn't snapped back to normal yet."

All women were afraid of the loss of love, Heather thought again. Men seldom understood, because they considered women possessive, when they were, in reality, possessed. All the time and money and effort that women spent in training themselves to find substitutes for love were dust in the mouth and ashes in the heart. Only, of course, young women growing up in a scientific age, with their biological functions explained and their emotions decried, would make the discovery too late.

Perhaps, Heather reflected, God in his mercy devised pain as a crucible to help women select the true values for themselves. No matter what learned professors thought about women's minds, their bodies could not be altered, although if you listened to the scientists you would not hear them admit this. Women, learning the limitations of their flesh, found for themselves what survived and what died, chose for themselves the things that could not be destroyed.

Patience had begun to learn, and she, Heather, held the true answer in the hollow of her hand. The most fortunate women in the world were those who had come through great tribulation and could still believe in love.

In the dim light Heather saw the long, lean outline of her husband's body in the lounge chair. "What did you tell Patience, Ross?"

"I think I tried to put my creed into words for her." Ross spoke slowly, as if he had to look back. "Real separation, to me, is the death of love. Any other—parting—well, it just isn't real."

But Patience probably worried when she needed sleep, he said a moment later, and Heather would turn into a pessimist herself, unless she shut off her mind and went to sleep at once. "Just this once I'll give you a pill," he conceded.

Chapter Twelve

BEFORE the war we had a phone in every private room, but they've never been put back in the—the—in this—" The student nurse floundered and looked distressed.

Patience finished the sentence cheerfully. "—in the cheaper rooms. I don't miss a phone—only now and then."

"Mr. Garrison said to tell you he'll get here sure before nine o'clock," the student nurse repeated. "He's been unavoidably detained."

"Did he say that?" Patience, glancing up at the small, dark-haired girl, suddenly laughed.

The young nurse, her duty accomplished, giggled. "He said he was tied up; I guess—" She broke off abruptly, her startled brown eyes widening as she stared at the figure in the doorway.

Patience saw a heavy-set figure, a white-haired man in a dark suit. He had pushed the screen aside and stood straight and tall, as if confident of making a good impression. In the subdued light his handsome face showed few lines, and his eyebrows were thick and black.

"Why—why, Dad Garrison!" Patience sounded surprised, even a little panicky. "This is my father-in-law, Miss Stevens."

The student nurse would have rushed past the visitor, but Joel Garrison placidly barred her way. "You're the little girl who's been taking such wonderful care of my daughter?" he asked in a beautiful, rich voice that flowed like heavy cream. "You've chosen a grand profession, my dear."

Miss Stevens murmured incoherently. The man was probably

a member of the Board of Trustees and accustomed to making speeches at the graduation exercises. She tried frantically to think of something to say, but a familiar voice in the corridor saved her the effort.

"I beg your pardon—" Miss Coburn poked delicately at the visitor's broad back.

"Miss Coburn, my father-in-law, Mr. Garrison." Patience admired the dexterity with which the little student nurse ducked behind the figure, as it turned, and made her escape.

Joel Garrison adjusted his tie and bowed. "I hope you know how much we appreciate the care you've given our little girl," he said.

It was his voice, Patience decided. Even the sturdy Miss Coburn was not indifferent to its caressing warmth, although she probably had him catalogued and classified at the first glance.

"You've got a splendid grandson, Mr. Garrison," the nurse was saying briskly. "You ought to stop by in the daytime and get acquainted with him."

He winced very faintly, as if she had reminded him of his age. But hers was a new face, and his gallantry did not desert him. Immaculately groomed—Vera believed in good tailors and barbers—he stood at the foot of the bed, holding his soft hat to his breast. "Yours is a wonderful profession—helping to bring life into the world," he said.

Corny. Patience could have blushed for him, except that one might as well blush for Hamlet. Joel was enjoying himself in his own way, cloaked in self-esteem. You could say this much for him—he put himself out to be charming in the same degree for Miss Coburn as for the eighteen-year-old probationer. "Anything in skirts," Jesse had once said, "evokes the knight-errant in Dad."

"Where the devil did I put that vaseline?" Miss Coburn, rummaging among the bottles on the washbasin, extracted a glass jar. "You sit down and have a nice visit with Mrs. Garrison," she suggested, her manner nicely adapted to the problems of senile decay. "She's doing fine, but she needs cheerful chitchat."

Her starched uniform rustled, her impersonal smile rated him as something of less importance than the jar of vaseline in her hand. She said, "I'm glad to have met you, Mr. Garrison," and vanished, pausing long enough to adjust the screen before the door.

"Well, my dear!" He advanced to the bed, bent down to kiss Patience's smooth forehead. "You look blooming as ever. How's the boy?"

He hated to say "grandson," and perhaps other men did, although since the war it had been the women, some of them unbelievably young grandmothers, who had been criticized for their sensitivity. The light from the headboard lamp, less kindly than the shadows, revealed the ruins of his handsome face in detail. The features seemed to have crumbled and to be held in place only by the heavy black eyebrows, straight as if measured by a rule. He was clean-shaven, and his skin looked ivory white. Not the dazzling white of his abundant hair—that was soapsuds white.

"Do you want to hear about Nicholas?" Patience asked gently. "Or has Vera told you everything? She's seen him, you know."

Joel's pale blue eyes smiled; he put his hand over hers as it lay on the counterpane. "You know, to tell you the truth, I'd rather hear about you," he said.

He didn't drink any more; he had stopped drinking when Vera married him. And perhaps he didn't exactly leer—she would be fair to him and admit that he didn't leer, Patience resolved—but his flowery speech was a tattered remnant of his past. He didn't pay any attention to a woman as an individual; he never paid her the compliment of studying her as a person and adapting his technique to her tastes. No, he had one vastly silly line, which he used indiscriminately and believed to be successful because he was too vain to know when he had failed.

"Nice little room you have here," he said, leaning forward so that he could see himself in the dresser looking glass.

Patience explained that she had wanted to be alone. "I could have been in a room with another patient, but I preferred this."

"More expensive this way?" Joel's smile indicated that he would never pry.

"A little."

"I wouldn't want to be shut away from people myself. Human beings have to help each other over the hard places." Joel's chair creaked under his weight. "Mind if I have a chocolate, dear?"

Patience urged him to help himself from the tin box on the lower shelf of the night table. "But I thought you were on a diet, Dad."

"Never overdo it. Like Jesse, for instance. I had lunch with him this noon and he's downright skinny. Clothes hang on him. I told him so. 'For Pete's sake, get some flesh on your bones,' I said. Made him eat liver and onions—he needs more blood." Joel bit into a chocolate, looked pleased. "Have to have soft centers on account of my teeth," he explained.

Jesse might be thin, but he was perfectly well, Patience said. "He's been examined for more life insurance, and the doctor wouldn't have passed him if he'd been too much underweight. Now Ross has really lost pounds and pounds—he was here tonight."

"Ross? I haven't seen him in a coon's age." Joel sat up, suddenly alert. "I would like to have seen him. Vera tells me Heather isn't so good. And Jesse intimated the same, but I couldn't get anything definite out of him. You'd think I was a reporter digging up scandal, instead of their own flesh and blood."

Patience soothed him. It was only that Heather wasn't to have visitors, that they wanted her to keep quiet. "She's always had so much company, Dad—I think she wore herself out. It may take time for her to regain her strength."

"I rather thought Jesse would be here," Joel said as if he had not listened. "I wanted him to come out to the house tonight, and he told me he had to see you."

Jesse would be tired enough without having to hear his father's aimless talk. Patience hoped fervently that Dad would leave before his son came. If Jesse had lunched with him, that must have taken care of anything he might happen to have on his mind. She and Jesse had so many wonderful plans, so many hopes to share, that every moment spent together was precious. It was absurd to say that at sixty Joel was spoiled, but he was. The droop of his mouth, the note of self-pity in his voice betrayed him. Whatever he wanted of Jesse, it would be something for himself; he looked upon both his sons as sources of supply. His attitude toward Vera was similar, and his constant demands upon her acknowledged nothing of her years of patient devotion.

"You'll be going home soon, I suppose," said Joel, raising his voice one rich note higher. Patience caught a brief glimpse of a nurse's trim feet and ankles flashing past the screen. "I was telling Jesse at lunch he's got something to work for now. A man doesn't know what responsibility is until he looks on the face of his first-born."

It was like him to be sentimental about Nicholas. A man undoubtedly could not see his first grandchild without being profoundly moved, but it was pretty silly for a grandfather like Dad to prattle of his responsibility for the first-born, or for the second, as far as that went.

Ross had been the first-born, and what had Dad done about him? Of course, Patience reminded herself, Jesse and Ross had been happy as long as their mother had lived—or up to the last few years of her life. Presumably home was always a pleasant place for small children as long as they had warmth and food and love.

Because Jesse would wish her to judge his father leniently, Patience tried to be kind. "You must come and see us in the new apartment, Dad. Vera will love it."

"I thought—" In the light the ravaged face showed startled for a moment.

"What did you think?"

"Oh, nothing. Guess I got it wrong. I thought you were going to live with your mother, that's all."

Patience, uneasy, surprised, raised herself on one elbow. "Why, Dad! Hasn't Jesse told you that we've rented an apartment on Birch Street? You know that row of houses that were remodeled two years ago? They're in great demand, but we finally got a top floor."

"You'll have your hands full with the baby, won't you? Why tire yourself out, going to housekeeping?" Joel added hastily that he was thinking of her. "You're pretty young to have so much responsibility."

Patience looked at him, gentle pity in her gray eyes. He was old, he had wasted his life, he couldn't even remember how sweet the beginning had been.

"When I think of making curtains and arranging our own furniture and cooking the things Jesse likes in that lovely kitchen, I am so happy I could sing," she told him. "We're going to fix up one room for Nicholas—a baby should have a room all to himself. I looked at samples of wallpaper before he was born, and Jesse is sure he can do the papering himself."

Joel seemed intent on selecting a chocolate from the second layer. "I always thought they asked a pretty stiff rent for those Birch Street apartments," he said.

It was probably just his way of trying to find out how much the rent would be, and his desire to know meant only that he didn't have enough interests of his own to keep him occupied. Patience conscientiously counted ten.

"We'll make it up on something else." Unconsciously she quoted Aunt Nellie. "It was only by luck that we got it at all." But something still plagued her. "What made you think I planned to go back to Mother's when I leave the hospital, Dad?"

He shrugged his shoulders, avoiding her glance.

"Has Jesse said anything about not taking the apartment?" Patience sounded alarmed. "He signed the lease—I know he did."

Joel tried to take her hand, but she jerked it away from him.

"Now don't get all upset," he begged her. "I thought, of course, that Jesse talked everything over with you. Vera always says there can't be secrets between husbands and wives."

Patience struggled with a hysterical desire to laugh. Dad, who had never been straightforward either with the unhappy little Avis or with Vera, who refused to surrender her pride, could talk about shared confidences in that lofty tone!

Then a sudden terror shook her. If something dreadful had happened and Jesse should be keeping the bad news to himself! All the unspoken fears, the imaginary calamities that she believed she kept under lock and key began a mad dance in her brain. At the pit of her stomach a cold, hollow spot had the weight of a stone.

"Dad! Where is Jesse? What's happened to him? If you don't tell me, I'll go out myself and find him!" Her voice was low, but the shadowed gray eyes had darkened almost to black.

Joel put the candy box on the floor. He patted the counterpane, murmuring, "Now—now, don't take on so," but his nervous glance was for the door as if he expected a nurse to rush in.

"Where's Jesse?"

"I don't know where he is. Anyway, there's nothing the matter with him."

"But you said—what was it you thought he had told me?" Patience, sitting up, caught a glimpse of herself in the mirror, her yellow hair sadly tumbled.

Joel wriggled uneasily. "Well—I'm in a little trouble."

"You!" The tension relieved, Patience fell back on her pillows, indifferent to any unflattering interpretation of her conduct.

He understood. For a moment something pathetic flickered in the once-handsome face, but he was silent.

Patience lay motionless, a blessed release flooding her heart in a velvet tide. Nothing mattered if Jesse was all right. She listened to the ticking of her small clock, heard the sound of the elevator gates in the corridor, thankful for recaptured peace.

What was it he thought Jesse had told me?

The shadow had only retreated, not dissolved. It filled every corner of the small room now, reached out, and enfolded Patience and the old man drooping in the chair.

"You'd better tell me, Dad. I'll only imagine all kinds of things."

He brightened at that. "That's so. I know how women are. And it isn't as if Jesse isn't planning to tell you. Because you'll have to know—sooner or later you'll have to know."

Patience wondered what he would do if she screamed. Her nerves must have a breaking point, but she hoped she could control herself until he had told his story in his own way.

"Does Vera know?" she asked, a little surprised at herself for asking.

"Jesse made it a point she isn't to know." Joel smoothed his hair, an aimless gesture and apparently unconscious. "If he gets me out of this, he says, Vera isn't to hear a word. I promised."

Dad had borrowed money from Jesse or Ross, or perhaps both of them. Patience waited, prepared for the details of the loan.

"I got into a little trouble down to the store," Joel recited. "A—a friend was hard up, and I let her—him—dip into the week's collections once or twice."

Vera had persuaded the owner of the city's largest independent tea and coffee store to employ her husband as a collector, the majority of the customers, housewives, preferring to settle their bills weekly and in cash.

"Well, I got in a jam, but I knew I could make it up on the horses." Joel's voice was without inflection. "And I would have, too, in the end, but you never have luck when you need it."

"What happened?"

"Well, Cummings was out of town for a month, and I didn't make any deposits. Figured I'd make a killing. But I hadn't by the time he got back, and I was in a hole for sure. I wouldn't have asked Jesse if there had been anyone else."

It was unjust, it was mean for this man to turn to his son when he knew that Jesse had the doctor's bill and the apartment rent and so many extras on his shoulders now. Dad, who had never done anything for his children, might at least have the grace to make no demands upon them. He had Vera to take care of him, hadn't he?

"I don't see why you didn't tell Vera," Patience argued. Her fingers began to twist a lock of her hair.

"Jesse seemed to think she might walk out on me." Joel made the statement almost apologetically. "Vera's been a little touchy since—since the last time."

Rather tardily Patience recalled the slip he had made in his pronouns. "You mean there's another woman—"

Not really, Joel disclaimed, but Vera probably wouldn't understand. "She leaps at conclusions. Always has."

He would never appreciate anything done for him and would probably be carried by someone as long as he lived. But perhaps there was still time to persuade him to have consideration for Jesse.

"Dad, you know Jesse has a lot on his mind—setting up our own home, and having the baby, and all. He has about all he can handle just now." One of the compensations of growing older must be that you learned how to influence people. You might even discover how to penetrate the hard shell of complete selfishness that enveloped your husband's father.

Joel said, "Oh, everything's settled. Jesse's been getting the money together, and he told me at lunch this noon it's all straightened out."

It was a nightmare, Patience told herself hopefully. She was having a bad dream in this tiny, crowded room, with Dad Garrison trying to tell her something that she could not hear. Whatever he had to say was just a few words farther on, but she was exhausted in her efforts to catch up with the key words.

"How much did Jesse—" She whispered the fuzzy sentence.

"Thirty-five—"

"Is *that* all?"

All these dramatics for nothing. And how like Dad!

"—hundred." Joel wet his lips.

"*What?*"

He eyed Patience resentfully. "I said thirty-five hundred."

"But—but Jesse hasn't thirty-five hundred dollars! Oh, Dad, what have you done to him!"

She wouldn't understand, he said; women couldn't be expected to understand. "I didn't come to upset you, Patience; if I hadn't thought Jesse had told you, I'd have kept my mouth shut. You won't run a temperature or get worked up over this, will you?"

"I'm all right." Patience had left him behind; her thoughts had raced forward to Jesse. Why hadn't he told her? When he came, what would he say?

Joel stood up, his pale eyes asking her to be kind. "I thought I'd find Jesse here," he repeated. "That's why I came. I can't see him at the house when Vera's home, so will you tell him I said I won't tell her? And I won't tell Ross."

"Mrs. Garrison?" The student nurse had brought a glass of fruit juice.

"My dear, if I were an artist I'd paint you as an angel of mercy." Jauntiness returned to Joel like a cloak mislaid and found. "I'm just leaving—can you show me to the elevator?"

He kissed Patience, and she heard him stop outside the door to speak to someone, presumably another nurse or some feminine visitor. Then his rich voice grew fainter as he moved on toward the elevator, and then it could no longer be heard at all.

Jesse! How could you do this to me! Patience, left alone, began to cry, the slow, hot tears a burning film that seared her eyes. Perhaps she had no real part in her husband's life; in that case she was married to a stranger, and Nicholas must grow up in a house that was not a home.

Impulsively she shut off the lamp. She could think better in the dark. The lighted corridor beyond the screen and the steps of passing people vaguely comforted her, keeping her in touch with reality. Only her personal world had rocked.

Jesse had not told her about his father, consulted her, or asked her advice. She was horrified, stunned at the thought of a thirty-five-hundred-dollar debt and hopelessly bewildered as to the source or sources from which her husband had secured that sum.

Dim and quiet, cool and peaceful and still, the atmosphere of the room imperceptibly calmed the throbbing in her mind. She lay passive, her brief anger spent. And remembered then that Lucy had laughed with her at the precautions taken to spare maternity patients mental anguish. It could be overdone, Patience admitted, grinning to herself; she was only one of many victims.

When Jesse came, she would know what to say to him. Perhaps something could be done about the money, too. No one should expect Jesse to carry the entire responsibility. He was too conscientious, and so was Ross. The parents who least deserved the love and charity of their children might be the ones who received it in fullest measure.

At the office the girls had often said that the poorest wives had the best husbands.

"You take a woman who drinks and plays around and runs a man ragged, and nine times out of ten she'll have a devoted husband who will put up with anything," Muriel Ames had said.

Another girl remembered an aunt whose husband had divorced her, remarried her, and for thirty years endured her infidelities with quiet dignity that protected her every escapade.

"And look at what men do to good wives!" Muriel complained. "The Social Service books are filled with cases of women deserted for no cause at all. I just can't understand men!"

But the girl who had cited the example of her aunt had confided to Patience later that she didn't think the answer was that Aunt Callie had had the luck to marry a good husband.

"I think she just married a good man," Betty said.

Chapter Thirteen

THE cook in the dinner wagon pushed a cup of coffee toward Jesse without interrupting his conversation with the customer on the next stool.

"So all I hear, when I'm home, is whether the kid should have a dog or not. My wife claims she has her hands full and besides she don't like dogs."

The young fellow seated next to Jesse grunted. "Something funny, if a person don't like dogs."

"Not women." The cook moved the mustard jar nearer to Jesse's ham sandwich. "Women haven't got much patience, that's a fact. My wife's always complaining she can't work with the kids underfoot, and I remember my mother was forever shooing us out of her kitchen."

The young fellow caught Jesse's eye, grinned. "Well, suppose you try serving short orders with a kid following you around," he suggested to the cook.

His mother had liked to have him and Ross in her kitchen, Jesse recollected; she seemed to take it for granted that boys should be on hand to lick the cake bowls and sample fresh cookies. She helped them to melt lead for "experiments" and showed them how to make flour paste for their scrapbooks. Surely his mother had been happy for the first ten years or so of her marriage—but Cousin Belle, who must have had a third eye used exclusively for probing, had been skeptical of her motives when she consented to get a puppy for her sons. Jesse, playing in the back yard, had heard the two women talking in the kitchen.

"You've got all you can handle now, without taking on a puppy," Cousin Belle's high-pitched voice scolded. "You know perfectly well that you'll have to take care of it. The boys will neglect it, and Joel isn't going to give up any of his comfort to help train a dog."

Jesse's mother murmured something.

"You love animals?" Cousin Belle had a laugh like a bark. "You mean you make a fool of yourself over dumb creatures. Let me tell you, Avis, there's something very wrong with people who waste affection on dogs and cats and such. Usually it means that they've been hurt by people and they won't run the risk of being hurt again. So they make friends with animals."

Cousin Belle knew everything and did not hesitate to pass her information along. Unfortunately she specialized in the dark side of life, so that no one spoke often to her of happiness for fear that she would either deride or destroy. She came frequently to sew for Jesse's mother, who said that her tailoring work was equal to a man's.

When the puppy died, Avis Garrison conspired with the boys to put off the funeral, and even to conceal the death, until Cousin Belle, who was due that morning, had gone home.

"Cousin Belle wouldn't understand, she doesn't care very much about dogs," Avis said.

Ross, helping Jesse to hide the box in the cellar, whispered that Cousin Belle would just dump a dead puppy or kitten into an ash can and put it out on the sidewalk. "Don't you let her see you cry, she thinks dead things are just trash," he admonished.

The cook was drinking coffee from a cracked cup, and the young fellow next to Jesse had finished his pie and gone. "If I had a different job, I could be home more and look after the kid myself," the cook said. "He needs a man."

For the two or three years following Avis's death, Jesse's recollections were of the cottage they had had at the beach, one of a row of small places rented furnished.

Sometimes they had a cook and sometimes not. Joel's friends

trooped down for week ends and the men took hold and helped with the meals when the cook left.

"I ain't going to cook in any house where the children's neglected," one of the many dissatisfied servants informed Joel one Saturday afternoon when she sought him out on the beach to ask for her wages.

Joel argued that his sons were not neglected. "They're being brought up right. I let 'em make their own decisions. That's all."

"The less supervision children have, the more self-reliant they are," Miss Ley chimed in. "Psychologists are beginning to teach that."

Miss Ley wore a scarlet bathing suit, and for all her figure was square and stocky she was an excellent swimmer. She had her own cottage, but she spent most of Saturday and Sunday on the sand with Joel.

"I say they's neglected," the cook persisted. She was a handsome, light-colored woman who never lost her temper or raised her soft voice. "When children are left alone in a cottage till three o'clock in the morning, I say they is neglected."

Joel remonstrated. That had been an isolated instance. He had been detained unexpectedly in town. "I should think you'd want to stay and look after them if you take such an interest in their welfare," he said.

"There are other things I don't like," the cook answered, and Joel hastily paid her and let her go.

A new cook came down from the city with Joel the following Monday and in her turn was shocked by the habits of host and guests. An elderly woman—perhaps Joel had engaged her with some vague idea of discovering motherly qualities in her—she talked to the boys as if they were her contemporaries.

"I never know how many there'll be for dinner," she would complain to them. "Your father must pick up people on the train. And then he fusses about the grocery bills—I can't run a hotel for nothing."

Mrs. Dehardt, it developed, was a "dry"; not only did Joel's drinking shock her, but she considered herself responsible for his cure.

"Your father's a nice enough man when he's sober," she told Jesse, "but he's laying the foundations for liver trouble with every drink he takes. How do you and Ross feel about it?"

Jesse looked blank. Ross, untangling a fishing line on the back porch, stared.

"I mean you'd like your father to be cured, wouldn't you? Wouldn't you like to have him talk sensibly at the table and be able to sit in his chair like a human being, instead of lopping all over?" Mrs. Dehardt demanded.

They would certainly like to have Dad the way he used to be, Jesse admitted. "Wouldn't we, Ross?"

Ross grunted. Apparently he did not take Mrs. Dehardt very seriously.

"I've got something to put in the coffee," she explained. "It's a sure cure. And your father and his drunken companions won't ever know they've taken it. There's no disagreeable taste, the package says."

For the first time Ross was interested.

"You mean you're going to poison Dad and everybody?" he asked, curiosity his only visible emotion.

Mrs. Dehardt was horrified. "My good gracious, what a thing to say!" she scolded. "Do I look like a person who would go around murdering anyone? This powder is perfectly harmless—I drop it in your father's coffee, and he loses all craving for liquor."

"Won't he even fall in a faint?" Jesse inquired, recollections of various movies refreshing his mind. "Maybe he'll spin round and utter a shriek."

They were heartless little beasts, Mrs. Dehardt informed them; she was sorry she had told them about the powder. "The least you can do is to keep still about it."

"When you going to do it?" the boys demanded in unison.

She groaned. "I don't know. Maybe tonight, maybe tomorrow night, maybe never."

Joel, not especially observant, gradually became aware at dinner that evening that he was an object of special concern to his sons. They stared at him over their mounds of mashed potato and eyed him above the rims of their milk glasses.

"Can't you take your eyes off me?" he shouted halfway through the meal. "Is anything the matter? Have I lost an ear or something?"

Emmet, the strange man who had come down to go out fishing the next day with Joel and his friends, laughed loudly. He felt as if he were in a zoo, he said.

"But kids always stare like that." Emmet spoke kindly. "Their eyes don't focus—a nurse told me."

Joel teased him about the nurse, and while they were all shouting and gesticulating, Mrs. Dehardt brought in the three cups of coffee. Joel liked to see the coffee poured at the table, but she thought that made too much work.

Jesse stopped himself just in time from asking if she had put the powder in. Afterward Ross said he had almost asked the same question. Mrs. Dehardt flashed them a significant, warning look as she left the room, but in spite of her protestations both boys expected their father to scream.

At his first sip of the coffee, he looked puzzled. His glance flickered to Emmet, then to the others, as if to determine whether they had noticed anything. They were drinking in gulps, and apparently Joel decided to take his cue from them; he drained his cup and threw himself back in his chair, prepared to smoke.

The boys, excused from the table, rushed to the kitchen, where Mrs. Dehardt sat eating her own dinner in lonely peace.

"Nothing happened!" Jesse sounded accusing.

"For pity's sake, will you hush up!" The exasperated woman dropped her fork with a clatter. "Nothing will happen—I told you. Your father will simply never drink another drop."

But Mrs. Dehardt was mistaken on two counts. Joel was violently ill a couple of hours later and blamed his troubles on tainted food. He and his friends managed to get off on their fishing trip at three o'clock the next morning, and they returned in what Mrs. Dehardt described as their usual shocking state. She was so bitterly disappointed that she left when her week was up, and the rest of the summer the boys and Joel led a hand-to-mouth existence broken only by the unannounced and whirlwind descents of Cousin Belle.

"How about a cut of cherry pie?" the cook offered hopefully.

Jesse declined pie, paid his check. He was thinking, as he walked the long block to the bus stand, that the worst of the troubled years—the time between his mother's death and his father's marriage to Vera—had been the sense of shame and the utter lack of security.

A kid wanted to be able to bring other kids into the house and not run the risk of having them stumble over a man in the final stages of intoxication. He wanted the neighbors to look up to and consult his father, instead of labeling him a chronic drunk and crossing the street to avoid being buttonholed by him. With a father like that and no one except the kid himself to deal with the bill collectors and the men and women who lived on an alcoholic's generosity, Ross had been his salvation, Jesse admitted—Ross, who refused to remember the scars. But Ross held the theory that in avoiding the mistakes of their father he and Jesse must inevitably commit others for which their children would suffer.

"About the best a parent can hope for is the epitaph, 'He Meant Well,'" Ross said.

He would have made better time by cab, Jesse admitted, glancing at his watch as he boarded the creaking bus. But things like the difference between bus fare to St. Luke's and cab fare happened to matter. Well, he'd count every penny, cut out smoking, go without lunch—anything to make it still possible for Patience to go to housekeeping in her own apartment. She insisted the baby's welfare depended upon it—funny how everything came round to the baby and his needs. Jesse squared his shoulders, tried to set his mind in order. He'd have to be on guard, talking to Patience—women had the strangest faculty for detecting whatever a man tried to hide.

It was late for visitors, and he was the only one to leave the bus at the hospital door. The quiet, lighted corridors of St. Luke's were familiar to him now. At night they always gave the impression of loneliness and of silence that muffled secret pain. He was glad to shut himself into the small, bright elevator that carried him to the third floor and his wife's room.

"Patience?" he whispered in the doorway. "Are you asleep?"

The light on the headboard clicked into radiance. Patience held out her arms. "Darling—why, your face is cold."

He sat on the bed, the yellow hair like a marigold against his shoulder. "I'm sorry I had to miss Ross."

"He left his love for you. He had to get back to relieve Heather's nurse. Heather's all right, I think—" Patience hesitated.

Jesse said firmly, "Heather is all right. And Ross is all right."

"Then I won't worry. It was only—"

Jesse held her away from him. "Let's look at you—how did the day go? Anyone tell you more cheerful tales about people and their sorrows?"

"No-o." Patience considered. She had been wise not to tell Jesse the story about the squirrels. *Better not say your father was here*—not yet.

"Have any company?"

She laughed, falling back against him, and her hair was spun gold on his dark coat.

"Darling, *everybody* came. It was lovely. And they all think Nicholas is beautiful. It isn't just because they care for us, he really is exceptional. Even the nurses say so. And they've seen hundreds of babies." Patience drew a deep breath. "Nicholas is so nice and firm—not flabby," she said.

Miss Coburn had removed the flowers for the night, and the dresser was ornamented only with the framed photograph.

Patience had told him she slept with it under her pillow, Jesse recollected.

"Who all were here, Patty?" he asked.

Patience held up a slender hand and counted on her fingers. "Aunt Nellie first—look at the carved pendant Uncle Luther made for me. Then Grandmother—Jesse, do you think I'll ever be a great-grandmother? Lucy came this afternoon—she's wonderful. And while she was here Grace Andrews dropped in. I don't believe you know her. She has such beautiful clothes."

"I know girls who have beautiful clothes," Jesse protested. "There's Heather."

Well, anyway, he didn't know Grace Andrews, Patience answered. "And Ross was here, of course."

"Dr. Guye will be reading the riot act to you. He didn't say you could keep open house."

Patience dismissed Dr. Guye with a sniff. "I feel wonderful. I lie here and plan all the things we can do, once I'm home. Be sure you have film to take the baby's picture. I want to start his memory book."

Memory books were precious to children once they were grown, she explained when Jesse confessed ignorance. "Lucy has kept books for Cinda and Ronnie, and Mother saved some things for me. No one but mothers will take the trouble to keep such records —I'm going to do all the things for Nicholas that no one but mothers will do."

She rested in the strength of Jesse's arms about her, possessed momentarily by peace, her nerves relaxed. To be young, to be happy, to be going forward into a future that included a husband like Jesse and a son like Nicholas, surely this was the fulfillment of her dreams. *Ask him to tell you that his father has no power to interfere.*

"Jesse?"

"Yes, dear?"

"Your father was here tonight."

She felt his body jerk convulsively. And for a moment he said nothing.

"My father was *here?*" His voice was too quiet, all the surprise deliberately ironed out. "How long ago?"

Patience thought it might have been half an hour.

"What did he want, Patty?"

So Jesse didn't think his father had come to see her or the baby.

"He said he wanted to see you. He was awfully disappointed when I told him he'd missed Ross."

Jesse sighed and, in that unconscious admission of weariness and anxiety shut up within his heart, betrayed his need for assurance.

"Oh, darling, I know—he told me about the money." Patience pulled herself free, faced her husband. "Jesse, I don't understand, but it's all right. Whatever you've done, it's all right."

A spasm of anger twisted Jesse's nice mouth. "Dad told you? When he knew you're not to be worried—he's never had a thought for anyone except himself, since the day he was born."

"Why didn't you tell me?" Patience could not avoid the reproach.

"Patty, how could I? You were going to the hospital any minute—"

Something flashed in the shadowed gray eyes. "You knew about it before Nicholas was born?"

His father had come to him about a week before, Jesse confessed. "I couldn't tell you—I don't see how he could tell you. And if Vera ever heard of it, she'd walk out and leave him flat."

"He isn't going to tell her—and he's promised not to tell Ross. Why don't you want Ross to know, Jesse?"

Because of Heather, who is dying, and he knows it and is shielding her from pity. Because he is the salt of the earth and sacrificed his boyhood to give me mine. Because it is the only way I can help him now.

"Ross has done his share," Jesse said.

She hated to keep asking questions, it sounded prying, but she still didn't understand—Patience bit her lip to steady it. "Would Vera leave your father if she found out?"

"Maybe not—although she's threatened to. Look, Patty, I wonder if I can make you see how I feel about Vera. She took over when things were pretty bad, made a home for Ross and me, tried to spare us in every way. Her eternal decency is what I can't forget. She spent a lot of her principal settling Dad's debts, and she's paid for half a dozen of his silly escapades since. Well, I figure she's human—she has a breaking point. If she ever did leave Dad, he'd be sunk for sure."

Patience thought of Vera, the little, fussy woman who, the family said, mothered her husband like a child. Vera was generous, she was kind, and she was supremely loyal.

"This is one thing she ought not to be asked to bear," Jesse said.

Miss Stevens, the student nurse, coughed. "I tapped on the screen, but you didn't hear," she apologized. "If I could get Mrs. Garrison ready for the night, you could stay a little longer, after," she explained not very coherently.

Outside in the corridor, Jesse found an empty bench. Trust his father to upset the applecart! Patience might have had to know about the loan eventually, but she certainly should have been spared the knowledge until she was stronger and at home. He had been too young to protect his mother from the selfishness of his father, Jesse reflected, but he had supposed that he could safeguard his wife.

Jesse put his elbows on his knees, rested his head in his hands. There must be an element of cunning in his father's nature, something mischievous and sly. How else account for his visit to the hospital? Jesse had lunched with him that noon to tell him that the money had been deposited and that the lawyer had straightened everything out.

"Vera isn't to know, or Ross," Jesse had repeatedly insisted, but it had not occurred to him to stipulate Patience, too.

Joel had asked few questions, had apparently been relieved and eager to talk of something else. Jesse, watching his father's absorption in his hot corned-beef sandwich, wondered if Cousin Belle would say that devotion to food was a sign of disappointment or frustration or merely one of the few interests of old age.

"No beer." Joel in the smoky little booth made a dramatic gesture of renunciation to impress the waiter.

Beer was strong drink to Vera, he confided to Jesse. "She won't keep anything stronger than spirits of ammonia in the house. After ten years she's still scared stiff that I'll begin drinking again."

"She can't forget," Jesse said. "Women are made that way."

Vera was a good sport in her own way, Joel conceded, but he quickly changed the subject. "You and Patience will have to begin to think of buying a house in the suburbs or country." The glance of his pale-blue eyes flickered. "Boys need a ten-acre lot to grow in—turn 'em loose, that's the ticket."

When I owe thirty-five hundred dollars! But the picture of Nicholas, aged ten days, or two years, or three, turned loose in a ten-acre lot provoked Jesse's grin. His father's adoption of the role of grandfather was about as practical as you could expect. It was like him to pose as an expert in handling boys; he had forgotten or discarded his unhappy failures; his sons, he probably reasoned, were witnesses for the soundness of his method.

"You and Ross had better health that winter you spent in the country than ever before," Joel said. "Nothing like roughing it to toughen up a boy, prepare him for adolescence."

Jesse stared, for a moment wondered if his father might be senile. That winter in the country, his mother, Ross, and himself huddled in the old farmhouse, three miles from town, on a back road, with no way of getting their supplies except on the boys' sleds. Was it possible that his father had forgotten why they were isolated in Maine; had he no knowledge of the hardships and the heartaches? Or had the knowledge been too painful to endure for twenty years, so that he had in desperation reshaped it?

"We're going to the country," Jesse had bragged to the boys on his block, when his mother had explained her sudden packing activities. "We're going to coast downhill and go ice skating."

"Will you have to go to school?" the other boys asked.

Jesse appealed to Ross, who expressed doubt. The general opinion was that in the country no one had to go to school.

The tension between his father and mother had been well concealed. His father helped with the boxes and barrels and trunks, promised to come up at Christmas time and go skating with them. He rode with them to the station to see them off, but in the excitement of the crowds and porters and the march through the iron gates only Ross noticed that their mother cried.

"I thought you wanted to come, Mother," Ross remonstrated. "I thought you told Cousin Belle it was your idea. You said you *liked* the country."

Avis Garrison dried her blue eyes and curved her lips in a smile. "I always cry when I leave home," she said.

Years later Jesse had tried to piece together the story behind the fantastic journey. Cousin Belle supplied a few details, but even she had had to guess at the truth.

"Your mother wanted to get away by herself and think things over, I guess," Cousin Belle hazarded. "She was too close to her problem, I remember her saying. Not that she ever mentioned your father's goings on. But she had an idea that if she removed herself she could think better, and I suppose she hoped he'd miss her and you boys and decide it wasn't worth breaking up his home for the cheap article he was playing around with. She was all wrong, of course, but I don't know as any other plan would have worked better."

The isolated farm in Maine must have belonged to someone in her family, although neither Jesse nor Ross had ever heard of the place afterward. But their mother had the key in her purse when they arrived at the tiny station, and the man who drove up a few moments later in a box sleigh called her by name.

"These your young uns?" he asked in the particularly silly manner adopted by adults.

Avis introduced her sons—"Mr. Bates is going to drive us to the farm"—and when everything was loaded into the sleigh, she and the boys sat down in the straw and covered themselves with the warm, smelly blankets.

Mr. Bates apparently considered his duty done when he had carried the boxes and barrels and two large trunks into the house. He had his chores to do, he said, and there was plenty of wood and coal ready to start fires.

"I got everything on the list you sent, but my wife said to tell you to air the bedding before you sleep on it. Things is probably pretty damp. Nothing's been used since last summer."

The chill of the house bit into even young bones. The Garrisons, accustomed to a heated city house, had never experienced such devastating coldness. Avis, her teeth chattering, her hands blue and stiff, built a fire in the kitchen range and heated canned soup for their first supper. The house, furnished and rented for the summer months only, had no electricity and no plumbing. Only one lamp had any kerosene in it, and the pump in the cast-iron sink was frozen.

"Don't you think it would be fun to sleep on the floor?" Avis suggested. "We'll bring the mattresses down here and have a fire all night to keep us warm."

There were blankets, for blankets were needed even on summer nights in Maine, but she had packed thick Army blankets to augment the bedding. Jesse held the one lamp while she and Ross tugged two heavy mattresses down the old staircase and arranged them on the kitchen floor.

"I wish now we'd bought a puppy to bring with us," Avis murmured, but not until several weeks later did she mention that she stayed awake most of that night, afraid of possible rats.

In the morning they discovered that a fine snow was falling, and the prospect of getting to town for the more perishable foodstuffs faded. They had kerosene, and Avis filled and cleaned a fine array of lamps so that their subsequent evenings were brightly lighted. She was an adaptable little creature and, without country experience, nevertheless seemed to know instinctively what arrangements would be most practical.

"This great big kitchen will be our living room," she planned. "We'll keep a nice big fire in the stove all the time. You boys can have the dining room for your bedroom, and I'll have the alcove for mine. The kitchen fire will warm them, or if it should be extra-cold, we'll build a wood fire in the dining-room stove."

The housework, with no electrical appliances and no running water for cleaning, laundry, or baths, must have been difficult for a city-bred woman, but she did not complain. Once Jesse found her crying with pain, after hanging out clothes in the bitter cold; her hands, stiff and numb, burned like fire as the blood returned to them. She learned, however, to hang her wash in the stiffly furnished parlor, and if the clothes were not so white, the boys never knew the difference.

"It's too much trouble to take a bath," Jesse objected, after one or two sessions in which he shivered in a tin washtub placed in front of the kitchen stove.

His mother agreed that it was a great deal of trouble but insisted that cleanliness was necessary. "You wouldn't want to be sewed into your clothes and never take them off all winter, would you?" she asked.

The suggestion rather charmed Jesse, but Ross was more fastidious. "I'd like to be clean, but I hate emptying the water out of the tub," he observed. "Why can't Jesse and I go out and roll in the snow, Mother? That ought to clean us up, and there wouldn't be anything to put away, afterward."

If they expected to live with her, they would have to use plenty of soap, Avis informed them. But she had already given up the task of bathing them every night and counted herself lucky if they had two full tubbings a week.

Her interest in the mail impressed and at the same time puzzled them.

"There's never anything in that old box, except the newspaper,"

Ross grumbled. "I almost froze my feet going out to the road. I should think once a week would be enough to go look in it."

But he said nothing to his mother, and every day he and Jesse plowed through the deep drifts in the lane that led to the main highway. The tiny flag on the box was always up, because the newspaper came daily, but letters were rare. Twice a week their mother wrote to their father, and they gave her messages to tell him, but very gradually they perceived that he did not write two letters a week, or even one.

"Will Dad be here for Christmas?" Jesse asked one morning at breakfast.

"He promised," Ross said.

Their mother, bundled into a sweater that matched her eyes, declared firmly that Dad always kept his word. "Of course, the weather might interfere with his coming. He isn't used to as much snow as we are."

The next week there were two letters in the mailbox, one for Jesse, one for Ross. Their father asked them to write and tell him what they wanted him to bring them for Christmas.

Jesse wrote for a new sled, a collar for the cat, and candy. Ross asked for fur-lined slippers for his mother and a toboggan. He told Jesse that he wanted a dog but he thought it would hurt the cat's feelings so he did not mention it.

The cat had come leaping across the fields one morning, propelling herself forward with the peculiar motion of a flying fish. She was white as snow, with amber eyes, and she acted as if she had been waiting for them to arrive and offer her a home. The boys named her Snow White and taught her to ride on their sleds.

Christmas in the country proved unexpectedly exciting, with mysterious bundles left stacked up against the post on which the mailbox was nailed and the box itself so stuffed with letters and parcels that the lid would not close.

Avis was busy from morning to night, cutting out cookies,

making wreaths to hang in the windows, cleaning the rooms they did not use, and laying fires ready to be lighted in the fireplaces and stoves.

"A fireplace doesn't give much heat in this weather," she said to Jesse, who followed her about, carrying the paper and kindling. "But the blazing logs look so pretty and Christmasy. I hope Dad will want to stay a week—you boys must take him skating. We used to skate together, before we were married."

She had hoped, too, that Joel would come up to spend Christmas Eve with them, and when he wrote that he had made other plans, she forgot to be busy and bustling for the rest of the day. But they were many miles from the city, she told the boys; Dad had to think of many things before he could take time off.

"If he doesn't get here right on Christmas Day, he'll come a day or two later," she said. "We'll save his presents for him."

"Can we light a fire in the fireplace and hang up our stockings?" Jesse asked. "Ross says we ought to wait for Dad."

But his mother said that Christmas Eve couldn't be postponed, and she helped them to hang their stockings and then, when they were ready for bed and wrapped in blankets, read them the Christmas story, as she had every Christmas since they had been old enough to listen.

Joel Garrison arrived two days later, bluff, handsome, laden with packages, and voluble as to the discomforts of his trip. He listened absently to the boys' eager recitals, accompanied them to the little pond they had discovered and kept swept clean for skating, but admitted that he had not brought his skates.

"Oh, Dad! We told you about the skating!" Ross scowled in disappointment, and Jesse considered socking his father in the eye with a good wet snowball.

"I couldn't carry any more junk. Besides, the pond's too small." Joel shivered. "Let's go back to the house—I'm petrified," he said.

Avis, who had been cooking and baking for a week, suggested an early dinner and then they could all go coasting. She looked excited and gay but, as Jesse remembered her, not exactly happy.

Her hands, red and rough, distressed her, and she was nervous about the stove, because you could never be sure how it would perform.

"While I'm getting dinner, you boys bring in lots of wood," she instructed Jesse and Ross. "Fill the wood box to the top. I want to keep a fire going all night; Daddy isn't used to a cold house as we are."

The wood box filled, they helped her set the table. Joel disappeared and was gone until she rang the dinner bell the boys had brought down from the attic. They had also discovered a polished hollow horn, which, Avis explained, had probably been used to call workers in from the fields.

"Did it belong to a cow?" Jesse asked, enchanted with the idea of such communication.

Avis thought that the horn had once belonged on a cow's head, but her knowledge of zoology was as limited as the boys', and she could not be sure. She regretted that the horn had been found, for the noises they made on it were hideous in the extreme, and she had hidden the thing before Joel was expected—his stock of patience, always small, would not expand to cover an interest in primitive customs.

The gate-leg table, opened and drawn near to the stove for warmth, seated four comfortably. Jesse thought the centerpiece of a spray of evergreen, set like a little tree in a glass bowl filled with English walnuts, and trimmed with strings of white popcorn, was beautiful.

"We're going to pop corn tonight, Daddy," he told his father. "We've got a big popper, and we make tons of it. Don't we, Ross?"

He and Jesse took a lively interest in the dinner. The turkey they had transported from a farm on the edge of town, using their sleds; the onions and potatoes and turnips they had carried up from down cellar, where they had to be covered with layers of bags to keep from freezing.

"We picked the nut meats out of the shells so Mother could make a cake," Ross volunteered.

Joel Garrison remained strangely silent. Even Jesse noticed his father's unresponsiveness, and he wondered if perhaps he disliked to eat in the kitchen. It was by far the best room in the house, and with the bright red curtains at the windows—Avis had made them—and with the red cushions for the chairs, it was very cheerful. She had scrubbed the rag rug, too, that covered almost all the floor. The dark-gray walls and the cupboards painted the same color troubled her, but she said she didn't dare change them without first asking the landlord.

She had, however, painted the wood box red, and Snow White liked to sleep on the black-hinged lid. The wood box, the stove, and a worktable occupied one wall, and the other walls were broken by two doors, four windows, a dish cupboard, and the sink, which was placed as far away as possible from the stove.

"We have to thaw it out nearly every morning," Avis said of the pump. "But some of the houses don't even have a pump."

Her Christmas gift, a five-pound box of chocolates, had been placed on the window sill, and Jesse and Ross could hardly keep their eyes from it. They considered it a magnificent present. If Avis was disappointed, she gave no sign; they would open the candy, she said, when they popped the corn that evening.

Neither did she mention that the heavy cream for the coffee and the brandied mince pie, together with the nut cake she planned to cut for supper, were extras. She and the boys lived on the simplest food, for, her sons learned afterward, it was part of her desperate hope that whatever she saved in their living expenses might be applied to the rising tide of debt.

"Now as soon as I have these dishes out of the way, we'll go coasting," she announced briskly, when Joel had finished his coffee and pie and had lighted a cigarette. "I hope you brought your windbreaker, Daddy."

Something in the way Joel cleared his throat halted her as she turned to carry a pile of plates to the sink. Jesse, about to lift Snow White from the wood box, and Ross, on his way to the cold room with the butter, swung around to face him, too.

"I might as well tell you, I've got to be getting back to the city." Joel stood up. "The man who drove me out this morning is going to take me back. There's a train at three-something I can make."

For a moment no one spoke. The tin alarm clock on the narrow shelf beside the stove ticked noisily, but save for that an absolute stillness pervaded the room. The same intent quiet ruled the out-of-doors—sometimes, Jesse fancied, outdoors was a thick blanket that wrapped itself around the house, like the hushcloth his mother put on the table beneath the cloth.

"You mean you're not going to stay one night?" Avis asked.

"I can't. You see, it's a bad time of year, and I have a lot to tend to. You're so isolated up here that a message couldn't get through. Maybe I'll run up again in the spring and spend a week. And if I don't, you'll be home by the first of April, so that's that."

Jesse watched his mother to see if she might cry, but she only put the soiled plates down on the table and picked up two cups and saucers. She didn't know what to do with them, either, and put them on top of the plates. "Why did you come at all?" she whispered.

"I always keep my word," Joel said. "I said I'd come up at Christmas, and I made it as close as I could. Now I know you and the boys are all right I'll be more at ease in my mind about you. Nice, snug place here, and you all look fine. The city's no place to bring up kids."

As if he had suddenly remembered his sons, Joel's gaze swung to the two lads, whose faces betrayed their lack of comprehension.

"Your old father has to get back to work, to make money to keep you tykes comfortable." His tone was that of an orator making a campaign speech. "Mind you take care of Mother and do as she tells you."

Avis swept a few crumbs from the table to the floor, using a folded napkin as a brush. Jesse was horrified at this action, so unlike his usually neat mother, but before he could say anything his father suggested that they all walk down to the end of the lane with him.

"The old codger with his horse and sleigh said he wouldn't come up this lane to fetch the Rajah of India," Joel chuckled. "I said I'd be down at the road by two-thirty."

"There isn't any train for the city in the afternoon," Avis said.

Joel had gone into the icy front hall, where he was struggling into his coat. "I can at least get a head start by going as far as the Junction and laying over till morning. Then I'll get a good train. By George, the fare up here almost broke me."

Ross looked at his mother.

"Shall we go down the lane?" He did not add, "Do you want us to?" but Jesse understood him as clearly as if he had said the words.

Avis understood, too. Her little red hands pushed the dishes about aimlessly, but her voice was steady. "You boys go. I have to wash the dishes. Hurry and get bundled up so you won't keep your father waiting."

In the rush of getting into their boots, buttoning up sweaters, winding mufflers around their throats, and hunting for the usual missing mitten, Jesse did not see whether his father kissed his mother good-by or not. He rather thought not.

Joel, who had been so silent at the table, was inexplicably talkative and gay as they plowed their way through the snow in the lane. They were lucky, he said, to be spending a winter in the country, and he only wished he could stay where everything was so peaceful and quiet.

"It's not much fun, bringing in wood," Jesse objected.

"And we almost freeze our hands, pulling sleds all the way to town and back," Ross added.

He thought the stores in the village delivered, Joel expostulated. But if they didn't, that was no real hardship. "You kids don't want to be soft. Why think of the Puritans who settled this country. They died off like flies in winter and thought nothing of it."

Jesse could not follow this reasoning, but he sensibly assumed it to be grown-up talk and not worth his attention. He and Ross waited with their father until Mr. Robbins, from the village, drove up with his long-legged gray horse. Joel climbed into the sleigh, tucked the robes around him and called "Good-by" as the horse, delighted to turn and head for home, swung the sleigh around.

"Well—" Ross shrugged. "He's gone."

"He didn't like it, did he?" Jesse remembered the look of relief on his father's face as he waved farewell. "He was glad to go, wasn't he?"

Ross began to tramp soberly up the lane, retracing his steps in the footprints his boots had just made. "He wasn't used to it. Remember we didn't like it, either, when we first got here? You like it now, don't you?"

"Some." Jesse, plodding behind Ross, fought an inclination to cry. "Mother wanted him to stay."

"Uh-huh."

They stumbled along for a few moments in silence, and then inexplicably the heavy, sorrowful feeling disappeared, and they were happy again. Jesse remembered the nut cake they were to have for supper; Ross recalled the beautiful box of chocolates.

"Do you think Mother will let us taste them, even if Dad isn't here?" he speculated.

"Let's ask her," Jesse said, and they started to run.

They reached the house breathless and in a fine glow, but in the kitchen they found only Snow White, asleep on the wood box. The dishes had not been touched; none of the food had been put away.

"Mother!" they shouted in sudden alarm.

Avis answered them from upstairs. "I'll be right down," she called.

They thought she had been crying, when she came down. Her face was blotched; her eyes were swollen and red. Her nose was red, too.

"It's so cold upstairs—it makes me look a fright," she murmured, catching sight of herself in the funny mirror hanging above the sink.

The three of them looked at one another uncertainly. The house was still, much more silent than it had been before Joel's brief visit. Jesse wondered if he could have made a mistake—perhaps his father had been there yesterday.

"Is it time for supper?" Ross asked, showing that he, too, felt confused.

"Supper?" Avis laughed, a strange, choked laugh that ended in a kind of croak. "Why it's only quarter-past-two. You've just had dinner."

She looked in the reservoir at the back of the stove and said the water was hot and that she ought to wash the dishes.

"But let's have fun—the dishes can wait till tonight. Let's go coasting till it's dark, and then we'll all pitch in and do the work—shall we?"

As she talked, she was carrying the butter to the cold room and putting it away with the remains of the turkey in a cupboard there that she called the food safe.

The boys were delighted and rushed to get their sleds from the back porch. Avis bundled herself up in her snow suit; when she came out, most of the redness had gone from her eyes, and she had powdered her nose.

They coasted until the short afternoon darkened at four o'clock. Then they tramped home to help wash the dishes, build up the fire, and enjoy cold turkey sandwiches and hot cocoa. In the evening Avis played parchesi with the boys and let them open her box of chocolates. They could each have two, she said.

"You may have two after dinner and after supper, every day, until they're gone," she announced. "In that way you won't be upset, and the candy will last a long time."

Jesse noticed that she ate none of the chocolates herself, and after he was in bed that night he remembered that no one had mentioned Joel. It was as if he had never been in the farmhouse.

The rest of the winter dragged past, with heavy storms isolating the Garrisons for days at a time. In the clear spells Avis walked with them to town to stock up on groceries, which must be toted home on the sleds. Fortunately none of them was ill, for they had no telephone, and the farmhouse was not equipped for illness.

Early in March Joel wrote to suggest that they might like to spend the summer at the farm, his argument, as Avis relayed it to the boys, being that the summer might make up to them for the hardships of the winter.

"We're going home," said Avis, her lips pressed close together after every word. "You've lost enough school already, and I must see what has happened to the house."

Once they were home, Jesse and Ross roamed the neighborhood with their friends and only vaguely realized that their father was away often and their mother seemed to have no time for anything but housework.

"She goes at it like a woman possessed," Cousin Belle told anyone who would listen. "Does scrubbing and cleaning that she could have someone else in to do. And she's losing weight—her eyes are the size of saucers."

Once Avis planned a party, two tables of bridge for Joel's birthday. She didn't want liquor served—"because you mix everything so strong now, Joel, and you drink more than anyone else"—but she lost the argument at the breakfast table. Joel said he wouldn't come home to the party if she insisted on serving cambric tea.

Avis worked all day, putting the house in order. She made a lunch for Jesse and Ross and sent them out to play Indians in their tent in the back yard. Then she scrubbed and polished silver and glass, unmindful of the July heat. In the afternoon she made sandwiches and arranged trays and the coffee service that had been a wedding gift.

"We'll have a cold supper early, so I can get everything out of the way," she said to Joel over the telephone. "I'll have your clothes all laid out, and you will have plenty of time for your shower."

Then, after all her work and planning, Joel was late. He came in at half-past-seven, looking hot and untidy and smiling the silly, loose smile that the boys had learned meant he had been drinking.

"Something came up at the last minute—I can't neglect business for anything as trivial as a card party," he growled. "Sure I'll shower and change, but I won't hurry. Well, suppose people are coming? Let 'em wait. This is my house, not theirs."

Jesse and Ross were hustled off to bed, but their room had baked long hours in the afternoon sun, and the heat kept them restless. Finally they decided it could do no harm to observe the party from the second-floor hall.

They had been asleep, although they would indignantly have denied it, and when they peered through the spindles at the top of the stairs, they were surprised to find the cardplayers eating.

The radio, directly behind their father, was tuned in to some station where hymns were being played. Jesse recognized "Faith of Our Fathers," because he sang it in Sunday school. The men and women who were eating at the card tables looked surprised, but Joel began to sing.

He had an excellent baritone voice, and apparently he knew the words. He sat there singing, a highball glass in one hand, his handsome, tragic face set in fixed, deep lines, his eyes seeing something far away. No one spoke or moved. The piano, a violin, and a woman's thin, sweet voice blended with his until, one verse finished, Avis glided in—perhaps from the kitchen—and shut the radio off.

That picture of his father was to remain with him through the years, Jesse had discovered. One other furnished a like clear impression. He remembered his mother's funeral, a year later, when he and Ross on either side of Joel in the church watched the coffin carried up the aisle from the altar at the conclusion of the service.

They followed the pallbearers, Joel with an arm thrown across the shoulder of each of his sons. The sun streamed through the great stained-glass window, and Joel threw back his head so that the light fell directly across his haggard face.

God forgive him, his grief was real enough, but I still think he dramatized the moment.

Someone touched Jesse lightly on the shoulder.

"It's all right, you can go in now, Mr. Garrison," the student nurse said.

Patience wore a white nightgown with frilled shoulder straps. She had put a net over her waved hair and tied it with a blue ribbon. And she smelled like a rose garden.

"Maybe I ought not to sit on the bed," Jesse suggested. "It's so darn prim and neat." But he seated himself, and she leaned against him, tucking her head under his chin again.

She said, as if there had been no interruption, "Jesse, how could your father steal thirty-five hundred dollars?"

"He didn't turn in his cash collections. And some of the other collectors, in a rush at the end of a day, left him their collections to deposit. In one way or another, Dad handled a lot of cash, mostly in small sums."

"Well, why wasn't he arrested?"

Jesse spoke slowly, careful to keep his tone even. "It took a lot of work. I had to see people. And of course his boss is an old friend of Vera's. That helped."

"But I don't see how you could get thirty-five hundred dollars! You make me drag everything out of you—your father thought of course you'd told me." Patience let irritation edge her voice.

"He did, did he? My father is—" Jesse broke off abruptly. His arms tightened around Patience. "I thought you could have an interval of rest, without worry or fear, Patty. You worry too much, anyway. It would have been time enough to tell you, after you were home."

He had borrowed the money to clear his father, Jesse went on. Vera's lawyer, Mr. Kennedy, had managed the details.

"I wouldn't borrow on my life insurance—that's for you and Nicholas," Jesse said. "But you know Drew Wright—he let me have it. I had no security, but he took my note. After a fight."

Andrew Wright had been Jesse's major in the Army. A rich, middle-aged man with a strong streak of sentiment that led him to keep in touch with every man he had known personally in the service.

"Did you hate to go to him, Jesse?"

Jesse was proud; he had refused Drew Wright's rather clumsy

offers to "set him up" in any business he might choose to follow at the end of the war.

"I hate to borrow, and of course I couldn't tell him the reason I needed money. Not that he asked. He was a prince." Jesse was silent a moment, remembering the instant, generous response to his question. "I had to force him to take my note."

Patience felt for a firm, thin hand, held it against her cheek. "But can we pay it back?"

"Darling, you're not in this. Just me. And I'll pay it back, without too much trouble."

Jesse, who had a horror of bills, who frowned upon charge accounts and shuddered at the thought of installment buying, could owe thirty-five hundred dollars and not turn a hair.

"How are you going to pay it back?" Patience asked.

"I've got an extra job. Three hours a night and Saturdays. The pay's good because of the hours, and it won't take me too long." Jesse was cheerful and brisk. "That's what held me up tonight—I had to settle the details."

Why, he doesn't expect any help from me. He's worked it out alone.

"You'll be so busy fussing around the apartment, you won't miss me. And I can do the painting and papering on Sundays," Jesse planned.

Patience said stubbornly, "You can't do it. You'll kill yourself. Besides, I won't see anything of you. Everything's spoiled." Which was not what she wanted to say at all, but the words were fashioned out of heartache and fear.

Jesse freed his hand from her clasp, laid his fingers gently across her rebellious lips. "Patty, if I can tell you how I feel about this, maybe you'll understand."

He hesitated for a moment, anxious not to deceive himself. You saw so clearly the injustice done you, but in your desire to avoid being unjust in turn you dealt other wounds as difficult to heal. You were clumsy, no matter how hard you tried to move delicately, and perhaps in parenthood you must always fail to some degree. But you could hope for your children's forgiveness when their own bewilderment challenged them, and there would be always one thing for which they might honestly thank you.

For life is a gift. There have been times when I doubted it, but now I know and my son will one day know, too.

"How do I know what my father thought and felt when I was born, Patty?" Jesse said aloud. "Maybe he was as humble and as exalted as I am when I think of Nicholas. And something later put him on the wrong track—who's to judge? There were times in the Army when I felt that I never wanted to see him again, but Nicholas has changed that for me."

Not, Jesse murmured, his lips brushing Patience's cheek, that he would wish his son to feel pity for him at the end—and yet pity was a kinder mood than resentment or hate. "There's no way to prophesy what the final judgment of your children will be."

When the time came for her son to judge his mother, what did she want him to feel for her? Patience, sheltered in her husband's arms, repressed an inward shiver. Not pity—she couldn't bear pity—but the lovelier grace of compassion, perhaps; all who were to be judged must stand in need of compassion and of mercy, too.

And yet compassion admitted only her mistakes, her sorrows, and her sins. She didn't want Nicholas to remember her for her failures, but rather for her gallant response to life. And suddenly she perceived that all her fumbling questions had been answered—she had only to open her heart to understand.

There is a way out—the brave will always find it.

The quiet bravery of quiet lives that touched her own—as well as all the lives beyond her ken—should teach her the power of courage and the might of love. She had demanded security for Nicholas; she had been prepared to expend frantic effort to ensure him protection against the unknown. And she had not believed that she could save him from unhappiness or guard him—as the Bible said—from dashing his foot against a stone. But now she knew: she had given him life and she would teach him to face it, and then for him there would be no real defeat.

I have never faced life. They've all sheltered me, first my father and mother, then Lucy. And Jesse—Jesse doesn't expect help from me.

"The thing to do," said Patience quietly, "is to cancel the apartment lease. We'll go back to living with Mother."

"Patty! Don't talk nonsense. You've talked about it for months—even ordered stationery with the address. Besides, the lease is signed. We're committed." Jesse ended on a triumphant note. "We're paid six months in advance."

Patience laughed, a gay, spontaneous ripple, more reassuring than a dozen words. "You can't trip me like that, Mr. Garrison. There were forty-seven applications for that apartment, including ours. Let the other forty-six fight for it."

"But you said you wanted to bring up the baby in your own way—"

"If he sees enough of you, he'll be all right."

Jesse's anxiety flowed through his kiss. "I will not have you uneasy and upset. This is my problem."

"You hurt me, when you talk like that." Patience pushed him away, twisted on the bed to face him. "I'm not a child any longer. I'm your wife. And you can't divide life, giving me all the sweet and keeping the bitter for yourself: we have to share what comes, together."

"But we'll manage the apartment, Patty. I can swing it."

"By killing yourself with extra work." Patience contracted her golden eyebrows to a frown. "No, the rent was too high in the first place—I should have had more sense. But now we'll pay that same amount to Drew Wright every month and turn over the six months' advance to him, too. Mother will approve—she never did think we should keep house."

Jesse was still arguing when the nurse reluctantly reported that the rules had been stretched to the breaking point, but Patience knew that he would accept her decision.

When he had gone, she lay awake for a while to think. A little of her mother, who, afraid of the echoes, still fought her own fears;

more of the future when she and Jesse should go back to her parents, their marriage fortified and with Nicholas, to whom she dared promise security, for she had learned all she needed, to set him free.

More than all else, she thought of the invincibility of love.

You never knew what you were to remember, until the fragments drifted to the surface of your passive mind. As a high-school freshman, searching for quotations for English class, she had copied into her notes a paragraph from a small, shabby book that had been her grandfather's. She had memorized the words for their music, indifferent to their meaning. And tonight, years later, because she was a woman and no longer a girl, they came to her in all their loveliness and truth.

" 'Love is not getting, but giving!' " Patience whispered to the darkness. " 'Not a wild dream of pleasure and a madness of desire. . . . Love is goodness, and honor, and peace!' "